TYPHOON

TYPHOON

Robin White

G. P. PUTNAM'S SONS
NEW YORK

This novel is a work of fiction. Names, characters, places, and incidents either are the product of the author's imagination or are used fictitiously, and any resemblance to actual persons, living or dead, business establishments, events, or locales is entirely coincidental.

G. P. Putnam's Sons
Publishers Since 1838
a member of
Penguin Putnam Inc.
375 Hudson Street
New York, NY 10014

Library of Congress Cataloging-in-Publication Data

White, Robin A.
Typhoon / by Robin White.
p.   cm.
ISBN 0–399–14935–X
1. United States—Foreign relations—Russia (Federation)—Fiction.
2. Russia (Federation)—Foreign relations—United States—Fiction.
3. Submarines (Ships)—Fiction. 4. Submarine warfare—Fiction. 5. Arctic
regions—Fiction. 6. Typhoons—Fiction.   I. Title.
PS3573.H47476T97   2003   2002031835
813'.54—dc21

Printed in the United States of America
1   3   5   7   9   10   8   6   4   2

This book is printed on acid-free paper. ∞

Book design by Lovedog Studio

I'm grateful to the submariners, Russian and American, active duty and retired, who knew what could be told and what could not.

And to Pete, who knew both the music and the words.

ROBIN WHITE, 2002

In the game of submarine cat-and-mouse,
the narrow margin of victory goes to the
proficient and the careful. A mistake—the
clang of a dropped wrench, the swish of a
propeller, even the pop of a light bulb—can
trigger an enemy torpedo. On these battle-
fields, warriors whisper.

**Vice Admiral R. Y. Kaufman,
U.S.N. (Retired)**

ARCTIC REGION

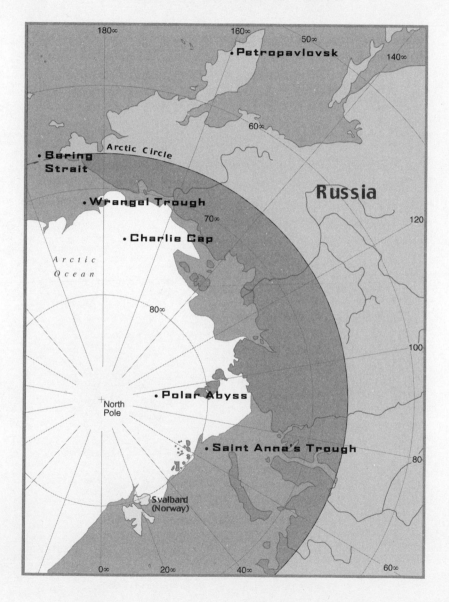

"NTINS . . ."

CHAPTER ONE
ACROSS THE BLUE LINE

Portland's navigator looked up from his plotting table and said, "Looks like a thousand yards to the Blue Line, Captain."

"It *looks* like a thousand, or it *is*?" said Vann.

Lieutenant Commander Whalley said, "It's probably more like nine-eighty, Captain."

"Mister Whalley," said Vann, "the navigator of this boat should know its position better than *looks like* and *probably.* Try again."

Commander James Vann raised a paper cup and let a few ice cubes slide into his mouth. He crunched them to bits as he leaned back on the small, padded shelf set into the forward edge of the periscope stand. It was like sitting sidesaddle on a motorcycle, but then it wasn't designed for comfort. It was there to give him a commanding view of the submarine's control room.

Vann could turn his head and take in everything at a glance. He could reach any of the boat's critical stations in seconds. The contact evaluation plot was mounted directly ahead on the forward bulkhead, with bearings and ranges to every target, every ship, inside *Portland*'s detection range. To its left, Vann could read the depth, speed and angle displays mounted over the ship's control station. Turn right and the fire control consoles for her main battery of torpedoes and missiles formed a solid phalanx along the starboard wall. Both the low-power attack and the high-power search periscopes were just a few steps aft, and the navigation plot was right behind them.

Back in the days of diesel smokeboats, someone had said you didn't board a submarine, you put one on. USS *Portland,* the last and final *Los Angeles*–class attack submarine in the fleet, was three times the size of a diesel, but it was still true. Civilians found submarines confining, but Vann thought of them as efficient.

Portland's control room was both. The space was lit by bright fluorescent lights. Within its curved walls there was no feeling of motion, no sense of the surrounding sea. It was like an airliner's cockpit blown up to the size of a two-car garage, stacked from linoleum deck to gray steel overhead with electronics, wire bundles, gauges and displays. Every square foot contained at least one thing too many—disorderly to the unacquainted eye, but like the organs and bones of a great undersea predator, nothing was there without a good reason. Nothing, and no one.

A dozen people worked here around the clock, their day split into three separate watches. The pole around which all this activity whirled was Commander James Vann.

"Nine hundred and ten yards to Russian water, skipper."

"Better." Vann demolished another cube and glanced at the multifunction screen above the helm. *Portland* was cruising three hundred feet beneath the surface of the southern Barents Sea, heading southeast at twelve knots. Norway was fifty miles behind them, the Russian coastline a dozen miles dead ahead. The boat's General Electric S6G reactor was putting out nearly 35,000 horsepower, driving seven thousand tons of steel silently through the sea. Immense forces were at work but the only sound Vann could hear was the whisper of fresh air from the overhead vents and the soft ticking of an old Hamilton deck chronometer.

Perfect, he thought. A nice enough goal in the civilian world. But here on *Portland,* Vann demanded perfection and he generally got it. It was rough on the men, but there were rewards: a junior officer who survived was prepared for anything. Vann's focus on performance had transformed *Portland* from a hard-luck boat into the leading fast-attack submarine in the Atlantic fleet.

Vann glanced at the old deck chronometer he'd brought to *Portland* from his last command. It was bolted to a small shelf at the ship's helm. He walked over to it, opened the glass lid, took a golden key off a hook and started to wind.

Though the Naval Observatory's atomic clocks beamed out time signals that were perfect to a billionth of a second, Vann insisted on the twice-daily winding of the old Hamilton. It was a ritual as important as entering *Portland*'s position in the logs, for it established Vann's place not on a chart but in history. The deck clock had faithfully stood watch over fifty years on the bridges of half a dozen American submarines. For Vann, there was a lesson in that. It was a kind of holy relic that honored precision, faithfulness, endurance and duty.

Vann wound the clock carefully, noting the steady rise of the power reserve needle on its face. When it registered correctly, he closed the glass cover and hung the key back up. A petty officer in Whalley's Operations Division would perform the same ritual later that day.

"Seven hundred yards to the Blue Line."

Vann would turn forty-four during this run, an old man by the measure of the submarine force, but then his path to *Portland*'s bridge had taken some detours. He had dark hair with gray streaks at the temple, brown eyes that looked black in the cold light of a submarine, and a thin, angular face that blended a nuclear engineer's calculated seriousness with an attack submariner's supreme self-confidence.

He was a "supernuke" who'd spent his career tending nuclear reactors. It was an unusual path to command in any navy of the world where engineers and captains occupied distinct and separate tracks. But the United States Navy wouldn't hand a man a boat unless he was first and foremost a competent nuke. Among such finicky, detail-oriented men, Vann was considered one of the best.

His first command had been a brand-new submarine out on an initial shakedown cruise. He'd brought her back to the yard with a list of rejected items seventy-five pages long.

The shipyard hated his guts, but the report earned him a solid gold reputation among submariners; a reputation that nearly foundered when his next command, the nuclear attack submarine USS *Baton Rouge,* struck an ice spur and nearly sank. Though the inquiry found him blameless, it took years before he went back to sea on *Portland*.

He'd found her in near total disarray. She'd been nearly run over by an oil tanker one night off Norfolk; she'd grounded on Nantucket Shoals when her navigator blithely drew a course that put a submarine with a thirty-two-foot draft in waters twenty-seven feet deep. Every one of her four departments—Operations, Weapons, Engineering and Supply—was in shambles. The bars along Norfolk's old East Main Street banned her crew as hooligans. The boat was a circus run by the clowns.

Vann's mandate had been simple: Fix it.

And so he had. Under his command, *Portland* broke all records for performance and operational readiness. No Atlantic submarine accumulated so many Battle E awards. Vann proved himself a master at evading antisubmarine forces. He'd sent a packet of periscope photos taken so close to the stern of an aircraft carrier you could make out the faces of sailors smoking on her fantail. Its captain lodged an official complaint, not that it went anywhere. Sneaking up on a carrier, the best-protected asset in the fleet, wasn't a problem, it was a badge of honor, and he became known around Norfolk as the "Invisible Vann."

Now he was back at the top of his game. When they returned to Norfolk, he'd leave *Portland* for a staff position, and then head off to command a squadron of submarines. It was a big step up and long overdue, but he'd leave reluctantly. Admirals politicked. On *Portland,* James Vann ruled.

Vann crunched the last few cubes thoughtfully. Everyone in Control could tell his mood by how fast he went through a full cup. It was a kind of barometer; a leisurely pace meant smooth sailing, fast and furious spelled storm.

He watched one of the two sailors at the helm swipe a sweaty palm across the knee of his dark blue overalls, known as a poopy suit. *Good.* A helmsman that wasn't sweating to keep his boat at precise depth and on course wasn't trying, and if you weren't trying you didn't belong here.

"Blue Line now six hundred yards ahead," said Lieutenant Commander William Whalley.

Whalley's chart was a paper copy of the electronic one displayed above the helm. It showed the southern shore of the Barents Sea, north of Murmansk, west of Port Vladimir. Two lines, one red, the other blue, paralleled the coastline. The red line stood well offshore and represented the Russians' generous view of their territorial waters. The blue line had been drawn by the United States Navy. It hugged the land, following the fjords and headlands with lawyerly precision. The area between them was marked DIS-PUTED, and carried a note: *Shipping Infringing upon Disputed Zones May Be Fired On Without Warning.*

"Four hundred yards. Turn-back warning, Captain."

"Log it." Vann knew Whalley was required to say those words, not that he intended to turn anywhere. It only meant there was still time to avoid a breach of international law, an infraction that carried a sentence of death if the Russians caught them and felt like imposing it. It was Vann's job to make sure they didn't get that chance. He'd already made the announcement over the boat's intercom, the 1MC, that from here on there would be no drills. It was all for real. "Helm. All ahead one-third." *Here we go.*

"Ahead one-third, aye." The helmsman spun the knurled knob of the engine room telegraph. Aft in the space known as Maneuvering, a pointer on the steam plant control panel moved and the duty throttleman acknowledged the order. He adjusted the propulsion turbine throttle valve to send a precise amount of nuclear-generated steam through the engine.

"Maneuvering answers ahead one-third," said the helmsman.

Steering a submarine was far more complex than flying a jet. It was a choreography of small corrections, checks and cross-checks accomplished by a skilled team. There were three bucket seats at the ship's control station, each equipped with a safety belt. The helmsman and planesman sat behind aircraft-style control yokes linked to the rudder and diving planes. The engine room telegraph was mounted between them. An overhead console held depth, angle and heading displays, the multifunction screen and a second, smaller screen, left dark for now. The diving officer sat behind them, double-checking every move they made.

The captain held out his empty paper cup. It was automatically replaced with a full one by the messenger of the watch, an off-duty planesman.

"Russian water in two hundred yards," said the navigator.

The final member of the team was Senior Chief Browne. He sat aft of the helm, facing outboard at the ballast control panel. There he managed the diving and surfacing of the boat and maintained its buoyancy and trim while submerged. He also kept a close eye on Wayne Choper, a young supply lieutenant standing duty as dive officer. A surprising number of young lieutenants seemed to come aboard a boat with a death wish. It was his duty to make sure their wishes weren't granted.

Browne had spent more time in submarines than anyone on *Portland,* including her captain. He'd been selected to become an instructor at sub school in New London, but then the opportunity came to make one more North Atlantic run on *Portland.* How he managed to get his papers changed so quickly was something of a mystery, but then the ways of senior chiefs were nothing if not mysterious.

Above Browne were the bright red Chicken Switches; actually, two guarded valves. Pull them and the boat's ballast tanks would fill with high-pressure air, driving out the water weight, sending the submarine blasting to the surface like an unguided missile.

Chief Browne had the relaxed, alert expression of a professional who knew a deadly serious business well enough to enjoy it. The small, wiry black man had a razor-sharp mustache and touches of gray shading his temples. On his left breast pocket was a medallion known as the "COB Cookie." An anchor, the letters *USN* and a single word: *COMMAND.* It was the insignia worn only by the chief of the boat, the highest-ranking enlisted man aboard. To the hundred enlisted men, he was the person who got things done. Vann might point the boat, but Browne made sure it got there and back.

Together, the four men of the ship's control party kept a submerged steel pipe three hundred and sixty feet long and thirty-two wide exactly where it was supposed to be: on course within a degree, at depth within a five-foot band, on speed within a knot and in perfect balance and trim. Precision was life-or-death in shallow-water operations off the barren Russian coast. The smallest inattention could send her broaching to the surface or plowing into the bottom, and everyone knew it.

"Crossing the Blue Line now," said Whalley.

"'Kay." Vann put his paper cup down and folded his arms across his chest. "Where's the XO?"

"Mister Steadman's in the wardroom, skipper," said Browne. COB kept track of the whereabouts of every member of *Portland*'s crew. He never went anywhere without a low-power radio clipped to his belt, a tiny earpiece installed in his right ear and a boom microphone at his lips.

"Get him up here, COB."

Lieutenant Commander Steadman, *Portland*'s executive officer, had a fan of Familygram messages spread out on the single table where the boat's fourteen officers took their meals. This morning he had the place to himself, which was just as well. This Familygram, sent to one of *Portland*'s enlisted crew, was a bad one.

> Linda cleared out storage, apt. Landlord says rent by Monday or he'll evict. . . . Mother

Normally, messages from home were very carefully screened. Divorce, death and Dear John letters weren't sent. But this Familygram, addressed to Radioman Larry Engler, had a deadline and so it had made it through. Something had to be done, and fast.

Now what? wondered Steadman. What was Engler supposed to do about a wife who'd left him? About a landlord who wanted his rent half a world away? For that matter, what could Steadman do about it?

Life on board *Portland* was clean, comfortable, detached. Except for brief excursions up to periscope depth you neither saw nor felt the sea that was always just a few feet away. Once you closed the hatch, the troubles of the outside world were supposed to vanish, but this one had come like a smart bomb looking for its target.

When he'd dreamed of life aboard a submarine, Steadman imagined serving aboard a high-tech jewel of a ship, utterly independent of the outside world. He'd imagined dicing with the forces of an evil empire, scouting the world's danger spots, striking America's enemies and vanishing back into the limitless deeps. His dreams never included the duties of marriage counselor, divorce lawyer, chaplain, landlord.

William Steadman had grown up in a working-class neighborhood in Providence, Rhode Island. He was seven years Vann's junior and two inches taller. He straddled the line between skinny and lanky. His hair was the shade of light brown that turns blond under the summer sun, though spending months underwater never gave it a chance.

His father owned the Silver Top, one of the last workingman's diners in Providence and so grimly real the city wanted to buy it for a parking lot. He'd told them to take a hike. He would sell only to one of his long-suffering waitresses who promised to change nothing.

Steadman had inherited his father's stubbornness, and while the Navy said it admired the quality it rarely rewarded it. What was true for the Navy was doubly true aboard *Portland*. This would be his last run as *Portland*'s executive officer, and perhaps the last run of his Navy career. He'd either leave with the CO's recommendation for Prospective Commanding Officers School in his pocket or else sit out his twenty years half asleep at some desk. Or resign. Vann had failed to recommend him once, and while it wasn't as damaging as a bad fitness report it would end up the same way. Lieutenant commanders didn't rise over the objections of their skippers.

The phone buzzed. The room was small enough to permit him to grab it off the bulkhead without standing. "Steadman."

"XO?" It was COB. "Captain wants you up in Control."

"Now?"

"Aye aye. Right now."

He hung the receiver back on its hook, then stopped and looked up at the intercom speaker.

What was that noise?

CHAPTER TWO

THE TEST

"What in *hell* is that?" Vann demanded.

It was the steady *squeak squeak squeak* of bouncing bedsprings, soft, rhythmic pounding and heavy breathing. Sounds that might be heard through the thin walls of a motel room on a Saturday night, not aboard a submerged nuclear submarine in hostile waters.

Senior Chief Browne spun a rotary switch. The performance continued. "It's on the 1MC. It sounds like the treadmill down in the Machine Room," he said. The space was aft of Control and down on the lowest of the submarine's three decks. *Portland*'s emergency diesel engine nearly filled the compartment. Tucked under its exhaust manifold between a hydraulic pump and an oxygen generator was the boat's "gym": a set of weights and a treadmill.

"Resolve it, COB," said Vann.

"Aye aye." Browne lifted a black phone off the bulkhead hook.

Lieutenant Rose Scavullo heard the ringer and ignored it. Machine One was owned by the Auxiliary Division. *Let those knuckledraggers answer it.* She started her final sprint, letting her feet pound the treadmill into a blurring ribbon, her breath coming faster and faster. Sweat flew off her face and darkened her gray University of Maine sweatshirt to black. The speed needle surged around the dial. It was as though she were running from some deadly predator hot on her heels.

Ever since she'd come aboard *Portland,* the Russian language specialist had felt trapped. After all, *Portland*'s living space was about the same as in a three-bedroom house, and she was sharing it with 120 men who didn't want her here and made sure she knew it.

The twenty-three-year-old linguist had her mother's glossy raven hair, her father's blue eyes and a Level Four qualification in Russian she earned for herself at the Defense Language Institute in Monterey, California. Five was the highest rating DLI awarded. No other student had come close. Her detailer gave her the pick of assignments. The Atlantic Fleet, the Pacific, NATO headquarters. Even the Pentagon.

Scavullo wasn't interested in shuffling papers and preparing transcripts from satellite intercepts. For a language specialist looking for action, a submarine was where you wanted to be. Surface ships had to steer clear of contested waters. Airplanes could be shot down. Only a submarine could move in unseen and unheard, put up an antenna and eavesdrop on radio transmissions.

The detailer bounced it right back. Women didn't serve on the boats. Where would she sleep? Where would she pee? He suggested a naval liaison posting at the National Security Agency, a plum Washington billet.

Scavullo had grown up in a Maine mill town and knew what hard work was about. She'd absorbed a simple faith that a person's worth was measured by achievement, not whether she peed standing up.

Scavullo put her graduation records and her request for submarine duty into an envelope and mailed them to her senator, a woman who happened to sit on the Senate Armed Services Committee, which decided on the Navy's budget requests. She expected it to be the end of her career. Two weeks later, new orders arrived by special Navy messenger. She was ordered to proceed to Submarine Base Norfolk and join USS *Portland*.

She'd arrived at the main gate in her dress white uniform at high noon on a blistering late-July day. The air felt like God Almighty had aimed His hair dryer on a point slightly south of latitude 37 degrees north, 76 degrees east. Sailing time was thirty minutes away.

She caught a crew bus for the short ride out to Pier 23. She got out into the ferocious heat, hefted her seabag and hurried to the guard booth.

Scavullo had worked out every day since high school. She weighed 120 sinewy pounds, but the bag was easily half that. Inside it was everything she'd need for months of enforced isolation: two sets of blue submariner's poopy suits, her khakis, five changes of nearly sexless white Jockey underwear. *It's the books,* she thought. She'd brought a four-book set of technical Russian and the damned things weighed five pounds each.

Scavullo stood before the guard, swaying under the bulk of her bag. Her dress whites were plastered to her skin with sweat. The sailor inside the air-conditioned booth ignored her. It was 12:15. She rapped at the glass again. He turned away.

Beyond the guard booth she could see the concrete pier, so glaring and white under the merciless sun it made the submarines moored to either side seem black and featureless as obsidian.

Finally, the window slid open. She handed the guard the manila envelope with her ID card and her orders, and noticed the silver "dolphins" of a qualified submariner over his breast pocket. "Lieutenant Rose Scavullo for USS *Portland*. Where do I find her?"

He slowly tapped her information into a keyboard, looked at his screen for what seemed like an hour and a half, and then said, "End of the pier. *Scranton, Montpelier, Oklahoma City,* then *Portland.* Better get a hustle on, Lieutenant. She's ready to go."

"I could use some help getting out to my ship. Any chance?"

"No, ma'am." He handed her documents back. "And submarines are boats, not ships. Have a nice day." The window slid shut.

She grabbed her heavy bag and dragged it through the gate, acutely aware of crossing an invisible divide. Behind her was the world of the regular Navy, ahead lay the submariner's world. A world that operated by rules Rose Scavullo had broken just by showing up.

Heat shimmered in waves from the hot concrete surface as she hurried by USS *Scranton.* She had her periscopes up and some sailors were applying gray paint to the shafts. They stopped their work and stared. Her uniform was soaked. Under her arms, down her back, two dark crescents under her breasts like signs shouting *Look here!* She felt their eyes on her back like four hot needle points of light.

Scranton, Montpelier, Oklahoma City. The submarines looked identical, except that the very last, *Portland,* was the focus of a lot of activity. Line handlers in orange flotation vests stood by on her decks. The gangplank, known as the brow, still spanned the narrow stripe of greasy water to her topside deck. It was festooned with red, white and blue bunting and emblazoned with a large white shield with USS PORTLAND on it. Beneath was a picture of a fierce red lobster holding a crushed submarine in one claw and brandishing torpedoes and Tomahawk missiles in the other, and the words HOME OF THE INVISIBLES.

Scavullo was a Mainer and knew about lobsters. A red lobster was a cooked lobster, not an auspicious mascot for a submarine.

A toot from an air horn. Men began hauling in the heavy lines.

Scavullo wasn't about to be left behind. She set off at a run and hurried across the brow. She came to a stop before a big, burly chief with a clipboard in his hand. His name tag said Babcock. A photographer in khakis stood behind him, sweating in the hot sun. There was a hatch open on the deck. She let out her breath. She'd made it. If the chief was going below, so would she. She dropped her bag, turned to the flag that hung limply from atop the sail, saluted the colors and said, "Lieutenant Scavullo reporting aboard." She handed him the manila envelope.

The photographer caught the moment for history.

"You almost missed the boat, ma'am," said Chief Babcock as he handed her papers back. "Just leave your gear with me."

"I can take it below myself, Chief."

"The skipper wants to see you first. That's him on the open bridge."

"I can take it up there with me."

"No, ma'am, you can't. There's no room. Trust me."

"Stand by to single all lines!" came the call from a man in immaculate dress whites standing in the open bridge.

She looked up. It was a good thirty-foot climb to the top of what used to be called a conning tower back when submarines spent most of their time on the surface. Now it was known as the "fairwater," or more simply, the sail.

"Don't worry," said the chief. "Your gear ain't going anywhere you aren't." He grabbed her bag and dragged it to the open hatch. "Down ladder!" he yelled, and then dropped it.

Scavullo watched it vanish, glad for the padlock she'd used to snap it shut. She walked across the curved deck to the base of *Portland*'s sail. The deck was warm, soft with rubber tiles. It felt more like an animal's hide than the hull of a warship.

The chief, the line handlers, the men on the pier all watched as she climbed a rope ladder dangling down from a small door set in the sail's port side. *Probably hoping I fall off.* She was sweating buckets as she swung her legs through the door and made her way up to the open bridge.

The chief had been right. The open cockpit was barely large enough for two people to stand in without brushing knees. She straightened herself and saluted. The Navy photographer below had a telephoto lens pointed up. The flag hung motionless behind them. The camera's motor winder whirred. "Lieutenant Scavullo reporting aboard, sir."

Vann picked up a microphone. "Stand by to answer bells." He turned and held out his hand. The photographer's Nikon buzzed. "You're late, Lieutenant."

"My apologies, sir. My flight was delayed and—"

"Look over there," said Vann, nodding at the staff car. "That's my boss, Admiral Graybar, and his chief of staff, Captain Welch. If I dinged the screw on a piling, you think they'd accept an apology?"

"No, sir."

"Correct. Maybe language school was different, but out here good intentions don't count. Performance will. Nothing is going to be held against you on *Portland* except failure. Remember that."

"That's all I want, Commander. I'll do better."

"We'll see." Vann picked up the microphone again. His voice boomed across the open deck. "Lift the brow!"

A crane swung the gangplank away.

Scavullo saw a tug standing by. It should be nudging *Portland* out into the harbor. Why wasn't it?

Vann checked his watch. When the second hand crossed the twelve, Vann picked up the mike and said, "Cast off lines two, three and four!"

Scavullo had a bird's-eye view of the operation, only what was she supposed to do? "Sir? Where am I supposed to go?"

"All ahead one-third." Vann looked right through her, his eyes on the narrow stripe of black water between *Portland* and the pier. The graceful screw at *Portland*'s finely tapered stern thrashed the water to foam.

"All stop!"

As the stern swung away from the pier, Vann called out, "Cast off the number-one line! All back one-third!"

Portland slowly angled out away from the pilings.

"Sound one long blast and three short blasts."

The air horn tooted its warning to traffic out in the channel as *Portland* shed her last ties to dry land and moved out into the sluggish current.

Wow, thought Scavullo. "Sir? Where should I . . ."

Vann seemed surprised to find her still standing there. "Go below and get yourself checked in at the yeoman's shack, Lieutenant."

"Aye aye, sir," she said. Then, more sheepishly, "Where is it?"

Vann turned and pointed at the main trunk hatch at his feet. "That way."

Scavullo looked down the hatch. The smooth-walled cylinder dropped away like the barrel of a large-caliber gun. She stepped through and started down. With each rung, the air grew cooler and more pungent with the smell of diesel, fresh paint, baking bread and a darker note that grew stronger. Sweat, urine, disinfectant, floor wax.

The ladder ended in a small antechamber just forward of the submarine's control room. The world of light, of open air, of color, had vanished. In its stead was a cramped, gray universe, a steel-clad basement. The floor was tiled in very clean linoleum. She looked around. Where was her bag?

Looking aft, she could see into Control. The sailors at the helm had a look of absolute concentration, almost devotional, as they stared up at displays Scavullo couldn't see.

Forward was a short, narrow corridor lined with identical doors. Where was she supposed to go? She saw a sailor coming her way. "Where can I find the yeoman's shack?"

He eased by and kept walking, not even letting his eyes register Scavullo's existence.

So that's how it's going to be. She started down the passage, passing a pair of doors, one decorated with a framed poster that exhorted the crew to "Zero Errors." Beyond lay a third door, also with a sign. MEN. It was hung on a brass hook. She flipped the sign over. WOMAN was printed, in pink letters, on the other side. At least she'd found where she was supposed to pee.

At the end of the passage, a massive steel ladder dropped down to the middle deck. She heard laughter rising from below.

She staggered a bit. The deck had begun to roll. Were they already out in the ocean? Down here there was no way to tell.

"Excuse me," said a thin, gangly lieutenant. He wanted to get by and descend the ladder.

She blocked his way. "Where's the yeoman's shack?"

He pointed down. "Middeck forward. By the Goat Locker."

"Thanks." She stepped aside and he vanished down the ladder.

Portland had just two main compartments: the engineering spaces aft and everything else forward.

The forward half was divided into three levels. The uppermost deck where she was standing was a place for working; the control room, the sonar shack, the radio room. Only the captain and the exec had staterooms up here. The middeck was home to the junior officers and senior chiefs, the galley, the wardroom. The boat's main living spaces. At the very bottom were crew's bunks, machinery spaces, cold storage compartments and the torpedo room. The Goat Locker was reserved for the senior chiefs.

She climbed down to the middle deck. Behind her was a large berthing space filled top to bottom with bunks. She guessed her cabin would be back there someplace. To her right were two doors, each a size suggesting a small closet lay beyond. One was labeled SHIP'S OFFICE and it was closed. She tried the handle. *Locked.*

The other door was identified only by a pair of bleached goat horns wired to the bulkhead above. She reached to open it, then stopped, listening.

". . . so I said, I know your kind, Engler. I could handcuff you, put you in a padded cell with two bowling balls and come back an hour later. One ball would be broken and the other would be missing. You got a true *talent* for fucking up."

Scavullo poked her head in. There were three men inside, two sprawled at a booth with coffee mugs steaming before them, the other, a wiry black man with a thin mustache, was standing with his hands on his hips.

"Excuse me. I think I'm supposed to check in with someone?"

The black man stared. "What the *hell* are you doing there standing like Little Red Riding Hood? You want to *check in*? Does this look like the Plaza Hotel? Do I look like some kind of *bellhop*?"

"I'm Lieutenant Scavullo reporting aboard, *Chief.*" She stressed his rank. Submariner or not, a lieutenant was supposed to outrank an enlisted man. "I could use some help. Commander Vann sent me to find the yeoman and I can't seem to. I left my luggage up on deck and I don't know where my cabin is either."

The black man went serious, fast as a thrown switch. "I'm pleased to *finally* make your acquaintance, *Lieutenant.* I'm Senior Chief Jerome Browne. You will call me COB."

Scavullo thought, *Oh shit.* She'd been on board less than fifteen minutes and she'd been treated like an idiot by the captain and proved herself one with the chief of the boat.

"The yeoman's shack is next door," said Browne. "He was waiting for you until it got so late he had a few other duties to attend to other than you. As for your *cabin,* Mess Management Specialist Williams will show you the way. You'll find your *luggage* waiting for you there. You can *check in* with the yeoman at the change of the watch. That's number one. Number two, you are what we call a *rider.* Riders should be seen and not heard. If someone is walking your way down a passage, you make a hole for them. With me so far?"

"Aye aye, Chief."

"COB. Number three. My idea of heaven is three petty officers first class and a lieutenant who does *exactly* what she's told. Your job is to make me think I'm in heaven. Got it? Class dismissed."

A sailor appeared behind Scavullo as though summoned by some invisible command. "Permission to enter the Goat Locker?"

"Granted," said Browne. He looked at Scavullo. "Go make sure your gear is properly stowed and then come back here for a briefing. And don't you *dare* be late."

"Thanks, COB." She gave a sheepish smile, turned and fled.

Her cabin was a bunk in a section of junior officers' berthing. The nearby tiers had been roped off and hung with blankets for her privacy. Her bag was there, just as Chief Browne promised. But when she checked the padlock, she found it had been clipped. She spilled the contents out onto her bunk. Four bras, four panties. Not five.

The phone buzzed again as the treadmill flew by beneath her shoes. Scavullo gave up. She was due up in the radio shack soon anyway. She picked up the phone. "Lieutenant Scavullo speaking."

Vann shot out a hand and Browne passed him the phone. "What in *hell* are you doing down there, Scavullo?"

"Sir? I was working out on the treadmill."

"And making enough noise to set off alarm bells from Murmansk to Moscow. Get your butt up to Control."

"Sir, I'm due in the radio shack in fifteen minutes. I'd like to get cleaned up and—"

"I want you on this bridge *now*." With that, Vann slapped the handset back into its cradle. "Jesus. Inside the *Blue Line*."

"Captain," said Browne, "someone rigged an open mike over the treadmill. That took knowhow. Scavullo didn't do it."

"You find out who did," said Vann. "I want a scalp over my door by the end of the next watch. I won't have this behavior, COB."

"Aye aye," said Browne, already thinking, *Engler.*

"Kee-*rist*." Vann stalked back to the navigation table. He took a sniff of the navigator's pungent aftershave and wrinkled his nose. The man was *not* suited to submarines. "What kind of water do we have?"

"Low." Lieutenant Commander Whalley was twenty-nine, plump and prematurely bald. A sandy fringe decorating a polished scalp. He claimed to have a sensitive sense of smell, though whether the cologne he used to cover the monkey-house miasma that passed as fresh air was proof of that or its opposite was open to speculation.

He'd attended Princeton and now his classmates were making tons of money at investment banks, Wall Street and computer start-ups. The Navy was run by idiots more intent on style than substance and he'd concluded that it was a waste of his very valuable time. "We're coming in at the bottom of the tide. The Tunnel's shut. The Pass is open but marginal."

"Those are opinions. Show me the numbers."

Since when is the tide an opinion? Whalley read off the fathoms as his finger traced the two covert passages into Kola Bay: The Tunnel was a narrow trench that began off Norway and snaked through shallow water into the bay from the west. The Pass began in the waters of the open Barents, meandered through a field of drowned hills and shoals, then sliced through a treacherous slot in the Murmansk Banks, a drowned mountain that blocked the mouth of Kola Fjord. There were no alternatives. The rest of Kola Fjord was as wired as a pinball machine. Make a noise in the wrong place and the whole coast would light up.

Vann stared down at the electronic chart. "How much water will we have crossing the Banks?"

"Thirty feet over the sail and the current will be really ripping."

"Ripping?"

"Four knots," said Whalley. "Sir."

"That's good." With that, he left.

Whalley watched the captain return to his perch. *Good?*

Vann scanned the helm's displays. Course. Speed. Depth. *Automatic,* he thought. It was COB's term for the proper running of his ship and Vann thought it was exactly right. He thought about Steadman. Vann had made one run with him and found him unready for command. This evaluation would be the hardest one yet. Failure meant the end of his career in the boats.

Some captains would have given Steadman an easier final exam. Not Vann. He was a link in a chain that went back to the beginnings of the submarine navy. He'd been taught by the last of a dying generation who'd earned their dolphins fighting the Japanese; crafty, aggressive men who brought their skills to bear on a different, colder war against Russia.

America had won that war, but then it let its military go soft, let it become an international police force, stopping drugs, saving crocodiles, refereeing disputes between bands of cave-dwelling Muslims. The regular Navy was becoming a laboratory for testing trendy social theories. The ranks were filling with the unfit, the illiterate, the poorly trained, with women who were turning warships into Love Boats.

The submarine service couldn't afford social experiments. There was no room for slackers. Submariners had a job to accomplish and took immense pride in doing it. Vann was part of that chain of honor and skill and he'd be damned to see it broken on *his* watch.

The XO appeared in the forward passage. "What's going on, skipper?"

Vann said, "We're inside the Blue Line, lined up on Route—"

"Sir?"

Lieutenant Scavullo stood in the aft starboard passage dressed in a sweaty civilian outfit. Vann glared at her as though she were a mess on his well-scrubbed decks. "Wait right there on that spot."

"Sir, I'm due to come on duty and I still need to get ready."

"Lieutenant," said Vann, "if the Navy ever makes you captain of your own ship you can do exactly as you'd like. Until then, you will do what the captain of this submarine would like. I am that captain. Clear?"

"Yes, sir."

"Come." Vann motioned for Steadman to join him at the helm.

Scavullo shivered in her sweats. The air from the overhead vents felt like an arctic blast. Apparently, it would be just fine if she caught pneumonia and died, as long as she did it quietly.

"Ma'am? I mean, Lieutenant?"

She turned to see a messmate carrying a folded blue poopy suit. "COB said you might be needing this."

The overalls were clean, dry and still warm. The boat's laundry was down in the galley. The washer and dryer would look small in an apartment, and so clean clothes were rationed out like gold dust. She looked in COB's direction, but he had his back to her, making a fine adjustment in the boat's trim. She sent a silent *thank-you* his way, then stepped into the suit, right over her sweats.

CHAPTER THREE

THE PASS

"You heard Scavullo's little performance?" asked Vann as he and Steadman huddled in the forward passage in front of the helm.

"I don't think anyone could have missed it."

"What's next? A panty raid? We're in *Russian water* and someone puts that *noise* over the 1MC? That's the kind of behavior that almost ruined this boat. If it doesn't prove you can't assign girls to submarines, I honestly don't know what will."

"She's supposed to be a good linguist."

"You don't think they bumped a better qualified man to prove a point? They're looking for a way into the tent, XO. Today it's a rider. Next it will be a radioman, or -girl. Looking at it from Washington, what's the difference? What if she gets pregnant? What do we do? Give her maternity leave in the torpedo room?"

"She knows what's at stake. I don't think she'll step out of line."

"That's an opinion. Here's a number: the pregnancy rate on mixed crews in the Surface Navy runs twenty percent per deployment. *Twenty percent.* You think all those girls planned to get knocked up? No," he said firmly, "Scavullo does *not* belong out here and we'll be doing everyone a favor if we prove it. Even her. 'Kay." Vann tapped the chart. "Next matter. We just crossed into Russian water. Our mission is to be in position to observe a major Russian fleet movement. It's their first exercise since they lost *Kursk*. I want you to take us in."

Steadman felt his heart tick over, then he said, "Into Kola?"

"You're supposed to be ready to assume command at any time. If you're not, that's another matter."

"I'm ready." Steadman didn't even have to think about it, which was good because when he *did* he wasn't so sure. All captains tested their XOs with simulated emergencies. But should *Portland* be caught *here,* it would mean more than just a failing grade.

Steadman felt the power, the responsibility of command. It was heady, serious and everything he'd ever wanted. He looked at the men at the helm, the fire control techs, the navigator. Poor Lieutenant Choper, the dive officer, was chewing gum so hard he looked like he was holding up both sides of an animated conversation.

"Well?" asked Vann.

Steadman took a deep breath and said, "I've got the conn."

Vann winked, then said, "XO's the command duty officer!"

Browne had guessed what was up from the beginning. He grinned as he called out, "XO has the conn!"

"Good luck," said Vann. He walked forward and resumed his perch, an observer and a judge.

"Sir?" said Lieutenant Choper. He was already standing up, ready to give his seat to a more skillful dive officer. Actually, he'd hand over responsibility to anyone.

Choper was a young and very green lieutenant from the Supply Department. He roamed *Portland*'s passages and compartments with a look of perpetual puzzlement. Which admiral had he crossed to merit this duty? He'd come from the surface fleet and wanted to go back as soon as possible. In the meantime, he was expected to come away from *Portland* knowing more than when he arrived, and it was giving him fits.

Choper was known as "Slice and Dice" for his inability to keep the boat's depth constant. He'd allowed *Portland*'s screw to cut the floating antenna to shreds more than once and was now so fearful of doing it again he could hardly think of anything else. "You probably want someone with a steadier hand, right?"

"Relax. You can do it," said Steadman. He walked back to where Scavullo was standing. "You'd better go warm up your radios, Lieutenant. You can start your work as soon as we put your antenna up."

She looked at Vann, then back. "Sir, the captain . . ."

"I have the conn, Lieutenant. Go."

She retreated aft to the radio room, unlocked the door with its security warnings and found her place in the small, cramped space before a radio console with a flickering blue display. There were three swivel chairs, and she took the middle one between a junior enlisted radioman, Larry Engler, and Lieutenant Michael Bledsoe, the communications officer.

Bledsoe had a white china cup brimming with steaming hot water. "You look like you could use something hot," he said. He held it up.

She looked at him. She had no friends on *Portland,* but even by that measure Bledsoe had been especially hostile. "What did you spike it with?"

"Nada." He handed her the cup. "Got a tea bag around here someplace." Bledsoe rummaged through the bookshelves above the radio consoles, then looked at Engler. "Hey, Pasha! You use up the last one?"

"Sorry, sir." Radioman Larry Engler looked sheepish. He was called Pasha for his thick, dark mustache. He worked out with weights like an inmate with nothing better to do. He wore glasses with clear, pinkish frames that gave him an undeservedly studious look. "You want me to go scrounge one?"

"Nah. I'll do it," said Bledsoe. "You cover." He stood up and left.

He wasn't gone a minute before Engler said, "Sir? I mean, *ma'am?* I found one." He held up a damp tea bag he'd rescued from somewhere. "Barely used. You want it?"

"Sure," said Scavullo. "Thanks." She put the cup to one side and began powering up her radio receivers. They were designed to vacuum up every stray signal beamed by Russian transmitters, record them for analysis and show on a screen the source and strength of each one.

She felt something heavy and soft on her shoulder. She turned.

Engler's naked penis had emerged from his poopy suit. It was draped over her shoulder, half erect but growing harder as she watched. She stared, not in horror, but in frank disbelief.

His eyes were hidden behind the reflection of blue data streams from her console. There was a quick rattle from the door handle. Engler zipped himself up in a flash. By the time Bledsoe stepped through the door with a fresh box of Lipton, Engler was seated at his console.

Bledsoe saw her expression. "Something wrong?"

He said it with so much empathy Scavullo knew Bledsoe and Engler had arranged everything. Report Engler and it would be her word against his. She turned her back to them and powered up the frequency scanners, receivers and recorders with a series of sharp, violent *clicks.* They sounded like small bones snapped in half.

Steadman joined Whalley over his charts. "Tell me you didn't know about this."

"I would have gotten us lost if I did."

"How bad is it going to be out there?"

"If we ground, we'll be able to get out and walk."

"I'd rather not."

"I'm with you. The Tunnel's totally shut." Whalley lowered his voice. "He might be testing to see if he can bully you into making the big mistake. You can say no. You can wait for higher water."

He could also volunteer for duty as naval attaché to Mongolia. It would amount to the same thing. "What about the Pass?"

"You'll have to see it up close to know. You okay with that?"

"Sure." Another automatic answer, but the truth was, there were easier places to demonstrate mastery of the art of covert submarine operations. Easier, and safer. They would soon be in water far shallower than *Portland*'s own 360-foot length, and the bottom topography was complex. The glaciers that bulldozed northern Russia flat had left a drowned obstacle course of canyons, mountains and shipwrecks, not a few of them Russian submarines.

"What about *him*?" Whalley nodded at Slice and Dice.

Steadman considered it for a moment, then said, "He might as well stay put. If we ground it won't be his skin we leave behind on those rocks."

"The pleasures of command," said Whalley.

"Right." Steadman rejoined Vann at the helm and scanned the displays while listening to the slow, steady crunch of ice. Unless you had a torpedo chasing you, the first rule when things got this tight was to *slow down*. The boat. Your thoughts. Everything. It was time for the *Invisibles* to live up to their reputation. "Helm. Make turns for six knots. Switch to the sound-powered intercom. Rig the boat for ultraquiet."

Quiet became *silent*. Loudspeakers went dead. Voices that were hushed became whispers. Off-duty crew retired to their racks.

Steadman could sense a curtain drawing over *Portland*. The coolant pumps stopped, allowing the nuclear fire in her reactor to simmer. *Portland*'s single bronze screw spun down to 48 RPM, a speed at which the great flower-petal blades sliced the water as silently as an Olympic diver slipping through the surface of a pool.

There were levels to this game. From that sunny summer day at the beach on Point Judith when he'd watched a submarine dive right off the coast to his selection for nuclear power school, the top had always meant command of an attack submarine. There was nothing more demanding, nothing more rewarding. Driving a ballistic missile submarine, a "boomer," was as boring as watching paint dry. Your main duty was to remain hidden. That made you prey. An attack-boat skipper was a hunter. Now the way to that goal ran straight through the Pass.

He put the sound-powered intercom to his lips. "Sonar?"

"Be just a second, XO," said Sonarman Schramm. "Bam Bam" Schramm lived in a tight space crammed with hot electronics immediately forward of Control and on the starboard side. If a submariner's world is confined to what his arms can reach, Schramm's world encompassed entire oceans. He could listen to whales a thousand miles away. He bragged that his sonar suite was so sensitive it could pick up his hometown radio station all the way from Nashville, though of course it couldn't. But then one day he'd astonished the other sonar techs by rigging a tape to do just that. One moment they were hearing the *swish swish swish* of a screw, the next, Hank Williams.

Bam Bam switched the high-frequency set from STANDBY to ACTIVE. Tiny, low-powered clicks too faint for the Russians to detect streamed from a transducer mounted beneath *Portland*'s spherical bow. The computer turned their echoes into an image that slowly built, line by line, into a picture on Schramm's screen.

The effect was like turning on the headlights on a dim night. Schramm could see the bottom scroll by on his screen, the boulders, the drowned hills. In theory, it allowed a submarine to make use of cover the way a soldier might run from tree to tree to cross a dangerous field. But a man carrying a rifle was one thing. USS *Portland* was another.

When the image was complete, Schramm said, "Coming at ya."

In Control, a clear, three-dimensional image of the bottom popped up on a television screen mounted above the helm. The false colors gave the icy Barents an almost tropical look. Azure blue marked flat sandy areas, tan for boulder fields, yellow for medium-sized obstacles and hot red for hills tall enough to pose a danger to *Portland*. As the boat moved, the closer objects vanished below the screen and new, more distant ones appeared at the top. Dead ahead was the red slope that ended at the Pass.

Vann crunched one final cube, then crumpled the cup, indicating he didn't wish a refill. "What's your plan, XO?"

You can say no. "We'll get closer and take a look."

"Get close enough to look and you might not be able to back out. Not with the tide running in. Still want to roll those dice?"

"I do. The Russians probably chose low tide for their fleet exercise hoping it would lock us out of the bay. If they think no one's looking, we have a shot at seeing something they don't want us to see. Maybe something important."

"Important enough to risk *Portland*?"

There it was. Did he turn back or take the bait? "Norfolk thought so or they wouldn't have sent us. If there's a way in, we'll find it."

Vann gave a poker-faced nod, but he thought, *Good answer.* "Then?"

"The bay drops off to three hundred feet on the other side of the Pass. We'll make sure we're alone. If they send out some boats, we ID them."

"What if they're not on file?"

"We underhull them and put them on file."

"Underhulling" meant driving your boat directly under another submarine: a dangerous place to be. Though he couldn't possibly hear *you,* you were in an ideal position to record everything about *him.* It was a little-known fact that every non–U.S. sub in the world, ally and enemy alike, had been underhulled by a stealthy, American attack boat. Vann was a renowned master of this black art.

"Very well," said Vann in a way that might mean *Good idea,* or just as easily, *It's your hanging.* "Who do you want sitting Dive?"

"Choper can stay. COB's got his eyes on him." Steadman concentrated on the screen above the helm. "Left ten degrees rudder. New course will be one seven five."

An undersea hill slipped to port. Another, taller one appeared to starboard. Steadman had them pointed at the narrow gap between them. A distant red slope grew higher, like a wave on the horizon.

"We used to do this with coded beacons and a stopwatch," said Vann. "You'd run from one to the next and hope to hell you saw it when the time came because if you didn't, you had no idea where you were. That was some hairy navigating. This is like flying low and looking out the window."

The second hill slipped behind. *Portland* entered a tight, sandy canyon. Steadman watched as the image on the sonar display changed. The screen showed less blue, less tan, more yellow and a lot more red. They were climbing an underwater mountain. Soon there was no room for turning around. No room for maneuver. No room for anything but hoping Whalley's tide numbers were pessimistic.

Schramm sent out another low-power sonar beam. "Conn, Sonar. Four hundred feet."

Whalley spoke up. "It shallows real fast out ahead." Then, to remind Steadman not to drill *Portland* into the Murmansk Bank, "No passes into the bay at this depth, XO."

"Sonar, Conn. Any close contacts?"

"Conn, Sonar. Negative," said Bam Bam. "But I'm starting to pick up that clanky old buoy at the mouth of the fjord."

The mooring chains that secured the first sea buoy out of Kola Fjord had broken in a storm, and the Russians had left the broken links and simply dropped a new chain and anchor. Now, when the sea state was right, the two chains rattled like a ghost in the attic.

'Bout drive ya nuts, thought Schramm. He blanked out the clatter with a filter and selected the passive broadband array. A green line immediately popped up on his octagonal "waterfall" display. "Conn, Sonar. I have a contact now bearing zero one three. Blade count looks about right for a twin-screw submarine. Sounds like a big 'un."

"A boomer," said Vann. "Probably a DELTA. Most of them are rusting at the pier or on the rocks."

On the rocks. Was that Vann's way of warning him not to do the same to *Portland*? "I wonder why they based their Typhoons up here? They have to be three times the size of a DELTA. It's pretty tight for a boat that big."

"Probably why they sold them to us."

Steadman looked at Vann. Was it a joke? "Sold them?"

"Congressional deal. The Nunn-Lugar Initiative. We paid the Russians to scrap their Typhoons before they auctioned them off. It came to half a billion dollars. Bought a lot of vodka, probably."

Whatever the Russians had spent it on, Steadman thought it sounded like a bargain. Typhoons were the largest submarines in the world, as big as a World War II aircraft carrier and so massively built the Russians considered them invulnerable. More, each dismantled Typhoon left the world two hundred nukes safer. "Sounds like money well spent."

"Personally, I'd rather put a Mark 48 under one of those big bastards. Then I'd *know* the job was done." Vann paused. "Maybe *two* Mark 48s."

"Conn, Sonar." It was Schramm. "Two high-speed contacts now, both triple-screws. The bearing looks good for Litsa Fjord."

Litsa Fjord was one of several that opened onto Kola Bay. It was insignificant on physical maps, but it loomed large on ones that counted nuclear sites, for it was ringed with Russian naval bases: Andreeva, Lopatka and Seal Bay, home to the rusting Typhoons.

"Bottom's rising rapidly," warned Whalley.

"Diving Officer, make your depth one hundred feet." Steadman could see it on the sonar monitor. The Murmansk Bank was a wall standing directly across their path. Its flanks were flocked with soft silt and slashed with deep, shadowed cuts. "Right rudder. Course one eight zero."

"Range to the Pass now eight hundred yards, XO," said Whalley.

On the HF display, the mountain rose higher, its contours more detailed. The sandy bottom was gone, replaced by a moonscape of boulders. Dead ahead, the shallow Pass was bracketed by rises marked in hot red. The HF display revealed a curious break in its bottom. A plunge, a deep crack, sharp-sided and terribly narrow.

"Still like those dice, XO?" asked Vann.

"I'd prefer to wait for higher water, Captain."

"No doubt. What about this?" Vann indicated the plunging notch.

"There's not much clearance down there."

"For a boomer."

Steadman recognized Vann's dig against the men who served aboard the big, lumbering *Ohio*-class ballistic missile boats. It was necessary work, but if they'd been any good, they'd be conning attack boats, wouldn't they? "You think *Portland* can squeeze through it?"

"You have the conn. If you want an opinion, I'd say if you take us over the Pass a seagull could take a crap on our decks. We're twenty miles from four of their five biggest submarine bases. You want to bet *Portland* they won't be looking?"

It's a bet either way, thought Steadman. For *Portland,* for Steadman's career, for 14 officers and 106 enlisted men. The pot couldn't get any more full. "It's a big risk unless we're in a war."

"A submarine is *always* at war. The only peacetime run we'll make is to the scrapyard. Until then, every submarine, every ship, every aircraft, is the enemy. Assume they feel the same way about us and you won't go too far wrong."

"Range now *three* hundred yards to the pass."

Steadman had the sense of a great narrowing in his life. Everything he'd trained for, necked down to the sharpest of points. Here. Now.

"Two hundred yards," said the navigator.

Vann was looking at Steadman intently, focused, as though watching something going on behind the XO's eyes. "Well?"

"Helm," said Steadman, "left ten degrees rudder."

Vann asked the question on everyone's mind. "What depth?"

"One hundred eighty feet. We're going to run that notch."

Vann gave Steadman a quick, conspiratorial wink.

Portland planed down deeper. The notch expanded in the HF screen. Steadman eyed it. The sides were sheer. The bottom a mess of boulders.

"Watch your lineup," said Vann.

Steadman saw the notch drift to starboard. "Right five degrees rudder," he said. The slot kept drifting. "*Hard* right rudder."

"*Line* up," Vann repeated. "You won't fit sideways."

"Range eighty yards," said Whalley. "You've got a following current."

The incoming tide was sweeping them right at the bank. Then it dawned on Steadman: *The rudder loses effectiveness with a following current.* He needed to put a good flow of water over the rudder, and fast. "Helm! Ahead two-thirds! *Move* the boat!"

"Sweet Jesus," said Slice and Dice.

Steadman reached for the collision alarm switch over the ballast control panel, but Vann's hand closed over his wrist.

"Keep rolling the dice, XO."

The great, graceful pinwheel of *Portland*'s screw spun up faster. The rudder began to grip. The image on the screen shifted.

"Hang on," said Steadman, though everyone was already braced. "We're going in." *Portland* entered the notch eighty feet from its bottom, forty from the wall to one side, and nineteen to the other.

CHAPTER FOUR

BELLING THE CAT

The submarine shot through the wall and into the deeper, inner waters of Kola Bay. The HF screen showed the ramparts of the bank falling away to a vast flat plain of sand.

"All stop!" said Steadman. He had grabbed a steel handle set into the overhead so tightly his hand had cramped. "Sounding?"

"Two hundred ninety feet."

"Diving Officer, make your depth two hundred fifty feet."

Lieutenant Choper stared at the screen above the helm.

"Hey! Wake up, Lieutenant."

"Yes, sir. Down to two five zero feet."

Chief Browne chuckled as he adjusted the ballast to maintain the correct buoyancy. His hands flew over the ballast control panel, a touch here, another there, tweaking, adjusting, anticipating what a few thousand pounds of water *now* would do to seven thousand tons of submarine in a few moments.

"Nice work, everybody," Steadman said to the ship's control party.

Vann scoffed. "You don't need to send them love notes."

"Yes, sir," said Steadman, though he disagreed. What harm did it do? "You've run that notch before?"

"Twice," said Vann simply. "You can see why the Russians never bothered to wire it. Who would try something that tight?" He allowed a small smile. "Were you really going to pull the collision alarm?"

"I really thought we were going to hit."

"Conn, Sonar. That boomer's definitely headed our way." Schramm was keeping one ear on the departing Russians, but he was listening a lot harder for signs that a quiet attack sub might be lurking nearby. "I'm picking him up real solid now. Designate the contact Sierra One. She's still running on the surface."

"What kind of a DELTA is she?" asked Steadman.

"No kind, XO. She kinda sounds like an OSCAR, but then the blade count is all wrong. Maybe it's all the fresh water in there, 'cause something's screwy." OSCARs were the Russians' newest cruise missile submarines. *Kursk* had been an OSCAR.

"Put it over the speaker," said Vann.

A low menacing rumble set against a waterfall's cascade emanated from the speakers above the helm. The steady *thrum thrum thrum* of double screws was loud and clear. Not the slash of a small, high-speed propeller, but a deep sound, a heavy, powerful rumble.

Steadman said, "The Russians buy the *Queen Mary*?"

Vann's face seemed carved from wax. "I'll take the conn, XO."

Steadman stepped back from the helm. "Captain has the conn."

"All stations make ready for periscope depth," said Vann. "Helm, make turns for four knots. *Left* ten degrees rudder. Sonar?"

"Searching." Schramm listened hard as the submarine did a slow, careful sweep. "Conn, Sonar. No close contacts."

"Very well," said Vann. "Diving Officer. Take us up to sixty feet."

Portland rose slowly, gracefully.

"Conn, Sonar. Bearing to Sierra One is zero one three. If she's just clearing the inner bay her range is about sixteen thousand yards. Designate escorts Sierra Two and Sierra Three. They're *Grisha*s for sure." Fast, heavily armed antisubmarine ships.

"Depth now sixty feet, Captain."

"Up the search scope. Let's have a quick ESM sweep," said Vann.

A slim antenna nearly impossible to spot broke the surface. It's job was to sniff for Russian radars.

There was a lot of activity to record this morning. A series of soft beeps and squawks came from the receiver. The electronics technician at the ESM console whistled. "Lots of activity. Two coastal radars, three ship sets. Two of them are Half Plates. Possible *Grisha*s."

Vann stepped onto the center periscope island. "Up the search scope."

When the search periscope's optical head broke the waves, a radio whip antenna rose with it. An instant later, radio signals began to flood into Rose Scavullo's computerized scanners. Radiotelephone. Ship-to-ship. Walkie-talkies. And though it wasn't exactly legal, the fainter whisperings of digital cell phones. Everything was vacuumed up and stored for later analysis.

Kola Bay was a target-rich environment for an eavesdropper. The radio traffic appeared on her computer display as vertical bars. The taller the bar, the more transmissions. The brighter the bar, the stronger the signal. It was the bright bar on the far right-hand side of the screen that drew her interest. Someone was doing a lot of talking on a cellular phone, and from the signal strength, he was not very far away.

She punched her frequency selector and began tracking the signal up and down the spectrum. In a few seconds, she had it dialed in. She ran up the volume and pressed the black headphones tight to her ears.

"... *too far, Kyt. Come to port now.*"

"*Da. Panimayu.*" Understood.

"*Port! Port! Port! You're headed for the rocks. Hard port rudder!*"

"*Panimayu.*"

There was a prioritized list of contacts every linguist heading for duty aboard submarines memorized. At the very top was *anything* that might mean another submarine was coming your way. *Kyt* meant "whale." What could "whale" be but a departing sub? She spoke into the open microphone circuit heard in Sonar and Control. "Conn, this is Scavullo. I'm picking up a two-way conversation that sounds like a submarine talking to a tug."

"We know about him." Vann put his eyes back to the search periscope and scanned the rocky hills guarding the mouth of the Litsa Fjord. By selecting maximum (24X) magnification, he could peer deep into the fjord itself.

Rows of drab concrete apartment blocks marched up a bare hillside. A loading crane leaned over a pier. Everything was still. It could almost be a view of an abandoned base. And then, something moved. He triggered the scope's video recorder. "'Here they come."

The sharp gray prow of a *Grisha* antisubmarine frigate emerged from around the rocky peninsula with a white bone of a bow wave in her teeth. A second *Grisha*. Then a black, rounded shape shouldered through the green sea.

"Son of a *bitch*," said Vann.

"Six seconds," said a quartermaster, keeping track of how long *Portland's* periscope was visible above the waves.

Vann turned away from the scope and said, "Down scope." The shaft was camouflaged and coated with radar-absorbent material. It was hard to spot, not impossible. "Run the tape," he told the quartermaster.

The monitor replayed the periscope observation.

Steadman blinked as the image appeared. "That's a . . ."

"It sure as hell is."

The Typhoon seemed to take forever to emerge from behind the arm of land. The eye couldn't grasp the true size of these behemoths. Like icebergs, what showed above water only suggested what was hidden below. A Typhoon was essentially two big titanium-hulled submarines welded together side by side and sheathed inside a steel skin that was strong enough to punch through nearly twenty feet of Arctic ice pack. Unlike other boomers, her missile compartment was located *ahead* of the massive, black conning tower. She wasn't pretty, but the captain of a Typhoon had more nuclear firepower at his fingertips than the prime minister of Great Britain.

Six Typhoons were built in the depths of the Cold War. One sat in a shipyard, unfinished. Three were barely afloat, more derelicts than dreadnoughts. A fifth had been badly damaged in a missile accident. The sixth and last Typhoon's luck proved no better: she'd suffered *both* a missile and a reactor accident that resulted in her permanent entombment in a tunnel blasted into a hillside at Bolshaya Litsa.

"I thought you said they were scrapping those boats," said Steadman.

"Washington thought so, too."

"Conn? This is Scavullo. If you can leave my antenna up a little longer, I might be able to tell you more about that submarine. They were doing a lot of talking and—"

"If I leave *your* antenna up, Lieutenant, the Russians will spot *my* submarine." He slapped the intercom handset back in its cradle.

"Conn, Sonar. I have a possible hull ID on that boomer. She matches up with Typhoon *Kara Sea*. She's listed as inactive."

"She looks pretty goddamned active today," said Vann.

Steadman watched the tape loop of the departing Typhoon. Scavullo said she heard a tug. Where was it? He looked at Vann. "What now?"

"Those sons of bitches took our money and kept that boat. We're going to go collect his scalp to prove it."

"Aye aye." Though Steadman thought Vann was taking the Russian's duplicity a little personally. Though he surely had a reason.

Steadman had read the Board of Inquiry findings. While commanding *Baton Rouge,* Vann had underhulled a departing Typhoon when the Russian skipper suddenly pulled a "Crazy Ivan"—a sudden, sweeping turn meant to expose a trailing submarine. Vann backed off. When the turn was completed, he moved right back in.

Then the Russian skipper did something totally unexpected: a *second* clearing turn. A "Double Ivan." Vann was forced into an emergency maneuver and in the ensuing scramble, *Baton Rouge* grazed a deep-keeled iceberg.

A sailor was thrown from his rack in the forward berthing area, broke his neck and died. The Typhoon slipped away. *Baton Rouge* limped home so badly damaged she never sailed again.

In submarines, doing a good job was no guarantee of promotion but screwing up nearly always got you fired. Vann's collision should have doomed him, but in the end the board decided that aggressiveness was not the worst characteristic in a fast-attack skipper. Against all the odds, *Portland* became his. But those who knew him from the old days called him *Double I-Vann*.

"Conn, Sonar. Sierra One's angle on the bow starboard twenty."

"Weapons. Firing point procedures torpedo, Tubes One and Two."

"Weapons ready," came the report from the torpedo room.

"Fire Control ready," said Lieutenant Keefe.

There was a pause long enough for all eyes to turn to Slice and Dice.

"Ship ready," he said at last.

"Try to remain awake, Lieutenant. Bearing and *mark,*" said Vann.

The fire control technician (FT) in charge of *Portland*'s weapons fed the data to a pair of Mark 48 torpedoes, knowing they would never be fired. "Bearing set. Range set. Solution is set. Tubes One and Two ready to flood." The Russian submarine was now burned into the torpedo's electronic brains. He wondered if a couple of Mark 48s could break a Typhoon's back, or just make him mad.

Vann said, "Up scope." The stopwatch clicked on as Vann swung the scope in another arc, then came to a stop. A flag snapped above the Typhoon's sail. At maximum magnification, tiny black dots could be seen moving on an open bridge big enough to hold all of *Portland*'s officers.

"Conn, Sonar. Range now twelve thousand yards."

The Russian ships carefully threaded their way out into open waters. The two escorts fanned ahead like eager sheepdogs sniffing for wolves.

"Six seconds."

"Down scope."

"Conn, Sonar. Sierra One is venting tanks."

Vann said, "So our satellites won't spot her. Too late. We did."

Then Schramm said, "Conn, Sonar. I'm starting to lose flow noise on Sierra One." He shook his head. A Typhoon's reactors were pretty quiet, but why bother quieting the plant in a submarine that big? You could run a Typhoon on fart gas and it would still make noise pushing the water aside. Moving, the boomer's flow sounded like a fountain splashing over rocks. But as she slowed, Schramm's passive sonar had to work harder to pick out the fainter machinery noises. "She's dead in the water."

"You think they know we're out here?" said Steadman.

"No way," said Vann. He was putting the pieces together, trying them one way, then another, checking for fit. "He's just letting those *Grisha*s run ahead and sniff around to make sure. They're violating a treaty that has brought them some major money and they don't want to get caught." Vann turned to the helm. "We'll let those escorts pass over and then follow Sierra One out to sea." It was a classic "Invisible Vann" move: let the opposition sweep over and pass out to sea, then cut inside.

As *Portland* crept in closer to the motionless Typhoon, Schramm heard a faint whine coming in through his passive sonar array. He focused hard on the sound, concentrating. The whine grew louder, clearer, then stopped with a *thunk*. "Conn, mechanical transient from Sierra One. I think our guy just popped a silo hatch."

"In the *bay*?" Opening the silo cover was the preparatory step to launching one of her RSM-52 intercontinental ballistic missiles, and that was done only out in the test ranges, or if you were planning on starting World War III. "Are you sure he's not rigging out his bow planes?"

Before Schramm could answer that he damn well knew the difference between a bow plane and a muzzle hatch, a low thud shuddered through Control, followed by the turbulent roar of burning rocket fuel and the waterfall hiss of a billion, billion bubbles. They were listening to the launch of a Russian ballistic missile, right through *Portland*'s hull.

"Conn, Sonar!" Bam Bam shouted. "That was a *launch*!"

Vann snapped, "Up scope! *Now! Now! Now!* Weapons! Flood One! Flood Two!" A missile launch might be a test or the opening shot of World War III. Vann had seconds to determine which one it was, and fast. The periscope went up in time for Vann to see a ball of hot orange fire and a cloud of white rocket smoke. "Sweet *Jesus*!" There was a bright flash, followed by the expanding flower of an exploding missile. Not a nuclear blast. That would have incinerated half of Kola Bay, and *Portland,* too. "They blew up that missile right overhead!"

In the radio room, Scavullo's scanners came alive as the periscope mast exposed her antenna again. Her screen lit up with radio traffic. She dipped into it and overheard someone on shore reporting an "explosion at sea." Then, a warning radioed to a patrol frigate to avoid the poisonous rocket fumes hugging the surface, followed by a message to stand by for another launch. A new voice answered:

"We should throw out our rockets by launching them someplace useful. Like Chechnya."

"Why not Moscow?"

Then, another voice, loud, and not happy. *"Who is on this frequency?"*

The air went dead. But Scavullo thought, *Throw out?* She grabbed the hot microphone. "Conn, Scavullo, they're not *launching* those rockets."

"Stay off this circuit!" Vann snapped.

"I mean, they're *launching* them, but they're blowing them up on *purpose.* They're *scrapping* them by launching them!" She selected the air band. Nothing. But the cell phone frequency was still active.

". . . like the fireworks? We have the best view. Not too close."

"We'll take it from here."

"Good luck, Whale. And don't forget me when you come back."

"Thanks for the help. We'll buy the first round. Whale, out."

The light bar on her display winked out. The connection went dead. She rewound her tape and played it again. If one Russian boomer was busy launching rockets, who was *Whale* to be seeing them, and not too closely? It had to be *another* submarine! She picked up the telephone. "Conn, this is Scavullo. There's a submarine leaving—"

"Isolate her," said Vann.

"Captain?" she persisted, "I think there's a *second*—"

"Isolate her!"

The line to Scavullo's console went dead.

She slapped her hand onto the console, then saw Lieutenant Bledsoe, the radio supervisor, smirking. She rushed over and grabbed the phone off the bulkhead beside him and yanked it off the hook by its coiled wire. The receiver clipped Bledsoe's upper lip. Just a light tap, but he looked as stunned as if she'd hit him with an ax.

"Are you out of your fucking mind?"

She ignored him. "Conn! This is Scavullo! There's another—"

"God damn it," Vann roared. *"Someone shut that bitch up!"*

Vann put his eye back to the scope in time to see the second missile break the surface and rise on a column of brilliant orange fire, smoke and steam. Like the first, it flew only a few thousand feet before exploding.

"The scope's been elevated *fifteen* seconds," said the quartermaster.

Steadman watched it on the periscope video feed. "The Norwegians are going to go bananas over all that rocket smoke."

Vann watched a third rocket follow the dirty gray trail of exhaust up into the sky. A fourth. Finally, he said, "Down scope. Okay, people. They're not supposed to sail those boats and they sure aren't supposed to scrap missiles by *launching.* Let's get some ocean under us and call it in. Nav?"

"Zero zero five to deep water, skipper."

"Helm, new course zero zero five."

"Conn, we've got a *Grisha* headed our way. Range now two thousand."

"Helm, ahead dead slow," said Vann. "Right ten degrees rudder. Diving Officer, take us down to three hundred."

The Russian frigate's active sonar began to lash her steel hull.

Ping! Ping! Ping!

"He's close," said Schramm.

"Rig the boat for depth charge."

The Russian ship stormed overhead, the angry *swish swish swish* of her triple screws growing louder, then fading.

"Conn! Sonar! Splashes in the water! Possible depth charges!"

Vann paused, then snapped, "*All* ahead *flank. Right* full rudder."

As *Portland* twisted away, a rain of slim steel cylinders descended, each two feet long and six inches wide. Deeper, deeper, from the green shallows down to where the light gave out to pure, cold black.

The first detonated over *Portland*'s stern with a sharp *crack!* The second went off directly over the weather deck aft of the conning tower, or sail. The third clunked down her sides and fell away. A dud.

Vann was furious. "Rudder amidships. Ahead two-thirds."

As the attack sub left the bubble-filled zone, a loud, metallic banging sounded in Control, like some diver striking the hull with a hammer.

Bang! . . . bang! . . . bang! . . .

"Conn, Sonar. Sound alarm." *Portland* had an onboard system for monitoring its own radiated noise, and the system was flashing an urgent warning. "We have a noisemaker on us," said Schramm.

A magnetic clapper had attached itself to *Portland* like a steel limpet. Streaming water forced a heavy metal disk to pound her hull.

Vann might be invisible, but he was no longer silent.

Bang! . . . bang! . . . bang! . . .

"Depth under the keel now three hundred eighty feet," said Whalley.

Vann's ears burned bright red. "We'll have to surface to pull that damned thing off." Once, a Typhoon had nearly ended his career. What would they say now? A second Typhoon finished the job?

Bang! Bang! Bang!

"We'll head for Norway. Helm, five degrees down on the planes. Diving Officer. Make your depth three hundred feet *smartly.*" He paused, listening to the infernal racket from that damned noisemaker, then said, "Take her deep."

■　　■　　■　　■　　■　　■　　■　　■　　■　　■

CHAPTER FIVE

GHOSTS

Captain First Rank Alexander Markov was up on the "Balcony," a small raised deck a short ladder's climb up from Compartment Four: the Typhoon's Central Command space. The Balcony was halfway up the sail from the control room, and it was by tradition Markov's alone. No one was allowed up here except by his specific invitation.

He pushed the thick rubber handles of the periscope. A motor growled, gears gnashed, and then, reluctantly, the massive instrument rotated away from the churning wake left by the departing tug. The crosshairs came to rest on a missile-loading crane leaning precariously over an abandoned pier. He pressed a trigger on the right handle, then called down, "Navigator, bearing, *mark*. Range, *mark*."

It was a formality. Markov knew exactly where they were. How many times had he sailed out of this fjord? Dozens, though never quite like this. Sailing a Typhoon to sea without a mob of tugboats to help? Markov had never pulled off anything like it, and neither had anyone else.

The navigator, Pavel Borodin, drew the new bearing line onto his chart. He prided himself on knowing his position within twenty meters, a tenth of *Baikal*'s impressive length. It was good discipline out in the open sea. Here, so close to the rocks and shoals, it was a matter of survival. His thin black hair was plastered flat to his scalp. A Nokia cell phone lay on the table, no longer needed. A picture of a red Volvo was pinned to the shelf above his chart table. He put a dot on the big paper chart. He let out a long breath. The last channel buoy was behind them. The first sea buoy was dead ahead. *Mother of God. We did it.* They'd sailed out of Litsa Fjord with decks awash, their sail cutting the water like a shark's fin, using only their periscope to navigate. And of course, the cell phone. How did Markov come up with *that*? "New course, zero five five."

"Just zero five five?" He let the periscope linger on the abandoned pier. The navigator had been issuing headings in *half*-degree increments as they slowly snaked their way through Litsa Fjord.

"Make it zero five *four,* then."

"Helm," said Markov. "You heard our navigator."

"Zero five four degrees." The young warrant officer, or *michman,* sitting at the rudder control moved a tiny joystick that belonged on a cheap computer game, not on the world's largest submarine.

Markov asked Belikov, the sonar officer, "Where's *Severstal?*" It meant "Northern Steel." *Kara Sea's* new name had been bestowed on her by a big steel company's charitable donation to the Northern Fleet. Markov thought, What's next? Would *Baikal* become *Pizza Hut?*

"Returning to base on the surface, Captain," said Belikov.

"And the American submarine?"

"Running away and making lots of noise."

Markov smiled. The Americans prided themselves on their quiet, their technical superiority. Yesterday, he'd have bet that none of this would have worked. Not the deception. Not their departure. Well, the sea was still a big place. It could still hold surprises. For him, even for the smug Americans. After spending a career playing mouse to their cat, he liked nothing better than a chance to stick his finger in the cat's eye.

He put his own eye back to the scope.

The view of the abandoned base was indistinct enough to allow Markov to people it with crews, to crowd the empty pier with the low, menacing shapes of submarines. The ones due out covered with snow, the ones just back from patrol jet black and glistening. All of them phantoms now. Broken up for scrap, hauled up on the beach, allowed to sink at the pier. Ghosts. Soon, Markov would join them, for when he returned from this run it would be as a civilian. Another ghost, though in Russia, the dead had a way of returning to the world of the living. *Baikal* had been reincarnated. Why not Markov?

Markov would make a young ghost at thirty-nine. He was a handsome man with full, dark hair, brilliant blue eyes and a bushy mustache that gave him a slightly raffish *mafiya* look. Looking like a criminal had its advantages these days. Certainly more than bestowed upon a captain, first rank, of the

Russian Northern Fleet. A fleet with too many officers and scarcely any ships worthy of the name.

Markov had climbed down the main trunk hatch of his first submarine at age nineteen. It was a smelly, cramped diesel that posed more of a risk to its crew than anyone. The reek of fuel oil permeated everything. The air, the drinking water, the food, his clothes. Eventually it seeped right into his skin. He could still summon the taste of fuel oil on his tongue.

He volunteered for nuclear boats and was selected for a communications posting. He went to sea and worked his way up until that incredible moment when he was blindfolded and hauled into the officers' mess, given a liter of ocean water to drink and ordered to kiss a heavy, swinging hammer suspended from the overhead frame. He'd cracked a tooth and emerged a qualified submariner.

His next voyage was nearly his last. He had the dubious honor of being assigned to an elderly Navaga-class missile submarine, the *K-219.* The boat had been launched when Markov had still been in grade school. Only her captain and chief engineer kept her running at all.

It was 1986, the end of the Cold War, the autumn of the year, when *K-219* suffered a seawater leak in a missile silo that spiraled into a full-blown chemical explosion, one that cut off all controls to her reactors and filled the hull with toxic gas. The captain ordered the survivors off the doomed ship and onto three freighters standing by. He remained aboard. There were American ships around and he was not about to let them grab his submarine.

Then Moscow ordered everyone back onto the submarine to save it at all costs. With water rising deck by deck, going back inside would have killed everyone, but the captain had the balls to countermand Moscow and scuttle *K-219* before anyone died trying to save her. Most of his men survived, but he was stripped of his commission and charged with treason. He lost his career and very nearly his life before a change in the political winds gave Moscow other things to think about.

Markov fared better.

He was chosen for submarine school at the top-ranked Leninsky Komsomol Academy. There he endured political instruction long enough to see it falter, then vanish, and he graduated at the top of his class. Four years later he went to sea as *starpom,* or executive officer, on a Typhoon. Then he was handed a Typhoon of his own. Commissioned under the Soviets with the soulless appellation of *TK-19,* it had been renamed for the largest lake in all the world: the "Sacred Sea" of Siberia, *Baikal.*

Baikal was just out of refit, which was both good and bad. The obvious faults had been fixed, but for every thing the workers had repaired, they'd broken, or stolen, at least one other. Computers. Sensors. Even copper wires and lightbulbs went missing. Just the same, what new captain can look upon his first ship with anything but love?

Under Markov's command, *Baikal* became the only missile ship that regularly arrived at its patrol station without an American hunter-killer submarine in trail. Markov did it with unusual tactics and by harnessing his greatest ally, the sea.

Two deployments later, Markov was ordered to take *Baikal* out with a gaggle of fleet officers up from Moscow. They were going to fire a brand-new missile in honor of Boris Yeltsin's birthday. Markov asked to see the test data. He was told the missile had been extensively tested.

In a submarine? A Typhoon?

When the engineers from the missile factory admitted that *this* was to be the very first launch from an actual submarine, Markov told them to go light their eighty-four-ton birthday candle someplace else.

The silo hatch yawned open. The missile dangled from a loading crane. His flotilla commander ordered him to allow the loading to continue. Markov was the best captain in the fleet. National prestige was at stake.

Markov respectfully refused. The commander in chief of the Northern Fleet ordered him to load that damned rocket. Once more Markov respectfully refused. That night, Admiral of the Fleet Koreodov called to find out whether Markov had gone crazy.

Markov felt the ghost of his old captain from *K-219* at his side. Besides, he was tired. His answer was less than respectful, and he was relieved of command on the spot. Another captain was found. The missile slid down into the silo, the muzzle hatch was sealed and *Baikal* put to sea, heading for the Novaya Zemlya test range.

The launch button was pushed and the missile exploded in a fury of flame and smoke. A slight misalignment caused it to jam. The rocket engine thundered, burning through the silo walls and sending a tidal wave of fire, water and poison smoke through the missile room. The captain managed to reach the surface and the crew fled the smoking, toxic hulk for rubber rafts.

In their haste, no one took note that one of her two reactors had failed to shut down automatically. With the pumps disabled, temperatures and pressures quickly built up to critical levels. A poorly welded coolant line gave way and the crippled *Baikal* erupted in a geyser of radioactive steam.

An oceangoing tug was dispatched and the giant submarine was towed into a tunnel built to hide Typhoons from snooping satellites. There, she was stricken from the registry and, except for the sea lions who had found a way into her tomb, she was forgotten.

Markov was also forgotten, but not forgiven. Instead of a new boat, he was given a training position at the Flotilla, teaching tactics and running the new computerized simulator for other officers. He often played the role of an American hunter killer ruthlessly tracking down a Russian enemy, and took no enjoyment sending their phosphorescent blips to the bottom again and again.

He heard someone scuffing up the short ladder from Central Command. Then a hand rested on his shoulder.

"Everything they said about you is true."

Markov looked up from the scope. A tall, distinguished-looking man stood behind him. Markov's blue coveralls carried a name tag that read, simply, KOMMANDER. This man's tag read K1-FEDORENKO: Captain First Rank Fedorenko. Markov thought, *Who invited you up here?*

Captain Gennadi Fedorenko let his hand linger on Markov's shoulder as though testing the fabric. "There's not one captain I know who would sail across a bathtub without tugboats nipping at his heels."

You need to spend more time with sailors, not spies, thought Markov. A submarine needed redundancy. *Baikal* had two reactors, two engines, two main pressure hulls. But two captains was a redundancy nobody needed. He'd seen Fedorenko's service record. He might be fluent in Chinese, but if he knew much about driving a submarine it had been kept well hidden. "I had plenty of help. A tugboat to keep watch above and a good navigator below. And don't forget the fireworks. The Americans had no choice but to pay attention to them."

"How did you come up with the idea of using a cell phone instead of regular methods?"

"The Americans already know our regular methods."

"So the old sea wolf can still come up with a new trick?"

"I'm not a wolf. I'm just a cat who prefers to walk alone." He turned back to the eyepiece, pushed on the periscope handle and let the instrument rotate him away from Fedorenko's hand.

Gennadi Fedorenko was just a few months older than Markov. His hair was yellow streaked with silver. His eyes were a pale gray that, like the northern seas, could cloud over and turn icy in an instant.

Like Markov, he'd attended the Navy's top academies. Like Markov, he'd served tours of duty aboard nuclear submarines. Unlike Markov, he'd opted for the political branch, a navy within the Navy.

Back in those days, every ship had its *zampolit,* its political officer, and no one dared make a move without his consent. In effect, he was a second captain who reported not to the Fleet but to the Party.

Fedorenko had been smart enough to sense the coming collapse, and agile enough to jump ship before it took him with it. He'd transferred to military intelligence, a line of work with better prospects than political discipline, and selected a specialty with a long history: China. Other enemies came and went, but the Chinese were eternal.

"How does it feel to be back in command of your own first ship?" he asked Markov.

"Like I'm driving my wife to a whorehouse."

"They're paying us a billion and a half dollars. It's a different matter."

No. A different scale. "Excuse me. I need to make another observation." He elevated the periscope until the bare, brown hills above the abandoned base filled the eyepiece. Then higher, until all he could see was the summer sky, hazy, white as alabaster. High summer in the far north meant endless, sunlit days and warm white nights. You never could get enough of summer, enough light, up here on the Kola Peninsula. He let the crosshairs drop back to a beacon mounted atop a rusted, skeletal frame that had once been painted in a red-and-white checkerboard pattern. "Navigator? Port Vladimir Light." Markov pressed a trigger in the periscope handle. "Bearing, *mark*. Range and *mark*."

Borodin drew another line, then said, "Captain? We're abeam the Bells." The clanking, rattling chains of the first sea buoy.

A cheer went up in Central Command.

"Save your lungs," said Markov. "We've got a long trip ahead of us."

"Why not let them cheer?" said Fedorenko. "The hard work is over. History was made today. This cruise will be remembered."

The hard work is over? Even if it were so, it was a stupid thing to say. You could never relax at sea. Not on a submarine, and especially not on *this* one. As for history, Markov had to agree. History would certainly take note of this voyage. It kept him awake wondering what it might say.

He slid down the short ladder to the main deck below, using only his hands, not even touching a rung on the way.

Fedorenko thumped down after him. At the bottom he turned and said, "Permission to leave Central Command?"

"Granted." Markov made his way to his chair, his ceremonial seat of command, and sat down in its smooth, blue vinyl.

Central Command was about the size of a Murmansk apartment and surprisingly snug for a ship nearly two football fields in length. He could reach up and touch the light gray metal console overhead where a framed plaque was mounted: SUBMARINE LIFE IS NOT A SERVICE, BUT A RELIGION. It had been a gift from K-219's captain. True then, and though the whole world had changed, true now.

From here he could swivel around and see the control stations lining both starboard and port sides. Active and Passive Sonar. Electronic Countermeasures. Ballast board. Radio and Navigation cubicles. Only the Weapons station was blank, but then Baikal hadn't sailed with any weapons, which was just as well. Misfiring missiles and torpedoes had put more Russian subs on the bottom than any enemy. "Belikov?"

The sonar officer pressed black headphones tight to his ears. Central Command was quiet by Russian standards, but any extraneous sound interfered with Belikov's job. He manipulated the azimuth ring until it overlapped the sound spike generated by Severstal. "No contacts."

"Rig the ship for dive."

The alarm rang three times as the officers in Central Command busied themselves with final checks. This cruise will be remembered. Markov thought. How? Like Quisling? The Norwegian had handed over only a few, outmoded ships to the Nazis. What would history have to say about the man who delivered Russia's biggest and most advanced submarine to the Chinese?

True, she would go without her missiles, thank God. And Markov knew that Russia needed the money. Admirals were paid $150 a month, when they could get it. His own salary amounted to less than half that. And a common seaman? The price of a life on the streets of Murmansk: twenty dollars. What would Russia not do for a billion and a half of them?

"Ship is rigged for dive," said Sergei Gasparyan, his first officer, or starpom. "Straight board. All hull openings are closed."

Markov examined the dive board himself. Not because he didn't trust his starpom. It was a matter of self-preservation. The first dive after laying up at pierside was always cause for vigilance, and it had been five years since the sea last washed over Baikal's back. Markov returned to his chair. "Make your depth fifty meters. Course zero two nine. Dive."

The raucous buzz of the dive alarm sounded again. There was a long, sad sigh of air rushing from cavernous ballast tanks that were larger than most submarines. Tons of dead water weight roared in from below, chasing the air out through the upper limber holes. The deck angled down, the air seemed to grow warmer.

The young officer at the helm moved his small joysticks slightly forward. His eyes were glued to the depth gauge and gyrocompass on the console before him.

"Depth thirty meters."

The water would only now be rushing over the open bridge at the top of his conning tower. *Let's hope we find all our leaks now,* thought Markov. Later, when they would be under a roof of ice, all problems would become more serious. *Baikal* was built to smash her way up through nearly twenty feet of it, but Markov could imagine a dozen ways she might end up on the bottom instead.

"Passing the one-hundred-meter line, Captain," said Borodin.

"Ahead on both engines one-third."

Two big screws shielded from the ice inside heavy shrouds spun up as a pair of 50,000-horsepower steam turbines absorbed power from the reactors. On the surface, *Baikal* could only wallow along at twelve knots. Submerged, she could go more than twice as fast.

Markov watched Gasparyan make a quick tour around Central Command, checking, probing, questioning. Gasparyan wore the white armband denoting his status as officer of the deck. He had thick black hair and a wisp of a mustache and a look of permanent suspicion. Markov liked sailing with a mistrustful *starpom*. An optimist made for pleasant company on land. In a submarine, he could get you killed. "Sergei? Have all compartments report their status."

Gasparyan pulled a small black microphone down from the overhead console. It was called a *kashtan*, "chestnut," though it didn't look much like one. He started at the bow torpedo room. "Compartment One, report."

"Torpedo room manned and ready," came the reply from a burly warrant officer named Lysenko. His compartment was located between the two main hulls in the upper bow, directly above the giant sonar sphere. The torpedo racks, designed to hold twenty-two weapons, were empty. "There's some seepage from Tube Six," said Lysenko. "The inner gasket crumbled. We can tighten it down but it should be replaced."

The torpedo room was usually manned by eight seamen under the direction of a petty officer and a compartment commander. But with no weapons aboard, the three torpedomen, all big, all brawny, had nothing to do but lift weights and read pornography. The Chinese would have plenty of weapons ready to load on board in Shanghai, and the three would earn a hefty bonus showing them how.

Still, a leak was not good news in any submarine. "Grachev?"

"I told you we should replace all those gaskets, Captain," said Chief Engineer Igor Grachev.

"You didn't tell me where to find new ones."

"The whole Navy is going to shit."

Markov smiled. When Grachev lost his gruffness, *then* he'd have something to worry about.

Usually, *Baikal* sailed with a propulsion engineer who worked under the chief engineer. Grachev was standing double duty. He was forty-one and divorced. He'd spent most of the last full year preparing *Baikal* for her final voyage, tinkering with balky systems, scrounging for spares from the idled Typhoons at Seal Bay, begging for what he couldn't steal and making do for the rest. He was the oldest nuclear engineer in the Northern Fleet, and so he was known as "Grandfather."

His short, iron-gray hair was as bristly as his personality. He wore a devilish salt-and-pepper goatee that was strictly against the rules; it interfered with the fit of an emergency breathing mask. But Grachev knew better than anyone that in a real emergency, say, a chemical fire, the piped oxygen flow to an EAB mask was usually the first thing to become contaminated. He wore his beard and dared anyone to notice.

Grandfather Grachev lived and worked in Main Engineering Control, immediately forward of Central Command. He'd papered a bulkhead there with photos of Russian women wearing short, tight outfits, gauzy underwear, bikinis and often less. They were Russian girls looking for a husband, and Grachev had vowed that one of these lucky girls would be his. Each member of the crew had been promised a sizable sailing bonus. Grachev planned to use his windfall to buy a wife. He'd invited the crew to vote for their favorite. A jar was filled with paper slips.

"Bottom now two hundred meters, Captain," said Borodin.

"Helm, take us down to one hundred fifty meters. Navigator. Plot a course direct to Saint Anna's Trough."

It was a two-day sail to the gates of the polar sea and slightly off the great circle route to Bering Strait, but making for Saint Anna's Trough would put deep water under them the fastest. Deep water was where a big submarine belonged, and *Baikal* was the biggest of them all. Though size wasn't everything. She had her weaknesses. *Baikal* wasn't maneuverable. She didn't part the sea, she *bulldozed* it. At certain speeds the water refused to flow over her tall rudder, rendering her almost impossible to steer. *Baikal* was solid as a mountain but she had to be respected.

"Compartment Two, report."

Rocket Alley was an enormous vaulted space forward of Central Command, home to twenty newly painted missile tubes. They marched down the sixty-meter-long compartment like a double row of massive yellow grain silos. Each was eight feet in diameter and thirty tall. Four- and eight-man cabins were tucked between them, each with its own sink and television.

"Rocket Alley manned and ready. All silos are dry."

"Make sure you keep tabs on their radiation badges," Markov said to Gasparyan. Not that a reminder was necessary. The whole crew knew that Rocket Alley was where the old missile accident had started. It was also where traces of the old radiation release could still be found.

The week before departure, with *Baikal* still in the tunnel, engineer Grachev took Markov on a final pre-sail survey. The boat looked, even *smelled* brand-new. Only Rocket Alley made the Geiger counters click. Not enough to kill, just enough to preclude lingering. News travels quickly in a submarine. The missile room was shunned. A sailing bonus was good only if you lived to spend it.

"Compartment Three, report."

"We're not sinking," said Grachev. Grandfather had moved aboard her for the last six months. It was a potent symbol. Even a wary conscript could see Grachev had suffered no harm from it.

Compartment Four was Central Command. Markov watched his officers go about their tasks with easy, economical motions. He'd drawn his inner circle from among his friends. Men he'd sailed with, knew and trusted. He'd let *them* pick the best junior lieutenants and petty officers. The rest had come from the moribund bases around Kola Bay.

"Bottom now two hundred eighty meters."

"Hold depth," said Markov. *One step at a time.*

Gasparyan said, "Compartment Five, report."

The huge, five-level space aft of Central Command was filled with mess decks, sick bay, fan rooms and at the bottom level, the sub's gymnasium and recreation center. An entire wall of the mess was decorated with a tile mosaic of a ship under full sail. A second wall was covered with a giant photo of the sun setting over the dark blue of Lake Baikal. Or was it rising? The gym came equipped with things never before seen in a submarine, American or Russian: a small waterfall, an aviary and even a swimming pool. Not a big one, and it was really designed to warm divers returning from the icy sea. But you could swim in it and better, the Americans had nothing like it.

"Compartment Five has a small leak from the TDU." The trash ejector. "If we dog it tight enough to stop the leak it might not open."

How many dried-out gaskets would they find on this cruise? "Seal it," said Markov. *Baikal* was designed to spend months underwater. A two-week run was a trip around the block. "We'll store trash in an empty freezer space."

Gasparyan relayed the order, then, "Compartment Six, report."

The aft engineering spaces were divided into two separate and identical hulls. Each contained a reactor and a pair of standby generators big enough to light a small city.

"Both reactors on-line and normal."

Gasparyan said, "Compartment Seven, report."

The turbines, engines and gearing that drove both seven-bladed screws were located in Seven, floating on isolation beds of coiled springs and dampened by thick rubber bumpers the size of heavy truck tires. A fact even Markov found astonishing: the great steel shafts, each the diameter of a tree trunk, stretched and twisted like taffy when the engines were run hard. Measured where they emerged from the reduction gears, the shafts were half a turn *ahead* of the hub and blades.

"Both engines connected. Spaces are manned and dry."

"Compartment Eight, report."

Baikal's stern was shaped like a beaver's tail and filled with hydraulic machinery to operate her rudder and aft planes. Beyond Eight was a maze of ballast tanks, an escape hatch, two thundering screws surrounded by protective shrouds and, finally, the sea.

"Eight is manned and ready. Aft escape hatch is sealed."

Gasparyan turned. "All compartments manned and ready, Captain."

Amazing. For a first dive to reveal only a few minor leaks was unusual enough in a *new* submarine. It was astonishing in one that had been buried in a tunnel for years. He picked up the intercom and broadcast his voice throughout the boat: "This is the captain. Well done."

His voice echoed through the half-empty submarine. Even with a full crew of 150, the interior spaces, the companionways, the decks, the mess areas were cruise-ship spacious to anyone used to submarine life. *Baikal* had sailed with just 107. Take away a third of her regular crew and she seemed almost haunted.

"Bottom now three hundred meters, Captain," said Borodin. "And our best course to Saint Anna's Trough is zero three one."

"Take her down to two hundred fifty meters. Course zero three one."

Markov was driving *Baikal* north to the Arctic Ocean. Soon enough they would encounter the marginal ice zone. The ice was Markov's friend. The Americans dominated the open ocean because they possessed a critical technical edge: they could hear Russian boats without being detectable by Russian sonar. But ice changed the equation. It turned the Arctic into a maze of hidden obstacles, floating mountains with keels hundreds of feet deep, chattering krill shrimp, rumbling pressure ridges. The noisy ice evened the odds considerably. It became a curtain behind which a careful captain could make even something the size of *Baikal* appear to vanish.

"Still picking up striker noise, Captain," said Belikov. "The American is running northwest at fourteen knots."

"No other contacts?" It wasn't unusual for several hunter-killer boats to be lurking off Kola.

Belikov pressed the big black headphones tight to his ears and closed his eyes. "None."

Markov thought, *Maybe the Americans are running out of money, too.*

"Captain?" It was Navigator Borodin. "You asked to be informed." He tapped the chart opened on his table.

More ghosts. The Barents was crowded with them. Markov put away the sailing orders and pulled down the *kashtan*. He clicked the microphone on. "Men of *Baikal*. This is the captain. We are at the point of nearest approach to where our brothers aboard *Kursk* were lost. There will be one minute of silence." He watched the red hand of the master clock sweep. "Mark."

The big submarine wasn't truly silent. Ventilation motors hummed. Coolant pumps thudded. But no one spoke a word until the red second hand ticked off sixty seconds.

When it was done, Markov picked up the *kashtan* again and said, "To the crew of *Kursk*, still on patrol."

The silence elongated, and then finally Markov said, "Helm? Let's do a clearing turn and make sure there's no one else around. Right full rudder, both engines ahead one-third. Belikov? Listen very closely."

Baikal lumbered around in a wide 360-degree turn, bringing her sensitive bow acoustic arrays to bear on any submarine trying to creep up from behind. It took a full twenty minutes before she was once again pointed north.

"No contacts, Captain," said Belikov.

"Take us around again. This time left full rudder."

"Why?" It was Fedorenko, returned with a glass of tea. "I thought the Americans were driven off."

"*One* of them was driven off," said Markov, irritated at having to explain himself in front of his officers and on his own bridge.

"Then we should leave the area before we attract another."

"We are leaving the area. Helm!"

"Understood." The rudder joystick went over and the submarine began a second clearing turn, a second "Crazy Ivan."

"Forgive me," said Fedorenko, "but our sailing orders say—"

"Captain, since you are familiar with our orders, perhaps you will do the honor of reading them?" He took the folded paper out and thrust it at Fedorenko before he had a chance to answer.

"Of course." Fedorenko cleared his throat and pulled down a *kashtan*. He stood at something near to attention.

"Men of *Baikal*," he began. "I hardly need to tell you that this voyage is unlike any other our Navy has attempted. No ship of this class has ever crossed the polar sea to the Pacific. We are like the legendary explorers who sought to open new trade routes to Asia. Russia is a nation of the north, and our ships and goods must be free to travel a northern route."

They are, thought Markov. *And we're making the delivery.*

"The Arctic stands in our path. But who knows the Arctic better than the men of the Russian Navy? Not even the whales. No surface ship can safely cross it. But a submarine can go where no others dare. Men of *Baikal*! This is our challenge!" He paused.

What is he waiting for? Markov wondered. *A cheer?*

"Now some of you know that foreigners had plans for *Baikal*. To this I say, *Not yet, my friends. Not yet.* The motherland has need for her, and for you. History will be made, and when you return home, you will not only be a little richer, you will have the thanks of your homeland to hold to your hearts forever." He stopped and clicked off the *kashtan*. "Captain? Do you have anything you'd like to add?"

Markov put the microphone to his lips, paused, then said, "This is the captain. I know some of you are here for the bonus, and there is nothing shameful in providing food for your families. And if there's a little left over, so much the better. As for history, I leave that to others. Instead, I speak to you as submariners."

Everyone in Central Command turned in his direction.

"Despite what you may have heard, there's a lot of work to be done before we reach the Pacific Ocean. No Typhoon has ever made the trip, and for good reason. Bering Strait is just fifty meters deep. This ship is forty meters from keel to sail. Captain Fedorenko is right. Finding a way through will be our ultimate challenge." Markov paused again and smiled. "And remember, if you screw up, if we sink, your wives and girlfriends will spend your bonus. And without even a body to bury, there will be a lot for them to spend. Think about that."

The men in Central Command swapped astonished looks. Then Borodin began to chuckle. Belikov joined in, then Gasparyan. They all knew he was right. Under the ice? Who would even *look* for them? It was their private nightmare, but Markov's joke took away some of its sting.

"Returning to course, Captain," said the helm.

Markov clicked off the *kashtan* and let it dangle from its cord. He nodded to the executive officer. "Sergei? Let me know when we reach the Central Banks. Captain Fedorenko and I will be in my cabin. You have the command." He stood and crooked his finger at Fedorenko. "Come."

The passage aft of Central Command was wide and paneled in birch. Only half the lights were burning. Markov swung himself onto a ladder and effortlessly slid down to the middle deck.

Fedorenko followed. "That was a stirring speech, but you know we should run while the Americans are too busy to look for us."

"What I know, Gennadi, is that it's not unusual for one American *Los Angeles* to come into Kola Bay while another waits offshore. And if it's not a *Los Angeles,* it will be a British T-boat."

"The oceans aren't teeming with schools of submarines, Captain Markov. A lot of effort is being made to assure our prompt arrival."

"All the more reason we should take our time. Follow me."

They went forward to Markov's sea cabin.

Inside was a bed, a desk, a chair with a 1960s "spaceship" style headrest sprouting from the top and an intercom with a big black telephone attached to it that could have been issued to a factory director in 1956. The designers of the submarine had included draperies to suggest a window, which was a stupid thing to suggest in a submarine and a fire hazard as well. Markov had ordered them all taken down and tossed into an empty freezer compartment. There were no personal touches except for a small, framed picture of his wife, Liza, another of his son, Peter, and a small vase filled with water. In it, a green sprig Liza had cut from a fragrant northern cedar to remind him there was a world beyond the sea, beyond the periscope, and that she wanted him to return to it, and to her.

Markov opened a small safe, withdrew a packet of papers and tossed them on his desk. "Here are our sailing orders. The real ones. Read them."

Fedorenko unfolded them. "I already have."

"Then do it for me. Aloud."

Fedorenko gave Markov a puzzled look. "From Commander, Submarine Flotilla Six, Admiral Popov, to Captain First Rank A. V. Markov, Commanding Officer of *Baikal*. Depart Seal Bay in conjunction with other fleet elements as briefed. Transit the Arctic Sea and arrive Anadyr Gulf, Grid Square twenty-two northwest, for rendezvous with Chinese destroyers *Hangzhou* and *Fuzhou* no later than thirteen August."

Fedorenko looked up. "That's ten days from now."

"I can count. Please continue."

"Proceed in company to Chinese territorial waters. Upon receiving proper signals, you will surface to take aboard a pilot for assistance in final docking, Shanghai East." He looked up.

"Finish it. There's not much more."

"Transfer command in Shanghai to Captain First Rank G. Fedorenko, who will remain behind as Liaison Officer in Command. Qualified officers and petty officers will be selected to remain as trainers. All others will return by chartered flight under the command of Captain Markov. While underway, Captain Fedorenko will be trained in the efficient operation of the ship."

"Imagine," said Markov, "finding an officer who can learn in days what it took me a career to figure out."

Fedorenko didn't rise to the bait. "While underway," he continued, "*Baikal* will operate under a regime of maximum silence. Every effort will be made to prevent tracking of your command by elements, surface or submarine, of foreign navies."

"I heard *maximum efforts should be made to prevent tracking and acquisition.* I heard nothing about sharing my command with you."

"I only wish to be helpful."

"How many combat patrols have you conducted?"

"This is a delivery mission, not a combat patrol. The Americans—"

"The sea is more dangerous than any American. A real sailor would know that."

Fedorenko stood stiffly. "You forget I am also a captain."

"You have my congratulations, Gennadi."

Fedorenko looked like he'd been slapped, which wasn't so far from the truth. "You're the master and I'm just a poor student. But allow this student to make a few observations. Our sailing orders are not suggestions. They're not wishes. Every deviation from them will generate a question. Was this step necessary? Was it useful? Or was it done to prove something personal?"

"Personal?"

"This was once your ship. Your first command. The Navy took it from you and this is your last chance to get it back, if only for a while. You aren't here for any bonus," said Fedorenko. "You're here to prove that everyone was wrong and that you were right."

"I'm a submariner, not a psychologist."

"I should think that a good captain would be both."

Markov could hardly disagree. Yet he'd be damned if he would share his command with some political golden boy. "We'll begin your familiarization when we reach the ice pack. You may go now, Gennadi."

Fedorenko started to leave, but then he stopped at the door and turned. "It's interesting how our sailing orders assumed you wouldn't stay on in Shanghai to oversee the transition. Have you wondered why?"

Markov had noticed that right away. "No."

"Maybe the Navy knows you better than you know yourself." With that, Fedorenko left.

Markov opened a paper chart of the Barents Sea. They'd stripped his office of all his files, his papers, even the photographs from the walls. There was nothing, no work, to return to. All he had waiting for him back in Murmansk was his wife and his son. And what would he do all day? Sit at the kitchen table in his dress uniform and tell them sea stories?

A simple red line marked his intended course, but nothing was simple about sailing *Baikal* across the pole. Once they were beyond the shallow Barents, the bottom plunged in a series of ever-deeper basins: the Nansen, the Amundsen, the Polar Abyss. The basins were broken by chaotic fracture zones and drowned mountains. On the surface, the thin, young ice that collected off Siberia grew thicker and heavier as it drifted toward Canada. Storms cracked it open, then slammed it back together into deep pressure ridges hard as armor plate.

Markov's course looked simple, but even without the added task of dodging other submarines it was anything but. Each kilometer was unique, each hour a new challenge.

His course brushed the North Pole, then dived through the shallow Bering Strait. He could make twenty knots and arrive there in a week, but he'd make a lot of noise doing it. On the far side of the world, two Chinese destroyers were waiting to escort him into the naval base at Shanghai East. It would take every one of the ten days he had.

The truth was, Fedorenko wasn't entirely wrong about timing. The Pacific Fleet couldn't keep Russian territorial waters free of Americans indefinitely. If *Baikal* was going to make rendezvous on schedule, he would have to make good speed across the Arctic, driving hard for the Bering Strait. There he would have to slow down. The approaches to the strait were shallow and choked with ice, even in summer. The margin between scraping his submarine's belly below and smashing her sail on a berg overhead would be a matter of meters.

Markov would have preferred to sail around the edge of the marginal ice pack, hiding in its grinding, grumbling noise. He would have preferred to lose himself in the middle of the empty Pacific and then sail into Shanghai alone. Not by tagging after some Chinese destroyer. But his preferences didn't matter. He had a rendezvous on the other side of the world. Professional pride was at stake, and so for better or for worse, it was an appointment he and *Baikal* would keep.

CHAPTER SIX

CASUS BELLI

4 AUGUST

Taiwan Oceanographic University, Taipei

The girl in the short denim jacket leaned over and said, "You're a senior? That's lucky. I have another year left."

James Lee Chen didn't answer. He wished she would turn around and pay attention to someone else.

But she found his distance intriguing. The hot August sun had streaked her face with sweat. She fanned herself with a protest sign with an old man's face, a diagonal red stripe and just three words: BIE DONG TAIWAN! Hands off Taiwan! "You have plans for after the demonstration? We're having a party."

James shook his head. "No plans."

"Great! Then you'll come. You have an accent. Where are you from?"

"Quemoy Island. My family are fishermen." *Were.*

Her interest faded. She raised a carefully painted eyebrow, moved slightly away, fanning furiously, as though James had suddenly taken on a smell. She leaned close to the girl standing next to her in line, and they quietly exchanged places.

A loudspeaker blared, *"They're on the way!"*

The students gathered for the demonstration stirred, a few signs waved. It was too hot to move much, to waste energy. The tropical sun was a physical force. It poured down on the courtyard of Taiwan's National Oceanographic University with almost liquid intensity. The air was windblown and dusty. Swirls of brown dirt were swept up in rising spirals. The campus was built on solid rock atop a hill overlooking Keelung Harbor. There were no trees, there was no shade. No escape.

Even by Taiwanese standards, NOU was a second-tier school, a place where the business of establishing career contacts was subjugated to the actual study of the sea. That was why James Lee Chen had chosen it.

He felt the sweat pour down his slim chest, plastering his T-shirt to his skin. It was completely soaked. His dark suit would be ruined, and that, too, made him sad. It had been an expensive gift from his family.

James Lee Chen had grown up on the tiny island of Quemoy, moored a scant three miles off the coast of mainland China. Taiwan had seemed as remote as Tokyo, while China was a dark wave rising on the western horizon, never breaking, always there.

In 1949, Mao sent thirty thousand troops of the People's Liberation Army across the narrow waters to claim it from the hated Nationalists. He neglected to consult the fishermen, who would have told him about Quemoy's sandy shoals and powerful tides. The troops were stranded in the shallows and systematically slaughtered.

From then on, only artillery shells crossed the disputed border. Quemoy's guns had fired on the mainland, and had been fired on in return. Though the big green loudspeakers that once shouted shrill propaganda at the mainland now played Taiwanese pop music, the beaches were still mined. Soldiers still sheltered under thick roofs of concrete and steel. Unlike other Cold War wounds, Quemoy had never healed.

Against such uncertainty, James found the sea reassuringly predictable. Its laws were consistent. Its principles well understood. You could set your watch to the tides. Taiwan's friends and enemies might change on any given day, but the Great Kuroshio Current never did.

The Lee family made the sea their life. Their oceangoing trawler *Shin Hwa* always returned to the island low in the water, her holds heavy with fish. The first share went to their fellow islanders. The second, by law, to the Nationalist troops stationed on Quemoy. The third usually found its way across the narrows to the mainland port of Xiamen, where fish dealers paid top prices. In an odd way, the Communists had sent James Lee Chen to college.

He turned. The concrete stairs leading up to the aquarium's cool, dark sanctuary were kept open by wooden barricades enforced by a double row of grim, suffering police.

Far below, James could see Keelung Harbor empty of its usual crowd of merchant shipping. It wasn't a natural disaster that had emptied it, but a political one. China had already taken back Hong Kong and Macao. Taiwan was the last plum left on the tree. How long could a few islanders defy a billion Chinese?

Beijing decided to grasp the tree and give it a good hard shake.

Taiwan's nineteenth annual military exercise, Operation Hangkuang 19, or "Chinese Glory," was scheduled for mid-August. For the first time ever, China scheduled war games for the same area, at the same time. Two armies, two air forces, two navies, could not pretend to fight each other in the same space without the battle turning real. Someone would have to back down.

Every cargo ship vessel that could leave Taiwan did so. In the scramble, little attention was paid when Chinese Maritime Police stopped a trawler off the port of Xiamen.

The little ship was boarded, seized and towed to the mainland. A news conference was held. A People's Liberation Navy captain announced that the vessel was stuffed not with fish, but with rifles, rockets, small arms and ammunition. The trawler was the *Shin Hwa*. The crew was tried one day and convicted the next. Under Chinese law, smuggling weapons was a capital offense. The executions by firing squad were covered live. A bill for the ammunition used was mailed to the Lee family.

A high-level Chinese delegation had traveled to Taiwan to "resolve outstanding issues regarding relations between the Province of Taiwan and the central government." The delegation was led by Wang Daohan, China's top official for Taiwanese affairs. A man with a passionate interest in sea snakes. The university's aquarium held a spectacular collection. It was his face that had been printed on thousands of cardboard posters.

"There he is!"

A motorcade appeared at the bottom of the street leading to the main gate. James Lee could see the bobbing helmets of a detachment of Special Police jogging beside the limousine.

The students began to chant. The police batons came out.

"BIE DONG!"

"TAIWAN!"

The motorcade veered away from the main gate and entered the campus from the side. Rocks sailed over the fence. The stones fell short, but flying objects of any kind clearly made the police nervous. They swung their batons in fierce arcs over the barricades, keeping the students from getting too close.

"BIE DONG!"

"TAIWAN!"

James Lee stood with his hands at his sides as the president of the National Oceanographic University got out of the black limousine. A stone sailed through the air and bounced off his bald head. The student who threw it fell under a storm of police batons.

"BIE DONG!"

"TAIWAN!"

Wang emerged from the car next. A short, rotund Buddha of a man with thin gray hair and a scalp glistening with sweat. Flanked by Special Police, he began walking to the aquarium steps.

"BIE DONG!"

"TAIWAN!"

It was the girl who gave Lee his chance. She screamed an epithet and threw her poster at him. Somehow, instead of fluttering to the ground, it sliced the air clean as a thrown discus and struck Wang Daohan's cheek, drawing blood.

The police mobbed her, yanking her over the top of the barricade, throwing her to the ground.

No one was looking at James Lee. The air was thick as water. The world beyond ceased to exist. There was no sound. He crawled under the wooden barricade, then stood. He pulled out a soggy sheet of paper. It was the bill sent to cover the cost of murdering his family.

A Special Policeman spotted him. His baton began an upward arc.

Lee moved in under it, close enough to smell the policeman's sweat, Wang's sweet cologne. He crumpled the bill into a wad and threw it. *"My name is Lee!"* James screamed so close his spittle flew across Wang's face. *"My father is Chen Ying Lee! Master of the* Shin Hwa!*"*

Wang Daohan's face seemed carved from marble. Cool. Impenetrable. His mouth formed the word, "Who . . ."

He never finished his sentence.

Five sheets of Semtex explosive were wrapped around James Lee Chen's waist. The pressure switch was underneath his watch. A wire ran up his arm and down his chest. The baton smashed down across Lee's brow too late. The young student had already balled his fist and brought it down against the face of his watch.

It was over in an instant, but the echoes of that terrible *crack!* would thunder around the earth, into space, and even beneath the sea.

Golden Horn Bay
Vladivostok, Russian Far East

The hills of Vladivostok stood above a cool summer fog blowing in off the Sea of Japan. It was just after five in the morning, and the largest city in the Russian Far East was barely stirring. A few fishermen dropped their lines into the oil-fouled waters of Sportivnaya Bay. Dogs prowled the empty streets, nosing through mounds of uncollected garbage so deep their bottom strata had composted to black, granular soil.

The soft gray mist blanketed the city, the docks, the fishing piers, the empty supply yards. It filled the bowl of Golden Horn Bay, home to the Russian Pacific Fleet, where concrete docks extended bony white fingers into cold, black water. The piers were crowded with warships of every size and shape, from aircraft carriers to liberty barges and everything in between. Most were derelicts, though it took a professional eye to tell the difference. All the hulls were scabbed with rust. Nothing moved except for the wheeling gulls and drifting fog.

Nothing moved, and then, something did.

A *chuff* of black exhaust rose from the gray guided missile destroyer *Hangzhou*. She'd been laid down for the Soviet fleet as an advanced ship of the *Sovremenny*, or "Modern," class. She'd languished in a St. Petersburg shipyard half-finished for years when a fresh infusion of cash turned her into the newest and largest ship in the Chinese Navy.

Hangzhou had the long, graceful lines of all *Sovremenny*-class destroyers. A clipper bow, a greyhound's sleek flanks. A helicopter hangar nicely faired into her aft superstructure. She had their heavy weapons, too: 130mm guns fore and aft, modern antiaircraft missiles, and stacked in angled tubes along her superstructure, eight Moskit missiles in quad mounts, Mach 3 speedsters designed to kill American aircraft carriers.

Lines were singled, then cast off. The big ship backed away from her berth under her own power. Bright pennants fluttered above her bridge. Her twin stacks sent shimmers of heat into the cool, gray sky.

The Russians sent *Hangzhou* off in excellent style.

She'd arrived at the Golden Horn with a long shopping list. The mayor of Vladivostok made sure the list was quickly and efficiently filled. He took a personal interest in the matter, as well he might: the mayor took in ten percent of everything the Chinese spent.

Destroyers of the Russian Pacific Fleet were stripped of their spares, their ammunition, their electronics, even their crews. Russian officers who hadn't seen pay in a year were hired as consultants. They came aboard to instruct the Chinese in the ship's complex systems and ended up running them. Russian weapons plus Chinese money was a winning formula, and *Hangzhou* bristled.

The warship's stern churned with froth as she swung her sharply raked prow out into the main shipping channel that led to Peter the Great Bay and the open waters of the Sea of Japan. There she would rendezvous with four *Kilo*-class attack submarines steaming under the protective wing of *Hangzhou*'s sister destroyer, *Fuzhou*. All six warships would turn north for the long run up to the Anadyr Gulf.

The destroyers would keep watch over the air and the surface of the sea. Their only vulnerability was to submarines, particularly American submarines. The *Kilos* were there to kill submarines.

CHAPTER SEVEN

WHISPERS

3 AUGUST

CFS Alert
Northwest Territories, Canada

Alert was remote, even by Canadian standards. The signals intelligence station was a small cluster of prefab buildings huddled around an airfield on the extreme northeast coast of Ellesmere Island, just 800 kilometers from the North Pole. That made Alert the most northern-inhabited settlement in the world.

From April to September, night was unknown. From October to March, there was no sun at all. The shore of the Lincoln Sea was a snowball's toss away, but it was usually invisible beneath a white plain of rumpled, pressure-cracked ice.

Alert had always been a hardship post. When the Cold War ended, much of the facility was shut down. Of the seventy-three hardy souls still stationed there, the "Frozen Chosen," only seven were still in the intelligence-gathering business and all of them worked for the United States Navy. They were there to tend SPINNAKER, an advanced system of hydrophones seeded across strategic gaps and submarine sea lanes at the top of the world.

The SOSUS (SOund SUrveillance System) lines down in the Atlantic and Pacific were very good. In calm sea states, they could hear planes flying *overhead*. But SPINNAKER was newer, and much better at filtering out natural sounds to focus on the beat of a submarine's nuclear heart.

SPINNAKER's thick fiber-optic conduit snaked out of the Lincoln Sea. It ignored Polaris Hall, the base's main communications center, and ran straight into the side of a windowless hut set behind a tall, barbed-wire fence. A big satellite uplink antenna towered over the hut, shielded from the elements inside a white geodesic dome.

A tone sounded at the SPINNAKER console. A printer chattered.

AAA/SC/5B: CONTACT LEVEL 3 . . . 12:23:31Z
BBB/SC/9D: CONTACT LEVEL 1 . . . 12:29:14Z
CCC/SC/12F: CONTACT LEVEL 1 . . . 12:47:03Z
DDD:END . . . . ???

SPINNAKER had picked up the sound of a submarine in the central Barents Sea. A twin-screw submarine, and that made him Russian. The subsequent contacts connected the dots and established his basic course and speed. The coded results were beamed up to a satellite, then bounced down to Norfolk, Virginia. There the biggest, fastest supercomputers in the world considered the submarine's acoustic fingerprints for only a few milliseconds before deciding that a Russian Typhoon, a ballistic missile submarine whose sounds matched no known profile, had put to sea, heading northeast.

USS *Portland*
off North Cape, Norway

Bang! . . . Bang! . . . Bang!

The striker was tireless. The pounding continued so long as the submarine moved, and with a pair of Russian frigates tailing her, *Portland* had to move.

The *Grisha*s finally stopped at the international boundary. The boat would have to surface to remove the striker, and Vann refused to do it under their eyes. *Portland* sailed on for Norway.

The racket was bad enough up in Control, but it was worse in the machinery spaces aft, closer to where the noisemaker had lodged. It made the engineering officer of the watch wince. The banging sounded like the noise made by pressure waves coursing through piping. The kind of "water hammer" that broke welds and spilled radioactive coolant and killed submarines; a problem American boats weren't supposed to have.

Bang! . . . Bang! . . . Bang!

Steadman's tiny cabin was located forward of Control, and so he had more of the submarine's bulk between him and the striker. With his door shut and his eyes closed, he could almost convince himself they were tied up at the pier, with yard workers making noisy repairs on *Portland*'s hull.

The cabin was roughly eight feet wide by ten long and paneled in sheets of imitation wood. The fittings were bright, shiny chrome. The effect was more Winnebago than marine. A teal blue bed folded up against the outboard wall. A laptop computer lay open on a fold-out desk.

He replayed the incident in Kola Bay. An American submarine caught and attacked inside Russian waters was going to make headlines. In the old days it could be kept quiet, but now if it wasn't already on CNN it soon would be. That meant diplomatic protests by the Russians and denials by the Navy with their usual *We do not comment on submarine operations.* Just because they wouldn't comment didn't mean they wouldn't investigate. Steadman also knew there had been no right move.

There was a knock.

"Come."

"Sir?" It was Rose Scavullo. She'd washed her face and combed back her dark hair into a ponytail. She was carrying a single piece of yellow lined paper, folded in half. "Do you have a moment?"

And then there's you, he thought. Bledsoe was still wearing a Band-Aid on his upper lip, and taking a lot of ribbing over being "beaten up" by a girl. It wasn't going to make it easier to convince him to drop his claim that she'd attacked him, which is what Steadman fervently wished he would do. "I'll meet you in the wardroom in five minutes."

"This is a private matter, sir. I'd rather not discuss it in the open."

"If it's about Bledsoe . . ."

"It's not. It's about what happened in Kola Bay." She shut the door, then unfolded the yellow paper. "This is a transcript of some message traffic I picked up during the Russian exercise. You should read it," she said, then remembered and added, "Sir."

Steadman thought, *With the door shut, she can say anything happened in here.* Would that thought even have occurred to him if Scavullo had been a man? He started to read. The first three entries were labeled *PHONE.*

". . . too far, Kyt. Come to port now."

"Understood."

"Port! Port! Port! You're headed for the rocks. Hard port rudder!"

He looked up. "This is the submarine you said was leaving port."

"Before I was thrown off of the command circuit. Keep reading."

The next three were labeled *SHIP to SHIP.*

"We should throw out our rockets by launching them someplace useful. Like Chechnya."

"Why not Moscow?"

"Who is on this frequency?"

Steadman looked up. "They actually *said* they were scrapping them?"

"They used a specific word: *v'brositye.* It means, 'we're throwing the rockets away.'"

"A word's not much to go on."

"It is if you know what it means."

"Would another linguist hear it the same way?"

"I don't know. I'm the linguist you've got."

Steadman was surprised. She was keeping her eye on the mission. Not personalizing it. "However you figured it out, it sounds like you were right. That was a good call."

"Thanks. Keep reading."

The third section, like the first, was labeled *PHONE*.

"*. . . like the fireworks? We have the best view. Not too close.*"

"*We'll take it from here.*"

"*Good luck, Whale. And don't forget me when you come back.*"

"*Thanks for the help. We'll buy the first round. Whale, out.*"

Steadman reread the last lines. It sounded like a continuation of the first voice intercept. A tug issuing helpful commands to a departing boat, trying to keep it off the rocks.

"Okay. I read it. What are they saying?"

"There was a second submarine leaving Kola Fjord, sir. One submarine launched missiles while another one sneaked by us."

"The transcripts don't say that."

"It's a logical inference. I tried to alert the captain and he cut me off."

"Is that when you hit Lieutenant Bledsoe?"

"If I'd hit Bledsoe, he'd have more than a Band-Aid on his lip."

Steadman could see the pulse beat in her throat. She was a fighter, all right. Did she know who, and what, she was fighting? He held up the yellow page. "Why are you bringing this to me?"

"Because when we get back to Norfolk, they're going to want to know how we let that second Russian submarine get by us. My job is to warn the commanding officer if I hear *anything* that suggests another submarine is around. I wasn't allowed to do my job. I don't want my evaluation tainted by the mistakes of others."

He read the passages again, hoping to find a flaw in her reasoning. "What's this about *phone*?"

"Digital cell phone. The spectrum band my intercept came from."

"I thought we're not supposed to listen in on phone frequencies."

"We're not supposed to sail inside Russian territorial waters, either. I can log the intercept as coming from anywhere."

"You'd alter your radio logs?"

"Sir, I knew what was happening out there. I had the right information and the captain ignored it. That's what counts, isn't it?"

"So is following orders. Commander Vann ordered you off the intercom. You ignored him."

"He was wrong, sir."

"You're a junior lieutenant unqualified in submarines. Commander Vann's a senior officer with a lot of operational experience. What makes you think you're fit to pass judgment on him?"

"Just take a look at what happened and make your own evaluation."

And take your side against the man who will recommend me for command. "I'll tell you how it looks to me. I think you deserve a commendation for figuring the scrap-by-launch deal so fast—"

"I *knew* you'd understand what—"

"—and a reprimand for listening in on unauthorized frequencies, and suggesting we alter the logs to cover it up. That's before I find out what happened between you and Bledsoe. Right now you're even. I'll discuss your second-boat hypothesis with the captain."

"It's not just my hypothesis, sir."

"You want me to call it women's intuition?"

Bang! . . . Bang! . . . Bang!

Her face flashed with anger. "Thanks for your time. I won't waste any more of it." She started to turn.

"Wait," said Steadman. "What happens ashore is out of my hands. But while you're here on *Portland,* for better or worse, you'll be evaluated on your performance. Nothing else matters."

"Really? Is that *your* intuition?"

"It's my promise. Don't assume everyone is waiting to ambush you. It can make the rest of the run harder than it has to be. You can go now."

His door clicked shut. Hypothesis. Intuition. Wild-assed guess. One way or the other, Steadman figured the odds of getting his own attack boat were now about as good as his making Chief of Naval Operations.

They were twenty-three miles off the Norwegian coast at Point Vardo when an alarm bell went off in the radio room aft of Control. The sub's trailing wire antenna had picked up the ELF (Extremely Low Frequency) code to rise to periscope depth to receive a special satellite transmission.

"Sonar, Conn," said Vann. "Any close contacts?"

"One trawler bearing zero one five. I've been watching him for a while, skipper. He's outside eight miles." Schramm entered the contact in his official log. He then pulled out a small notebook and wrote the time, followed by *trawler, S-015 R + 08, adv CO.*

Keeping a private, duplicate log was totally against the rules. They could hang him for it. But when they got back home, people were going to wonder who screwed the pooch off Kola. Official logs could be altered. Schramm's would show that he'd warned Vann about those *Grisha*s.

"Come to periscope depth," said Vann. He took a large cube of ice and cracked it in his teeth. Submarine captains were chosen for their coolness, their accuracy, their confidence. Aggressiveness was rewarded. Recklessness was not. Sure, he'd left the periscope up too long, but what choice did he have? *Missiles in the air.* Was it a live fire drill, or some rogue captain deciding to start World War III? Scenarios just didn't get any hairier. He had to observe that Typhoon, even at the risk of getting tagged, and do it while trying to deal with that hysterical girl.

Bang! . . . Bang! . . . Bang!

"Sixty feet, skipper."

Crunch! "Up scope." He put his paper cup aside.

The search scope slid up from its well. Vann swept the horizon. There was nothing but gray mist, gray sea. "Nice fog bank. Radar?"

"Target bearing zero one six, range seven miles."

"Conn, Radio. New message traffic received," said Lieutenant Bledsoe. The satellite antenna atop the periscope had picked up the coded whisperings from Norfolk. "I'll have it confirmed in a couple of minutes."

"Send our sitrep back up the instant you're finished."

"Aye aye."

"Diving Officer. Surface the ship," said Vann.

The shipwide intercom squawked, *"Surface, surface, surface."*

With the rumble and swoosh, high-pressure air replaced water inside *Portland*'s ballast tanks. The attack sub began to rise. Soon, the roll of the open sea made itself felt inside Control. It was not a pleasant sensation for men accustomed to her rock-steady decks.

"Let's go pull that son of a bitch off our back," said Vann. "Have the XO and Chief Browne join me on top."

Steadman arrived at the bottom of the main trunk ladder after Vann and the two lookouts had already climbed out onto the open bridge. At the very top, the inner hatch had opened downward, the outer hatch swung up, revealing a beautiful circle of pearl gray light. What submariner didn't relish the sight of the sky, the smell of fresh sea air?

Steadman climbed up the sail and out into the small, open bridge. The lookouts were on station, though in the fog there was little for them to do. It was dank and cool, but the fresh air was sweet after breathing *Portland*'s manufactured atmosphere. There was no land in sight. A low fog hid the sun completely. Water hissed up her black sides as she rolled in the small seas, then fell away in sheets of foam.

Browne climbed out of the open hatch a few seconds later. He carried a black pry bar. His orange personal flotation vest was already strapped on. He had another slung over his shoulder.

Even up on the open bridge, Browne wore his short-range radio and earpiece to keep in touch with other parts of the boat. Browne never stood still. He was always making rounds, appearing to be everywhere and nowhere. One minute in Control, then in the engine room, later on the mess decks, the sonar room, the torpedo room, the radio room. As Browne liked to say, he had more rooms to take care of than a hotel.

Vann said, "I want that striker gone, COB."

"Aye aye, skipper." Browne hefted the bar and looked at Steadman. "You ever see one up close, XO? Might not get another chance."

COB wanted to talk about something. Steadman glanced at Vann. The captain nodded.

Steadman turned to clamber over the lip of the open bridge, but Browne handed him a float vest.

"Mighty long swim to the beach, XO," he said.

Steadman put it on, wondering how COB had known to bring the pry bar without being told. And how did he know he'd left his vest below?

They climbed down to the weather deck and clipped their "monkey tail" safety lines into the recessed safety track.

"You got to pay attention to your habits, sir. That vest should go on the minute you head topside. It shouldn't be a matter of *thinking*. It ought to be . . ."

"Automatic?"

"See, when things go sour it ain't your *thinking* that'll save your butt. It's your *habits*."

"I'll remember that."

Submerged, *Portland* was a deadly predator. But on the surface, she wallowed like a floating hot dog in even the calmest sea, low to the water. Her hull was covered with tiles that became slick when wet, and a single slip would put a man over the side. Even in August, the Barents was cold enough to kill.

The slim, black hull tapered as they made their way aft. The stern was riding too low to spot the striker. Waves rolled clear over the hull just forward of the tall black rudder.

"So how's Scavullo making out?" asked Steadman, fishing.

"Bad," said Browne. "It started when she came aboard and it hasn't quit. See, she's trapped with a bunch of guys who don't know how to act in front of her, who don't want her around and there ain't *no* place for her to hide. Excuse me." Browne spoke into his microphone too softly for Steadman to hear.

A rumble shook the deck. A valve had been opened, sending high-pressure air into the stern trim tanks, forcing out the water. The submarine began to ride higher in the sea.

"So you don't think putting women on the boats will work?"

"It's gonna work on this boat because I'll *see* to it. But if you want my personal opinion, no, sir. Not until the Navy *wants* it to work."

"The Navy sent her here."

"Yeah, but they had to know that putting her and Vann together was like dropping a mouse into a snake pit. That's no *experiment*. You *know* what's going to happen."

"You think she's been set up?"

Browne took a deep breath and let it out slowly. "Way back when, a man like me would be hauling dinner and peeling potatoes. But the boats, they're different. Anybody here, he passed the same tests as everyone else." He opened his flotation vest and tapped the dolphins pinned to his breast pocket. "This is *all* that counts. Nobody *ever* set me up to fail. You see what I'm saying?"

"The fix is in?"

"All the way."

The magnetic clapper emerged from a boil of white foam. A crude, rusty tin can with stabilizing fins at one end and slots for water to flow through on the other. It was surprisingly small; about as big as a child's sand bucket. "Not much to it."

"Enough to sink a CO." Browne watched the waves slosh around the black hull. "Skipper worked hard to come back after *Baton Rouge*. They forgave him once. Doesn't mean they'll forgive him twice."

"The Board of Inquiry cleared him over *Baton Rouge*."

"Yeah. I read that report."

"You were with him on that run. They miss something?"

Browne seemed to be reaching down inside himself for the right words to say something difficult, something unpleasant. He took a deep breath, then let it out. "Sir, I've sailed with a whole bunch of captains. You can say I've made a study of them. Some want to be your best friend. I call them smiling menaces because a leader's got to cut some wake. Commander Vann's got the opposite problem. He'll take over your job because he doesn't really trust you not to screw it up and make him look bad."

Steadman thought of Vann's poster, *Zero Errors*. "Vann turned *Portland* around. What's wrong with that?"

"I'll tell you. See, on a boat, someone's *always* making some kind of mistake. Captain's got to set up a system to catch them and correct them. Not turn them into a capital offense. All that does is encourage people to *hide* and that's *seriously* dangerous."

"Was that a problem on *Baton Rouge*?"

"It sure as hell was. I'm not saying that sonar tech shouldn't have warned Vann about the ice. But ask yourself why he *didn't*. What kept him from screaming like a stuck pig that *Baton Rouge* was gonna hit something?"

"Panic?"

"I'll tell you something scarier than a collision. It's a man who's afraid to tell the captain he's wrong."

A wave rolled over the clapper. It gurgled and swirled in white foam.

"Everything happened fast," said Browne. "We were tailgating that Typhoon and then he swung around and came at us like a big old freight train and we're sittin' on the tracks. CO orders hard over rudder and fifteen seconds later we hit. The flooding alarm sounded. We got toxic gas from seawater mixing with the batteries. We take a steep down angle. I saw good men crying while the captain chewed out that ST for not warning him about that ice."

"Vann wasn't trying to save the boat?"

"He was trying to save something, I guess." He unclipped his safety line. "If I go over the side, be sure to throw me a line."

"Can't run the boat without the COB."

"You remember that when they give you one." Browne eased down off the weather deck to retrieve the striker. He thrust the pry bar under the magnetic lip and heaved. The thing let go at once.

"COB," said Steadman, "I want you to get to the bottom of what happened between Scavullo, Bledsoe and Engler."

"Engler's old *Portland*."

"He's got problems. His wife moved out on him. I just saw the Familygram today. She left without paying the rent and the landlord's going to put his stuff on the street next Monday. How do you think we should handle it?"

"I'll send up some smoke signals and see what can be done."

"We're a long way from Norfolk."

"We have our ways." By this he meant the network of other senior chiefs, the true rulers of the United States Navy. "Engler's a pain, but he's still one of us. Let's bring the skipper his prize."

They rejoined Vann up on the open bridge. Browne held up the noisemaker. "What do you want done with it, Captain?"

"Throw it into the ocean, COB. We're not on a souvenir hunt."

"Aye aye." Browne heaved it far over the side. It hit with a splash, and with a last defiant *clack!* disappeared.

Baikal
Persey Rise
Central Barents Sea

Markov handed control of the ship to Gasparyan and went forward to have a quiet talk with his chief engineer.

Main Engineering occupied the forward section of the compartment located immediately beneath the massive sail, sandwiched between Central Command and the vaulted missile room. Every mechanical system in the vast boat could be run from this one spot, where Grachev sat like a spider at the center of a nuclear web.

Markov entered the crowded space through its aft door. There was a large circular waterproof hatch leading directly forward to the missile room. Two other doors in the port and starboard walls connected the Command Capsule with the two outer hulls containing the crew's cabins. The rest of Main Engineering, every available centimeter, was paneled in controls, gauges, switches and ranks and rows of identical dials. Four seats were upholstered in cheap blue terrycloth. An open spot above the reactor temperature controls was decorated with photos of pretty young women: finalists in Grachev's search for a mail-order bride. Every crewman got a vote. Markov read the two at the top, Angelika from Sevastopol and Fatima from Bishkek.

Angelika's photo showed her leaning back on a rock on the banks of a small river. She wore the mere suggestion of a pink string bikini. The Kyrgyz girl was a soulful young woman with long brown hair and huge dark eyes. She was dressed in a conservative black dress and flat shoes.

"How is it coming?" asked Markov, taking a seat next to the engineer.

"Angelika is ahead two to one."

"I can see why."

"So will everyone. You put your bonus money down on a girl like that and some *mafiya* jerk will come along and make her a better offer and it's goodbye, Angelika. Still, it might be fun for a while."

Markov shifted the subject. "I want you to put together a training program for Fedorenko. Has he spoken with you about staying on in Shanghai?"

"That little shit."

"You told him no?"

"Look, if they want to pay us for sailing to China, fine. But teach them how to use this ship? Never. You wouldn't, would you?"

"I'm still considering my options."

"Options." Grachev snorted. "You'll walk off the deck in China and go home with the enlisted men."

"What makes you so sure?"

"Simple. I know you."

Markov stood and patted the chief engineer on the shoulder. "You're right."

"Wait," said Grachev. "You haven't voted."

Markov looked at the two front-runners, the Olgas, Tatianas and Lenas. "A girl from Bishkek would be more reliable."

Grachev grinned. Plainly, it was what he thought, too. "Reliability counts," said the chief engineer. "I knew you'd understand."

CHAPTER EIGHT

THE CALL

USS *Portland*

Lieutenant Bledsoe and Radioman Engler were still on duty in the radio room. Bledsoe wore a small bandage on his lip. Engler was diligently studying a schematic diagram. It was enough to make anyone who knew him suspicious.

Engler was a short, heavily muscled man with close-cropped hair, a pirate's bushy mustache and a reputation as a fighter. You didn't go to bars with Engler and expect to come back to the boat clean. If the place was too peaceful, Engler would haul off and slug a stranger just to get things started.

Steadman stepped into the radio shack. "Message decoded yet?"

"Almost," said Bledsoe as he worked the KG84 encryption machine. "It'll be done in a minute."

"I want to talk to you about this morning. Meet me in the wardroom when you come off watch." Steadman went down a deck, then forward to the wardroom.

A wide-screen television there showed a map of the Taiwan Straits. Ominous arrows, red and blue, arced across the screen and met in the middle of the Taiwan Straits.

Steadman saw Lieutenant Dan Keefe, *Portland*'s weapons officer. "What's going on?"

"Some big shot from Beijing got blown up in Taiwan. It looks ugly."

Steadman watched the screen. It showed an aircraft carrier launching jets. "Nice to be on the other side of the world."

"I'll say." The weapons officer was like a librarian who hated the idea of books being checked out. Keefe's Tomahawks and Mark 48s were kept in a state of ready perfection. The idea of allowing them out of his control bothered him.

The carrier deck on the television faded, replaced by a reporter standing in front of the Great Hall of the People in Beijing. It was nighttime, and there were a lot of lights burning in tile offices behind him.

"In response to the assassination of a high-level mainland diplomat in Taipei, Beijing released a short message: *The people of Taiwan Province stand on the abyss of war. Order must be restored.*"

Damn, thought Steadman. *That's not the way diplomats talk.*

"The Ministry of National Defense has declared a maritime exclusion zone in the South China Sea. Commercial shipping is leaving the area as an American battle group races to the scene to deter Beijing from taking Taiwan back by force. . . ."

"This have something to do with the flash from Norfolk?" asked Keefe.

"Quiet!" came half a dozen voices.

The Beijing correspondent was replaced by another reporter standing in front of the White House fountain.

"Today, the president ordered a second U.S. carrier battle group into the area, and the Pentagon has shifted the carrier already there, the USS *Kitty Hawk,* into the area designated for the Chinese war games. The Secretary of Defense called the movement a prudent, cautionary measure. In a statement read thirty minutes ago, the Chairman of the Joint Chiefs of Staff added that sending in two carrier battle groups represents a signal to the Chinese that we want the situation to return to normal."

If they can read our signals, thought Steadman. "Keep watching," he said to Keefe, then returned to the radio room, where Bledsoe handed him a sealed envelope. "Eyes only for Vann," he said.

"I'll see that he gets it."

Vann was still topside on the open bridge. Steadman handed him the envelope. "We picked up a CNN broadcast, skipper. A mainland Chinese diplomat was assassinated in Taiwan and Beijing is making noises about invading. Seventh Fleet is going in again to separate them."

"Not our ocean. Let COMSUBPAC worry about it." Vann slit open the envelope and read it. He looked up and handed it to Steadman.

Z090043Z3AUG2001
NLOB*NLOB*NLOB
EYES ONLY FOR VANN
FM: COMSUBLANT
TO: CO USS PORTLAND

INFO: COMSUBPAC, CINCPACFLT
SUBJ: SPECIAL OPERATIONS

1: UNK TYPHOON-CLASS SSBN DETECTED CENTRAL
   BARENTS, PROC NE 14 KNOTS
2: INTERCEPT RED SSBN PRIOR NANSEN BASIN
3: ASSUME COVERT TRAILING AT COMBAT RANGE
4: ESTABLISH ID OF RED SSBN AND RPT
5: UNODIR MAINTAIN TACTICAL CONTACT
6: IF SSBN ENTERS PACOM CHOP DIRECTLY CINCPACFLT
7: WARNING: CHINESE AIR AND NAVAL FORCES EST 200NM
   EXCLUSION ZONE FROM ALL CLAIMED TERRITORY, INC
   TAIWAN
8: WARNING: COMBINED RUSSIAN-CHINESE ASW FLEETEX
   CURRENTLY UNDERWAY PETROPAVLOVSK SOUTH
   ANADYR GULF NORTH
9: COMM: GUARD SPECOPS BROADCAST LIMA FIVE AT
   DESIGNATED SCHEDULE
10: THIS IS IMPORTANT. GET IT DONE, JIM . . . GRAYBAR
    SENDS

These were marching orders, and they came right from Vice Admiral Graybar, commander of Submarine Force Atlantic. Steadman reread the message.

An unknown Typhoon? Schramm had identified the one they'd seen launching rockets as the *Kara Sea*. It meant Scavullo had been right, a *second* Russian submarine was on the loose, and Norfolk was sending *Portland* after her.

"They must have slipped that boomer out while we were running for Norway," said Vann. "Maybe that missile-launching exercise was designed as a cover."

She thought so, too. "Skipper, you need to talk to Scavullo about this."

"Why? She's the reason they were able to pull this caper off. They spotted my scope while we were dealing with her hissy fit in the radio room. They tagged us and forced us to leave the area while they sailed this second boat out free as a bird. *Talk* to her? I don't want to even know she exists until we get back to Norfolk. Then we'll let Graybar *talk* to her about her behavior. You know the last time a Russian boomer left port without one of our fast attacks in trail? Never."

Just wait until they find out that she knew it and you wouldn't listen.

Vann stared off into the fog, looking southeast toward Russia. "We'll have to cut the corner and get ahead of him." He turned to Steadman. "Have Whalley plot a course for Galiya Bank and get us heading that way flank, then meet me in my stateroom." He turned. "Clear the bridge!" Vann spoke into the intercom. "Prepare to dive!" He looked up once more at the sky, took a last breath of clean, fresh air, then said to Steadman, "Let's move the boat."

Browne heard laughter coming from the Goat Locker. He opened the door and the two senior chiefs inside went guiltily silent. He tossed his flotation vest onto his bunk. "Okay, what's goin' on in this space?"

The leading chief from the Torpedo Division was Arthur Babcock but he was known, for reasons lost to time, as Bobby. "We were just talking about the girl."

"The girl's a lieutenant, asshole."

"Yeah. That's the one. We were thinking that if the Navy really wants to make this female thing happen, they ought to do what they do with the boomers. You know, have two separate crews assigned to each boat. They have Blue and Gold now. Why not Blue and Pink?"

"You been burning the midnight oil, Bobby."

"There's just a couple of problems. I mean, how they gonna figure what shoes to wear with their poopy suits?"

"So?"

Babcock covered his mouth and made an announcement in a squawky voice. *"Announce casualty and gather all hands on the mess deck to confer and commiserate!"*

The second chief spoke up. "Of course, a Bad Hair Day Drill will be a cast-iron bitch."

"Announce casualty, gather all personnel on the mess decks," said the torpedo-man. *"All hands to the base beauty salon."*

"But it could get worse," said the second chief. "I mean, what would happen if they found a spider someplace?"

Browne turned to Babcock. "Well?"

"Spider Drill. Evacuate the boat and call the Marine boarding party to come and kill that horrible thing."

Browne gave them the toothy smile of a crocodile contemplating lunch. "I'm glad you all have such good senses of humor. See, if I hear those jokes again on this boat, you're both headed for sensitivity training. I guarantee you, a good sense of humor will come in handy."

Portland scribed a curved white wake as she swung her bow north. Faster, faster, her single propeller churned the water to a frothy boil. Fifteen, twenty knots. The wake vanished as she slipped beneath the gray water of the Barents, heading northeast. Twenty-five knots. Twenty-eight. Submerged, she could run even faster, though the rock-steady decks gave no hint of her power, her speed.

Stepping through the hatch from Control to the passage leading forward to Vann's stateroom, Steadman might have been negotiating a well-lit tunnel carved out of living rock.

Vann's door had a plain white sheet of paper on it with just two words: *ZERO ERRORS.* He knocked.

"Come."

The walls of Vann's cabin were covered with more imitation wood paneling. The single bed was folded up into a kind of table and booth. A framed photograph on one wall showed Vann shaking hands with a frail old man. It was Rickover, the creator of the Navy's nuclear fleet. Beneath it was a quote from the prickly old admiral: *"An engineer must have the courage of his convictions."*

A pair of blue curtains framed a small mirror mounted above a tiny sink. To one side was a television monitor that allowed Vann to see what was going on in critical areas of the boat: Control; the sonar room; the maneuvering, torpedo and engine rooms; even scans from the periscope. A multifunction display mounted on an arm beside the table glowed with streams of red data.

Vann nodded at the booth. "Take a seat and let's figure how this is going to play out."

Steadman slipped behind a small Formica table.

Vann sat down and pulled the multifunction display out, tilting the screen until they both could see it. Their knees brushed. "The Russians and the Chinese cooked something up, XO. It's a coordinated operation. The only question is, what are they trying to accomplish?"

"Where does the Typhoon fit?" asked Steadman.

"Where indeed." Vann shook his head. "Congress will want to know why they gave the Russians half a billion dollars to scrap those Typhoons and the

Russians are sending them out on patrol. Will they blame themselves? No. The Navy will turn to me. To us."

Steadman remained silent. Vann was probably right.

"It might not be anything official," said Vann. "They'll call it an evaluation, but trust me, XO, the knives will be out and the blades will be so sharp you won't feel the cut." Vann tapped a key. A map of the Arctic Ocean appeared.

"Sir, Lieutenant Scavullo intercepted some chatter between a tug and a departing boat back in Kola. She thinks she heard that second boat leaving the fjord."

Vann squinted as though a bright light had been switched on. "Is she claiming she knew that second boomer was out there?"

"The transcripts suggest it."

"*Suggest?* Look. I had missiles in the air. I had patrol boats coming down my throat. It could have been the opening shots of World War Three. You want me to stop and listen to the speculations of a girl riding a boat for the first time in her life? And then she went off the deep end. You were there. You heard."

"I was there," Steadman agreed. "I heard."

"If she'd let us do our jobs we wouldn't need her suggestions. We would have picked that second Typhoon up on sonar. Then there's Washington." Vann said it as though the very word had a foul odor. "She's got more friends there than we do, XO. That's why we're going to have to stick together to make sure this comes out right."

Stick together? "I'm not sure I follow you, skipper."

"From here on we can't tolerate any more mistakes. Every misstep on our part makes us look like clowns and her like Joan of Arc. She can cook those transcripts and who the hell will know?" Vann paused, then, "About the Typhoon. There are just two ways we can disgrace ourselves. One is not to pick him up again. The other is to find him and then lose him. I don't intend to let either one happen. There will be no acceptable excuses. There will be no equipment failures. Only personal failures."

"Yes, sir."

"Okay. Next item. I'm recommending you for Prospective Commanding Officers School. Congratulations. You earned it."

There it was. Everything Steadman wanted, within his grasp.

"Of course, if they knock me off the wall over what happened today, my evaluation of you won't count for much. That's why we have to stand together. After we nail this guy, let's sit down and go over our recollections about what happened today. Just to make sure."

"I'll ask COB to assemble the logs."

"Okay. Just remember the logs won't mean a lot in a political fight." He looked up. "We both know what really happened back there, don't we?"

Steadman saw something in Vann's eyes he'd never seen before. "Not yet. But we will."

"I'm headed for a staff slot and a squadron. You're headed for PCO school. That's what we want, isn't it?"

"Yes, sir, it is." But what was Vann really asking?

"Good. Now. What did COB find out about that business with Scavullo? Who rigged that microphone?"

"He's still working on it."

"What's taking him so long?"

"He wants to be certain."

"Lieutenant Hennig owns that space," he said, meaning the officer in charge of the Auxiliary Division. "Tell him I want the treadmill stowed until I have a name."

"Sir, it's the only exercise machine on board."

"The area is posted off limits until I have that name." Vann tapped the keyboard again and two pie-shaped operational areas were highlighted. The North Pole itself was at their juncture. A blue dot at the lower left edge marked *Portland*'s position. A red circle in the central Barents Sea marked the last known location of the unknown Typhoon. "Norfolk thinks he's running for the Pacific."

"They've never sent a Typhoon into the Pacific before."

"Doesn't mean they won't try to." The captain called up a different screen. "The Russians are beating the bushes chasing our boats away from their coast. And look. The Chinese sailed a new destroyer out of Vladivostok. She's headed north."

"Rendezvous?"

"That's how it looks. Probably south of Bering Strait."

"If this Typhoon is really headed for the Pacific, he's got to start hustling." Vann looked up from the screen. "Go on."

"Bering Strait is a nightmare for a submarine that big. He'll have to pick his way through dead slow. He's got to start making better time if he hopes to meet up with those Chinese ships. They can't wait around up there forever."

"Better time means more noise."

"Yes. If we sprint ahead and find a polynya, we can surface and get an update on his position." A polynya was a patch of ice-free water in the Arctic. "We can wait for him, then we fall in trail."

Vann paused long enough to make Steadman wonder whether he'd said something stupid, but then the captain nodded. "I'll buy it. Tell Bam Bam we'll need a polynya by this time tomorrow."

"Aye aye, skipper." Steadman turned to leave.

"XO?"

"Sir?" said Steadman.

"I want you to assign someone to tag after Scavullo. I don't mean into the head. The last thing we need is her screaming harassment. But we've got to have the goods on her. We need documentation. When she steps out of line, I want it on the record."

"Aye aye, Captain." Steadman couldn't think of a more onerous duty. "I'll try to find someone."

"And don't forget about the exercise machine," said Vann. "I want it gone by next watch."

CHAPTER NINE

IN FAST ICE

4 AUGUST

Baikal
Galiya Bank

Navigator Borodin's small cubicle in Central Command was separated from the large compartment by a simple curtain. A gooseneck lamp illuminated a paper chart of the waters around Franz Josef Land. Borodin slowly, painstakingly entered *Baikal*'s speed, course and elapsed time since the last known fix into his navigation log.

A NAKAT-M navigation computer that was state of the art in 1986 displayed the same chart and the same data, but it was surely nothing to depend on. When Borodin was finished, he'd have a position estimate he'd be willing to bet his life on, which was what it amounted to anyway.

He put a tentative dot, in light pencil, on his chart and compared it with current depth soundings and gravimeter plots. Gravity seemed so uniform, so reliable, but a sensitive instrument could detect minute variations. A map of those variations helped Borodin establish *Baikal*'s precise location. It was slow, tedious work, but absolutely reliable.

They were skirting the Galiya Bank, a shallow rocky spur extending into the Barents Sea from Franz Josef Land. The pole itself was just three days' sail ahead. After that, they'd be headed south, but when you were at the pole, *everywhere* was south.

For now, they were in a zone of brash ice and bergs drifting in the prevailing northerly current. Very soon now the edge of the polar ice pack would appear, a chaotic jumble of noise and a good place to hide.

Borodin ran his calculations again, and only then was he willing to commit a dark dot and a sacred line to his paper chart. The shallow Galiya Banks were passing to port. They could end up on them and have some hope of escape. Not so out over the Polar Abyss, where the bottom was five thousand meters deep. Run into trouble up there and they'd simply vanish from the world of men forever.

The curtain behind him was pulled wide. "Are you having problems with the navigation computer, Borodin?"

Borodin turned. Fedorenko had a habit of showing up uninvited. It reminded him that the captain was no submariner; submariners responded to tight quarters with a greater respect for privacy. "I don't like to trust computers, Captain."

"A captain who is fearful of his shadow and a navigator who doesn't trust his tools. At least you're not using a sextant."

"I brought one."

"No doubt you did. You *do* know where we are?"

"I do."

"Then show me." Fedorenko gave a cursory glance at Borodin's computer monitor, then the chart, but then his eye stopped on the photo of the red Volvo pinned above the table. "Your car?"

"When I get back."

"You know, there will be plenty of work to be done when we arrive in Shanghai. You could stay on as an instructor and when you return you could be driving a BMW. Even a Jeep."

And look like a gangster? "I'll think about it."

"Do that, Borodin." Fedorenko examined the paper chart, then the computer screen. "You and the computer seem to agree."

"Not quite." Borodin pointed to the white cross. "If the computer is right, we're about to go aground on Galiya Bank. If I'm right, we'll pass to the east by two and a half kilometers."

"When did you last update the NAKAT with a satellite fix?"

Borodin looked up with real surprise. It was an intelligent question. *Maybe he knows more than I've given him credit for.* "I'm sneaking satellite fixes each hour."

"It seems to me that a ship with two navigators is never sure of its position. Who is right? You or the computer?"

What about a ship with two captains? The cross inched closer to the shallow bank. Then it merged. Borodin looked up. "It appears that I am. If you'll excuse me." He reached for the *kashtan* microphone. "Captain? This is Borodin. We're passing Galiya Bank. Turn to zero one five."

Markov sat in his raised chair. He swiveled to face the two officers at the helm. "Come to zero one five. Maintain ninety meters."

Fedorenko stepped out of Borodin's cubicle and into Central Command. He glanced at the speed display. "We're standing still."

"That's about to change," said Markov. Ahead, the broken sea ice was replaced with *fast ice,* a flat, uniform shelf that spanned the sea between the scattered islands. Fast ice held firm right through the summer. It was very smooth, very even with few embedded bergs and likely none. Markov needed to make better time and this was a good place to start. "Sonar? What do we have overhead?"

"Still choppy, Captain," said Belikov. "The ice firms up in about two more kilometers."

"Captain? This is Borodin. Sounding is now four hundred meters under the keel."

Nothing below to hit, and soon, nothing above. *All right.* Markov clicked on his *kashtan.* "Grachev?" he called to his engineer. "How are your engines?"

"So far so good. And they're your engines, too."

"Captain Fedorenko would like some more speed."

"Would he also like to arrive in Shanghai? These engines haven't been run hard in years."

"Passing under the edge of the fast ice," said Belikov. "Thickness is steady at one point five meters."

Baikal could explode up through such a thin layer with barely a pause. "That's exactly why I need to know what they can do. Ahead two-thirds on both engines. Turns for twenty-four knots. Open her up a bit, Igor."

"Why not? The atoms are free." Grachev reached over and pulled a pair of levers that allowed more steam to flow through the coolant loops. More steam out meant more cold coolant in, and cold water is more dense. Dense water absorbed more radiation from the cores, raising temperatures and producing more power.

Steam flashed through the turbines. Far astern, inside their protective shrouds, the bronze screws began to spin faster. It took a lot to move nearly forty thousand tons of submarine. Speed came on gradually, solidly. More than anything, the boat felt *unstoppable.*

"Seventeen knots."

"Belikov?"

The sonar officer looked up from his big, circular screen. It was filled with amorphous green blobs, drifting clouds, sudden flashes. "Just our own echoes."

The submarine's noise caromed off the ice above. The sounds might reveal to a careful listener that *something* was out there, but beyond a few kilometers, *Baikal* would simply vanish in a blizzard of echoes.

"Nineteen knots."

Belikov watched as the bright returns on his screen faded, then went out as water noise blanked out his sensors. "Sonar is degraded."

"Very well."

"We can't see what's ahead," said Fedorenko, a look of worry on his face. "How do you know we won't hit something?"

"I know ice," said Markov.

"Twenty knots," the helmsman reported.

A small rumble made the huge sub shudder.

Markov had expected it. Turbulent water was flowing back from *Baikal's* sail and striking the tall rudder. It was something that happened to all Typhoons until speed straightened the flow out again.

"Twenty-two knots, Captain."

The shudder should have stopped. But it didn't. Markov felt the jolts right through the soles of his shoes. "What is it, Igor?"

"There may be a problem with one of the propellers, Captain."

"What kind of a problem?"

"Twenty-four knots."

The deck was jumping in a definite rhythm. *Bump bump bump bump.* Like driving on a flat tire. A bulb popped out of a fixture and crashed to the deck's green tiles.

A water-intrusion alarm sounded. A red light flashed at Gasparyan's damage control console. The *starpom* punched a button to stop the noise. "Water in the Number One shaft tunnel."

The propeller shafts? Spring a leak there and the sea could flood the engineering spaces. "Grachev . . ."

Suddenly, as though a switch had been thrown, the rumbling stopped. The deck became rock-steady.

"What did you do?" asked Markov.

"Nothing," said the engineer. "Number One shaft was just flexing under the torque load. Everything is normal."

Normal? There were five shaft rings meant to keep the sea out of *Baikal,* and even at rest, on the surface, they leaked. "What about the through-hull seals?"

"I'm pumping it out faster than it's coming in."

"Twenty-six knots."

Baikal was flying just beneath the ice roof.

"Captain, seawater temperature is rising," said Gasparyan. He was reading a figure transmitted back from the trailing sonar probe. "The ice is thinning. We may be under a small polynya."

Unusual, thought Markov. Normally the ice shelf extended unbroken well beyond the northern coast of Franz Josef Land. He turned to Fedorenko. "Come with me. I'll show you something."

Markov climbed the ladder up to the balcony above Central Command. It was pierced by the two thick periscope shafts. A pair of heavy watertight hatches were set into the bulkheads on opposite sides of the space; they led into a pair of escape capsules mounted on either side of the sail. It would be a tight fit to get even his reduced crew into the capsules, but Markov doubted anyone would complain if they had to use them. Another ladder went up to the heavy hatches that sealed the hull from the enclosed bridge, and the sea.

Markov grabbed the handles of the command periscope and the shaft rose with an audible hiss. The cold metal steamed in the humid air of the submarine. Markov touched a switch and a bank of high-intensity lights went on atop the sail. "We're in a warm zone. The ice is thin."

"Thin or thick, you can't put a periscope up through it," said Fedorenko. "What is it?"

"Look for yourself."

Fedorenko put his eye to the lens, but he jumped back as though he'd touched a live wire. "Markov!"

The lights had illuminated an endless plain of vivid turquoise, a world of blue-green ice, hurtling by a few meters overhead.

"Look again." Markov killed the lights.

Fedorenko approached the eyepiece as though it might bite. He saw the last glow of the lights fade away to soft purple.

"See how the ice lets daylight through? Like stained glass in a cathedral. I never get tired of looking at it."

"I've seen frozen water before."

"You're a romantic, Gennadi."

Bam Bam Schramm powered up the BQS-15 under-ice sonar and sent a discreet ping upward. The BQS-15 knew where the surface was. Any hard return shy of it represented the thickness of the ice layer.

A few seconds later, the return was displayed: *4.6*. Nearly five feet of ice separated them from the light and the air. He plotted the number, which was just a little more than the one he'd obtained an hour ago.

Portland was running north at well over her best advertised speed of thirty knots. He'd been ordered to find a thin place to surface, but from the looks of things, the ice roof was hanging in there, uniform and thick.

Schramm pressed a button, and the BQS-15 sent another ping of focused energy upward. The thickness of the sea ice popped onto his screen: *3.6*. He checked the sea temperature. *29.2*. Not exactly swimming weather, but definitely warmer.

The water here was a mixed bag of temperature and salinity. Shallow currents born in the warm Gulf Stream mingled with the frigid deep outflow from the arctic. Sometimes a warm whorl spun off the current and remained together long enough to thaw the roof of fast ice. That was a polynya. He glanced at the temperature display. *30 degrees*. He grabbed the intercom. "Conn? Sonar. The ice is starting to thin out. Temperature's up a little, too."

Steadman had the conn in Control. He picked up the yellow intercom. "What have we got overhead?"

"It went from almost five feet down to under four in a couple of minutes. Stand by." He took another reading. *31 degrees*. "Temperature's still rising. We got us a polynya."

"All stop," said Steadman. "Right full rudder!"

Portland gave up her speed slowly, reluctantly, as she entered a wide, sweeping turn.

"Helm, left full rudder," said Steadman. It was called a Williamson Turn, and it was meant to bring *Portland* back to a spot precisely beneath the sky-light of thin ice.

"Left full rudder," said Slice and Dice. Punching through the ice was not something supply lieutenants really needed to know how to do, was it? He fervently wished someone else was sitting behind the helm.

"Ice layer is now two and a half feet," said Schramm.

"Current is variable one six five at two knots," said Whalley.

"Helm, rudder amidships. All stop." Steadman selected the captain's stateroom on his intercom. "Skipper? We've found a polynya. I recommend we surface through the ice."

"Very well. We've got a satellite window coming up in twenty minutes. Make sure we're ready to receive messages."

Steadman switched to the boatwide PA system, the 1MC: "Stand by to surface through ice."

Senior Chief Browne didn't have the duty at the ballast control panel. But surfacing through ice was a delicate, dangerous operation. Rise too slowly and you risked getting stuck. Hit the ice too fast and you could break something. It had to be done just right, and so no one was surprised when Browne showed up and took over the BCP.

Steadman was relieved to see him. "Rig in the bow planes."

"Sir?" said Choper. "I think someone else should take over."

"You're doing fine, Lieutenant," said Steadman. "Relax."

"Relax. Aye aye, sir."

A few moments later, Browne said, "Hull is set for surface through ice, XO."

"Blow depth control," said Steadman. "Start her up."

"*Surface, surface, surface.*"

A low rumble sounded. The seven-thousand-ton submarine began to rise from the darkness, heading for the green filtered light overhead.

"One hundred feet. Twenty feet per minute up."

"Too slow," said Steadman. "I need thirty-feet-per-minute, COB."

"Shifting ballast," said Browne. Water was pumped out of the bow trim tanks. You had to sneak up on the right buoyancy. Let it get away from you and you could rocket upward so fast nothing would stop you until you hit.

"Depth now fifty feet. Thirty-feet-per-minute rise."

Forward in the sonar room, Schramm took the opportunity for a last listen on his passive narrowband sonar. They hadn't run this slowly in a day and a half and *Portland*'s own flow noise was gone. If there was something to hear, now was the time to hear it.

There was a muffled thud from overhead. Then, with a small shudder, the sail pierced the ice.

Schramm blinked. In the instant before *Portland* broke through the ice with the sound of a million glass windows shattering, he heard a faint, distant rumble, and though it was gone in an instant, he'd heard that sound before.

He tried to listen "through" the noise by electronically steering the sensitive bow sonar sphere down 40 degrees to blank it out. Whatever he'd heard was gone.

Steadman stood in the open bridge. *Portland*'s sail was a black tower rising from the middle of a shattered ice field that extended in every direction as far as he could see. It rose, then fell, responding to waves generated by distant storms.

"Bridge, Sonar."

"Go ahead, Bam Bam," Steadman answered. His parka was already buttoned against the cold.

"It's not real solid but I thought I heard something as we hit. If I had to guess, I'd say it was plant noise. I'll listen again when we dive."

Plant noise. An icebreaker with a load of tourists out looking for polar bears? Or another submarine? "Anything now?"

"Zip."

"Keep listening."

The surface detail cleared the ice away with shovels, brooms and bare hands. Plates two feet thick were strewn across the weather deck aft of the sail. The bridge was cleared, and the mottled, camouflaged periscope rose to expose the UHF satellite antenna.

Vann was studying an on-screen chart of the Arctic when the decoded message arrived. He unfolded the crisp sheet of paper.

Z041630Z4AUG2002

NLOB*NLOB*NLOB

IMMEDIATE

FM: COMSUBLANT

TO: CO USS PORTLAND

1: TYPHOON-CLASS SSBN NOW IDENTIFIED BAIKAL, PROCEEDING NE 20 KNOTS

2: RENDEZVOUS WITH CHINESE ASW FORCES VICINITY PETROPAVLOVSK IS NOW CONSIDERED LIKELY

3: INTERCEPT BAIKAL AND DELAY TRANSIT BERING STRAIT BEYOND 10 AUGUST

4: ALL PRUDENT MEANS TO ACCOMPLISH THIS MISSION ARE
   AUTHORIZED

5: WARNING: USS HOUSTON ATTACKED VICINITY
   PETROPAVLOVSK BY RUSSIAN ASW. HOUSTON
   WITHDRAWING

6: JIM . . . WATCH YOUR BAFFLES. THE BASTARDS ARE
   PLAYING HARDBALL—GRAYBAR SENDS

Vann felt his neck redden. *Baikal?* Memories echoed, merged, faded. *Baikal* was the boomer that had forced him into the ice. The Typhoon intel said had been so badly damaged in a missile accident she'd never be able to sail again. Alive and making twenty knots for the pole?

Vann sat back at his small desk and switched off the lamp. The screen illuminated his face with red light. The Chinese had always looked to Moscow for modern weaponry: tanks, fighters, ships. Now they were making noises about taking Taiwan. What did they need most?

To keep the U.S. Navy at arm's length. A Chinese Typhoon would surely fit the bill. No American president would trade Seattle for Taipei. Though it was dumb of the Russians to give the Chinese so potent a weapon. Who knew where those missiles would be pointed when . . . But then he stopped. *The bastards didn't give it to them. They sold it.*

He reread Graybar's orders. *Delay transit Bering Strait beyond 10 August . . . All prudent means authorized . . .*

How did you prudently delay a ballistic missile submarine? Harass him? Lash him with active sonar? The Russians had taken a poke at Houston. So now what was prudent?

Whatever worked.

He blanked the screen and pressed the intercom button. "Conn. This is the captain. I'm on my way. Prepare the boat to dive."

CHAPTER TEN

AMBUSH

Baikal
Saint Anna's Trough

Belikov was listening on passive sonar to the otherworldly chorus of whales. Sometimes "biologicals" sounded almost human, other times like creatures from the depths of the cosmos, which in a real sense they were. Was there a market for a record of them? No Russian company would bother, of course. But what about England? America?

Belikov was born in Leningrad. He'd seen it become Petersburg once more. By any name, it was a city founded as a window to the West. A farm boy from Kiev always had shit between his toes, a brat from Moscow might think of power and deals, but a Petersburger naturally took a broader, more international . . . *What?* He sat bolt upright and manipulated the filtering controls. "Captain! Sonar contact."

"Range?"

"Close." The sonar officer shook his head. "It's gone now. It could have been a berg."

But you don't think so. "Let me listen." Markov pressed one earphone against the side of his head. The cushion was warm. Markov heard the keening of a distant whale, the snap and pop of a billion tiny shrimp. The steady gnashing of ice plates grinding against one another.

"What's wrong now?" said Fedorenko.

Markov glanced at him, then away. "Belikov heard breaking ice."

"This is the polar sea," said Fedorenko. His expression said, *Am I the only sane person here?*

The black conning tower slowly sank beneath the ice as compressed air jetted up from her ballast tanks, expanded in the open air and fell as a shower of soft, white snow. Green water sheeted across the ice. Soon the scar left by *Portland*'s surfacing would knit itself together and erase all sign of her passing from the world of light and air. Ahead, directly off the bow, the continental shelf ended at Saint Anna's Trough, a plunging chasm that ended some twelve thousand feet below at the Polar Abyss.

Vann stepped in from the forward passage. "I've got the conn."

"Captain has the conn!" Browne called out.

Vann noticed Choper sitting behind the helm. "Take a hike, Lieutenant. Go fill out some forms. Mister Steadman will sit dive."

"Yes, sir!" Choper was only too happy to leave.

"Make your depth one hundred fifty feet," said Vann. "Turns for eight knots. Right ten degrees rudder. Sonar, Conn. Let's clear baffles right away."

"Aye aye," said Schramm. His display was already beginning to clear. The sea immediately under the ice was a mix of both salt and fresh water, a condition that made long-range detection all but impossible. But down deep in cold, clear waters even faint sounds could propagate for hundreds of miles.

Steadman saw the orders in Vann's pocket. Usually, Vann would share them with him, but he hadn't yet and it wasn't up to Steadman to ask why. "Did Norfolk have a position report on that boomer?"

Vann nodded. "He's in the neighborhood."

"Bam Bam thought he heard something just before we surfaced. It wasn't solid enough to designate but it sounded like plant noise."

Vann snatched the intercom mike. "Sonar, Conn. What did you hear and why was I not informed?"

"Ah, it came and went too fast to develop a bearing and the ice makes everything squirrelly anyway. I told the XO it wasn't solid."

Vann raised an eyebrow at Steadman, then said, "From now on deciding if something is solid is above your pay grade. You detect. I will evaluate. Clear?"

"You got it, Captain." Schramm thought, *Who put a poker up your butt?*

"Depth now one hundred feet."

Vann stood behind Steadman, his eyes swiveling like a tank barrel hunting for a target. His gaze came to rest on the Hamilton deck chronometer. The winding needle had fallen to LOW. "Who had the duty to wind this instrument last watch?"

"ET Bedford, Captain," said Steadman.

"ET Bedford is now assigned to mess duty. He can wash dishes until he learns to take his assignments seriously."

"Sir, Bedford is an electronics tech first class. He—"

"Was. As of now he's not." Vann picked up a microphone and sent his voice out over the 1MC: "This is the captain. As most of you know by now, the Chinese are making noises like they want to take Taiwan back. They may have their heads together with the Russians this time, because one of our boats, *Houston,* was attacked while she was operating in international waters and forced to withdraw. In COMSUBLANT's words, the bastards are playing hardball. Well, we know a thing or two about the game ourselves."

Attacked? thought Steadman. *Houston* had the reputation of being a hard-luck boat. Bad things always seemed to happen to her. But what did Vann mean by "attacked"? Did someone drop depth charges on her, or a noise-maker? There was a world of difference between the two.

"What's our job?" Vann continued. "Right now, Norfolk thinks a Russian boomer is headed for the Pacific where she doesn't belong. Our job is to find her and stop her. If she's smart, she'll see us coming and run for home. But if she wants to play games, we'll remind her that she's taking on the varsity team. We've been chosen to deliver a message to our Russian friends: You're playing way out of your league. It's a message *Houston* can't deliver. But *Portland* can and will. That is all."

"One hundred fifty feet," said Steadman. He replayed the captain's words. "Captain, how are we going to stop that boomer?"

"First we find him." Vann switched the intercom to Schramm's station. "Sonar, Conn. What have you got?"

"Still searching." At least now he knew why Vann was so spring-loaded. Schramm knew the sonar supervisor on *Houston,* and the CO was right. It was like someone taking a poke at family. Schramm swept the frigid waters for stray sounds. Detecting a submarine under the ice was always a bitch.

A flicker showed up on his scope. He electronically steered the array in the direction of the faint whisper. "Conn, Sonar. Stop turn now." Schramm punched a button, selected a more tightly focused frequency filter and closed his eyes.

It was like looking at a faint star. Stare at it and it vanishes. Look off to the side and there it was. A faint, pulsing *swish swish swish* hiding beneath a blanket of random noise.

Bam Bam smiled. *Gotcha.* "Conn, Sonar. I've got faint screw noise bearing zero five five. If you can give me a couple of legs I might be able to come up with a range."

"Right ten degrees rudder," said Vann. "Turns for eight knots."

Target motion analysis was a kind of team trigonometry problem that demanded both skill and thoroughness, only not too much. Run multiple legs to nail down your quarry and you ran the risk of losing him. Run too few and you wouldn't have a firing solution.

Portland crept north. Streams of pale light filtering through the broken ice sheet faded to black as the roof turned solid and thickened.

Lieutenant Keefe at the fire control console watched sonar data points stack up on his screen. When he was sure he had a real target and not just noise, he looked up at Vann and said, "I have a curve."

"Left ten degrees rudder," Vann ordered.

Portland swung onto a second ranging leg.

Schramm watched the azimuth change on the sonar contact. The angles were coming together a lot quicker than he would have guessed. Soon, he had a squat triangle with a Russian boomer at its apex. *Fuck,* he thought. *He's close.* "Conn, Sonar. This guy is definitely inside twenty thousand yards. Warning. I'm starting to pick up noise from the marginal ice. If he makes it that far we could lose him in the weeds."

"I've got the second curve, Captain," said Keefe.

Vann watched the sonar contact dots stack up on Keefe's screen. Two legs was thin, but there was that marginal ice ahead, and once the Russian made it that far he'd be hard to dig out. "Any ID yet?"

Schramm compared the faint new sound with the recorded ones in his archives. "The spectrum doesn't match any known boat."

"Try *Baikal.*"

Chief Browne looked up from the ballast panel. *Baikal?*

"Conn, Sonar. It's close, but no matchup with *Baikal.*"

"How far to the ice line?"

"About thirty thousand yards."

"Then this is where we stop him," said Vann.

Schramm listened to the *thrum thrum thrum* of distant screws, the faint, cataract tumble of water flowing over steel. The signal was noisy with echoes and biologicals. "Conn, Sonar. Designate the boomer Sierra Five. I show blade count and bearing change consistent with a Typhoon running at eighteen knots, range nineteen thousand three hundred yards."

"Ahead two-thirds," said Vann. "Turns for twenty knots."

As *Portland* rushed to close the distance, Vann thought, *A polynya in the roof of the world. It all comes down to a few degrees of heading, a few fractions of a knot.* A small difference in either one would have put the Russian missile boat outside *Portland*'s detection range. Vann took a breath, then said, "Sound Battle Stations Torpedo."

An urgent electronic tone sounded throughout the boat, then, *"Man battle stations! Man battle stations!"*

Portland plowed into the steady northerly current. Rushing in from astern, she'd be all but undetectable to American sonar, much less Russian.

"Conn, Sonar. Range to Sierra Five is now fourteen thousand yards. Bearing unchanged. I'm picking up flow noise on him pretty good now."

"Let's flood tubes One and Two while we can still do it quietly."

Lieutenant Keefe punched two buttons and waited as a low cataract rumble of water echoed through the boat. "Tubes One and Two are flooded."

Goddamn! You can't just shoot him, thought Steadman. You didn't fool with the other side's nukes unless you thought World War III had already begun, because it was a good way to start it. "What exactly are we doing, skipper?"

"We're going to keep him out of the Pacific."

Steadman looked at the folded orders in Vann's pocket. "How?"

"I'm not going to play chicken with a forty-thousand-ton boomer. He'll run us over. We can't tap his screws and disable him. His props are shrouded in steel rings. We're going to underhull him. We're going to document him from bow to stern so that there is *zero* question about who he is, or what the Russians are trying to pull. If we get his attention and slow him down, fine. If not, I'll make the next call."

"Sir?" said Keefe. "We could maneuver in his baffles and fire a water slug." He meant flooding a torpedo tube and using ram pressure to eject a column of water. It made an ominous rumbling that could be heard a long way off and mistaken for a real torpedo launch. "He'd have to stop and pay attention to that."

"Until he didn't pick up any torpedo screws, then he'd laugh and fire a real fish right back down our bearing. Sonar, Conn. Where is he?"

"Range to Sierra Five now twelve thousand yards. He's *real* close to the bottom of the ice. I'm getting target spread and multiple reflections," said Schramm. The sonar was painting a picture not of a point source, but *multiple* acoustic contacts coming from various parts of the approaching submarine. If you knew what to look for, it was like watching an acoustical X ray.

Vann was being evasive. Steadman wanted clarity, and he wanted it *now*. "That's a Russian strategic missile boat, Captain."

"Norfolk gave us a mission. How it gets done is up to me."

"Even if it starts a war?"

Vann pointed a finger at Steadman and said, "You're forgetting what I said. Submarines are always at war. The rest is politics."

"Just the same, I'd like to see those orders."

"That's your right." But Vann's expression didn't match his words. He had the look of a man whose puppy had just taken a nip out of him. He yanked the folded orders from his breast pocket and showed them to Steadman, then turned his back.

Steadman scanned the message body.

3: INTERCEPT BAIKAL AND DELAY TRANSIT BERING STRAIT BEYOND 10 AUGUST

4: ALL PRUDENT MEANS TO ACCOMPLISH THIS MISSION ARE AUTHORIZED

What a trap! thought Steadman. Here were orders that could justify anything, as long as it worked and you weren't caught. But what if it didn't work? If something went wrong, it wouldn't be Norfolk's fault. It would be Vann's. *And mine.* He folded the sheet up and handed it back. "These orders seem pretty ambiguous."

"I'm the captain. The way *I* read them is what counts."

Steadman bit off his quick answer. The orders contained the word *prudent*. Ambushing a Russian boomer in peacetime didn't fall into that category. "If we shoot him, all the other options go away."

"What options?" Vann's mouth turned down in a sour grimace. "We've got a submarine out there headed for the ice. If he makes it we may not be able to find him again. Where is he going? Someplace where they're shooting at Americans. Is that war enough for you?"

Steadman looked at Vann, at Chief Browne. At the young sailors at the helm. Everything in *Portland*'s control room was about clarity. Everything was measured and precise. Every action from starting up the reactor to pumping the sanitary tanks had a checklist and a NAVSEA publication specifying each step, each switch, each valve position in excruciating detail. But what if there was no right answer?

"Conn, Sonar. Sierra Five's angle on the bow, starboard five, range nine thousand seven hundred yards," said Schramm as the ghostly collection of noise marched toward the center of his screen.

Vann turned away from Steadman. "Firing point procedures, tubes One and Two."

"Weapons ready," came the call from the torpedo room.

"Solution ready," said Keefe. *He can't be serious.*

Vann turned to Steadman.

"Boat ready, Captain."

"All ahead one-third," Vann ordered. "Let's go get him, people."

Baikal

Markov went to the sonar officer's console. "Gone?"

Belikov nodded. "Nothing. It must have been a natural sound. If a machine had made it, we'd still be hearing something."

Markov wasn't convinced. In a soundless forest, the sudden snap of a twig meant something. "Helm, make your depth one hundred fifty meters."

As the big missile submarine planed down into the black depths, Markov said, "Left full rudder. Belikov? Listen closely. We may not get another chance."

USS *Portland*

"Range to Sierra Five seven thousand yards and closing," said Schramm. The distorted echo of a Russian Typhoon was growing across his screen as *Portland* moved in behind him.

"Take us down to three-fifty," said Vann.

"Five degrees down on the planes, three hundred fifty feet," said Steadman.

"Sonar?" said Vann. "I want this guy's signature on file. Be sure to save the tape."

"Aye aye. Range now five thousand yards."

As *Portland* drove straight up the Typhoon's wake, Schramm turned away from his screen for a second to make sure the system was recording properly, and when he looked back, the image had changed. He blanched when he realized what had happened. "Conn! Sonar! Crazy Ivan! Sierra Five's turning to port!"

"All stop!" said Vann. *Portland* would remain motionless until the Russian sub returned to her original heading.

"Conn, Sonar. Sierra Five is passing down our port side now. Range three thousand. He's below us, but not by much."

"We'll match his depth when he passes us again heading north," said Vann.

Steadman was growing more uneasy with every second. Moving in close was like tailgating a big truck on an icy road. If the truck touches his brakes he might swerve, but you would surely hit him.

Baikal

"Returning to heading, Captain," said the officer at the helm.

"Hold depth at one hundred fifty meters." Something was still bothering Markov. A sound where there shouldn't be one followed by dead silence. He glanced at his second in command, Gasparyan. He was about to read something out over the shipwide intercom, probably the watch change.

"Set readiness condition two on deck level two," the executive officer announced, then put the *kashtan* microphone away.

"Captain?" It was Belikov at the sonar console. "Heavy ice eight kilometers directly off the bow." A steward poured Belikov a glass of tea. The sonar officer drained it in a swallow.

Something made Belikov's line twitch, thought Markov. Sometimes it's a fish, but usually not. "Helm?"

"Captain?"

"Take us around again. Right full rudder this time."

USS *Portland*

"Conn! Sonar! Crazy Ivan! This time to starboard!"

A Double Ivan? Steadman turned to Vann. "Sir?" They were too close. *Portland* would have to back down, and fast, or risk a collision.

A Double Ivan? Vann knew Russian tactics. They performed their clearing turns one by one, spaced like clockwork, as though taking some unpleasant medicine. *Except for one I was trailing on* Baton Rouge. It was the same boomer. Could it be the same captain?

"Range two thousand yards," said Bam Bam.

Steadman said, "Captain?"

"Conn, Sonar. The range is still closing."

"Very *well*," Vann snapped. "*Left* full rudder!"

Portland was still skidding into the Typhoon's screws.

"Conn, Sonar. Range now one thousand yards."

"Skipper?" It was Chief Browne. "We'd best move our butts *now.*"

"Range now *five* hundred yards."

He couldn't avoid a collision without backing off, and hard. But if he did, *Portland*'s propeller would churn the water into bubbles and froth that even Russian sonar could detect.

There was no choice.

"Helm," said Vann. "Engine all back. All back emergency."

The young enlisted man at the helm didn't need any further encouragement. The engine annunciator rang *BACK EMERGENCY*. There was a juddering vibration as *Portland*'s screw bit the water in reverse.

"Conn, Sonar. We're cavitating."

"Very *well*, Sonar." Vann sent his thoughts at the Russian captain. *All right. It's not what I planned. But here I am. It's your move.*

Baikal

"Captain. Contact bearing zero zero three and very close. A single-screw submarine."

A Los Angeles. So there were hunters in this forest after all. "Right full rudder." *Baikal* began to turn her tail away from the contact. "Five degrees rise. Make your depth one hundred twenty meters."

"He was following us too closely," said Belikov.

Markov thought, *That was his first mistake. He won't make it again.* And how long had he been there? Since Kola? "What's the course to the ice line?"

"Zero zero three, range seven kilometers."

"New course zero zero three. Ahead two-thirds." His boat was built to strike a berg head-on. The American was not. "Let's see how well the American likes the ice."

USS *Portland*

Portland's screw thundered in reverse and began to bite.

"Range *four* hundred yards," said Schramm. "He's above us and all *over* my scope. I don't know if we're underhulling him or he's overhulling us." *How much water does a Typhoon draw, anyway?* "Here he comes." Schramm's display showed a giant steel overcast eclipsing his sonic world. The Typhoon blotted out everything like a towering thunderhead.

Vann could actually hear the low, powerful throb of the Russian boomer in Control. Like an earthquake that went on and on. He reached up and touched a steel handle. He didn't need sonar. He could feel the alien vibration right in his own fingers. The heavy swirl of the Typhoon's passing rocked *Portland* like a dory in the wake of a passing freighter.

Control was absolutely silent. Then, "Range opening," said Schramm. "Bearing and speed unchanged."

Vann looked up at the pipes and conduits running along the overhead. As though he could look through the steel, through the rubber tiles of *Portland*'s hull, and see the passing Typhoon.

"Conn, Sonar. Sierra Five is making a beeline for the heavy ice."

Dumb. "How far is it now, Bam Bam?"

"Eight thousand yards."

In the dark of the night, when the doubts would float behind his closed eyes like glowing phosphors, it wasn't the Board of Inquiry, the bashed-in bow of USS *Baton Rouge,* the shame of sending a boat to the scrapyard. No. It was a Typhoon and its captain he thought about most.

All prudent means are hereby authorized.

Let him get lost in ice and there was a good chance he'd make Bering Strait. He'd reach that cleared corridor and then nothing could touch him. And then?

It wouldn't be a sonar technician's fault. Or even that girl's. Vann would have failed and failure was not an option. "Sonar, Conn," he said. "Let the range open to four thousand yards. On my command, one ranging ping on the active set. Maximum power."

Then what? Steadman wondered. He sent a silent, fervent wish at the Typhoon racing north: *Don't run. Turn back. Stop.*

In the blue glow of the sonar room's lights, Bam Bam was also wondering what Vann had in mind. An active ping would surely get that Typhoon's attention. He powered up the SADS-TG active sonar set. *Forget getting his attention,* he thought. *Portland*'s active sonar wouldn't just be *heard* inside that boomer. It would *thunder.*

Baikal

"Contact is lost," said Belikov. "Last range two kilometers astern. He's not following us, Captain."

Is he frightened? The American had to know the only chance he had of trailing them was to stay so close that not even the ice could interfere. Why was he holding back? "Watch for him to go deep and sprint ahead of us."

Fedorenko hurried back to Central Command. "What is it?"

"An American submarine."

Fedorenko said, "You can't allow him to follow us."

"He didn't ask for my permission." Markov turned to the sonar console. "Helm, all ahead full on both engines. No. All ahead *flank*."

USS *Portland*

"Conn, Sonar. Sierra Five just stepped on the gas. Twenty knots and accelerating."

"He's running for it." *You'll never make it.* Vann said, "Weapons. Reset tubes One and Two for short-range attack mode, swim out at thirty knots. Enable the seekers at one thousand yards then step them up to fifty knots to impact. Doppler mode all the way."

Lieutenant Keefe had a "shopping list" of attack options on his console screen. There were really too many of them; he could command the weapons to perform underwater ballet if he chose. All well and good in the open ocean, but here, so close to the ice, even the improved ADCAP torpedo had problems picking targets out of the clutter. The only way to stack the odds in *Portland*'s favor was to put blinkers on his torpedoes, to force them to ignore everything that didn't move, like the ice, and pay attention to the one thing that *did*.

He glanced at the fire control technician's console. From the tight stack of dots on the screen, their target was running, which was dumb. Mark 48s could run a whole lot faster.

Two lights on the torpedo board changed from red to green.

"Presets accepted, Tubes One and Two are ready in all respects." The torpedoes would now disregard stationary targets and home in with ruthless precision on anything that moved.

"Range to Sierra Five now three thousand eight hundred yards."

"Stand by, Sonar," said Vann.

Schramm flipped open the safety cover to the active sonar. His finger rested lightly on the button.

Baikal

"Speed now twenty-four knots."

The great submarine was rocketing under a thickening roof of ice.

Chief Engineer Grachev cursed, then pulled his seat belt tight around his waist. Why bother putting all the time and sweat into bringing the ship back from the dead when you were going to smash into the ice?

Belikov drained the tea he'd been nursing and put the empty glass down on the deck between his boots. At least it wouldn't fall.

"Where is he?" asked Fedorenko.

"Patience, Gennadi," said Markov.

USS *Portland*

"Bam Bam, single ping, max power," said Vann. "Hammer him."

"On the way." Schramm triggered the active sonar.

A high, crystalline *PING!* burned through the cold, clear depths and kept right on going. It refracted as it passed through the layer of confused water near the ice, but a forty-thousand-ton submarine at close range was impossible to miss.

PONG!

The Typhoon's obituary flashed on the bottom right corner of Schramm's display. "Solid solution! Range four thousand one hundred yards. Depth one five zero feet. Angle on the bow starboard six degrees."

"Match final bearings and shoot," said Vann calmly.

"Jesus," Steadman whispered.

"Firing One and Two," Keefe answered with a catch in his voice. Touch the big red button on his panel and a Russian submarine, and her crew, would die. Submariners. Men like himself. He'd never fired a warshot in anger, but training took over and carried him across the unknown. He pressed the button, waited, then hit it again.

With a shudder, two jets of water spat out a pair of Mark 48 ADCAP torpedoes. They trailed fine guidance wires as their small screws spun up with a furious wasplike buzz. "One and Two fired."

Vann's face was radiant. "Watch those fish, Mr. Keefe! When he hears them he'll go deep. Be ready to chase him down. Make ready Tubes Three and Four and flood 'em. Stand by to fire decoys."

A Mark 48 swims at 1,300 yards per minute. Keefe's fire control computer said that the Russian boomer had two minutes and eighteen seconds left to live.

CHAPTER ELEVEN

IMPACT

Baikal

Belikov's ears were still ringing with echoes of the active sonar pulse when he heard a new sound, a high, fast buzzing that sent a jolt of raw electricity right through his headphones, his ears, straight into his brain. For a precious second, he was speechless. He kicked the empty tea glass away from his feet and it shattered against a bulkhead. *"Torpedo in the water!"*

Markov turned and stared. "What?"

"Two torpedoes in the water astern!"

Fedorenko started to say something but Markov shoved him roughly aside. "What range?"

"Both inside three thousand meters!"

Markov's thinking leaped like a spark flashing from pole to ground. He couldn't turn and run. The torpedoes would turn inside and catch him. He couldn't dive. They could dive deeper and faster. His moves had been reduced to just one, and it wasn't a good one. *Mother of God. We won't make it.* But Markov said the words anyway: "Both engines ahead emergency!"

USS *Portland*

Ping! Ping! Ping!

"First fish has gone active," said Keefe. The torpedo's own sonar would now guide it to their target. "Second fish has gone active."

"Dead man walking," said Vann. "Cut the wires. Close the outer doors and reload with ADCAPs." He had to expect the Russian would shoot back, and if he did the shot would be coming up the wake left by *Portland*'s own fish. It was time to be someplace else. "Helm. Left full rudder! Ahead *flank*!"

Portland's torpedoes would find their own way now.

Ping! Ping! Ping! Ping!

"Torpedoes have gone active," said Belikov.

"Good," said Markov.

"What's good about that?" Fedorenko yelled.

"The Americans can't change their mind about how to kill us," said Markov. *I think.* He sounded sure of himself, though he wasn't. "Belikov? How deep is the marginal ice line? I want it to the *meter.*"

Belikov looked at his sonar display. The edge of the polar ice pack showed as a glowing, undulating line on the screen, illuminated by the reflected sonic energy from the torpedoes and growing brighter as he watched. "Thirty-two meters at its deepest, Captain." They would graze it unless Markov did something, and fast. What did he have in mind?

Markov stood behind Belikov's console, watching the screen. He checked the Fathometer display. The distance from the bottom of their keel to the top of the sail was 90 meters. The keel depth was now 120 meters. They had 30 meters of water, or ice, overhead. He turned to the two officers at the helm. "Rig in the bow planes." He fought to keep his voice even, calm, though his mind wanted nothing so much as to panic, his mouth to scream, his bowels to let go in fear. "Helm. Take us five meters deeper." Markov stared at the flickering depth display. One hundred twenty-one meters.

"They're shooting at a ship of the Russian Federation!" Fedorenko sputtered. "Don't they know what that means?"

"You can register a complaint at the embassy."

"You can't sit and wait for those torpedoes to blow up!"

"That's exactly what we're going to do," said Markov. "Find something to hold on to, Gennadi." He turned back to the Fathometer. One twenty-three. One twenty-four. One hundred twenty-five meters. "Engines all stop!" said Markov. "Sound the collision alarm!"

As the *whoop! whoop whoop!* blasted through the boat, Markov reached up and grabbed a steel handle set into the overhead, right next to the framed plaque: SUBMARINE LIFE IS NOT A SERVICE, BUT A RELIGION. It was never more true than now, for they were well beyond the zone of science and reason. They had entered a place familiar to mariners since the beginning of time. A zone of faith, of miracles.

"The ice line is now fifty meters dead ahead, Captain."

"All right. Get ready to blow ballast. On my command."

"Twenty meters."

We're too fast, thought Markov. Get forty thousand tons of ship moving and it wanted to *keep* moving. They were still coasting at fourteen knots. Too fast to hit something head-on with the bow, but the armored sail was built with breaking the ice in mind.

At that instant, the forward lip of the conning tower brushed the pack ice. With a solid *crunch,* the boat was shoved deeper. The deck tilted and Central Command was filled with the scream of bending steel.

The submarine struck again, this time farther aft along the top of the sail, a headlong collision that ripped the ice apart. The impact barely slowed them. Fedorenko was thrown to the deck. He sprawled under the sonar console, finding something to hang on to at last: Belikov's legs.

The lights blinked off as their breakers tripped, replaced a second later by the feeble red glow of battery-powered battle lamps. The hull was filled with the thunder of breaking ice. Then, the battle lamps winked out.

"Blow ballast!" Markov yelled. *"Everything! Blow it all!"* He was hanging from the steel handle like a subway rider in the middle of a train wreck. The framed plaque came loose and smashed to the green deck tiles.

Markov tried to read the indicators above the helm but the compartment flashed with a hundred red alarm lights. Water was coming into a missile silo, or perhaps one of the big ballast tanks inside it had ruptured. Batteries had spilled acid, reactor power flux was varying wildly. Any one of them a first-order emergency anytime but now. Their sail was carving a long gash into the roof of ice. They were slowing, he could tell by the sounds from overhead. Slowing, slowing. They had to rise up the far side of the ice keel. He had to put as much of its bulk between his ship and those two relentless weapons hunting for him. And then he had to play dead, and play it so well those torpedoes would find something else more appealing.

He realized the roar of the collision had faded enough to hear the torpedoes' furious pinging. He looked at the speed display above the helm. It had to be broken. The warning lights still flashed red, but a single digit glowed above them all, a steady beacon in an exploding galaxy of light: zero.

USS *Portland*

One moment the seeker heads on two Mark 48 ADCAP torpedoes were locked onto a moving submarine. The next, their target dissolved into an expanding cloud of broken ice.

Ping! Ping! Ping! Ping!

The fine guidance wires were cut. The torpedoes were on their own. Their preset commands left no room for contemplation. Moving targets were to be attacked, and so they shifted their attention to a car-sized chunk of ice the Typhoon had broken loose. It was rolling up the near face of the ice keel. It was moving. Their steering fins shifted, their screws spun up to a victorious *scree!*

Schramm heard the sound of *Portland*'s two torpedoes as they moved in for the kill. Any other place but here, two Mark 48s fired at close range at a target as fat as a Typhoon were not going to miss, period. He wasn't so sure about *these* two. All torpedoes had problems dealing with ice. Not that he'd trade places with the Russians. The idea of *one* ADCAP ranging him on active was enough to make him sweat.

He'd never heard a fish detonate in anger before, much less two, but he was sure it would be loud. His passive sonar had automatic filters to block such sounds, but he took one earphone off and made ready to slap the other one away. He manually jacked the gain way down.

A voice over the 1MC said, "Twenty seconds left to run on One."

Then, "Fifteen seconds."

A rumble shot through *Portland* like distant thunder. Schramm looked up at the overhead. *That's too fucking soon. . . .* He listened to the tremendous *crash!* of a wrecking ball smashing its way through the biggest china shop in the universe. The collision went on and on, lighting up his sonar display like the Fourth of July. High frequency. Low. Wide and narrow bands . . . *That's not our fish! That's . . .*

The rumble suddenly cut off as though a switch had been thrown, to be replaced by the tremendous roar of six hundred and fifty pounds of high explosive going off, followed by the blast of the second Mark 48. When the blast ebbed, Schramm got back on his passive set to pick up the sounds of the dying Typhoon. He listened hard for the rush of flooding compartments, the eerie groan of steel under immense pressure. But all he could hear was the sound of a billion bubbles and the grumble of shattered ice. *Where is he?*

Vann grabbed the intercom. "Sonar, Conn. What have you got?"

Schramm tried to filter out the sonic chaos. "It's a dead zone out there. I can't make out *squat.*" His fingers flew across the manual filter controls. His screen showed only a snowstorm of sound left by the double explosions. "Ice. Bubbles. Reflections . . ."

"Christ. Do I have to look at your screen myself? I want *bearings.*"

"Captain, if you want bearings all I can give you are bad ones."

Vann's face reddened. "There was a forty-thousand-ton submarine out there, Sonar. Where did he go?"

Baikal

Terror was like thunder to a bolt of lightning. First came one, then the other. The ambush, the desperate run, the explosions had flashed through Markov's mind. Now that there was a pause, he felt terror rumble through him. His hands were shaking. Power alarms were going off as the Typhoon's complex systems tripped off-line. It wouldn't shock him to learn that his ship had been cut in two by those torpedoes, that half was already plummeting to the bottom while he stood there, safe for the moment, wedged like a pick against the roof of ice.

Markov had to get control back, and fast. Of his ship. Of himself. He had a window of opportunity to escape before the Americans could find him and attack him again, and it was very small. Perhaps as much as ten minutes, maybe as little as five. "Helm! Flood bow and stern trim! Take us back down to one hundred fifty meters! Gasparyan?"

The *starpom* had a folding outline of the ship open and was marking it with a grease pencil. "Damage reports are coming in, Captain," he said calmly, as though it were just another drill.

Markov grabbed the *kashtan* microphone. "Igor," he called to the chief engineer, "how's the ship?"

"We've got water in the Number Two battery bay. If it rises enough the batteries will start putting out chlorine, but I'm pumping it out faster than it's coming in. And there's water inside Silo Sixteen. The ballast tank inside it is probably split."

"Anything critical?"

"This ship can take it if you can." Grachev clicked off his *kashtan* and scanned the row of meters that showed how much water had accumulated in the Typhoon's bilges. Only the one beneath Silo Sixteen worried him. It registered a definite rise. He punched a round button beneath the meter to run the pump at high speed. The sump wasn't large. The pump was powerful. The level should have started dropping immediately.

The needle didn't move.

Grachev tapped the gauge with his finger. Someone would have to go down there and see where the water was coming from. If they were lucky, one of the water ballast tanks installed to offset the absence of a rocket had sprung a leak. If it wasn't, then it could be the sea, and not even Grachev could stop the sea.

The battle lamps came back on in Central Command. Fedorenko lay sprawled, a thin trickle of blood seeping down from his hairline to the deck's green rubber tiles. Markov reached for the *kashtan* again to summon Pavel Ossipov, the cook. He hadn't been able to hire a real doctor for *Baikal*'s final run. A real doctor could earn money without sailing derelict submarines over the top of the world to China. And so he had to make do with a mess cook who'd taken a brief course as an emergency medical assistant. "Sergei," he called to his *starpom,* "have someone take Fedorenko to his cabin."

Gasparyan already had his *kashtan* in hand.

Pavel the cook showed up with two sailors carrying a stretcher. The beefy *michman* had a red bruise on his forehead nearly the same hue as his hair. Apparently Fedorenko was not the only one caught unprepared. They loaded him onto the canvas and hauled him aft.

"We're pinned against the ice," said the ballast officer.

Markov was running out of time. The noisy ice, the billions of bubbles left by the explosions made a kind of acoustic curtain, and he had to exit the stage before it rose and left them naked. Before Belikov heard the next torpedo in the water. *My God! How could the Americans dare to do this?* He had to get word to Fleet. But that would come later. "Flood main ballast to the thirty-percent line."

With a hiss of escaping pressure, a torrent of seawater rushed into the lower ports of the Typhoon's main ballast tanks.

Time seemed to grow as heavy as the boat itself. Something snapped overhead, and with a sudden crunch, the deck tilted, then stopped. They were still stuck fast.

"Flood to the forty-percent mark."

The hiss and rumble continued.

Another lurch, another sudden stop.

"Flood to fifty percent," said Markov. They should be dropping like an anchor. He couldn't flood main ballast much more without losing the boat's reserve buoyancy. If they didn't break loose soon, he'd have to rock the ship back and forth by pumping fore and aft and hoping no one would hear, which even he knew was unlikely.

There was a tremendous *crack,* and the deck seemed to fall away beneath Markov's boots.

Someone shouted, "We're free!"

Baikal began settling fast, bow first. The deck tilted down. One hundred and fifty meters came, and passed.

"Rig out the bow planes," said Markov. "All ahead slow."

"Depth now one hundred eighty meters."

Markov could feel the hull resisting the growing water pressure. *Like a walnut in a vise.* The bulkheads creaked. A sad groan sounded from somewhere aft. He couldn't blow the ballast tanks dry. The Americans would hear that. He couldn't keep diving, either. A Typhoon was tough, but she had her limits. Her official test depth was four hundred meters. Her official crush depth was five hundred. And that was when she was *new.* That was *before* she'd been torn open and welded back together like some monster on a madman's operating table. Before she'd struck an ice keel at a speed that would have doomed a lesser ship. Who knew where the hull would collapse *now?*

He had to arrest the dive and silently steal off into the Arctic sea, and right away. "Engines ahead one-third. Full up on the planes."

"Bow planes are still not extending, Captain."

"Two hundred meters."

Fuck, swore engineer Grachev. Two lights were burning on the hydraulics console that controlled the boat's bow planes. They were huge, hydrodynamic wings that allowed the ship to swim at an even keel through the water and both of the lights were red. The bow planes were stuck.

"Igor . . ." said Markov. "I need those planes out *now.*"

"I'm not eating cakes up here."

Markov glanced at the Fathometer dial. The needle was still unwinding. "Depth now two hundred fifty meters."

The chief engineer cycled the hydraulics. There was a *crunch* as the bow planes tried to extend. He retracted them, then commanded them to open again. Another *crunch,* heavier than before. He knew why Markov needed them. There wasn't much time left. Soon there would be too much external pressure to blow the ballast tanks dry. You could try to force compressed air into them from now until doomsday and it wouldn't do a thing. Then there would be nowhere to go but straight down.

Another *crunch,* a shudder. The lights still burned an obstinate red. He clicked the intercom. "You'd better blow ballast while you can."

"Depth now three hundred meters."

Markov listened to the hull protest. They were now in the realm of very large forces, an invisible world where steel could stretch like taffy and shatter like glass. The hull was really singing. Not a mournful dirge. Just the opposite: Its tone climbed note by note, octave by octave, like an overtightened string. The green tiles on the deck at his feet were curling up at the corners as the steel underneath took on a distinct curve. He knew any leaks they had were growing worse with every meter of depth. At some point . . .

"Three hundred fifty meters."

There was a loud *crack!* Markov jumped, for it sounded like something giving way. He was about to give the order to blow the ballast dry when Grachev's gruff voice came over the intercom.

"They're coming out!"

Grachev's status lights were no longer red. First one, then the other turned green. The planes were emerging.

Markov said, "Helm! Full up on the bow planes!"

"Three hundred eighty meters."

The helmsman had already pulled his joystick all the way back. The maximum deflection was 40 degrees. He pulled back hard, as though by bending the joystick a few more precious degrees of travel might be found.

"Three-ninety."

Another voice said, "Mother of God."

"Coming level! Speed five knots!"

Markov watched the Fathometer steady, then begin to rise. He let out a very long breath. "Belikov?"

"Sonar is blinded by broken ice, Captain."

Let's hope their sonar is blind, too. "Set course zero two zero. Ahead dead slow. We'll stay deep. I don't want a single sound from this boat. Igor? Can we maintain this depth while we look for leaks?"

"You won't have to look for them at this depth. They'll find *you*."

But it reminded the chief engineer of the water collecting beneath Silo Sixteen. "The water's still coming into Sixteen."

"How bad?"

"When things settle down, I'll go take a look."

"There's radiation up there."

"I'm aware of the conditions," said Grachev. How much radiation would he take checking on a leak? Surely not so much.

"All right, Igor. Tell me what you find and don't spend too much time looking." Markov hung up his *kashtan* and found himself with time to think.

Why were the Americans trying to sink him? It had never happened during the Cold War, at least as far as Markov knew. What was different now? Why weren't they terrified that Moscow would learn of the ambush? It terrified Markov what Moscow would do when they found out. And find out they would. "Sergei? Can we extend any of our masts? We need to get off a report."

"We've lost hydraulics to the periscope masts and the communications antenna. They won't extend." He looked up from his greaseboard outline. "They might not even *exist*. Someone will have to go up and see."

"On the surface?"

"There's no other way."

Grachev handed control of Engineering to a bright young lieutenant named Demyan, grabbed a new radiation badge from his private stock and went forward to the big circular door at the forward end of Compartment Three. He opened the watertight hatch and stepped into the central passage running between the double row of missile silos.

Everything about a Typhoon was built on a scale that started at big and grew to overwhelming. Rocket Alley was a tall, narrow passage that was longer than most other *submarines*. It extended forward more than a hundred meters, some three hundred feet. Open metal catwalks spanned overhead. Only a few lights burned. He snapped on a flashlight.

Fat yellow cylinders marched off into the gloom. The twenty silos were as tall as five-story buildings. The tubes disappeared into the bilges below and into the curved hull high above.

Grachev marched down the center aisle to Silo Sixteen.

The inspection panel at the bottom was secured with a padlock machined from a solid block of stainless steel and, as an extra precaution, bolted around its periphery. The bolts were laced with lock wire to keep them from turning, and there were lead seals as proof against tampering. A placard warned the panel could be opened only by direct order of the commander, Northern Fleet Submarine Flotilla Six.

Grachev snorted. Who would go poking around a silo if they didn't have to? It was bad enough when there was a rocket in there; the damned things were three stages full of chemical poisons and, of course, ten hydrogen bombs tucked under their nose cones. Grachev, like most submariners, preferred not to think about them at all.

But it was worse now that each silo contained a cylindrical tank filled with tons of water ballast. Rockets didn't leak, at least those with solid fuel. But a water tank welded by a drunk yard worker?

Grachev let his light fall on the yellow skin of the silo. The lead seal was intact. He touched the metal. Cold. The pump should have no trouble keeping up with a few drops. So why was the water level not going down?

He switched on his radiation meter. It clicked merrily. *Let's get this done before I'm sterile as a mule.* He used his flashlight to tap the inspection hatch bolts to make sure they were all properly snugged down. If all that was holding back the ocean was a few bolts, he wanted to make certain they were all as tight as they . . .

One of the bolt heads moved.

He grabbed it with his fingers. It was loose enough to turn.

Those idiots! The yard workers had put their safety wire through it, they applied their lead seal, hung their ridiculous warning sign and snapped their lock shut, but they'd never tightened the bolt!

He took out a pair of cutters and snipped the safety wire. The warning placard fell to the deck. His master key opened the heavy padlock. *The Commander of Flotilla Six can kiss my radioactive ass.* He threaded the bolt all the way out.

If a muzzle gasket had come apart, the sea would be raging out of the bolt hole like a high-pressure jet. It should have blown the damned thing out of the hatch like a machine-gun bullet. Instead, there was a small, steady trickle. *Maybe we're lucky.* It had to be the ballast tank, and a leaky tank was an easier problem to solve.

He walked to the nearest intercom station. He clicked the *kashtan* on. "Captain? This is Grachev. I'm at Silo Sixteen."

"Have you found the leak?"

"Yes. There's not as much water coming in as I thought and it's not under any pressure. It has to be a hairline crack in the tank. I might be able to weld it up. I can't tell without pulling the whole inspection panel."

"You need me to send someone with tools?"

"Actually, I won't," said Grachev as he spun another loose bolt with his fingers.

"What does that mean?"

"You'd better come forward and see for yourself."

Markov knew you weren't summoned by the chief engineer without reason. He went forward and found Grachev sitting on the deck, leaning against the silo. The radiation meter was clicking away altogether too fast for comfort. "How did you thread out those bolts?"

"They were never tightened." He stopped. "Who were the bastards who tried to kill us?"

"Americans," said Markov.

Grachev stared down the row of yellow silos. "The Americans don't seem to think giving *Baikal* to the Chinese is such a great idea." He spun the remaining bolts out and dropped them to the deck, then grasped the hatch's handle.

"If they knew so much, they'd know my ship isn't going to China armed." Markov stood back against the flood that was about to gush forth. "Igor, are you sure that's safe?"

"Pah." The inspection hatch swung open. He was right. There was no gush, only a splash, then a trickle. Grachev pointed his light inside, then stuck his entire head through.

"The ballast tank is leaking?"

"No." His voice echoed, muffled by the thick steel of the silo. He pulled his head out and spat. "Look." He handed him the light.

Markov got down on his knees and peered through the open hatch. He could hear the hiss of a seawater leak from somewhere up in the silo. But Markov's attention was focused on the curved, salt-streaked metal panel just inside the hatch. Not the skin of a ballast tank, but of an RSM-52 intercontinental ballistic missile.

"I'd say the Americans know more about your ship than you," said Grachev.

CHAPTER TWELVE

THE BEAST

Portland cruised at her best silent speed of twelve knots. An American submarine would find it almost impossible to detect her beneath the crashing, rumbling ice. A Russian boat would have no chance at all. That was fine by Vann, for the only thing more dangerous than trying to kill an enemy was sharing an ocean with one who'd survived your attack.

Inside Control, the distant rumble of explosions gave way to a silence so deep it seemed like the very air had been sucked out. Even the ticking of the old deck chronometer was muffled.

That was too damned fast, thought Steadman. He stood behind the helm with both hands on the back of the planesman's seat. A chasm had opened up at his feet, a divide that put him on one side, and the captain, and his future, on the other.

The weapons officer was puzzled. Keefe had just fired two absolutely perfect torpedoes at a big, fat target they couldn't possibly miss, except that they had. Whalley watched with an anxious eye as the dot marking *Portland*'s position marched into the deeper waters of Saint Anna's Trough. Above, the ice was growing too thick for surfacing. Below, the continental slope plunged to depths no submarine could plumb and hope to return.

Only Chief Browne at the ballast board seemed perfectly normal. COB had his earpiece in and was speaking softly with Chief Babcock in the torpedo room. But he kept glancing at Vann the way a driver with miles to go eyes a gas gauge bouncing on empty.

"Captain?" said Steadman.

Vann reached over and yanked the intercom mike from its cradle. "Sonar, Conn. Can Sierra Five be playing dead up in the ice pack?"

"No, sir. I should be seeing a fifty-hertz buzz from his electricals. He's either on the bottom or too far away to hear."

Then we can forget about catching him, thought Vann. Most games of cat and mouse begin and end with a pounce. This one had not. *Why?* Vann looked right at Steadman. "Bam Bam, how fast was Sierra Five moving before she disappeared?"

"Close to twenty knots."

Hitting the ice at *half* that speed would have doomed *Portland,* yet Vann was convinced his quarry had survived. Wounded, limping. But alive. "How close did our fish come before they lost lock?"

"They'd already gone active. Call it inside a thousand yards."

"They were running at thirteen hundred yards a minute. If my math is right, if we'd fired *two minutes sooner,* both fish would have hit." Vann turned to Steadman. "How long were we discussing our orders, XO? Would you say one minute? Five? We can consult the deck log if you're unsure."

"I guess a couple of minutes. Why?"

Vann held up two fingers in a V sign. "Two . . . wasted . . . minutes. The difference between success and failure." Vann's neck burned red. "We just fired on a Russian submarine. Their friends in Moscow will view that as an act of war if they find out, and because *you* wanted to engage in a debate they just might. Do I have to remind you what that could mean?"

"Commander, fifteen minutes ago that Typhoon had no idea we were around. We were in good shape to track and trail her."

"Our orders said stop her. Not track and trail her."

"No, sir. The orders said *delay her* and keep her out of the Pacific until after August tenth. We were to use prudent measures. Sir, sinking a Russian strategic missile boat is not a prudent measure."

"In submarines, the only thing that's *imprudent* is failure." Vann turned his back. "Sonar, Conn. I'm going to take us around the detonation zone. Is there any reason you can't reacquire Sierra Five?"

Yeah. He could be halfway to the fucking North Pole, thought Bam Bam. "We'll need to maneuver inside ten thousand yards to pick him out of the ice, Captain."

"How deep is the freshwater layer?"

"There's a break in the salinity curve at two hundred feet."

"Then we'll stay shallow where he won't hear us and troll the fat line below. If he's alive, you will find him. If he's dead, find where he sank."

"Aye aye." Though Schramm was a lot less confident than he sounded. The "fat line" TB-16 towed array was a heavy sonar detector they could trail behind on a cable half a mile long. The trick wouldn't be in hearing something. The ocean was full of sound. The challenge would be in figuring out where the sound was coming from.

Vann glanced at Steadman and said, "Call Choper back up here, XO. He's a nitwit but at least he knows when to keep his mouth shut."

"Sir, that boomer could be waiting to ambush us up ahead. We fired on him and he might feel like returning the favor."

"I'll say it just once more. You're relieved. Now clear out."

Baikal

Markov left Grachev in Rocket Alley. He stepped through the aft hatch to Main Engineering, but instead of going on to Central Command, he walked to the portside passage and climbed down a ladder to the middle deck. There he made his way aft along a silent passage to his own cabin. Only the battle lamps were burning, and in their dim red light it was far too easy to imagine foaming walls of green water rushing through the Typhoon's broken hull, the rifleshot *crack* of collapsing bulkheads, the frantic screams of the dying. Or worse, the stunned silence of the not yet dead as they rode the hull down.

He came to his cabin door. *When did they load that rocket on board? How many are there?* It had to have happened when he and Grachev were summoned to Moscow to meet Fedorenko. *Are they unarmed?* There could be as many as ten hydrogen bombs nestled under the nose cone of each RSM-52, or none. His boat might have *two hundred* warheads on board. Only Moscow knew, and they'd plainly found no reason to tell *him*.

Grachev was right. The Americans seemed to know more about his ship than he did. It meant they would do everything to prevent him from reaching China. Most likely they'd trailed him all the way from Kola, waiting until he reached the ice to shoot, figuring, not unreasonably, that the ice would keep their secret forever.

Two thoughts moved inside him now: *I won't do what the Americans expect,* and *Fedorenko knew.*

He opened his door and stood for a moment. The lights were off. He took a deep breath and smelled the sweet green scent of northern cedar, the sprig Liza had sent him off with. To remind him of her, of the fact that there was a world worth returning to. He slapped at the switch and the cold fluorescent lights buzzed on.

The collision with the ice had sent the vase with its cedar sprig tumbling to the deck. The water had spilled but the sturdy glass was intact. He picked it up, went to the tiny sink and opened the tap, letting the water flow until it was no longer the color of old blood. He refilled the vase and set it back in place on his desk, noticing that the digital depth display mounted on the wall had gone blank.

Markov had heard plenty of sea stories told by retired captains late at night at the Submariner's Club in Saint Petersburg. He'd witnessed the agonies of *K-219* firsthand. The Cold War had not always been so cold. Men— Russians, Americans—had died, lost by fire, by explosion, by drowning, by collision. The circumstances of their deaths were kept locked away in Washington, in Moscow. Not even their own families knew the truth inside the sealed folders inscribed with the names of lost ships, of crews on eternal patrol: *K-19, K-219, Kursk, Scorpion* and *Thresher. Baikal* had been seconds away from joining that ghostly fleet.

He grabbed the heavy black telephone and dialed the sonar operator. "It's Markov. Any contacts?"

"None detected," said Belikov. "But it's getting very quiet astern."

"They won't follow their own torpedo. They'll sprint ahead, then wait." *Unless they know we can't shoot back.* Then they'd steam up his baffles and shoot again and again. *That means they don't know we can't fire back.* It was a temporary advantage. Eventually they would realize it. Markov had to make good his escape before that happened. "We're going to run parallel to the edge of the ice for ten more minutes, then turn south."

"South?"

"Have Borodin plot a course back for Seal Bay. And not the same one we used coming up here. We'll hug the eastern coast of Novaya Zemlya."

"It gets very shallow there, Captain. We'll have to take it slowly."

"You have your orders." He clicked off the phone, then dialed the *starpom* in Central Command. "Sergei?"

"Gasparyan listening."

"How deep are we? The repeater in my cabin is broken."

"Three hundred meters and level."

"Take us back above the salt layer, but we can't make a sound doing it. Plane up to one hundred fifty meters. Slowly."

"Understood." Then, "Captain, are we really going home?"

"If we're lucky," he said, then slapped the phone back into its cradle. They'd have to get beyond the ice, surface and rig an antenna to transmit a message back to Northern Fleet headquarters. He knew they'd have only a short time. The noise of their surfacing would be impossible to mask. The Americans would find them.

But *Baikal* trailed a long wire designed to hear extremely low-frequency signals. They could be picked up underwater, even beneath the ice, but they were restricted to simple messages. If he could find a transmitter, then *Baikal* could dive and listen for a response. He picked up the phone and called Grachev. "Igor?"

"Main Engineering. What is it, Captain?"

"How long will it take you to rig a new antenna?"

"It depends on how badly you mangled the old one."

"I'm serious. I want an answer."

"I'm serious, too. We hit hard enough to wipe out the periscopes, but the antenna is mounted farther aft. If there's anything left of it, no less than an hour and no more than a day."

They'll find us. "An hour is too long. I need a better estimate."

"I need a wife. Unfortunately, we'll both have to wait. But I've been thinking. We could use a Beast instead."

It was the name Russian submariners gave to the ship's rescue buoys. Two red-and-white disks were mounted on the outer hull, one at the bow, the other far astern. The Beasts were released by detonating explosive bolts or automatically should *Baikal* sink to a fatal depth. Both contained radio transmitters that beamed *Baikal Baikal Baikal* on the international emergency band. Special satellites would pick up the signal, determine its location and trigger an alarm in Moscow.

A Beast might work. Though it would draw the attention of the Americans like a . . . Markov stopped. *Bell?*

"Captain?"

"Is there any chain on board?"

"Where are we going to dock?"

"I'll tell you what I have in mind. . . ."

When Markov was done, Grachev said, "It's risky."

"Tell me what isn't. Go find that chain." Markov put the phone down. Where was the American submarine? Markov was like a blind man locked in a cell with a killer. Listen for the slightest sound, the smallest scuff, for you will never see the next attack coming.

His black phone buzzed.

"Markov."

"Captain, Gasparyan. We're passing under the edge of the pack ice now. Borodin has us headed for Point Zhelaniya. Is that correct?"

Baikal could hide off the northernmost spur of Novaya Zemlya. Its rugged coast was a maze of banks and rocky inlets. A commander would have to be crazy to enter waters that tight, that dangerous. *Or desperate.* "Yes. What's our depth?"

"Two hundred meters, rising slowly on the planes."

"Good. I didn't hear a thing. Now find some open water. It doesn't have to be an ocean. Just enough to . . ."

Markov heard a distant, muffled *thump.* He instinctively turned.

"What in the name of God was that?"

USS *Portland*

Bam Bam had nearly half the TB16's cable reeled out. The heavy end, packed with sensors and directional hydrophones, sagged down into colder, clearer waters. His green "waterfall" sonar display began to fill with the random snow of ocean noise. The top of the screen was marked off in degrees, showing the bearing to the sounds.

What's the noisiest creature on earth? In the undersea world, there was nothing as loud as the snap, crackle and pop of billions of shrimp. The sea surrounding *Portland* sounded like nothing so much as the world's biggest popcorn machine. A whale song shifted up and down the spectrum in eerie harmonies. The bearing said the whale was off the bow, slightly to port, but Bam Bam knew it could be one mile away or fifty.

Sound traveled in mysterious ways through the sea. Three things made all the difference: temperature, salinity and depth. A warm zone could bend sound like a lens, a layer of fresh water could reflect it. So could the dense, icy water at the bottom of an abyss. Schramm had all three to contend with. And Vann.

A new vertical line appeared on the left-hand side of his screen. Natural sounds came and went in a kind of random flicker. Always there, but no pattern. Something made by a machine had rhythm.

Bam Bam watched the line fade, then return. Once, twice, a third time, then it vanished. He picked up his microphone. "Conn, Sonar. Possible mechanical transient bearing two four eight."

"Put it over the loudspeaker."

A random, watery slosh, followed by a low *thud . . . thud . . . thud* emerged from the intercom speaker. Schramm was about to suggest they switch to the more discriminating sonar array in the boat's bow, but he held his tongue. If Vann wanted something, he could fucking well ask for it.

"Can you estimate his range?" asked Vann.

"Not close." *You want a better guess? Make it yourself.*

"All right," said Vann. "Helm, left five degrees rudder. New course two five zero. Sonar, switch to the bow sphere and see if we can pick him up again. Secure from general quarters."

"Switching." The acutely sensitive sonar sphere in the bow began flooding Schramm's console with information. The sphere looked like one of those glittery disco balls from the eighties, except that instead of mirrors the fifteen-foot globe was studded with hundreds of directional hydrophones for passive listening, and powerful transducers for active searching. A long access tunnel connected the sphere with a hatch set in the forward elliptical bulkhead near the chief's lair, the Goat Locker.

Short of crawling into a torpedo tube, no place on the boat was as confining or as frightening as the sonar tunnel. You were neither in the boat nor quite outside, and you shared the long, dark pipe with thick, high-voltage cables.

Schramm watched his display for the odd sounds he'd heard. He wouldn't say it because he couldn't prove it, but he had a hunch that boomer was still alive.

Scavullo lay in her bunk listening to the air whispering from a small vent. She'd heard Vann's little pep talk over the ship's intercom and dismissed it. He'd screwed up down in Kola and now he was rallying the boys around the flag, and himself.

But then *Portland* echoed with strange noises, rolling rumbles punctuated by whooshes of compressed air and long silences. She'd felt the ship maneuver, heard the engine surge, then subside. Were they chasing someone or running away?

"Secure from general quarters. Secure from general quarters."

She rolled out of her bunk. Everything was absolutely normal out in the empty passage. The overhead lights burned, the temperature was constant. She heard hurrying footsteps behind her. It was Wallace, a junior-grade lieutenant from the communications division and Bledsoe's understudy, though with none of his malice. He carried around a pocket Bible and took the question *What would Jesus do?* very seriously.

"What's going on?" she asked him.

"Gotta run." He didn't stop to chat.

Scavullo followed him aft to a ladder. He headed for the middeck galley. She went all the way down. It was here on the bottom deck that *Portland* seemed less like a basement and most like a ship. Down here the great steel curve of the hull was perfectly visible. Just a little over one inch of HY-80 steel separated you from the ocean, and it took no great effort to imagine what was on the other side.

She made her way aft to the Auxiliary Machine Room. There were no A-Gangers around. The treadmill was folded up against a bulkhead and secured by a strap. She pulled a loop of stainless steel safety wire out of her breast pocket and formed it into a pick. Someone had put a microphone near the treadmill. A microphone had a wire. Scavullo didn't trust anyone else to find it. Like the sign up in the officer's head said, it was *men* against *woman*.

She ducked beneath the emergency diesel's exhaust manifold. The pipe vanished through the overhead. There were no wires. No microphones. No evidence there had ever been one.

It was here someplace.

A tool locker was mounted to the hull close to where the treadmill once stood. Inside it was a sign decorated with a skull and crossbones, a warning that the tools were the property of the Auxiliary Gang.

Scavullo noticed something else. The locker was made with straight sides but the hull behind it had a curve. She let the locker door fall shut and ran a finger under it. There was a crevice, narrow at the corners but a good quarter-inch wide at the middle. Scavullo bent the tip of her safety wire into a hook and slipped it up behind the locker.

The hook caught on something. She gently pulled down a twisted, double-strand wire. Red and black. It could have come from a doorbell. The copper conductors were too small to carry much electricity, but a microphone didn't use much. She pulled the line until it went taut. It was still connected. She traced it until it vanished into a conduit that went up to the middeck.

Even though she had been on board for two and a half weeks, *Portland's* densely packed geography was filled with uncharted land. Scavullo had only a dim sense of which compartment was overhead. It could be the officers' wardroom, the crew's mess, the galley, even the small trash area where garbage was packed into metal jackets and fired into the sea. But there was no doubt about what was above all of *that* on the upper deck.

The radio room.

She felt ridiculous for not having realized it sooner. Who could rig a microphone better than a radioman? *Engler.*

I'm going to nail his sorry ass, she thought as she paced off the distance to the ladder going up to the middeck. *Twenty-six.* She climbed up, stepped out onto the deck and headed aft, silently counting.

Ten steps took her to the door of the wardroom. She looked in and saw Wallace wolfing down a sandwich while he studied a diagram of the boat's antennas and masts. She kept on going.

Five steps more and she was beside the entrance to the crew's mess. Ahead, the passage ended at a circular watertight door. There was just one such hatch inside *Portland,* and it opened onto "Nuke Alley," the tunnel that connected the forward spaces with the reactor and engine compartments aft.

The hatch was set in a heavy, shielded bulkhead. Not even Engler could run a wire through it. That meant the microphone wire was threaded up through the galley or *Portland's* freezer compartment.

She entered the mess room and found it empty. The big banner that proclaimed *Portland* the HOME OF THE INVISIBLES had been taken down. The cooks were piling up cold cut sandwiches that could be grabbed and downed in a hurry.

She walked behind the ship's laundry, under the hatch leading up to the escape trunk, and found herself standing next to the insulated door to the freezer hold. She pulled the door open. Cold mist streamed by her feet. The lights were on. Scavullo went in and let the thick door close.

Coils of liquid vapor cascaded down over a wild jumble of crates and cardboard boxes. The walls were frosted with ice and padded with insulation. The needle on a thermometer bolted to the wall pointed at four degrees above zero.

Between the stacked boxes were narrow slots barely wide enough to slither through, and behind them were tall shrink-wrapped pallets of frozen peas, pizza crusts, chicken nuggets, fish fillets. Scavullo went to the far wall. The insulation had been cut, then patched with silver tape.

Her fingers were growing numb as she plucked the tape away and peeled back the blanket, revealing the red-and-black wire. Above her, where the freezer coils snaked back and forth, she spotted it entering an air grille, where it vanished.

The door to the galley opened and a cook peered in. "What the fuck?"

Scavullo turned.

"You aren't allowed in here. Get a move on, Lieutenant."

She walked out under his hostile stare and climbed up to the top deck, hugging the wall to keep anyone in Control from seeing her. She hurried aft. The door to the radio shack was closed. Beyond, the passage became a dead end, blocked once again by the reactor bulkhead. There was only one compartment left on this side: the fan room.

The fan room door was posted with a hand-lettered notice: *SOUND KILLS!* It opened onto a tiny airlock, barely big enough for one person to stand in, and designed to keep the tremendous din of the fans from escaping. A second door lay within. The entire compartment floated on springs to isolate noise. She opened the outer door and stepped in.

The inside door was secured with a curious knob that had to be unscrewed before it could open. It was posted with a sign that reinforced the message:

EAR PROTECTION REQUIRED BEYOND THIS DOOR
94 DECIBELS—NO UNAUTHORIZED PERSONNEL

She could hear the hum from the other side of the door. All those decibels were being kept in check by a massive amount of insulation. The outer door closed. She unscrewed the inner door and went inside.

For ears accustomed to the hushed silence of a modern nuclear boat, the sudden onslaught of howling blades and roaring electric motors was a physical shock. She could feel all ninety-four decibels beating on her ears. It resonated in her chest. Another sign warned of dangerous high voltage.

Equipment was arranged around the compartment in the shape of a U. In the center of the room, a big steel cylinder rose like a missile silo. Scavullo got her bearings and recognized it as the emergency escape trunk she'd seen down in the mess area. Narrow walkways hugged the meager space between the cylinder and the surrounding equipment.

She walked down one leg of the U, across the compartment, then back up the other side to where a large blower motor was mounted on springs and rubber disks. Heavy power cables were bolted to its housing, protected by rubber boots. A placard read 450 VOLTS AC. Beyond it, on the outer hull where a duct rose up from below, she found what she was looking for.

Engler hadn't been as careful up here. Why would anyone notice a small twisted wire emerging from one small duct and diving into another? The submarine was laced with miles of wires and ducts. There was no way to tell by just looking, but she could guess that one of those ducts went down to the freezer room, and the other went to the radio shack. She grabbed the exposed section and pulled.

The fan room lights went out.

A deep mine, a cavern. What is so utterly black as an unlit compartment inside a submarine? She could make out electric blue flashes projected through openings in the fan motors. They flickered in a kind of cold blue fire. She'd have to navigate back across a blacked-out room without electrocuting herself.

She was reaching out to find her way back to the door when the blue flashes on the wall in front of her were eclipsed by a looming dark mass. She put her hands up instinctively as a fist buried itself in her stomach. She fell, gasping. Something heavy struck the thin metal of the fan housing with a sharp, resonant clang. Scavullo flattened herself to the deck. The blue sparks inside the motor were close and bright. She felt something cold on her cheek. Metal pipe. Hovering close above her, blue lightning glinted off eyeglass lenses. She grabbed at them and felt Engler's mustache instead.

She rolled as the pipe slashed down hard. It caught her shoulder blade. Her vision doubled, her bones shook. She caught an end of the pipe and held on with all her strength. It wasn't enough.

Engler pulled her to her feet, then shoved her back against the fan housing. She lost her balance and fell across the top. The terminals jabbed into her side. She tried to stand but Engler's hand grabbed the belt of her poopy suit and yanked her back down to the deck. A second punch to her stomach blew her breath out.

Two powerful hands shoved her legs open. Before she could react, a hand slipped inside the gaping fly. She tried to lock her legs together but he was already between them, ripping at her underwear.

She tried to kick him but she was trapped. There was no way forward, no way back. She clawed at Engler's face but the pipe slammed down across her neck. She tried to scream above the roar of the fans but she couldn't even hear herself.

He moved against her, forcing her thighs far apart. She could see the cold flicker in his glasses. She could smell the high-voltage ozone from the roaring motors. One end of the pipe rested against the rubber boot that protected the power terminal. The other touched the deck. In between was her own neck.

Scavullo's reaction was automatic and instantaneous. She reached over and yanked the rubber boot off the terminal.

There was a loud *pop!*, a dazzling spark, two exploding stars filled his eyeglasses with hot, liquid light. The pipe flew away. He screamed loud enough for her to hear over the roaring motors. The air was filled with the stink of electric smoke, melted insulation, hot copper and burning hair.

Then he was gone. One minute, two. Scavullo jumped up with her veins pumping pure adrenaline. Her neck tingled where the current had raced by. She'd been blinded by the flash. But when the phosphorescent clouds behind her eyes cleared she was alone. Alone in a room full of roaring machinery, isolated by springs, dampened by insulation. Alone with her enemies, locked inside a steel prison guarded not by walls and fences, but the sea.

Bam Bam noticed the blue lights of the sonar shack flicker. He looked around to see what might have caused it. A submariner might happily sleep with his head against a torpedo and never think twice about it, but let the fans falter, the lights flicker, let there be an unusual sound, and all his senses went on high alert. "What was that?"

"Routine maintenance," joked another sonar operator.

"Piss-poor time to screw around with the lights," he said, then looked back at his screen. "Hey. When did this show up?"

A faint green line pulsed with life.

COB noticed the flickering lights and made a quick call on his low-power radio to a chief in the engineering division. "Skipper, the engineer reports a ground in the fan room."

"When were the water sumps last drained? You know condensate backs up and shorts those motors, COB," said Vann.

"I'll send someone to find out what happened."

"Conn, Sonar," said Schramm. "I'm picking up a faint fifty-hertz contact." The characteristic hum of a Russian electrical system. "It was *real* faint but the bearing was close to where that first sound came from." *Why didn't you run for it?* "If it's our guy, he ain't heading north no more."

Vann watched as the contact evaluation plot was updated. *Where's he going? Back to Kola? Maybe we did get a piece of him.* "Let's move in and check it out," said Vann. "Helm, right five degrees rudder. New course three zero zero. Well done, Bam Bam. Meet me in my cabin in five minutes."

Well done? Bam Bam nodded for one of the other three sonar techs to take over his console. "On my way," he said, wondering what Vann had in mind.

CHAPTER THIRTEEN

THE WORD

Steadman stared at the light on his small desk. Had it just dimmed, or was he imagining things? He'd taken *Portland* through that gap down in Kola and come out the other side certain of his future: command school, a final run made with a boat full of senior captains and then a fast attack of his own. Now he'd just been thrown out of Control, and like as not the Navy.

He got up and headed for the wardroom down on the middle deck, climbing down the ladder mechanically. What had he done wrong? He'd demanded clarification. He'd doubted Vann's authority to shoot. When action was called for, Steadman hesitated. Who was right?

The wardroom was just forward of the galley. Bedford, the electronics tech who'd forgotten to wind Vann's clock, the young husband who missed his wife so much he was known as "Tripod" for the way he woke up every day with the unmistakable evidence of his longing, was guarding the door.

Tripod looked miserable.

"What are you doing hanging around down here, Bedford?"

"Sir, the captain asked me to tail Miss, I mean, Lieutenant Scavullo."

"She's in the wardroom?"

"Aye aye. Listen, if saying I'm sorry about that clock will help, I'll do it. I'd rather do garbage duty for the rest of the run than tail after *her.*"

"I'll see what I can do to get you a new job."

"I'd appreciate it." Bedford held up his hand to show Steadman his gold band. "What's my wife gonna think when she hears I'm hangin' with some girl? I don't want her to have to worry. You can put a good word in with the skipper, can't you?"

"Sure." Steadman thought, *No way,* and went in.

Rose Scavullo sat at the single table with a mug in front of her, filled to the brim. A tea bag sat unopened on the table. Her eyes were red. She looked frightened. Her neck was smudged with soot.

Steadman slipped into the seat across from her. "What's wrong?"

"I had to find someplace." She held on to the mug with both hands. "With a door."

Steadman touched her mug. It was cold. He went to an urn and filled her mug with hot water, then another with coffee for himself. He sat back down and pushed her mug to her. "I'm listening. Talk."

"I went looking for the wire. I found it. But then . . ." She stopped.

"What wire?"

"The bug down by the treadmill. I traced it to the fan room. Someone tipped him off. It had to be the cook. I think they're in it together, because the wire went through his freezer, and then . . ."

"Tipped who off?"

"Engler." Scavullo told him some of the story. Enough to get the point across. But there were sentences, whole paragraphs missing.

Steadman listened and when her words dried up, he said, "If half of what you say happened is true, Engler's headed for a Captain's Mast and a court martial when we get back. You have my word on it."

"It'll take two weeks to put back in at Norfolk. I can't hide out that long." She looked up and seemed to focus on Steadman for the first time. "Aren't you supposed to be in Control?"

"I got thrown out." He hesitated, then thought, *What does it matter what I say now?* "We just fired two torpedoes at a Russian submarine. Probably the boomer you heard down in Kola. I didn't think it was a great idea and I questioned it. I was relieved."

She stared, trying to see if he was serious. "You just sank a Russian submarine?"

Steadman noted her use of the accusatory *you*. "No. Both fish went after the ice. I think he got away."

"Doesn't Vann know what shooting at Russians means?"

"He didn't do it on a whim," said Steadman, angry at having to defend something he didn't believe in. "We received orders."

"To start World War Three?"

"They left room for interpretation. I read them one way. Vann read them another. The rules say the captain makes the call."

"Shouldn't he radio Norfolk to clarify them?"

"That's not how this business works, Lieutenant." Steadman took a sip. "At sea, the captain is judge and jury."

"And executioner?"

"We're under the ice pack. There's a boomer out there that's either running for its life or waiting to shoot back. Nobody's going to phone home. If we break contact to send a message, that Typhoon will be gone. You know what would happen if he gets off a distress message? What's going to happen when they take one of *our* missile boats down? You think everyone will understand it's just evening the score?"

"You said the orders weren't clear. If you let Vann get away with this, it won't be just his fault."

"I'm not letting him get away with anything."

"You're not stopping him either."

"Correct. Now I'll tell you why I can't. It's called mutiny."

Baikal

Markov found Engineer-Lieutenant Ivan Demyan waiting in the passage outside his cabin. He was a nuclear reactor specialist, and one of Grachev's hand-picked team.

"Captain?" said Demyan. He had wide-set blue eyes, the wheat-yellow hair of a pure Slav and the open face of a farm boy. "Can I have a word with you, sir?"

"Not now." Markov tried to edge by the beefy young lieutenant.

Demyan didn't move. "It's important."

Markov knew Demyan from the candidate files Grachev had sent along. Demyan was one of those rare officers who didn't mind dirty hands. "All right." He stepped back into his cabin. "You've got two minutes."

Demyan followed, then shut the door. His face clouded. "Sir, I heard we're going back to Kola. Is it true?"

"Who told you?"

"I'd rather not say."

"Do you care if we go south instead of north?"

"It makes a difference to me, sir." He paused. "To my family."

"You'll be seeing them that much sooner."

"But I can't do that."

"Can't?"

For an answer, the young lieutenant rolled up the right sleeve of his blue coveralls.

Markov sucked in his breath. A dark, irregular mass had erupted from the soft skin inside the engineer's elbow. Large as a squashed prune, its surface was mottled, its circumference surrounded by angry red. Markov could see it pulse. "Have you shown that to a doctor?"

"There's no point. I looked it up myself. It's called nodular melanoma. The fast-growing kind. I tried to be careful around the reactors but I guess I must have slipped a few times." He shrugged as though he'd gotten paint on himself and not a potentially lethal dose of radiation.

"Skin cancers are treatable, Demyan. They'll cut it out and you'll be fine. When we put in at Kola, you're going straight to the hospital."

"With what money?" Demyan said bitterly.

"The Naval Hospital in Murmansk is free."

"All they give you is a bed to die in. There's no medicine, no treatments, no doctors. *Baikal* is more comfortable and I can make sure my wife and daughter will be taken care of."

Markov stood back. "Your bonus?"

Demyan nodded. "The half we got is a start, but they're going to need it all." His eyes glistened as he reached into a pocket and brought out a tiny photo wallet. "Look. See how beautiful they are."

Markov looked. *The wife.* A pretty woman, very young, her hair drawn back, standing in front of a rough wooden wall hung with garden tools. *The dacha.* A girl of about four. *The daughter.* "Don't believe everything you hear about naval hospitals. There are some good people there willing to help."

"It's too late, Captain."

"Demyan, you're an engineer, not a doctor."

Demyan gave Markov an impatient glance, as though they weren't speaking the same language. He reached over and rolled up his other sleeve. His left forearm was spattered black, as though he'd stood too close to a roofer at work and had been splashed with hot tar. He looked up. His face said, *Do you understand now?* "When I'm dead my family will have to leave the base, our apartment. Everything. Where will they go? What can they do? I have to give them something. I figured on staying in Shanghai and making money until I drop. They could throw me on the trash heap, but she'd have the money. They could start life over. Look at her face, Captain. What kind of life will she live? How will she eat? You know what I'm saying. I can't let that happen. I can't."

Markov folded the little wallet shut. "Does Grachev know?"

"He'd *kill* me! We're supposed to be more careful. Please don't tell him." He rolled the sleeve back down. "You're captain. You decide where the ship goes, but . . ." He stopped talking, the pressure behind his words gone. There was nothing left to say, nothing left to beg for.

"I'll think of something. Don't worry. You have my word. I'll think of something. And stay out of the reactor compartment."

"I'm sorry I let you down."

"Go."

Demyan gave Markov a sheepish smile and then left.

Markov waited at his door, wondering how he'd solve Demyan's problem. He'd hand him his own sailing bonus, but Demyan would not be the only one counting on the money Fedorenko had promised. *Fedorenko.* He opened the door, expecting a line of other unhappy sailors, but it was empty. He walked down the quiet, dim passage to Fedorenko's cabin and without knocking, opened it.

Pavel the cook was painting a cut in Fedorenko's forehead with iodine. The former naval attaché was on his bunk with a bloody cloth in one hand, his eyes closed. Markov said, "How is he?"

"Another bandage should stop the leak."

"Pavel, you're needed in the galley."

"I have everything there under—"

"Go."

"Understood." Pavel hurried off. Markov kicked the door shut.

"My head feels like a nut in a vise." Fedorenko opened an eye and touched the gash in his forehead. Fresh blood welled up through the purple iodine. "The ship is all right?"

"You should have grabbed onto something when I said to."

"I'll listen next time." Then, Fedorenko gave Markov a one-eyed glance. "The American submarine?"

"Gone. Temporarily."

"They're crazy if they think they can get away with this." Fedorenko dabbed at his scalp. "It must be reported to Moscow."

"We're heading for a place to surface. If we live long enough to reach it we'll make that report." Markov pulled out a chair from the tiny desk and sat. "As for who is more crazy, I'm not so sure."

Fedorenko's face went professionally blank. "What do you mean?"

"The Americans didn't put those rockets in my silos. They're only trying to keep them from the Chinese. Who's crazier? You tell me."

"Rockets?"

Markov tried to read Fedorenko's expression. "I examined Silo Sixteen. There was no ballast tank. There was a three-stage, eighty-five-ton rocket. An RSM-52. Imagine my surprise."

"A rocket? You're sure?"

"Please. You knew all along what was in there. Apparently, so do the Americans. I'm the only one they left in the dark."

Fedorenko shook his head. "This is shocking news, but I have no special knowledge of such matters, and frankly speaking, why would I need any? We're delivering a ship. You agreed to sail her. Nobody pointed a pistol at your head. Who cares what's inside those silos?"

"I didn't agree to sail her armed, and the Americans didn't try to murder us because we're hauling beets."

Fedorenko balled a fist. "The Americans are unbelievable. Why should we have to ask permission for anything? We're a sovereign nation and this is a matter for sovereign nations to decide. This ship will go to Shanghai whether they like it or not."

"No. *Baikal* will go where its captain decides."

"That decision has already been made."

"At sea, my word is law."

"Technically. Now let's speak practically. You don't want to go to Shanghai? Then where will you go? Turn around and run back to Seal Bay? They'll just find another captain. And then there's your own future to consider. You'll be known as the man who stole a billion and a half dollars from Russia's pocket. When the lights fail, when the trains stop, when the schools freeze and the hospitals close, who will they blame? If Moscow doesn't put a bullet in your head, there will hundreds of others anxious for the honor."

Markov knew Fedorenko was almost certainly correct.

Fedorenko could see Markov waver. "Stop talking treason. If you aren't careful, you'll end up like your old captain from *K-219*. In a cell. Is that what you want?"

"He was acquitted."

"Not because he was innocent. I can guarantee that you will not be so lucky. Be sensible. You're a captain of the Russian Northern Fleet. You have your orders. You accepted them. The time for questions has passed. And think about your wife, your son. A traitor for a husband, a father who refused to help his country. Is that what you'd condemn them to?"

Markov felt his heart begin to thump. "My family is not involved."

"I can see in your face you don't really believe that."

He felt something move inside him, something resolve. He reached for the telephone and dialed Central Command. "Sergei? This is the captain."

"Listening," said the *starpom*.

"Stand by to answer bells for emergency reverse. Both engines."

"They'll hear us digging holes in the sea from here to Murmansk."

"Stand by to execute." He looked down at Fedorenko. "How many rockets are on board my ship? Are they armed? Do you have the release codes to jettison them?"

Fedorenko peered at Markov as though he were slowly coming into focus. "What is this? Suicide?"

"This is my ship. I need to know what's on it."

"Or you'll help the Americans kill us? You'd commit this crime against your own men?"

"Their families already have half their sailing bonus. Russian submariners have died for less."

"They've died carrying out their sacred duty, which is more than they will say about you. I don't believe you'd do it. Not for an instant."

Markov put the phone to his mouth. "Sergei?"

"*Wait!* Put that damned telephone down!"

Markov held it, but moved it away from his mouth.

"All of them. If you don't believe me, go ahead and let the Americans kill us. I can't stop you."

Twenty intercontinental ballistic missiles. "The rockets are armed?"

"You'll have to ask Moscow. I have no—"

The phone came up.

"*I don't know!* The deal was negotiated at the highest levels."

Markov held out a hand. "The codes."

"Why would they give a launch key to me?"

Markov leaned close. "You're one evasive answer away from finding out how long it will take American sonar to hear us."

"*No!* I'm not wearing any keys and I don't have one stashed and besides, what good would a single key do? It takes three to launch a rocket and Moscow would never trust one man to hold them all."

Fedorenko was right. A rocket could be launched only after three men— usually the captain, the security officer and the head of the weapons division—agreed to insert magnetic cards into three separate launch consoles. Unless the computers read the correct codes from all three cards within one minute, the rockets might as well be welded to their silos. There wasn't even an emergency provision for jettisoning them. "What about the radiation in the missile compartment?"

"Emitters in the bilges. It's not much. Only enough to keep out the curious. It's harmless."

To Demyan? "You admit to sabotaging my ship."

"Your ship?" Fedorenko sat up. "The Chinese government bought *your* ship, Captain Markov. One and a half billion dollars. I think they have the stronger claim."

"The Americans bought it first. That didn't stop you from selling it again, did it?" Markov put the phone to his mouth and said, "Sergei?"

"Markov! Don't be—"

"I'm coming to Central Command now. What's our depth?"

"Ninety meters. There's an open lead in the ice in three kilometers."

"Call Grachev and tell him to stand by to surface." Markov slapped the phone back into its cradle. "Thank you for your cooperation," he told Fedorenko. With that, he left.

USS *Portland*

Schramm glanced at his sonar display one last time. *Nothing.* That 50-hertz line had better pan out. If the contact proved to be false, if the Russian was running in another direction, they'd never find him again.

He left the blue-lit sonar room and headed down the short passage to the door bearing the poster *Zero Errors.* Schramm knocked.

"Come."

Vann was sitting at his little fold-out table, studying a screen filled with streams of red data. It gave his pale skin a distinctly sunburned glow. A big, spiral-bound notebook lay closed on the table, along with a yellow marker pen.

Schramm recognized the book as the quartermaster's log. "What's up, skipper?" He was feeling pretty bouncy after telling Vann off, then getting an *attaboy* from him.

"Sit down. I want to discuss that last approach with you."

Schramm sat down. *Where's the XO?*

"I didn't want to say this in the open, because it would have to be written up. But you let us get *way* too close to that Typhoon. I can't conn the boat and run your sonar console. I depend on you for timely warnings. That means catching problems early. Not when they're about to become an emergency. You see something developing, you holler. If nobody pays attention, you jump up and down and scream."

It didn't take an ear finely tuned to nuance and tone to put Schramm on guard. "I know all that, Captain."

"Then why the *hell* didn't you do it?" Vann opened the deck log. "I've marked four different points in the engagement when the officer of the deck had to make a snap decision without the latest sonar information up on the contact board."

"Sir, plotting those contacts isn't my job."

"Don't union-shop me, Schramm. I won't stand for it. It's pretty clear you had critical information while we were operating in the dark."

Schramm looked at the logbook, wondering what Vann was talking about. "Sir, I wouldn't put a lot of trust in some quick notes and time hacks kept while we were maneuvering and shooting. Those logs always get cleaned when things settle down later."

"I want to be fair with you, Schramm," said Vann gravely. "I instructed the XO to make certain everyone on this boat knew that from here on, there could be no slacking off. Did you have that conversation?"

"Not in so many words, no."

"You've heard my message now."

"Loud and clear." *XO's in the doghouse for sure.*

"Good." Vann nodded at the logbook. "Now, I want you to go over the deck logs. Pay close attention to where I've highlighted them. I want you to make sure your sonar logs match them *exactly.*" He pushed the notebook across the table to Schramm. "You might find you overlooked something in the heat of the moment. As you said, things always have to get aligned after the fact. You may come out of this better than I thought."

What the fuck? He wants me to cook the books? "Maybe so, skipper. I'll take a look." Schramm touched the notebook. Curious to see what Vann was getting at. Curious, and a little frightened, too.

"You work with me, I'll work with you," said Vann. " 'Kay?"

"You got it, Captain."

"We're a team again, Schramm. See that you stay on it."

CHAPTER FOURTEEN

MESSAGE IN A BOTTLE

Baikal

"Open water in three kilometers," said Belikov.

Markov hoped so. Though he didn't know what Grachev would find up in the sail, he could guess that *Baikal* wasn't in any condition to break through serious ice.

Belikov reached over and adjusted the circular sonar screen until it displayed a detailed forward view rather than the usual full circle. "We shouldn't see much more than brash and blocks."

Brash ice was more slurry than sheet, though larger chunks could be hidden in it. And under a late summer sun it would be growing softer, not hardening.

"Five degrees right rudder. Align the ship with the lead."

Grachev showed up dressed for the surface in a heavy sweater and oil-skins. He was carrying a black iron socket wrench. Lysenko, the brawny warrant officer from the torpedo room, followed him with a length of heavy chain draped over his broad shoulders.

The chain was a piece of their "storm rider," used to help secure the submarine to its pier during heavy weather. Its links were thick as good sausages. He grunted as he lifted his leg through the hatch and stepped into Central Command.

Markov watched to see who was carrying the storm rider's tail.

It was Demyan. The young engineer wore only a slicker over his blue coveralls and he was sweating buckets. He tried to step through the hatch but his boot caught on the coaming. With a clank of chain, he tumbled against the bulkhead and sagged to the green deck tiles.

"Quiet!" Grachev snarled.

Demyan gave Markov a quick glance, then staggered upright and leaned back to let the bulkhead support him.

Markov thought, *That chain weighs as much as he does.* A strong, healthy man would buckle, yet Demyan was standing. *How the devil is he going to climb up on deck?* "We'll use the forward buoy," he said to Grachev. The Beast mounted at *Baikal*'s bow was a hundred-meter walk across the top of the missile hatches, but the deck was wide and flat. The Beast at the stern was only half as far, but it sat on a part of the hull that ramped steeply down to the water. "Retract the bow planes," said Markov.

The bow planes slid into their protective slots without a hint of the trouble they'd given coming out.

Markov turned to Belikov. "Any contacts?"

"None detected." It was true if not very reassuring.

"All stop," said Markov.

The engine annunciators came back to ALL STOP. *Baikal* drifted, its enormous momentum carrying it southeast.

Markov glanced at the plaque over his chair: SUBMARINE LIFE IS NOT A SERVICE, BUT A RELIGION.

It had been true aboard Markov's old submarine, the old *K-219*. It was still true. Submarine service was a religion, one that couldn't be easily explained to someone from the outside world. Duty. Honor. Sacrifice. *Look at Demyan.*

He was standing with chains wrapped over his neck and across his shoulders, ready to carry out orders that would put his family on the street without a kopeck. Why? Because Markov had asked him to.

He glanced at the clock. It was 0720 Moscow time, the only kind of time a Russian submarine kept. "Come to periscope depth."

"Captain . . ." said Grachev.

"I won't raise the scope until you've had a chance to inspect it." But old habits were hard to break. Markov wished he could raise the satellite antenna and broadcast a full, coded account of what had happened. *No.* He wished to be home in bed with his wife, wondering how he'd find a job to see them through the coming winter.

"Periscope depth, Captain," said Gasparyan.

Markov turned to his chief engineer. "We'll stay in contact by radio."

Grachev patted the small, low-power handheld clipped to his belt. "Too bad the signal won't reach Murmansk."

"I'll give you one-minute time checks. I want you all back down with the hatch sealed and the boat ready for dive inside fifteen minutes." Then he noticed that none of them were wearing life vests. "Where's your flotation gear?"

Grachev shrugged. "Vests won't do much good with all that chain around our necks. Besides, nobody's going swimming."

"Clear water around the boat," said Belikov.

Markov looked to the young officer at the dive board and said, "Blow bow and stern ballast groups. Blow them dry. Surface!"

The alarm bell rang three times, and Grachev put a hand on the ladder that went up to the commander's balcony, and on to the hatch to the O1 deck, the bottom level of the sail.

The submarine broke through a thin skin of brash ice into the bright, golden light of a polar dawn. The sea was dotted with floating chunks the color of purest sapphire. Ocean swells heaped the brash into thick, gelid hillocks that rose and fell against the black hull with the dry, rasping sound of poured sand.

First the battered tip of the sail broke through, then the rounded, ice-breaking base, followed by a distant *sshhh!* ninety meters aft as the tall rudder emerged. A torrent of water and ice cascaded off her rubber-coated flanks. Low in the east, the sun burned yellow as kerosene, all glare and some heat. It illuminated *Baikal's* steaming, glistening decks.

Even before she stopped rising, the main hatch inside the Typhoon's sail fell open with a *clank!* that echoed inside the cavernous space. Grachev was the first one to climb out onto the O1 deck.

The inside of the sail was an enormous, free-flooding compartment. Water drained swiftly away through the scuppers, but solid crystals of brash ice remained behind to form a slick, treacherous surface.

"Let's go!" Grachev shouted down the ladder. He pulled the handheld radio out. "Captain? I'm on top."

"How does it look?"

Grachev looked up. "Not good." He should have seen a round circle of sky at the top of the ladder leading up to the open bridge. It was now a definite oval. The inside of the conning tower looked like a giant had taken a sledge hammer to it. Rivets were missing, sheets bulged inward. Frames that had once been true were curved. The underside of the enclosed bridge was folded aft like the bellows of an accordion.

"Two minutes," said Markov. "Tell me what you see."

"The open bridge looks the worst. I'm checking the deck hatches now." Grachev slogged across the slush to the forward hatch leading out to the missile deck. He tried to undog the locks, but the handle wouldn't budge. "Forward One is jammed." Grachev tried a second hatch set into the side of the sail. "Port Two is jammed. I'll check the last hatch."

Directly across on the starboard face was Starboard Three, the last hatch out to the weather deck. Beyond it was a narrow, flat catwalk going fore and aft.

By putting his shoulder into it, Grachev forced it open. He watched water sheet down the black hull and into a sea shrouded with a thin, smoky fog. He leaned out. *Fuck.* The collision had forced a section of the sail to bulge like a squashed cardboard box. It made the already slender catwalk impossibly narrow. "Captain? Starboard Three works. I can open it, anyway. I'm not sure it will close. But the way forward is blocked. The sail is really bent out of shape. We'll have to use the Beast at the stern."

"Come back down. You can climb up the forward escape trunk."

"That will take too long. We're already up here." Grachev eyed the outside deck. The walking area was no more than two meters wide. There were no railings, no safety tracks to clip into. Greasy swells loomed out of the fog, heaved and fell back against *Baikal* with a hiss.

"Gasparyan's on the way up with a safety line, Igor. What about the masts? If the antenna is all right we can forget the Beast Buoy."

That was the good thing about Markov. Some officers might as well be carved out of wood. Talk to them all day and nothing would register. Markov was different. He knew what that catwalk was going to be like without Grachev having to tell him. "I'm going up to the attic now," he transmitted, then grabbed the ladder going up to the exposed bridge. Grachev gave it a hard shake. It didn't budge.

He climbed thirty feet up to the enclosed bridge. It was a good deal smaller than it had been before. The forward lip of the sail had taken the first blow from the ice and had been squashed down almost to the deck. The portholes were gone. *Amazing.* To think they'd hit something this hard and *survived.* No other submarine in the world would have.

He climbed the final rungs to the outer bridge. The sprayscreen, the foghorn, the lights used to see under the ice, they were simply gone. Where ten men in heavy weather gear could once stand, there was only room for Grachev. He peered over the torn lip at the sea far below.

Broken rafts of gray ice merged with gray fog, darkening in the distance. The sky overhead was blue pearl. Tendrils of mist wrapped *Baikal* as the relatively warm water clinging to her hull steamed in the colder air. Aft, the heavy door that protected the radar and satellite communications masts had been torn away. The masts themselves leaned back in their wells, staring uselessly at the sky. It would take a real shipyard to make them move again. The nearby general-purpose periscope was a total loss, its optical head a blind, black hole. The smaller attack periscope and the satellite antenna that fed Borodin's navigation systems were farther aft, and they appeared to have survived. "Captain? You've got the attack scope and the satellite navigator."

"That's everything?"

"We're alive. Believe me, if you saw this you'd say it was enough."

"Engineer Grachev?" came the echoing cry from inside the sail.

He looked down. They'd hauled the chain up the trunk to the O1 deck. Gasparyan was there with a coil of safety rope. "Use Starboard Three! We're going aft!"

His handheld radio crackled. Markov's voice said, "Six minutes. Are you down on deck yet?"

Grachev said, "There's nothing more to see up here." He climbed back down and picked up the heavy wrench he'd left.

Gasparyan handed him the coil of safety rope. "Don't get lost. It's a long swim home."

"Don't you know? I'm the chief engineer. I can walk on water."

"Not that far," said the *starpom*. He climbed back down into the main trunk.

"Okay," Grachev said to Demyan and Lysenko. "There's no easy way out to the foredeck. There's no easy way aft, either, but it's shorter."

Demyan shifted under the heavy chain. The links clanked like a set of manacles. The aft Beast Buoy was mounted just forward of the tall rudder, right where the hull sloped down to the smoking water.

"There are five bolts that hold the Beast to the deck," Grachev explained. "I'll take care of them while you two attach the chains *exactly* the way I said." He hefted the wrench. "If we're lucky, the bolts won't be frozen and the chains will pull it right over the side."

"The bolts are going to be rusted," said the torpedoman flatly.

"Then Gasparyan will blow the Beast off from Central Command." The Beast sat on what amounted to a live mortar shell designed to shatter the hold-down bolts and send the buoy to the surface from the deck of a sinking submarine.

"Eight minutes," said Markov.

"If they can blow the Beast from below, why not let them?" asked Lysenko. "That way we wouldn't have to go out on deck at all."

Grachev stared, then said, "Tell me. What's that necklace around your shoulders?"

Lysenko's eyes slowly registered understanding. "You mean the chain?"

"You're smarter than you look, Lysenko." Grachev rolled his eyes and looped the rope around Demyan's waist, then tied it off with a slipknot. He paid out a meter, then did the same for the torpedoman. He tied himself to the very end. "Let's go." Grachev walked to the open Number Three hatch. "The deck's going to be a fucking skating rink."

Grachev stepped through the hatch and found the footing better than he'd expected. It was drier outside the sail than in. The brash ice had flowed freely off the sloped hull, leaving only a few diamond-clear chunks to worry about. The rubber tiles felt secure. He kicked a brick-sized piece over the edge of the catwalk and watched it slide down to the sea.

"Ten minutes."

They kept close to the sail for ten meters, and then the catwalk merged with *Baikal*'s broad, sloping afterdeck. Grachev ventured out onto the great ship's backbone, where a narrow walkway was marked off in white stripes.

It was an easy downhill walk, but then, just forward of the two vanes meant to direct the flow of water into the propeller shrouds, Demyan's shoe caught on the edge of a rubber tile and he fell. The chains spilled from his arms. They rattled down the hull, pulling Demyan along behind.

The torpedoman hollered as the safety rope went taut. He planted his boots, but between Demyan and the chain, a lot of mass was in motion and the deck was growing steep. He squalled as he went down.

Now two men and five meters of heavy chain were sliding down the deck to the water and Grachev knew he'd be pulled off his feet, too. He sprinted down to where the flow vane emerged, grabbed on to it and held on for all he was worth.

The rope yanked at his waist and tried to tear him off the vane, but Grachev refused to budge. The rope stretched, threatened to snap, then relaxed.

The radio squawked, "What's happening?"

Grachev couldn't answer. The torpedoman was still cursing, but Demyan was up on his knees pulling the chain hand over hand. When the end with the snap ring on it appeared, it was wet with the sea. Grachev's fingers ached with cold. He had to force them to release, joint by joint. "Both of you! Get those chains secured!"

"Igor?"

"We're running ahead of schedule," said Grachev.

The Beast was the size of a manhole cover, painted in an hourglass pattern of white and red with the word *DANGEROUS* in several languages around its perimeter. In the center was a black, circular plate where the radio antenna would extend by way of a small explosive charge. Once erected, a rescue strobe would flash and marker smoke would be released. Five bolts secured the buoy to the deck.

Lysenko had been correct. The heads were flaked with rust.

Grachev pulled out his wrench and began to attack the first bolt. With a loud grunt, it began to turn. Once started, it turned more easily. Four bolts grudgingly came out. He tossed them over the side. He inserted the socket over the fifth bolt and pushed.

It didn't move.

"The last fucking bolt," cursed Grachev. "Come on, torpedo pusher. Help me with this bastard." The torpedoman took hold of the handle. *"Now!"* They pushed. There was a crack.

The handle snapped.

Grachev cursed again, then threw the broken handle over the side. He took out the radio. "Captain, the chains are on. We got four bolts out but the fifth won't come. You'll have to blow the last one off."

"All right. Get back into the sail."

Grachev pushed the chains over the side. They rattled and clanked down the hull, struck the sea with a splash, then went tight.

Walking uphill was easier. They made it back to the open hatch without a slip. Grachev said, "We're ready. Go ahead and blow it." He heard Markov say something to someone down below, then his voice came back loud and clear. "At the count of five, four, three, two, one and *mark!*"

At first nothing happened. "Now what?" But then there was a white flash, a muffled *tonk!* they could feel right through their boots. *Finally.*

But when he looked, the Beast was still on deck with its antenna extended, sitting in a cloud of billowing yellow smoke. A weak strobe began to flicker from the top like a flashlight with moribund batteries.

Grachev stepped out through the hatch. "Wait for me here," he said. "I'm going to kick that bastard over the side myself."

USS *Portland*

"Whoa!" said Schramm. His octagonal screen showed a bright green vertical line where there had been none. He replayed the sound through his headset.

A sharp, fast *thud,* followed by a fading echo as the sound reverberated through a maze of ice.

"Conn, Sonar, something just blew up out ahead. Bearing zero zero eight."

"Torpedo?"

"No, sir. It was way too small and over too fast. But then it kind of rang for a while like a big old bell. Like something going off inside a hull."

Vann didn't need to wait for the contact to show up on the master plot to know that the new sound came from the same general vicinity of the two previous contacts. One, two, three. *They were running for open water and something blew up.* That was a stroke of pure luck, because it meant that when the Russians found the wreck they'd only see signs of an internal explosion. *Just like* Kursk. But Vann wasn't going to leave matters to luck. "Sound General Quarters! Ahead two-thirds!"

Steadman heard the General Quarters tone sound over the 1MC and felt *Portland* heel and accelerate. He opened the door to the radio shack. There wasn't a lot of radio work to do with the boat underway submerged, and Lieutenant Bledsoe, the head of the communications division, was there by himself. "I'm looking for Engler," he said. "Have you seen him?"

"I sent him down for a bite to eat, XO."

Steadman had just come from below and he knew the radioman wasn't in the mess. There was something in Bledsoe's look he didn't like. Something that said he knew perfectly well where Engler was and saw no reason to tell Steadman. "Engler could be in serious trouble. If you know something you'd better say it now, Lieutenant."

"If I find something, you want me to tell you or the captain?"

"I'm the exec, Mr. Bledsoe."

"Still?"

"Just bring it to me," he repeated, and he left to find Engler.

Baikal

Grachev swore as he hurried aft. A biting wind blowing off the ice fields swept the yellow smoke away. The strobe continued its feeble flashing. It was only when he was standing next to the Beast that Grachev wondered about the color of the smoke.

Yellow?

Mortar smoke wasn't yellow. Marker smoke, the kind meant to draw the eye of a rescue ship, *that* was yellow. He looked at the extended antenna. The explosion, the smoke, they were from the gas charge meant to blow the antenna upright. The main charge, the mortar, hadn't fired.

He spun on his heel and began to run when a tremendous *crack!* struck him from behind. A gust of hot wind plucked the engineer off the deck, and Grachev was flying.

Demyan was gathering the safety rope into a neat coil when the pressure wave of the blast swept over him. It was as sharp as the first report had been muffled and much louder. He didn't wait to look out through the open hatch, to assess, to judge. He headed aft at a dead run.

"Hey!" shouted Lysenko the torpedoman.

The entire stern was hidden by a pall of gray smoke. The chains had dragged the distress buoy over at last, and it bobbed in the sea off the starboard side. Demyan burst through the veil of smoke and stood over the black hole where the Beast had once been bolted.

Unburned charge bubbled and glowed like new lava. Where was the chief engineer? "Engineer Grachev!" Demyan turned. "Engineer Grachev!" He edged closer to the starboard side.

The strobe on the Beast seemed to be revitalized by its short, violent flight. It flashed faster and brighter. Demyan heard a faint cry from behind him. It was coming from *Baikal's* port side.

Grachev was in trouble. He'd yelled as loudly as he could but his voice had been swallowed up by the great, rubber-tiled hull that towered before him like a wave. He was dressed for the cold, not for a swim, and his heavy jacket, his boots were pulling him under. One moment he'd been standing on the deck, and the next he was trying frantically to stay afloat in the ice-choked water.

The first shock of it was gone, and now he could feel the cold invading him, draining him. He tried to paddle over to the hull. It took all his will, all his determination, all his stubbornness to gain any distance. A swell rose up from behind and swept him against it, but then it surged back, spun him around and shoved him away. When he twisted to face *Baikal* again he was no closer than he'd been before.

He had to kick his boots and beat the brash ice with his fists to keep his chin above water, and every time he stopped kicking he sank a little deeper. His mouth, his nose. He tried to peel his coat away but to do that he had to stop paddling and in an instant, Grachev was under, his breath rising around his head in thick, gelatinous bubbles.

He fought the impulse to surrender and kicked back up to the surface. He tried to twist out of his heavy coat and only managed to get snarled in it. He tried to take a quick gasp of air but he was too late and the first slug of water poured down his throat. He gagged and sank deeper.

He looked up to the surface. He felt as though he were rising, not sinking, rising like a balloon above a pale green landscape that was turning darker, darker. He would fight the sea for every meter. He reached out his arms to the light, took a fist of icy water in each and pulled.

He was still pulling when the dark green landscape far above him exploded in a galaxy of white foam.

Demyan hadn't planned on jumping. He hadn't planned on anything, which was just as well. If he'd thought about diving over the side into water this cold, he'd never have done it. He'd looped one end of the safety line through a recessed cleat on the deck, tied some sort of a knot and taken one step off the flat top of the hull. A second step landed him halfway down the port side of the hull, where it was too steep to walk. The third brought him into open space high enough above the waves to give him time to realize it was a long way down, time to feel the growing speed of the fall, time to take a deep breath.

He landed feet first, still holding on to one end of the yellow safety line, directly atop the rising bubbles he'd spotted from above.

The shock of the cold struck him like a fist. Stunned, Demyan rose to the surface, took another deep breath and dived, letting the line pay out as he descended deeper, deeper. It was growing too dark to see, and still no chief engineer. He could hear the clank of the chain from the Beast. Demyan clawed at the water with one hand, kicking in fast, hard strokes. There was only one chance. If he had to go back up for another breath Grachev would be gone. His lungs started to burn, he'd have only a few more seconds, a few more meters' depth, and then . . .

His hand brushed against something soft. He reached out and grabbed a handful of hair, then lost it. His body was screaming for oxygen, but he dove deeper, sweeping his arm ahead of him. He found a jacket sleeve. Demyan grabbed it and started for the surface, afraid for a moment that it was nothing, that it had fallen off Grachev or worse, that he'd pulled it off. But then he felt resistance, felt weight on the other end, and kicked hard for the mirror green surface.

CHAPTER FIFTEEN

BAIT

USS *Portland*

A new green line blossomed on Schramm's sonar display, a loud, clear blast, transmitted cleanly and directly from its source. Then, a different kind of noise.

Clang . . . Chunk! . . . Clang! Clank! The beat was irregular, the origin obvious. Someone was on the surface banging metal on metal, and after the explosion he'd picked up earlier, he had no doubt about what it was, or what it meant. "Conn, Sonar. Explosion in the water bearing zero zero two. I'm picking up beaucoup transients on the same bearing. He could be on the surface."

We've got to get there fast and kill him before he makes that report, thought Vann. "Man battle stations torpedo."

Steadman hunted for Engler from the torpedo room at the bottom of the bow to the radio shack at the aft end of the top deck and came up empty. Engler was either hiding out in the engineering spaces or else he'd disappeared. He climbed up to the middeck to make another sweep and found him sitting at a table in *Portland*'s mess area.

He grabbed him by the shoulder hard, and Engler came up ready to fight. He cocked an arm and almost took a swing before he saw it was Steadman. The fist came down. The murderous look only receded. It didn't go away. His hand was bandaged. "What are you doing here, Engler?"

"Lieutenant Bledsoe said I could grab some chow."

Steadman nodded at the bandage. "What happened to the hand?"

"I spilled hot coffee. Cookie saw the whole friggin' thing. He won't get into no trouble, will he?"

Steadman motioned the cook over. "What happened to Engler?"

"I told him to be careful. The coffeepot was *red* hot. But you know you can't tell this joker nothing and now look what happened."

"Who bandaged it?"

The cook glanced at Engler, then back. "I did, sir."

Steadman eyed the cook. They were lying. "Come with me," he said to Engler.

The radioman slowly, insolently stood. "We goin' someplace, XO?"

"The Goat Locker." Then, to the cook, "Meet us there in ten minutes."

"What the hell, XO?" the cook protested. "I got a meal to prep."

"Wrong. You've got a date with the chief of the boat."

Steadman was about to pick up the intercom mike and get COB headed for the Goat Locker, when an urgent tone sounded over the 1MC, followed by *Man battle stations! Man battle stations!*

Engler grinned. "Guess it's gonna have to wait."

Baikal

"Igor! What's happening up there?" Markov turned the volume all the way up but got only static for an answer. He handed the radio to Gasparyan, his *starpom*. "I'm going up on deck. If Belikov picks up a submarine, *any* submarine, call me at once. If you don't get an answer, call me one more time, then rig the ship for dive and get out of here."

"But, Captain . . ."

"I mean it, Sergei. If you hear anything, don't wait around one extra minute. Dive the ship and run for the ice. Understood?"

Baikal's executive officer was about to protest that they couldn't outrun a torpedo, but Markov was already heading for the main ladder.

Demyan rose to the surface, gasped for air, then started hauling up on Grachev's sleeve. It was heavy as a bag of boulders. Each pull put his own head back under and he could feel his strength ebbing. He looked up and saw the burly torpedoman high above. Then, a second man dressed in blue overalls joined him.

It was Captain Markov.

Demyan kicked back to the surface. "The rope!" he screamed up at them, then sank. He struggled back to the surface. *"PULL THE ROPE!"*

Lysenko and Markov began to haul in the yellow rope together. It went taut, Demyan felt a tug at his waist, and he was pulled to the great black wall of *Baikal*. Grachev trailed behind lifelessly, but at least Demyan stayed above water. Nearer, and then his boot struck the hull.

The feel of something solid, something familiar, under his feet sent a fresh surge of energy through Demyan. He was still in a frigid sea with a drowned engineer in tow. He was still looking up at ten meters of curved hull. Hope can look cold and dead as yesterday's ash, then give it a chance, even a small one, and it can flare back to life.

Lysenko did the heavy pulling. He spread his legs wide and put all his strength, all his back, all his thighs into each haul. Markov secured each newly won length of line by passing it through the cleat.

Demyan found himself walking up the rubber hull on his own two feet. As he rose, Grachev's dead weight made him teeter, made the rope stretch, but there was no way this was not going to work. There was no way at all. The climb was vertical, then a little less so. He walked up the port side until his eyes were level with the deck. Two more steps and he'd make it over the top. The black water was pulling at him, calling to his shaking muscles to give up, to let go of Grachev, to live. He looked up at the torpedoman for help.

Lysenko couldn't hold the rope steady and grab him. There was one last thing Demyan had to do, and though he had no more strength, no more energy, he lunged up over the shoulder of the hull and collapsed on the deck, still holding Grachev's leg and arm in a grip that refused to surrender.

Markov untied the rope from Demyan's waist, then tried to pry Grachev's arm away from Demyan. "Let go of him, Demyan!"

Demyan stared up at his captain, uncomprehending.

"Let him go!" It was like yelling at a wall. Markov was about to strike Demyan to make him let go, when the radio at his waist squawked.

"Captain? This is Gasparyan! Submarine approaching from the northwest!"

"Demyan! Let go!"

"Captain Markov? Answer!"

Markov grabbed the radio. "We're coming! Rig the ship for dive! Flood the tanks *now!*"

Lysenko pried Grachev away from the young lieutenant and slapped the chief engineer facedown to the deck with his head over the side.

The two ventilator scoops began to retract down into the deck. There was a clank of shutting valves.

"Lysenko! What are you doing?" Markov demanded.

The torpedoman didn't answer. Instead, he straddled Grachev and pushed down hard between his shoulders. A trickle of water flowed out of his open mouth. The trickle grew to a foamy stream.

The forward main ballast tank erupted with a long, sad sigh of compressed air that sent a jet of fog into the pale sky. Then two more geysers rose from the base of the tall conning tower. Markov could feel the ship start to settle. "We've got to get below now!"

"Wait!" Lysenko flipped Grachev onto his back and blew his lungs full of air, then pressed down on his ribs, hard.

A fourth jet of air roared skyward from the stern ballast group.

Markov pulled Demyan to his feet. The young engineer was shaking. "Can you move, Lieutenant?"

Water streamed down his face. He nodded.

"Then *run!*" He turned to the torpedoman "You get Grachev's legs! I'll take his arms! We'll have to take his . . ."

Grachev's eyes fluttered. He coughed and sprayed Lysenko's face with foam and spittle.

White water boiled up at the stern as the tall rudder began to sink into the sea.

Markov knew they didn't have much time. "Grab him!"

The torpedoman picked Grachev up in his arms. They caught up to Demyan just as the narrow catwalk outside the sail came level with the sea. Markov was the last one through. He stepped into the conning tower, slammed the reluctant hatch shut and ran for the main trunk, chased by the flood surging across the deck.

He jumped down into the hatch and pulled the chain after him. The heavy clamshell clanged shut overhead and icy water showered his face. He grabbed the locking wheel and spun it. The shower became a spray, the spray a trickle, and then stopped.

"Keel depth forty meters!" came the call from below.

Markov climbed down to the periscope balcony, then to Central Command. "Where's Grachev?" he asked Lysenko.

"*Starpom* Gasparyan and Engineer-Lieutenant Demyan carried him to sick bay, Captain. He was cursing and fighting them every step."

"You saved my friend."

"Demyan was the hero. All I did was pull on a rope."

Markov thought of Demyan's wife, his child, the money that would mean a normal life for them. And the life they might lead without it. "Demyan will be taken care of," he said, and then walked over to where the sonar officer sat hunched over his display. "Where's that submarine?"

Belikov manipulated his receiver. "Northwest. Coming straight in."

Markov noticed that Belikov had taken down the picture of the Volvo he'd intended to buy with his own bonus. "You think they hear the Beast?"

"Listen." Belikov turned up the volume on the passive sonar set and put it over a loudspeaker.

Markov heard the *clang! clink . . . clink!* of the chains as the Beast Buoy bobbed in the swells. "How fast are they coming?"

"Better than fifteen knots. I had a blade count on him for a while but then I lost it."

Too fast. The American wasn't hunting. He was moving something the *mafiya* called the *kontrolniy vuistrel,* the "control shot," a second bullet to the head to finish the kill.

Clang! Clink! Clang!

Now the chess game would begin again, only this time both players, not just the Americans, knew the stakes. Markov assembled the pieces on the board. His own submarine was damaged, unable to communicate, unable to shoot back. *He thinks we're on the surface making repairs. He'll learn the truth soon enough.* When the American captain realized he'd been fooled, Markov needed to be outside his detection range. Where to run, and how fast? *The ice is easiest to hide in, but stay around and he'll find us.* Check. *Run for home? It's quieter to the south. But unless we get a head start, he'll pick us up before we can escape.* Check and mate.

Somehow he needed that head start. Somehow, he had to put the Americans on the defensive. But how? The captain of a missile submarine is trained to hide. The American was an attack captain, a professional killer. He looked at the screen. *He wouldn't dare run straight for us if a Russian attack submarine was around.*

Markov felt the crystal of an idea begin to grow. He turned to the two officers at the ship's control station. "Helm. Left ten degrees rudder. New course zero three zero. Make your speed four knots."

"Northeast?" The helmsman seemed puzzled. Home was to the southwest.

"Northeast. Ahead one-third on Number One engine. All stop on Number Two."

The helmsman twisted the engine telegraph, then glanced back at Markov. "You said all stop on Number Two?"

"All stop and disengage the screw." The port propeller would now "windmill" in the watery stream flowing by it. Markov thought through the game one, two, three moves ahead. He picked up a *kashtan* microphone and called Main Engineering. "This is the captain. Secure the Number Two reactor. Emergency scram."

As the duty officer in engineering acknowledged the odd commands, the sonar operator looked up from his circular screen. "Captain, if you do that we won't be able to run very fast."

"We're not running. We've got two OK–650 reactors. Two engines. Two screws. Divide them in half and what's left?"

"Half a Typhoon."

"Or all of a shark," said Markov.

USS *Portland*

"Conn, Sonar. Contact now bearing two eight zero. Range fifteen thousand yards. He's sitting on the surface in an open lead in the ice." Vann had steered *Portland* on a ranging leg to the southwest and Bam Bam was fairly certain of where the banging was coming from, but he was growing increasingly wary about what it was. *No steam, no flow, no mechanicals, no tonals, no 50-kilohertz hum. Just somebody beating on metal.* He listened. The sound wasn't natural. Whales didn't hammer on steel. But if it was coming from a work party clearing away debris on a damaged Typhoon, why couldn't Schramm hear the Typhoon itself?

Vann said, "Left ten degrees rudder. Come to one four zero degrees."

"Left ten degrees rudder, one four zero degrees, aye," said the helmsman.

"Mister Keefe," Vann said to the weapons officer. "Make Tubes One and Two ready in all respects."

"Making One and Two ready in all respects, aye," said Keefe.

A rapid ballet scored for sweating torpedomen and multiton weapons began in *Portland*'s torpedo room. Moving quickly, the TMs shifted two 3,400-pound torpedoes off their storage racks and onto the loading trays. They were massive weapons with dull silver hulls and bright green noses. Once the Mk 48s were in position, hydraulic rams pushed them forward through the breech doors. The data transmission wires were connected to their tail spools, the circuits tested, and then the breaches were sealed. As a final step, a sign was hung from the ready tube: WARSHOT LOADED.

A green light illuminated on Lieutenant Keefe's weapons console, then another. The boat's fire control computer was now connected with the guidance systems on board each torpedo. "Tubes One and Two loaded with ADCAPs, Captain. Systems checkout is underway."

"Flood One. Flood Two."

Once more *Portland*'s hull rumbled with tons of rushing water.

"Firing point procedures, Sierra Five, Tubes One and Two," said Vann. "Short-range attack mode. Disable Doppler and run them in at max speed. There's no point in being subtle and we've got to make sure he goes down fast."

Keefe tapped a series of commands into the fire control console.

"Conn, Sonar. Contact's angle on the bow starboard three. Range fourteen thousand six hundred yards."

"What do you mean *contact*? Is he my Typhoon or not?"

"I can't ID him from what I got up on my screen, Captain."

"You designated him Sierra Five before. He's still Sierra Five."

"Aye aye." *If you say so.* But Schramm slipped out his private log and made another note. As he did, a faint vertical line glowed to the left of the zero-degree mark. He let the acoustic filters sift the sound, clean it up, then put it up through his headset.

It was the faint, regular beat of a propeller.

A second green line blossomed, a third.

Where did you come from? Schramm listened closely to the *swish swish swish* of a screw. Was he hearing the damaged Typhoon at last? *No.* It took a lot of listening, a lot of experience, to be able to distinguish one class of submarine from another. But there was no way to confuse the sound of fourteen propeller blades for seven. *Shit. We've got a second boat.* "Conn, Sonar. New contact bearing three five zero. Evaluate it as a single-screw submarine."

Vann paused, then snapped, "What kind?"

"Stand by." Schramm sent the new sounds into a sound spectrum analyzer. The computer considered it for only a second before confirming Bam Bam's suspicions. "Single reactor, single screw. The analyzer is calling him an *Akula*. Designate him Sierra Six."

Akula. A Russian attack submarine whose name meant "shark."

Baikal

"Range twelve kilometers."

Markov watched as the American submarine rushed in after the Beast Buoy. "One ping, one-third power," he said.

Belikov lifted the guard on the transmit key. The active sonar button was warm to the touch and his finger was slick with sweat. It slipped the first time he tried to push it, but not the second.

Ping!

A brilliant green line flashed onto Bam Bam's sonar screen.

"Conn, Sonar! Active ping from Sierra Six bearing zero one zero! It sure sounds like a Skat set." A Russian sonar used by several types of submarines, including the stealthy *Akula*s. "Signal strength puts him outside thirty thousand yards, skipper. No way he could have us."

He's not looking for us. He's hunting for the Typhoon. Attack now, or run for a better position? Sierra Six was an acoustical ghost slowly taking the ominous form of an *Akula,* an attack submarine very nearly as silent as his own. Vann listened to the soft ticking of the old deck chronometer, weighing his moves. It was possible the Typhoon had already gotten off some kind of a message. Why else would the *Akula* come sniffing? Vann could not allow him to find that Typhoon. But retreat now and that *Akula* would move in to escort the damaged Typhoon back to Kola. The whole world would learn what had happened up here under the ice.

Vann couldn't allow that, either.

If he's hunting for the Typhoon, he's not close. Yet. He can't know what happened. Yet. And he's not sure where his big brother is. Yet.

There was still time to complete the job Norfolk had given him.

"Open the outer doors Tubes One and Two," he said to the weapons officer.

Keefe pressed two buttons on his fire control panel. Two red lights went green. "One and Two are ready in all respects."

"Sonar, Conn. Firing observation, Sierra Five."

Schramm wished he had more to go on than that rattling and clanking. He wished he could creep up on it and listen hard for the other normal submarine sounds that *had* to be there. He would have preferred to swim one torpedo out and let its own sonar find the floating hulk of that Typhoon, but there wasn't time for that now. Not with a second Russian boat sniffing around. "Angle on the bow starboard ten. Range ten thousand three hundred yards."

"Match final bearings," said Vann. "Shoot One. Shoot Two."

Keefe pressed the large red firing button. There was a low rumble as *Portland* spat out first one, then a second torpedo. They immediately accelerated to full speed, their screws buzzing like angry wasps as they streaked away into the dark green sea.

"One and Two are on the way," said Keefe. He was watching his screen for the instant when the torpedoes' seeker heads would pick up the unmistakable shape of a Typhoon bobbing on the surface. "Run time eight minutes twenty seconds."

CHAPTER SIXTEEN

THE SARDINE CAN

Naval High Command Headquarters
Moscow

When *Baikal*'s distress signal went up it was heard by three Russian search-and-rescue satellites; one rising over Finland, a second directly overhead Novaya Zemlya and a third setting over the North Pole. The signals were bounced down to an antenna farm outside Moscow and triangulated and the results routed over a land line to Naval Headquarters in downtown Moscow.

The signal's journey from buoy to satellite to Moscow took less than a minute. But once inside the Ministry of Defense's imposing building on Yanesheva Street, everything slowed. The message had to be written out by hand and authenticated. The duty officer gave it to a messenger, who carried it from the Naval Communications desk on the fifth floor to the Emergency Action Center, known as the "Sardine Can," three levels underground. The elevator was not in service. He took the stairs down to the large, low-ceilinged room of bare concrete walls, polished wood tables, red telephones and multicolored maps.

While this was being done, a phone call was placed to Northern Fleet Headquarters in Severomorsk, just outside Murmansk. The Ministry's list of warships carried *Baikal* in the category of *inactive . . . pending decommission*. She was sitting inside a tunnel up at Seal Bay awaiting the scrapper's torch. Had one of her Beast Buoys come loose and drifted out to sea?

Precious minutes evaporated in Severomorsk as Northern Fleet staff scrambled to deal with Moscow's questions. In the end, they passed the inquiry directly to the commander of Submarine Flotilla Six up at Seal Bay, Admiral Vyacheslav Popov.

Six minutes after the satellites picked up the distress beacon, Admiral Popov's telephone rang. The great-grandson of a famous Tsarist naval officer, Popov the younger was as short, balding and plump as his ancestor had been tall, silver-haired and patrician.

His breakfast had just been delivered to his desk on a silver tray. Tea, rolls, sausage, sweet Volgoda butter and strawberry jam. Outside, weak, gray light struggled through a chill fog rolling in off Kola Bay. The hilltops were still glazed with last night's hard frost. In Petersburg they were celebrating summer's "White Nights" as though winter would never return. Here, winter was never far away.

He ignored the buzzing phone and glanced at the clock. It was a quarter past eight, and he was already regretting getting out of bed. Popov had just thrown a Norwegian journalist and his cameraman out. At least, that's who they said they were. Of course they were spies.

Norway had lodged a formal complaint over the unannounced launching of missiles the other day. They were calling it a toxic attack on the ecology of Barents Sea, a plot to get rid of inconvenient poisons while the world's attention was focused on Taiwan.

The little bearded bastard even brought photographs of dead fish. Dead fish! Popov had tossed them back in his face. The oceans were full of fish and some of them were bound to die. Besides, it was none of Norway's business. The launch had taken place in Russian waters.

Now there was a flotilla of protest boats bobbing off Kola Fjord, sometimes darting into Russian territory to take "chemical samples" or to "monitor for radiation." Western submarines were on the prowl, triggering acoustic alarms by the hour, sniffing about to determine what exactly had happened. Between the Norwegians above and the submarines below, you couldn't take a piss over the rails without some snoop snapping your picture.

The telephone finally went silent.

Good, he thought as he dipped a spoon into the jar of jam, stirred it into his tea and picked up his copy of the English-language *Moscow Times.* It was folded open to the apartments-for-sale page. Popov would shortly receive a substantial facilitating payment from the State Arms Export Agency for helping arrange the sale of one of his missile submarines to China. Indeed, the "sailing bonuses" of its crew came right out of his pocket, and Popov was not known for his generosity. The sizable remainder would be Popov's ticket out of Seal Bay forever.

Popov swiveled in his chair to gaze out onto the gray buildings, the collapsing docks, the half-sunk derelicts that constituted his flotilla. When the State Arms Export Agency came to him with a proposal that would take him away from this, who could blame him for saying yes?

The telephone rang again.

Popov cursed, tossed the paper aside and picked up the heavy black receiver. "What is it?"

He listened, his bushy dark eyebrows nearly joined together in a scowl. "Where did you get this information?" He listened again, then said, "Most probably it's a mistake. Yes. Tell Moscow that exactly." He hung up, scribbled a quick note on a piece of paper. *It better be a mistake.* When he was through, Popov dialed the flotilla radio section.

"Radio room, listening."

"Has there been any communications with *Baikal*?" asked Popov. "Nothing, Admiral. The situation here is perfectly normal."

"You think so?" Popov looked at the Moscow newspaper, then glanced out his window at the bleak fjord. "Try raising them on the normal channels. If they don't answer, use the submerged communications net." He picked up his note. "Send someone. I have a message for Captain Markov."

Baikal

"How far are we from the Beast?"

"Five thousand meters, bearing now one five eight," said Belikov.

A sudden commotion made Markov look up.

"Get your hands off me or I'll throw you down a ladder!"

Chief Engineer Grachev and his assistant Lieutenant Demyan were grappling in the aft hatch. Grachev was wrapped in blankets and his hair was soaking wet. He left a puddle on the green deck tiles where he stood.

Grachev shoved Demyan away and glared at Markov. "You can't just flip a switch and shut down an atomic reactor like a lightbulb. What idiot ordered it?"

"I did," said Markov. "It's nice to see you on your feet, Igor."

"Ramming icebergs wasn't enough? You had to see if you could blow up my reactors, too?"

"If you'll just calm down, I'll explain what I—" But Markov didn't get to finish the sentence.

"Captain!" yelled Belikov. "Torpedo in the water!"

Grachev said, "Not again."

A second green spike brightened on the sonar scope. "Two torpedoes!" said Belikov. "Both weapons are astern bearing one seven zero. Range seven thousand meters." Belikov watched the green lines slowly shift away from the center of his screen. "I have bearing changes on both torpedoes!" He looked up from his screen, realizing now what Markov had planned all along. "They're heading for the Beast!"

USS *Portland*

"Both fish are running hot, straight and normal," said Lieutenant Keefe. "Forty seconds left."

"Have they acquired Sierra Five yet?" asked Vann.

"No, sir. Not yet."

"There's a forty-thousand-ton submarine sitting on the surface out there, Lieutenant. He's had two internal explosions and they're beating on the hull. All he's neglected to do is to send us an engraved invitation. What do you *mean* 'not yet'? Are you sure you used the proper preselects on those weapons?"

"I used the ones you said to, skipper. The ice might still be shielding him. They might not pick him up until they're right underneath his keel."

Vann slapped the back of Keefe's seat and grabbed the intercom microphone. "Sonar, Conn. What's Sierra Six doing?"

"I'm seeing some bearing change. That *Akula* was off to the east but it looks like he turned around. He could be headed back our way."

Keefe said, "Thirty seconds left."

Vann added up the tactical picture. His weapons hadn't picked up the Typhoon yet, but they would. It was the largest submarine ever built, sitting dead in the water, not a ghost. Vann was already thinking beyond its destruction. Even if they didn't pick up the sounds of his running torpedoes, that Russian attack submarine would hear them go off and know that the rules of the game had changed. When that happened, Vann had to be someplace else. It was noisy to the north. Silent to the south. Silence favored the quiet American submarine. *We'll head south.*

"Twenty seconds," said Keefe. "Both fish are picking up mechanical transients on Sierra Five's bearing now."

At last. That banging *had* to be the Typhoon. There was nothing else it *could* be. "Steer both fish onto those transients, Mister Keefe." The *Akula* would expect *Portland* to hide in the ice to the north. Vann would sprint south, drift and listen. And if the second Russian came looking for trouble, Vann would oblige him.

"Ten seconds to go."

"Cut the wires," Vann snapped. "Close the outer doors. Reload One and Two with ADCAPs. Helm, new course one eight zero."

Bam Bam Schramm was about to turn down his acoustic receiver to keep the torpedo blasts from damaging it when a bright green line blossomed on his scope. A sonar pulse, and strong enough to make Schramm worry that the Russian attack boat wasn't looking for his friend anymore. "Conn, Sonar! Active ping from Sierra Six!"

"Five seconds to go."

Vann thought, *Too late.* The detonations would roil the sea between *Portland* and the *Akula*. In a few seconds there would be no way on earth that *Akula* would hear anything but the sounds of a dying Typhoon. "Helm, all ahead flank. Do not cavitate. Make your depth eight hundred feet. Move the boat!"

The first torpedo swam up from the black depths, heading for an area of dim green light overhead. Somewhere in the middle of the open lead was the object it had been commanded to destroy, one that obliged the torpedo by advertising its precise location with a muffled underwater clang. The ADCAP's seeker head pulsed with sonar energy, and it soon detected a tiny dot floating on the surface slightly to port. No matter that a dot was not a submarine. It adjusted its steering fins accordingly as it hurtled up to the light. The dot became a tiny disk, the disk swelled. The torpedo shot up like a rocket on a tail of streaming bubbles, the second weapon following right behind. Up, vertical, the weapons' sonar pinged faster, faster. The torpedo's nose brushed against something metallic. It shoved the weapon off track, but a full throw of its rudder slewed it back. It struck the Beast Buoy eight inches off of dead center and 650 pounds of high explosive scalded the green water a brilliant white.

Schramm's display lit up in stabbing flashes and curtains of light. "Conn, Sonar, two explosions in the water bearing two six five!"

A cheer went up in Control, but Vann didn't join in. Instead he listened to the rumble of the distant thunder as it came straight through the hull. Echoing, fading, then gone. The eerie moans and pops of a sinking, collapsing submarine would be next. *Finally,* he thought. *It's done.* "Sonar, Conn. Stand by to record him going down. Mister Whalley?"

"Sir?" said the navigator.

"What kind of a bottom is he headed for?"

Whalley put his finger on the chart and looked up. "He's over an eighteen-hundred-foot ledge, skipper. If he misses it, the bottom of Saint Anna's Trough is about three thousand feet deep."

They build those bastards tough. He might not crush before he hits bottom. Vann thought about her captain, her crew. They'd been on the surface long enough to put people over the side. Did the Russians equip their boats with rafts? Given the sea temperature, anyone in the water was already dead. They might be the lucky ones, for anyone still alive inside her hull was going on a long, dark ride down.

Baikal

The Typhoon was much closer to the double explosions, and they were both sharper and louder. "Left full rudder!" Markov ordered. "Igor! Maximum turns on one engine! What's our speed?"

"Eleven knots," said Gasparyan.

"Igor! Is there any more speed available?"

"Sure. Use both engines," growled Grachev as he raised more steam from the one reactor Markov wanted on-line. He eyed the gauges measuring neutron fluxes inside the reactors. One needle was in the blue "cold" zone. A radiation storm was raging in the other power plant, its needle into the yellow caution band with the red limit line close by.

As *Baikal* swung her bow north, once more headed for the ice, the intercom by Markov's chair buzzed, and the attention light flashed. He snatched the *kashtan* down. "Captain."

"Sir? Radio message coming through over the trailing wire."

They heard the Beast! If they were luckier, the message would say that the Navy was sending ships north to find out what was going on and to escort *Baikal* back to Kola. "Go ahead. Read it."

"Proceed Anadyr Gulf grid square twenty-two northwest for escort."

Markov waited for clarification, and when none came he said, "That's the whole message?"

"Yes. Everything."

They had to understand that a Beast broadcast meant his ship was too damaged to communicate over normal channels. Markov let the *kashtan* dangle from its coiled wire. Was it stubbornness or stupidity, or did Moscow prefer them to sink? Wearily he asked, "Where is the American submarine?"

"South, Captain," said Belikov. "He's running due south."

USS *Portland*

Portland shot out from beneath the overhanging ice and into clearer waters.

"All stop," said Vann.

"All stop, aye," said the helm.

COB Browne sat at the dive board right behind the helm. He had his handheld radio out and was speaking softly into his mouth microphone.

"Sonar, Conn," said Vann. "We're going to drift to give you a chance to listen to Sierra Five go down. I want his sinking marked as accurately as possible. Someone may want to go down and take a look at him someday. Can you hear him flooding?"

"No, sir. We're still moving too fast to hear much of anything except the *Akula*."

"Where is she?"

"Still off to the east. I show blade count now for eighteen knots but there's something screwy. Her screw's spinning up real fast but she's not making enough speed."

"Can she be farther away than you thought?"

"Not likely, skipper. That last active ping nailed her data pretty good."

Ten knots, thought Vann. *Why so slow?* With a couple of live torpedoes in the neighborhood, that Russian attack boat should be running flat out at better than thirty knots. Just the same, forcing the Russian *Akula* to withdraw was icing on the cake.

"Speed now twelve knots."

At twelve knots she should be able to hear a Typhoon die. Perhaps it was the ice. Perhaps a thermal layer was refracting, distorting the sound. But unless that Typhoon had put a chain gang out on the ice sheet and ordered them to make noise, Vann was certain he'd just carried out his orders. He turned the intercom selector. "Radio shack, Conn. Send someone up here on the double. We've got an after-action report to transmit to Norfolk at the next satellite broadcast window."

"Aye aye, skipper," said Lieutenant Bledsoe. "Engler's on the way."

Vann leaned back on the small seat set into the forward edge of the periscope stand. He listened to the ticking of the old deck clock and let out his breath slowly. "Well, COB. What do you say?"

"Something blew up out there," said Browne. *I wish I knew what.*

"What you heard was the sound of *mission accomplished.*" Vann felt tons of dead weight rise from his shoulders, his soul. *Forty thousand tons,* he thought. *And four years.* He no longer had to wonder. He no longer had to wear *Baton Rouge* around his neck like a stone. It left him buoyant. He could even admit that Steadman hadn't been entirely wrong about the orders Norfolk had sent. They *did* hand him a turkey of a mission along with a stout rope to hang from if he'd failed.

But Vann hadn't failed. He'd been resolute when challenged, dogged in the face of doubt. The message he would send back to Norfolk would heark back to a World War II tradition, when a boat would return from a war patrol flying an upside-down broom from her periscope shears. It meant she'd put all her torpedoes into enemy hulls; a "clean sweep."

True, *Portland* had fired only four ADCAPs, but those four torpedoes had swept away a great deal more than just a Typhoon. Vann had spent years atoning for the mistakes of others. Now he would no longer have to wonder what people were saying, or worse, whispering.

Engler hurried up from the radio room. "Message to send, Captain?"

Vann ripped a small sheet of paper from a pad and jotted down the simple, sweet message:

Returning to Norfolk with a broom lashed to our sail.
Vann sends

He handed the note to the young radioman and noticed the bandage on his hand. "What's with the hand?"

"I burned myself on some hot coffee, Captain," he said sheepishly.

"Have Chief Cooper look at it." Cooper was the boat's independent duty corpsman, her doctor.

"Aye aye." Engler walked by the dive board and nearly made it. But Browne stopped him with an arm across his path.

"Let's have a little talk, Engler."

"What about, COB?"

"I will see you in the Goat Locker," Browne said too softly for Vann to hear. "You'll find out."

Vann picked up the microphone for the 1MC. "This is the captain. Secure from General Quarters." His voice rang out through the boat. "To all of you. Well done." He turned to the navigation plot. "Mister Whalley? I'll be resting in my stateroom. You have the conn. Keep a weather eye out for that *Akula* and try not to hit anything."

"Okay, Captain," said Whalley. He stepped away from his charts and walked up to the helm.

Whalley didn't deserve it but Vann was feeling magnanimous just now. And why not? There was no cleaner sweep than one that erases a man's doubts, or his past.

CHAPTER SEVENTEEN

THE GOAT LOCKER

USS *Portland*

Senior Chief Browne sat alone at the small table in the senior chiefs' private lair. There was a quick, sharp rap at the door. He slipped a small piece of paper into his breast pocket, then placed his low-power radio on the table. He wrapped a rubber band around it to hold the transmit key down and shouted, "Well? You waiting for an invitation?"

It was Engler.

"Shut the door. What we're going to talk about here is not for general distribution."

The radioman slouched in with a studiously blank expression on his face. "What's up, COB?"

"You are. Tell me something, Engler. Who am I?"

"What's that supposed to mean?"

"It's a simple question. Answer it."

"You're the COB. Chief of the boat."

"Okay. That's good. Now *what* am I?"

Engler cocked his head. "What's the game?"

"Games are over. School of the boat is now in session." Browne stood up slowly. At five-foot-eight he was not a big man, but Browne seemed to keep unfolding like an accordion, taller, taller, more imposing, until his presence filled the small space. "I am the senior chief of this boat. I am God's designated hitter here on earth. I make things happen. I can change your world, Engler. For better or for worse. Still with me?"

"I hear you."

"Keep listening. This whole *boat* used to be filled with clowns like you, and I mean from the top down. You got an advanced degree in attitude but you still haven't learned the basics. That's why trouble follows you around. On liberty, on the boat and on the beach. You don't have *Navy* problems. You got *life* problems."

"What do you know about it?"

"Plenty." Browne stepped around from behind the table. He took out the sheet of flimsy paper from his pocket and walked over to the muscular radioman until he stood no more than a foot away. "Go on. Read it."

Engler stiffened. His instincts were spring-loaded to *fight*.

"Son, I know what you're thinking. It won't be worth it. You've got enough to figure out as it is." Browne gave the folded Familygram to the radioman. "Here."

Linda cleared out storage, apt. Landlord says rent by Monday or he'll evict. . . . Mother

Engler looked as though he'd been stung. "That *bitch*!"

"Seems like you got another problem. They're starting to add up. Now I can help you out or cut you loose. It's your move."

Engler crumpled up the Familygram and threw it at Browne's feet. "I'll hunt her down and *kill* her. I don't need your help."

"That's where you're wrong. You can stay wrong or get right. Getting right means telling me what I want to know."

"I thought you knew everything," Engler sneered.

"I will eventually. You can speed up the process. Right now you can start with what happened in the fan room."

"I'm not an electrician. I ain't into fans."

He nodded at Engler's bandaged hand. "Looks like they been into *you*."

"I spilled hot coffee on my hand. Ask Cookie. He'll tell you."

"I already did and if you think he's going to keep helping your sorry ass you're dead wrong. Four hundred fifty volts grounded out for no good reason, Engler. It made the lights on the whole boat flicker and left scorch marks on the sheet metal. Must have been a pretty good spark. How'd you do it?"

Engler shrugged. "I don't have to tell you squat. I know the regs."

"You know some of them but I know them *all*. The ones that get written and the ones that don't. You familiar with Article Ninety?"

"I ain't a sea lawyer."

"It says that any person who strikes a superior commissioned officer shall, in time of war, be punished by death. If the offense is committed at any other time, by such punishment as a court martial may direct."

"Someone get hit?"

"Lieutenant Scavullo, and she says you did it. Add a charge of attempted rape—"

"I wouldn't give that dyke a poke if she begged for it."

"So what's your side of the story? I'm waiting."

"I spilled coffee on my hand. That's my fucking story. Anyway, what was she doing in the fan room? That's posted off limits."

That was true. "Why don't you tell me?"

"Fucking bitch has been nothing but trouble. She probably shorted something out in there and now she wants to blame me. Fuck her. No way."

Now we're getting someplace. "Okay. Maybe she did cause that ground. I'm ready to hear the rest."

"There ain't no rest. That's all I got to say. You want to know what she was up to, ask her, not me."

"I did. *She* says you were in there, and *she* says you assaulted her. That means *you* are headed for a court martial. With your record, I *guarantee* you will be taken off the boat and dropped into a brig."

"I've been in brigs before."

"This won't be the same as having the Shore Patrol kick your ass out of a van after a fight. See, she's the first woman on the boats. She's got people back in Washington watching us with a magnifying glass. Remember Tailhook? If she sneezes the whole submarine force comes down with the flu. That's *my* family I'm talking about."

"I ain't worried."

"You will be. See, those brigs, they're run by senior chiefs. I know all their names, their birthdays, and whether their sisters kiss with their eyes open or shut. You get into some trouble on the beach and I think you're worth helping, you *will* get treated right. You piss me off and you'll get put in with the biggest, baddest motherfucker they got. He gonna take one look at you and decide your name is *Mary*."

"I won't be there forever and then I'll know who to come see."

"I wouldn't be so sure, Engler. I can get you shifted from Navy brig to Navy brig so fast your paperwork won't *never* catch up. So as you ponder your immediate future, you might want to ponder this: you're one lie away from spending the rest of your Navy career as a human condom."

Engler laughed. "Kiss my ass, COB. You can't touch me. Ask Bledsoe. He'll set you straight."

Bledsoe? "No officer is going to back you up."

"Just talk to Bledsoe. That's all I'm saying." Engler turned to leave but

Browne grabbed him hard by the shoulder and spun him back against the bulkhead.

"I ain't done talking, Engler. And you ain't done listening."

Engler's good hand was pinned between his body and the door. Browne had his bandaged hand in a grip that was hard enough to burst the burn blisters. His bandage darkened, his face was contorted in pain and rage.

"From day number one you have been a sniveling, two-faced waste of a good submariner's air," said Browne calmly, evenly. "You are a lying, mealy-mouthed zit-picking lower-than-whaleshit *puke*." Browne stared straight into Engler's eyes. "I don't understand. They say ignorance is bliss. So why ain't you looking blissful?"

"I'm warning you."

"My my," said Browne, "I can see how you ran your wife off. But I ain't your wife and you got *one* chance to tell me the truth, the whole truth and nothing but the truth so *help* you God. I want to know what the *fuck* you were doing in the fan room and who told you to do it. Was it Bledsoe?" Browne let go of Engler's burned hand. "It's time to come to Jesus on this, Engler. If you were ordered to do it, then you've got a solid-gold way out."

Engler twisted away and grabbed the doorknob.

"I'm not done with you, Engler."

"Piss off." The radioman slammed the door in Browne's face.

Jesus, thought Browne. An officer and an enlisted man conspiring against another officer. This was something foul, something dirty, and it would only get dirtier. He walked back to the table and plugged his earpiece back into the small radio. "You heard him?" he said into his mouth microphone.

"I heard him," said Steadman. He was alone in the wardroom with a radio on the table. "What about the cook?"

"He went along with the coffee story."

"They're lying, COB."

"I think so, too. The question is what we can do about it."

"If Bledsoe's involved, we've got bigger problems than Engler," said Steadman. "Is the captain still in his stateroom?"

"Aye aye. Whalley's got the conn. Skipper's resting. He left orders not to be disturbed. Why?"

"I'm going to go disturb him."

Markov stepped through the watertight hatch into Main Engineering and found Grachev hunched over the reactor consoles, his hands manipulating pump and pressure controls like a pianist on a keyboard. He'd changed into a dry set of light blue overalls, but the red-and-white armband denoting his position as engineering officer of the watch was still sopping wet. Demyan sat at a battered wooden desk in the middle of the compartment, recording temperatures and Pressures as Grachev called them out.

"Primary and secondary system pressure is down point six."

Demyan consulted a table. "Coolant temperature should be three hundred fifty degrees Celsius."

Grachev tapped a small, circular gauge. "Three fifty-eight. It's close enough. Congratulations," said Grachev without looking up, "you're a lucky man, Captain. You didn't break anything."

Markov noticed that the mail-order-bride photos had all vanished. "Go bring us some tea, Lieutenant," said Markov. He waited for Demyan to leave, then slipped into a blue-padded chair beside his chief engineer. "I thought we'd lost you back there."

"Did you come for tea or talk?"

"Talk." Markov handed him the slip of paper with Popov's message. *Proceed Anadyr Gulf Grid Square 22 NW for escort.* "What do you make of it?"

"Popov gets paid if we make it to Shanghai, so of course he wants us to go. Otherwise, if we're damaged enough to use a Beast Buoy, he'd just as soon we die quietly."

"So where does that leave us?"

"Safe so long as the Americans think we're already dead." Grachev smiled. "You made them think we were an *Akula* by cutting our power in half. It wasn't smart, Captain. You could have split the reactor with thermal shock. But it was clever."

"Not enough. We drove them south." Markov glanced at the empty notice board. "Where did your girls go?"

Grachev pointed to the trash can. "If we make it out of this with our skins, they won't be handing out any money."

We'll be lucky to stay out of prison, thought Markov.

Grachev said, "They don't want us in Kola, and we can't stay here forever. It leaves us with only one direction."

"North. Then the Pacific. If we're lucky, we might even make Petro-pavlovsk. But there are a few little problems to solve first," said Markov. "There's Bering Strait. No one has ever tried to sail a Typhoon through it before."

"If it can be done, you can do it."

"And the rockets?"

"You'll figure something out. You're the captain. If Fedorenko gives you any trouble we can stuff him into a silo and open the hatch. The rocket will get wet but so will he. Come to think of it, that solves two problems at once."

Markov was about to laugh, to dismiss the suggestion for the joke that Grachev intended, but then he grew serious. "We *could* flood the silos. The rockets and their warhead would be ruined."

"Flood all twenty silos and you have two thousand extra tons of weight on board. We'll go straight to the bottom. Are you willing to sink the ship to kill those rockets?"

"No."

"Then unless you can figure a way to get the Americans to kill the rockets but not us, we're stuck delivering the ship."

Demyan arrived bearing a silver tray with two cups, a thermos of strong black tea and some sweet crackers.

"You said something interesting," said Markov.

Grachev eyed Markov warily. "What?"

Markov looked up suddenly. "How badly do you think the Americans want to keep *Baikal* out of Chinese hands?"

"You know the answer."

"I do," said Markov. "But I wonder. Do they?"

USS *Portland*

Commander Vann switched the fluorescent lights off and his small reading lamp on. It cast a warm, intimate glow across the paperback book on his lap: *Delilah,* a naval yarn set in Asiatic waters in the years leading up to the First World War.

Though *Delilah* was an old, four-stack destroyer burning dirty coal, though her fires were kept lit by half-naked stokers working amid the flames, it was hard for Vann not to feel a connection to the world it portrayed. And nostalgia. Her captain was truly a king, not just enforcing American policies but crafting them. He wasn't a manager. He was a kind of demigod answerable only for his failures.

As Vann read, the walls of his cabin, the cheap-looking imitation wood, the harsh chrome trim, receded. Only the bright status monitor served to remind him of where he was: in a ship three hundred feet from the world of light and air, moving silently at sixteen knots, headed slightly west of due south.

There was a knock at his stateroom door. "What the devil?" He slapped the book shut and swung his legs onto the deck. "Come!"

Steadman opened the door.

"I'm surprised," said Vann. He didn't get up from his bed, nor did he offer Steadman the only chair. "I thought you'd have too much pride to come here." Vann nodded at *Delilah*. "Ever read the book?"

"No, sir." Steadman shut the door.

"There's a character who shows up for duty with a seabag full of books. He's smart as hell about history, philosophy, literature. But what's he going to wear when his dungarees get dirty? See, he hadn't thought it through. He's got a first-rate education and third-rate common sense."

"Captain, I didn't come here to talk about dungarees."

"No, I expect not. I'm sorry, Willy, but after what happened today I have no choice but to withdraw my recommendation for you to go to command school. When we were given a dirty job, you wanted to chew the orders over and hope they'd taste different. It's a sign of a man who's unsure of himself, not of a commander. Strike two."

"I didn't come to talk about command school either. There's been an assault on board. A serious one."

The book went down. "Assault?"

"Lieutenant Scavullo was attacked in the fan room."

"Jesus. What was she doing in there?"

Steadman was taken aback. Vann's question wasn't wrong, but it wasn't the first thing that should have come to his mind. "She found a microphone wire next to where the treadmill was set up. It went up to the fan room. She was tracing it when she was attacked."

"Finding that bug was supposed to be COB's job."

"Scavullo got to it first."

"And she says someone assaulted her?"

"Someone knocked her to the deck with a piece of pipe. There was a struggle and the pipe must have touched a terminal because one of the fans grounded. And I think there could be more to it."

"Or less. She was snooping around a space that was posted off limits, where she had no reason to be, while a Russian attack boat was hunting for us. A time when *any* excess radiated noise might have killed us all. Hell. If I'd caught her in there I would have dragged her out by the scruff of her neck. Who is she saying did it?"

"Radioman Engler."

"Engler," Vann said as though to himself. "Any witnesses?"

"No. But I saw her right afterwards. I'm convinced something happened."

"What's Engler's story?"

"He claims he was elsewhere."

"Anyone back him up?"

"A cook, but I think he and Engler are coordinating their stories. Sir, I saw the look on her face. I think Engler was in the fan room with her. I think he tried to rape her and she fought him off."

"Whoa. Is she crying *rape* now?"

"No."

"Jesus, XO. Nobody saw anything. Nobody's confessed to anything except Scavullo, who admitted she was someplace she wasn't supposed to be. Engler's a bad apple but he says he was someplace else and he's got a witness. You know she has it in for us. Don't you think she's got a motive for making all this up?"

"Someone assaulted her."

"Someone *may* have assaulted her. Or not. In the absence of any evidence, why would you assume her story's true? Don't you have enough on your shoulders right now without helping her smear mud on the whole submarine force?"

"I saw her face. I know Engler. And if half of what I think happened really did, then this is a problem that can't wait for Norfolk."

"What are you recommending?"

"An informal hearing. Take written statements and put together a case for your action at mast."

"Engler has the right to refuse to cooperate, you know."

"Then he can face a court martial back home. I don't think he'll risk it. They're more likely to squeeze out the truth."

"The truth is, she's been nothing but trouble from the beginning. Maybe Engler got frisky and maybe Scavullo cooked it all up to explain away her

failures. 'Poor little me. How could I do my job when everyone was harass-
ing me?' Have you considered that possibility?"

"I haven't dismissed any possibilities."

"Well, don't ignore what's right under your nose. We're not going on any
witch hunts with a war about to break out in the Pacific. Take testimony as
you see fit and put it all together. I'll take a look and decide what needs to be
done. But don't dawdle, XO. We've spent too much time on that girl as it
is." The intercom buzzed. Vann snatched the phone off the bulkhead. "Yes?"

"Captain?" It was Bledsoe. "Message traffic coming in from Norfolk."

"Did you send up my contact report?"

"Aye aye, skipper. Message sent and confirmed."

"All right, Mister Bledsoe. I'll be right there." He hung the phone up.
"Let me be frank. Assigning Scavullo to *Portland* was a mistake that will not
be repeated. First that business down in Kola. Now she's sticking her nose
into places she's not permitted to go. She's got your ear. I hope to hell that's
all she's got."

"I have no personal reasons to pursue this matter, Captain."

"Well, like I said, I hope not. But either way when we get back she'll be
leaving submarines forever. You don't have to."

"No?"

Vann took a long, deep breath and let it out. "I know what happens when
people stop believing in you. After *Baton Rouge,* I fought back because I
knew I was right. In the end, I earned myself another shot. You can, too. I
can recommend that you be sent out under a different captain. You might
hit it off better with someone else. But not if you insist on taking Scavullo's
side. You'll become radioactive. Way too hot to handle." Vann stood, folded
up his bunk, let the table drop down in its place. "You've got to choose,
Willy. Your career or Scavullo. Think it over."

"Why don't we let the facts speak for themselves?"

"If you find any."

Bledsoe was hunched over the encryption console. The printer was chattering, stopping, chattering, as the message was decoded. "Be just another second, Captain."

"Are you recording anything off the commercial satellite?"

"Got a CNN update on China, skipper," said Bledsoe.

"What would we do without CNN?"

Bledsoe ripped a sheet of paper from the printer and handed the decoded message to Vann.

Z00043Z6AUG2002
NLOB*NLOB*NLOB
FM: COMSUBLANT
TO: CO USS PORTLAND
INFO: COMSUBPAC, CINCPACFLT
SUBJ: SPECIAL OPERATIONS
SECRET

1: PROCEED BEST SPEED CHUKCHI SEA
2: ESTABLISH BARRIER PATROL WRANGEL ISLAND WEST PT
   BARROW EAST
3: IDENTIFY AND REPORT ALL RUSSIAN SSN/SSBN TRAFFIC
   BOUND FOR BERING STRAIT FOR TACTICAL HANDOFF TO
   COMSUBPAC
4: ROE OPTION BRAVO IS AUTHORIZED AGAINST ANY, RPT,
   ANY PLAAN UNITS TRANSITING BERING STRAIT
5: UNODIR NO ACTION AGAINST RUSSIAN UNITS IS
   AUTHORIZED
6: ALL PREVIOUS ADVISORIES RE PRC/RUSSIAN NAVAL
   ACTIVITY ARE STILL IN EFFECT
7: HOSTILITIES WITH PLAAN FORCES ARE CONSIDERED
   POSSIBLE BUT NOT CERTAIN AND COULD BEGIN
   WITHOUT, RPT, WITHOUT FURTHER WARNINGS
8: TAKE ALL MEASURES CONSISTENT WITH THE SAFETY OF
   YOUR COMMAND
9: WELL DONE TO PORTLAND AND VANN FOR SHOWING
   LOST TYPHOON THE WAY HOME. SOURCE INTEL
   SUGGESTS SHANGHAI AS HER FINAL DESTINATION. HERE'S
   HOPING THEY ALL WISE UP AND HEAD FOR THE BARN . . .
   GRAYBAR SENDS

Rules of Engagement Option Bravo stink, thought Vann as he folded the paper. Option Bravo meant he was supposed to give the Chinese the first shot. *Not a chance.* Vann was not going to risk *Portland* while he waited for an engraved invitation written on a torpedo's nose.

Vann folded the slip of paper, reached over to the 1MC intercom and picked up the handset. A tone sounded throughout *Portland.* In every compartment, in the galley, in the engineering spaces, in the head and in the sleeping berths, *Portland*'s sailors stopped what they were doing and gazed up at the nearest speaker.

"This is the captain," said Vann. "I know most of you were looking forward to liberty in Norfolk next week, but COMSUBLANT has other plans for us. He's sending us across the top of the world to keep Russian forces out of the Pacific and Chinese boats out of the Atlantic. We've already taken on the best that Russia has, and you all know the results. As for China, the United States Navy has drawn a line across the Bering Strait and God help anyone who tries to cross it. Now I want to read something COMSUBLANT just sent." Vann unfolded the paper. "To USS *Portland* and Commander James Vann for actions taken against Typhoon *Baikal*: *well done.* Vice Admiral John Graybar, Commander, Submarine Force, United States Atlantic Fleet."

Bledsoe raised an eyebrow. That wasn't what the message said.

Vann picked up the handset again and punched in the code to Control. "Conn? This is the captain. Dive the boat to eight hundred feet and head us for the Chukchi Sea. All ahead full."

By the time Vann made his way down to the middeck wardroom, the smell of fresh popcorn was spilling out into the passage from the galley. A big bowl was brought in from the mess. Steadman, Keefe and every other officer not on duty waited for the show to start. The crowd parted for Vann, but Steadman stopped him just outside the door.

"What is it now, Mister Steadman?"

"I heard COMSUBLANT's *well done.* I was wrong about those orders. You were right." He offered Vann his hand.

Vann took it and quickly let go. "Welcome back to the team." He stepped into the wardroom and said, "Roll it."

The screen flickered, and the network's Beijing bureau chief appeared. The Great Hall of the People was behind the reporter, bathed in white-hot sun. No sound came from the speakers. Beneath her was the caption, *Live from Beijing.*

"What happened to the sound?" someone asked.

It swelled, distorted and became too loud, then clear. ". . . with the noon deadline approaching there have been no signs of a settlement. They're taking the murder of Wang Daohan very seriously here. We've been told that an official note was passed to the American embassy this morning containing some very specific language. It referred to Beijing's right to combat terrorism in the same way that the United States did after the nine-eleven attacks. It ended with a warning that any actions taken by foreigners on Chinese territory will be considered an act of war."

The image on the screen flipped, then went dark as the snippet of tape copied from the satellite came to an end.

"Damn!" someone groused.

The officers all turned to Vann.

"Well, gents, it looks like the Chinese are determined to do something stupid. It's a good thing they won't have a Typhoon to point at our heads when they do." Vann turned to Steadman. "What's your view on the matter, XO?"

Steadman felt the gaze of his fellow officers fall on him and cling like a bead of sweat. He'd been wrong about Norfolk. Maybe he'd been wrong about killing that Typhoon, too, though it sure didn't feel like it. Not even now. "I'd have to agree, Captain."

Vann winked, a secret bargain with Steadman made. Made, and met.

CHAPTER EIGHTEEN

THE MAST

7 AUGUST

USS *Portland*

Steadman held the screening hearing in the wardroom, taking statements from everyone who'd seen Scavullo or Engler in the time leading up to, and after, the incident in the fan room. He had Scavullo now. They were seated at the same long table where he'd seen her right after the attack. Engler would be last.

"That's everything you want to say?" he asked her.

"Yes, sir. That's everything," she said.

He'd assembled Engler's trail from the moment Lieutenant Bledsoe had let the radioman leave his watch early to when Steadman had found him in the galley. It was a trail with a ten-minute gap. Engler had either spent them scalding himself with coffee or cornering Scavullo in the fan room. Which?

"You need to know how this screening process works," he said. "I'll assemble the facts and make my recommendations to Commander Vann. I can dismiss the matter but I can't impose punishment."

"I understand that."

"The stronger you can make your case, the easier it will be for Vann to take action."

"You mean the harder it will be for him not to."

Steadman didn't answer that, but it was true. "Engler could spend the rest of the run handcuffed to a torpedo rack if you'd only tell me what really happened in there."

"You have my statement."

Steadman had pushed her, but Scavullo would come to a point in relating what had happened in the fan room, then stop. "You understand the captain's word will be final?"

"I also understand what would happen if I cried rape. It's the excuse they're looking for to keep us out of submarines forever. I won't give it to them, sir. Besides," she said, "I wasn't raped and I refuse to speculate about what radioman Engler had in mind." She paused. "If anything."

"I could order you to see Chief Cooper for a physical exam."

"I don't know who that would embarrass more."

Steadman closed the manila folder. "Okay. Engler assaulted you with a pipe in the fan room. He grounded it out on a fan terminal and you fought him off."

"That's what happened."

Just not everything. "You can stay in my stateroom until the captain decides how to handle Engler. I'll try to minimize any contact you might have with him, but . . ."

"I know. It's a submarine. I just want the rules to work the way they're supposed to. You think there's a chance?"

"We're going to find out. Dismissed."

Ten minutes later there was a knock at the door.

"Come!"

It was Engler.

"Be seated," said Steadman as evenly as he could. Innocent until proven guilty was not part of a Captain's Mast. It all came down to what you believed, or whom, and Steadman had already made up his mind.

Engler swaggered in and sprawled in the chair.

"Want some coffee?" asked Steadman.

"Is it the same stuff the guys drink in the mess?"

"Exactly."

"Nah. I'll skip it."

Steadman went over to the urn and refilled his mug. "You understand why you're here?"

"I know what she's saying. Doesn't make it true."

"The captain and I will decide what's true. Right now you are suspected of showing disrespect toward a superior officer, assaulting an officer and insubordinate conduct toward a petty officer. Those are violations of Articles Eighty-nine, Ninety and Nintey-one of the Uniform Code of Military Conduct. If you make any misleading statements to me now, that's a further violation of Article One-oh-seven. These are all serious charges. You have the right to remain silent and to demand a full court martial. Anything you elect to say can be used against you. You understand all that?"

"Sure."

Steadman returned to the table and took a sip, letting the weight of those words have an effect on Engler. "When I'm finished, I'll make a recommendation to Commander Vann, and he'll decide what to do with you. It could be Captain's Mast or a summary court martial."

"So what's this? A half mast?"

Steadman leaned over the table and stared at the radioman until the smile went away. "We're one flash message away from a state of war with China. Committing the offenses you're charged with during a war carries a sentence of death."

"I didn't assault nobody, sir. You have the waivers?"

"I forgot. You've done this before."

"Hell, sir. I been before so many masts I got it memorized. I'da been an admiral by now if they just quit busting me back to E-3."

"There are worse things to be than an E-3, Engler." Steadman pushed two sheets across the table. "By signing these waivers you're handing the commanding officer of this boat the authority to decide how to proceed on the charges you're facing. You still want to proceed?"

"I ain't worried about it."

"Sign." Steadman pushed over a pen.

Engler scrawled his name at the bottom of each sheet, then shoved them back. "Everybody knows I didn't do it."

"Not everyone." *But nearly.* Steadman opened a file. "I've taken statements from the crew. People who knew where you were or thought they did." He flipped through several sheets, then looked at Engler. "Now I can see how a messmate in the galley could know where you were. I could even imagine that someone down in the machinery room could have spotted you. But I've got statements here from people in the maneuvering room, the torpedo room. Even some A-Gangers working aft. They all seemed to know your whereabouts. How do you explain it?"

"It's like COB, only backwards. He knows where everyone is? Everyone knows where I am. Hey, can I change my mind about the coffee, sir? It ain't every rag hat gets the XO to pour his coffee."

"Help yourself."

You could see things rattle around behind Engler's eyes, behind his expression. "That's okay. I don't need it that bad."

"Then let's start with what happened from the time Lieutenant Bledsoe excused you from standing the rest of your watch."

"I left the radio shack and went down to—"

"How? Which ladder did you use?"

Engler paused, weighing his answer, then said, "The ladder by the three-inch launcher. You know, aft of Control."

"Scavullo came up that same ladder. Did you see her?"

"Nope."

"You went straight from the radio shack to the galley?"

"I went down to my rack first."

"What for?"

"I was tryin' to decide whether to rack out or grab a bite to eat. Everybody saw me. You can't disappear in Rat Alley, sir."

And it's filled with all your pals. Rat Alley was the name of the enlisted berthing area on the bottom deck, just forward of the auxiliary machine room. In a city, it would be a neighborhood you'd avoid after dark. "Where did you go then?"

"Straight to the mess. Cookie had some fresh coffee and rolls." He held up his hand. "You know what happened then."

He told you Scavullo found your wire. "How would you characterize your working relationship with Lieutenant Scavullo?"

"How would I do what?"

"What's it been like working with her?"

A shrug. "Okay."

"No problems?"

"Well, she uses this soap. It's like perfume or something. Closed up in the radio shack, all those consoles radiating like crazy, it gets pretty heavy. LT told her to quit using it."

"You mean Bledsoe?"

"Yeah. Lieutenant Bledsoe."

"Did she?"

"No, sir. She said it smelled better than he did."

"Has the corpsman taken a look at your burn?"

"I don't need to bother Chief Cooper."

"He should probably look at it. For the record."

"Nothin' to see."

"Tell you what. Show the hand to me."

"Show you what?"

"The burn. Unwrap the bandage, Engler," said Steadman. "I want to see it for myself."

Engler didn't want to comply with Steadman's request, but it would become an order if he didn't and then what? He started unwrapping the bandage, though slowly enough to get the message across that he was only doing it because he had to.

The bandage went around Engler's right hand from wrist to knuckles. When he was finished, Engler held up his hand like a witness taking an oath on the stand.

Steadman examined it. The welts were on the inside palm, stretching across the pads at the base of his fingers in a straight, red line. The thumb was unmarked.

"Nasty-looking," said Steadman. "How did you manage to splash hot coffee in such a straight line?"

The hand came down. "Beats me."

He waited for Engler to say more, and when he didn't he asked, "What happened next?"

"I hollered. Cookie came running. Everybody in the mess heard me yell. You can ask them. They'll tell you."

"Did the cook tell you he'd just seen Lieutenant Scavullo?"

"No, sir."

"He didn't mention she was snooping around the cold box?"

"No shit? What was she doing in there anyway? Tryin' to cool off or something? Maybe it's a female thing, you know, hot flashes."

"I don't think so."

"Anyway, I got the hand washed off and wrapped and that's when you showed up looking for me. Then we went to general quarters and, well, that's all I know until I hear from COB she's yelling I raped her or some crazy-ass thing like that."

"She's not making that claim." Steadman pulled a wire out from under the table. "Know anything about this?"

"It looks like a wire to me, sir."

"COB found it in the cold box. It ran up to the fan room, and from there into an air duct feeding the radio room. How do you think it got there?"

Engler shrugged, not the least bit curious. "Beats me."

Steadman put it down, reached under and picked up a length of pipe about fourteen inches long. The surface was covered with fine, powdery rust.

"COB found this in an emergency equipment locker." He held it carefully by one end, then rolled it across the table. "Pick it up."

"Why?"

"Because if you don't I'll order you to. If you still don't that's refusing to obey a lawful command. I won't need to hold a hearing to nail that one on you. It's your choice."

Engler picked it up. "So what?" He was about to let go but Steadman reached over and closed his hand around the pipe, then let go.

"Now open your hand."

Engler dropped the pipe as though it were red hot. It left a powdery orange line across the pads of his fingers: a mirror image to the burn blisters on his right.

Steadman said, "Perfect fit, Cinderella."

Engler glared up defiantly. "That don't prove nothing."

Steadman walked back to his side of the table and stood. "Is there something more you'd like to say for the record?"

"Yeah," said Engler. "I heard Scavullo's been hangin' out in your stateroom. Is that gonna be in the records, too?"

"Get out, Engler."

"Well, you've been very thorough, Mister Steadman." Vann closed the file and tossed it to his bunk. They were alone in the captain's stateroom. "I think we can apply Articles Eighty-nine and One-oh-seven. But you haven't made the case for assault."

"Engler's guilty as hell. I think you should bring him up before a summary court martial today. The evidence—"

"Hold off. Engler mouthed off to you and to COB and he'll lose two weeks' pay for it. The business about having her in your stateroom was out of line, though you left yourself open to it. Engler's whereabouts have been vouched for. She's the only one who says different. The pipe business? Nobody saw him with it." Vann paused. "We'll bust him back two grades. What more can I do?"

"You're making a mistake, Captain."

"We're through, Mister Steadman," said Vann.

CHAPTER NINETEEN

THE ICE PICK

United States Embassy
Beijing

In the world of diplomacy, receiving an unscheduled summons is never good news. And so it was with real foreboding that the U.S. Defense Attaché to China, a retired admiral named Richard Mauldin, and Captain Bradley Kaplan, his naval affairs deputy, left the embassy to find out how bad the news was going to be.

Mauldin and Kaplan hurried out of the three-story embassy building, heading for a black Chevrolet Suburban idling by the main gate. It was 12:20 Beijing time, and they were bound for the twenty-story pile of Stalinist masonry that was home to the Chinese Ministry of Foreign Affairs.

The Suburban pulled away from the gate and out onto the crowded street, Towering over the swarming cars, the darting taxis, the flocks of Flying Pigeon bicycles. Though Beijing drivers were notoriously aggressive, they parted for the big American machine.

"Take a look," said Captain Kaplan. He pointed behind them. A blue police car was pacing them, neither drawing close nor falling behind.

"Are they chasing us or escorting us?"

"Probably both," said Kaplan. He'd been in China long enough to know how things worked. Beneath the facade of chaos, nothing happened without a reason, though it usually took a great deal of effort and interpretation to figure out what that reason might be.

The Suburban pulled up to the curb at the Chinese Foreign Ministry. The police car parked nearby. The Americans were met in the lobby by a deputy from the Department of North American Affairs, who escorted them up to see Lu Shumin, its director.

They found Lu at work in his office, a space furnished so aggressively in Danish modern it might have been airlifted whole from Copenhagen. There were two envelopes on his polished desk.

The deputy ushered the two Americans in and shut the door behind them.

Mauldin was fluent in Mandarin, but he could look at Lu's face and know that something unpleasant was in the offing.

"I have two messages for the American ambassador, the American president and the American people," Lu began. "The first is from the president. The second is from Admiral Shi Yunsheng, commander of the Ninth Fleet, People's Liberation Navy."

"Will we need the services of a translator?" asked Mauldin.

"No, Admiral, you will not," said Lu. "Both messages are quite short and written in terms that you will understand." Lu picked up the first envelope and opened it.

Here it comes, thought Kaplan.

"From the president of the People's Republic of China to the President of the United States. Foreign intervention on Chinese territory will be repelled by all means necessary. Terrorism will be wiped out." He paused and looked up. "Taiwan will be liberated."

It's war, thought Kaplan.

"Can we have a copy of that, Mr. General Director?"

"You may have the original, Richard." Lu slid the first envelope across the table.

"And the second message?" asked Mauldin as evenly as he could. He could feel the spin of history under his feet.

Lu opened the next envelope and pushed it across the smooth table to the Americans.

Mauldin took it. It was strangely heavy, as though the message within had been written on a piece of stiff cardboard. He opened it warily and slipped out a small, rectangular plastic card. It was not much bigger than a credit card but twice as thick, with a magnetic stripe on one end, a neon-bright red band on the other. In between was a black shield, an unfurled white flag with blue diagonal stripes and some small text in Cyrillic. "What is this?"

"Your experts will tell you," said Lu. "I advise you to show it to them quickly. You may go."

Mauldin slipped both letters into his briefcase and both Americans stood up and left.

"What's with the Russian ID card?" asked Mauldin when they were safely back in the Suburban.

"May I look at it?" asked the naval attaché.

Mauldin dug it out and handed it to Kaplan.

"The flag is a Russian naval pennant. *Severnyi Flot* means 'Northern Fleet.' "

"What's a Chinese admiral doing with a Russian naval ID?"

"That admiral's a submariner. I think that could be significant. And it's not an ID card," said Kaplan. "It's a nuclear release key off one of their Northern Fleet ships. Either a major surface combatant or a boomer."

Kaplan turned the card over and pointed to the second line of text. "*Dlya Trenirovky*. It means 'for training.' "

"So it's a dummy release card. Why give it to us?"

"To make us wonder who's got the *real* key." Kaplan handed the card back to Mauldin. "I think we'd better do a fast head count of Russian boomers." He looked at the release card. "If one is missing, if the Chinese have it . . ."

"They get to keep Taiwan," said Mauldin.

Baikal
Polar Abyss

Baikal churned northeast at a steady sixteen knots, her course an arc scribed across the top of the world. Markov was keeping close to the edge of the ice pack, hiding in the constant grind and grumble.

This was the true north. Up here the world grew small, and they were cutting across lines of longitude every four and a half hours, so fast that Borodin had to struggle to keep up his hand plot. The shallow Barents Sea, the frozen islands of Novaya Zemlya, the barren Siberian shore, were all behind them. They could turn to port and reach the pole in under a day. The Chukchi Sea lay forty-eight hours dead ahead, with the impossibly tight funnel of Bering Strait just beyond.

But right now Markov and his men were alone in a universe every bit as hostile as the vacuum of space.

Markov watched the pen on the recording Fathometer plummet. Three thousand meters. Four. Nearly five thousand meters of water lay beneath *Baikal*'s keel. This was the Polar Abyss, and that meant that it was time to make one last check. "It's too quiet," he said to his sonar operator.

"What's wrong with quiet?" asked Fedorenko. He was standing near the big circular hatchway leading aft, his unofficial "observation" station in a compartment where it had been made plain he was neither needed nor wanted.

Belikov knew what Markov was thinking, even if Fedorenko didn't. "The overhead ice is four to six meters thick. The deep layer is very cold and very clear."

"I asked a question. Will no one answer me?" Fedorenko felt like a steward waiting to be invited into a private meeting.

Markov swiveled in his chair to face Fedorenko. "Right now we're sailing over the deepest waters of the Arctic basin. Tomorrow we'll be in the shallows dodging icebergs. So now is the time to listen for the Americans."

"You've had us going around in circles ever since we left Kola Bay. Besides, the Americans think we're dead."

"I wouldn't. I have to assume they wouldn't either. Excuse me." He plucked the dangling *kashtan* microphone. "Borodin, what kind of a current do we have?"

"Following current, Captain. About a knot and a half."

"Very well. Helm, left ten degrees rudder. All stop on both engines. Set the bow planes to five degrees rise."

Baikal turned its wide flanks to the pushing current as it planed up out of the depths. The roof of ice was too thick to transmit much light. Just an indistinct green glow.

"Bow is passing through north," said the helm.

"Captain," Markov said to Fedorenko. "You've been training with my officers. Would you like to stand duty as assistant to the officer of the deck?"

"If you'll tell me what you're planning."

"I'm heading our bow into the current."

"For a clearing turn?"

"Clearing turns won't help us here. The Arctic Sea is too noisy and American hunter-killer boats are too quiet. Even in ideal conditions, our sonar can't hear them very well."

"You said the noise of the ice would protect us."

"I said that it would improve the odds. Our best chance to hear something is to come to a full stop and shut down our engines. There will be no flow noise across the hull and our own noise will be essentially zero." Markov smiled. "We're going to turn *Baikal* into an ice pick. A nuclear-powered ice pick."

"Speed is now under two knots, Captain," said the petty officer at the helm.

Markov picked up the *kashtan*. "Igor?" he said to his chief engineer. "Ballast the boat to rise dead slow."

"If you hit the ice hard you could sink us," Grachev complained.

"That's why I said dead slow, Grandfather." He turned to Fedorenko. "You can stand by the Fathometer and call out every ten meters of depth change."

"Keel depth passing one hundred meters," said Fedorenko.

Markov made the quick, almost instinctive calculation. "We should hit at forty-four if the ice is where Belikov thinks it is."

"Keel depth ninety meters."

"Belikov, we'll pivot the ship counterclockwise for you after we're positioned against the ice."

"Understood." Belikov adjusted his sonar receiver to make best use of the quest conditions.

"Excuse me," said Fedorenko, "but if we shut down the engines, how will you pivot? The docking motors?"

"They make too much noise. We need absolute silence." *Baikal* had two thrusters built into her hull, one at the bow, the other at the stern and used to push the giant ship against a pier. "Depth?"

"So how will you turn the ship?"

"By using the sea."

"Sixty meters."

"We're rising a little fast, Captain," warned Grachev.

"Then slow us down."

"What do you think I'm doing?"

"Fifty meters!"

"Flood the ship down!" Markov commanded.

"Forty meters!"

Thick curtains of bubbles rose from the Typhoon as Grachev tried to fill her ballast tanks with water. But it was too late. As the ship rose, the water pressure diminished and the air in her ballast tanks expanded, pushing out the sea as fast as Grachev could let it rumble in. Faster. "She's broaching! I can't hold her!"

Markov grabbed the collision alarm lanyard and pulled. The raucous alarm sounded an instant before *Baikal*'s crumpled sail struck the ice with the sharp, loud *crack!* of a toppling oak. The ship shuddered, tilted, then bounced back down off the ice.

Grachev's hands flew across the ballast control board. Now there was too much weight. He sent a long, solid blow of high-pressure air into both main tanks that stopped the submarine's plummet. The ship hung motionless for a moment, surrounded by a halo of rising ice fragments drawn down by the Typhoon's mass. Then, *Baikal* began to rise again.

Fuck. Grachev added ballast, slowing the ascent. "Here we go," he said to Markov. "I'll blow her out just before we hit to keep us from bouncing again."

"Keel depth fifty meters," said Fedorenko. He was hanging on to a steel bar with both hands.

"Now, Igor," said Markov. "Now."

There was a roar of high-pressure air and a rumble of water forced out of *Baikal*'s cavernous ballast tanks.

"Forty meters!"

The sail hit the ice a second time but with her ballast tanks half empty. *Baikal* pressed up against the roof.

"The ice is holding overhead," said Belikov.

Markov looked up to the overhead console with its gauges, its wire bundles, the framed plaque. The eerie groaning of steel was gone, replaced by the crunch of something heavy being dragged across crusted ice. "Reduce steam through the plants to minimum, Igor. Switch the ship to batteries."

The lights in Central Command blinked, then came back.

"Ship is on battery power," said Grachev. "You've got one and a half hours before we have to restart the kettle."

"You may wish to observe Lieutenant Belikov," Markov said to Fedorenko. "He will be the center of attention."

As Fedorenko left to look over the sonarman's shoulder, Markov listened as his ship began to grow quiet. The whine of the turbines fell to a whisper. Only the cooling fans made their presence known. He could hear individual switches turned, buttons pushed, clear across Central Command. He could even hear that Belikov was coming down with a cold. Markov had been told that this was how an American submarine sounded underway. It would be astonishing if true.

"We're starting to pivot," said the petty officer at the helm.

Markov saw the digital heading display shift by one degree. Not much, but then each increment meant some forty thousand tons of steel had been put into motion by the gentle, silent force of flowing water. A knot and a half of current didn't give much of a push, but applied over the vast acreage of the Typhoon's hull, it was enough. "Belikov?"

"No contacts detected."

"Because there's nobody out there," said Fedorenko. "And at this rate, there will be no escorts waiting for us in the Pacific, either."

Good, thought Markov. *I don't need to steam up some destroyer's wake.* He'd rather go it alone and lose himself in the vastness of the open sea. "Do you agree, Belikov?"

"Not yet, Captain."

Good answer. "Keep listening."

CHAPTER TWENTY

BLIND RUN

USS *Portland*

Browne shut the door to the Goat Locker and faced Steadman. "So?"

"He's docking Engler's pay and busting him back two grades."

"That's *all*?"

"I think Bledsoe and Engler have their heads together on this, and they both could be taking orders from Vann."

"You'd best be careful with ideas like that, Mister Steadman," said Browne. "Number one, Norfolk just sprinkled gold dust over him. Whatever happened down in Kola, he made things happen up here. Nothing succeeds like success."

Steadman had to agree. The *well done* from COMSUBLANT had been clear enough.

"Two, the captain *ought* to make the call. It's your job to alert him to the facts. It's his job to act on them."

"What if he's wrong?"

"He's still captain. He still makes the call. I hate to say it, but unless someone talks, you got nothing to work with."

Steadman listened to the throb of the engine. He could feel the power coursing through the boat. *Portland* was rocketing through the ocean at nearly forty knots, as fast as some torpedoes could swim. "Then we've got to find a way to get Bledsoe and Engler to talk."

"If Bledsoe's got something cooked up with the captain, he won't talk to you about it. I could lean on the cook . . ."

"No. We snag Engler, all the others will fall into our laps."

"I already tried that."

"Scavullo hasn't."

"*Scavullo?*"

"He hates her, COB. Putting them together might break something loose."

"Might break more than that."

"We can protect her." He nodded at the low-powered radio Browne carried. "He'd say something to her that he'd never say to us. We'll listen in. If it goes bad, we can be there in ten seconds."

"Ten seconds is going to feel like ten *hours* to her. Be a big risk. She willing to take it?" asked Browne.

"Let's go find out."

Baikal

Lieutenant Belikov watched ghostly phosphorescent shapes appear, then vanish on his circular sonar screen. With the reactor pumps shut down, the engines still, the ventilation fans secured, the generators off-line, *Baikal* was as quiet as she could ever be. Without screw noise, without the raspy roar of water flowing against her hull, entire bands of her acoustic spectrum were totally blank.

"Belikov?" said Markov.

"The bow array is sweeping through five degrees per minute," said the sonar operator.

Three hundred and sixty degrees divided by five. That's the hour I gave Grachev, thought Markov. Well, faith might go a long way but it wouldn't extend the charge in your batteries, and once they were drawn down to a critical level, there might not be enough left to restart the reactors. Then, with a layer of ice overhead too thick to break through, they'd be trapped.

"Captain," said Belikov, "I may have something." A green line glowed on Belikov's screen. Unlike the random snow of natural sound, it pulsed with a regular and obvious beat. "Possible contact bearing three four zero."

Markov walked over to the sonar station.

Belikov pointed to a number flashing in green numerals. "The blade count shows three hundred and twelve revolutions per minute. That translates to nearly forty knots."

Forty knots? Markov could see the bearing shift even as he watched. "How far away do you think he is?"

Belikov pushed a bang of lank hair off his sweaty brow. "It's just a guess, but I think he's running deep and fast. He's making enough noise to wake the dead and he doesn't care who knows it."

Fedorenko joined them. "What is it?"

You don't sprint like that if you're hunting. Markov slowly smiled. "Some good luck for a change. The Americans still think we're dead."

The messenger of the watch had really screwed up with his wake-up calls. The good news was that Bam Bam Schramm got an extra half hour of sleep. The bad news was that he was now late, and so he had to jump out of his rack, throw on his shoes and poopy suit and hightail it to the sonar shack to relieve a very weary Sonarman First Class Niebel as watch supervisor.

When Bam Bam settled into his familiar seat and put his feet up on the console, he saw that he'd forgotten his socks. He gave it a mental shrug. His octagonal screen was solid with sound, all of *Portland*'s own making. The noise made by all that high-speed water flowing over her hull could blank out the most sensitive receivers. Schramm was just putting in time.

The sonar shack was dimly lit and midnight quiet. Bam Bam went to a bin filled with manuals and rummaged around until he found what he was looking for: a George Strait CD, *The Road Less Traveled*. He returned to his console and slipped it into a player he'd patched into the exquisite sound machinery the Navy had so thoughtfully provided him. He switched on the CD player, placed the large black sonar headset on and leaned back with his eyes shut. He was surrounded by sound, every note, every nuance. It was better than a front-row seat in a concert hall.

"*Schramm!*"

His eyes popped open. *Jesus!*

"Get your feet off that sonar console and sit up!" said Vann.

Bam Bam's feet dropped to the deck like two shot birds, but not quite fast enough.

"Where are your socks?"

"I guess I'm not wearing any, sir."

"You *guess*?"

"I got a late wake-up from the messenger and I had to rush up here to relieve—"

"You can't stand a professional watch without socks. Who had the duty before you?"

"Niebel, sir."

"Call Niebel back here to stand your watch until you get yourself properly dressed."

"He's probably already in his rack, skipper. He looked pretty beat when—"

"Then call the chief of the watch to wake him up."

"Aye aye," said Bam Bam, thankful that Vann hadn't noticed the CD player at his feet. He picked up the phone and informed the chief of the watch that Niebel was wanted back on duty. He held the phone away from his ear as he heard the answer. Bam Bam looked up at Vann. "He wants to know why."

"You tell him that the captain of this boat has ordered it."

"Aye aye." Schramm relayed the dictum.

"What is that gear under there by your feet?" asked Vann.

Oh shit. "A CD player."

"You're listening to music? What if there were a Russian *Akula* out there waiting to put a torpedo into us?"

We'd never know it. "I figured at the speed we're making through the water, my sonar's shut down tighter than a bull's asshole in fly season."

Vann reached down and yanked the CD player away by the cords. "I can't make you hear a Russian boat," he said to Bam Bam. "But by *God* I can make you listen."

Sonarman Niebel appeared at the sonar shack door. He came in without asking permission, his eyes red. "Why do you need to be relieved?" he asked Schramm.

"Skipper here says I'm not wearing any socks."

Niebel looked at Vann, then leaned against the bulkhead and pulled off a shoe, then a sock. He balled it up and threw it into Bam Bam's lap, then did the same for the other. "Here," he said, and then stomped off barefoot.

Baikal

The green spike on Belikov's sonar screen kept up its rapid pace around the screen. "Captain, target bearing one seven zero relative. He's definitely a *Los Angeles.* He'll pass inside six kilometers."

Six kilometers, thought Markov. *If we were making any sound at all he'd find us.* It reminded him of something Grachev had said, about how it would be ideal if they could only get the Americans to kill the rockets but not *Baikal.* It was a great solution, except for one detail: How do you negotiate with your executioner?

"Target passing abeam," said Belikov.

Keep going, Markov silently urged.

USS *Portland*

Socks or no, Schramm's screen was still nothing but noise. This was one hundred percent pure, government-inspected chicken shit. *White out.* There was nothing to hear but the roar of the sea flowing by *Portland*'s hull and the steady, lulling thrum of her engine. Sure, there were some frequencies that might make it through all that racket. But they would have to be real close and what were the chances of that up here?

Fuck Vann. Maybe he could force him to listen, but he sure as shit couldn't make Schramm *look.* He let his eyes close. The skipper would murder him if he came by. But Vann had to know what forty goddamned knots did to sonar reception.

Even if Bam Bam's eyes had been wide open he might have missed the faint, pulsing line that briefly appeared on his screen. A thin white wisp of noise that flickered once, twice, and then vanished like a glowing cigarette tossed into *Portland*'s churning, phosphorescent wake.

Baikal

"He didn't even slow down," said Belikov.

"Like a bullet," Fedorenko remarked.

Yes, thought Markov. But bullets weren't usually fired blindly at nothing. One had whistled over Markov's head. What did it mean?

He plucked the *kashtan.* "Igor? Restart both reactors now. Ready both engines to answer bells." He clicked the intercom off, then back on. "Navigation?"

"Listening," said Lieutenant Borodin.

"Lay a course for Bering Strait."

CHAPTER TWENTY-ONE

THE TRAP

"Where you thinking of doing this?" asked Browne as he shut the door to the Goat Locker. He had the usual radio strapped to his waist plus a spare.

"The radio room."

"Wallace has the watch. Where do you want him?"

"I'll leave him some manual revisions in the wardroom."

"Aye aye. I'll send him down to get Engler out of his rack first," said Browne. "Engler's gonna be spring-loaded to the pissed-off position when he sees her, you know."

"I know."

"Does she?"

"Better than anyone."

They climbed up the ladder from the middeck level to officers' country. Steadman took just two steps aft, then stopped.

Browne said, "What's wrong?"

"I left Tripod guarding my cabin door." Three long strides brought him to his door. He pulled on the handle. The door was still locked. He pounded on it. "Lieutenant!"

Browne had his master key out in a flash. He was about to insert it into the lock, but the door swung open.

Scavullo had washed her face in the tiny cabin sink and brushed her long, dark hair back into a neat ponytail. The smoke smudges on her neck were gone. The sweet smell of flowery soap wafted out into the passage.

Finding a well-manicured rose-bush blossoming down in *Portland*'s bilge would have seemed no stranger.

"I needed to wash up, sir," said Scavullo. "I went down below and brought some of my soap up. I hope that was all right."

No! But Steadman said, "Did Bedford go with you?"

"Two steps behind me all the way." She looked down the passage. "He was out here a minute ago. I heard him talking."

"I'll go find him," said Browne, anxious to find a reason to leave. COB knew there was no reason on earth to find her presence in the XO's stateroom suspicious, but a pretty girl behind an officer's locked door smelling sweet triggered something that was beyond the reach of reason. He handed the spare radio to Steadman. "Let me know if we're on."

Scavullo's eyes darted between them, a questioning look on her face. "On?"

"Let's talk." Steadman ushered her back in and shut the door. Outside, the smell of her soap had been strong. In here it was overpowering. "I tried to get to the bottom of what happened in the fan room. I didn't make much progress. The only thing we know is that you were in there and something happened."

"I wasn't in there alone."

"So you say."

"What does the captain say?"

"He's docking Engler's pay and busting him two grades."

"For assaulting an officer?"

"No. For showing disrespect to me and to COB."

Her dark blue eyes turned darker until they looked nearly black. "That moron went after me with a pipe."

"There's no evidence of that unless you give us some."

Her hand flew to her belt. "Call the corpsman. I'll show him the marks he left on me. You want to see my torn underwear? How about blood where his fingernails scratched me?"

"Take it easy, Scavullo. You don't have to convince me. We need *Engler's* cooperation."

"Then you can forget about it."

"Maybe not," said Steadman. "Let me explain . . ." When he was done he said, "It's up to you, Lieutenant. It's going to be nasty. Nobody can make you do it, and I wouldn't blame you if you said no."

"Will it be enough? I mean, will Vann pay attention to it?"

"He'll have no choice," said Steadman.

"Then I'm in."

Browne went up to the door to the radio room. It was decorated with security warnings and locked. He rapped on the panel. It opened at once and the narrow, beaky face of Lieutenant Wallace appeared. He had a thick binder in his hand.

"The XO sends his regards, Lieutenant," said Browne. "He'd like to see you in the wardroom to discuss some manual revisions."

"Now?" said Wallace. "But I have the duty, COB."

"What are you studying?"

"The USC-38." The satellite communications receiver. "I'm having a hard time following all the connections from the mast."

"Wisdom abides in the mind of a man of understanding, but it's not known in the hearts of fools."

Wallace blinked. "Proverbs fourteen. You know your Bible?"

"I look for help wherever I can find it. Like the good book says, without counsel, plans go wrong, but with advisers they succeed."

"I guess I could use some new advisers."

"It's your lucky day." Browne pushed his way inside. "I can draw a USC-38 schematic in my sleep. When you're done seeing the XO about that paperwork, find me. We'll go through it."

"Thanks, COB. But who'll stand my watch while I'm away?"

"Engler. Go get him out of his rack. I'll wait till he shows."

Wallace looked scared at the prospect of rousing a man with a hair trigger filed down to a wicked point. "Engler?"

"Ephesians four: twenty-seven. Give that old devil no opportunity. Let him labor at honest work. The change will do him good."

Wallace laughed and, reinforced with scripture, left for the netherworld of the berthing area down on the bottom deck.

Browne waited until the door clicked shut, then went hunting for a place to stash the radio. The snug compartment was lit with cold blue fluorescent light and packed with tan equipment racks, storage bins, flickering computer displays and humming printers. He found the spot where the USC-38 binder had been stowed.

Browne unclipped the radio at his waist and placed it in the open slot. The fit was perfect. He pulled it out and keyed the microphone. "Ready," he said, then locked the transmit key down and slipped the radio back in.

A few minutes later there was a knock at the door. It was Scavullo. He pulled her in and shut the door. "You sure about this, Lieutenant?"

"No."

"Honest answer. Just remember, I'll be listening. So will the XO. You even *think* you need help, you *holler.* Got it?"

"It's automatic," she said with a smile.

Browne caught his own words bounced back from this unfamiliar source and smiled. "Lieutenant, you still don't *smell* like a submariner. But you *are* beginning to sound like one." With that, he left her for the XO's stateroom. The hook was baited. It was time to go fishing.

It's been said that a submarine is a miniature municipality. The skipper is the mayor, the wardroom is its city council and the COB is the sheriff. Rated submariners were the responsible citizens—at least, most of the time.

At the absolute bottom of this social structure were the nonrated enlisted. Most of these untouchables had their berths down on the lower deck in a densely packed passage forward of the auxiliary machine room.

The area was known by many names. Those who lived there called it the Alley, and themselves Alley Rats. All officers above the rank of ensign knew it as the Headache Factory. By any name, if something went wrong, this was where an officer would look to find the usual suspects.

Among such men, Engler enjoyed an elevated status. A rated radioman didn't have to live among the untouchables. He'd *chosen* to. His reputation as a bar fighter and a prankster who could taunt officers with impunity made him their hero.

The lights in the Alley were kept low. It was into this dim no-man's-land that Lieutenant Wallace ventured. He slipped quietly by a tier of occupied racks and into a narrow passage that echoed with the discordant rumble of snores.

A curtain pulled open. "It's Baby Jesus."

More curtains opened. An instant later, the passage was filled with hoots, catcalls and whistles.

"Lordy!" someone called out in a tremulous, revival tent shout. "Someone pass me a snake! I feel the *need* to handle a serpent for the *Lord*!"

"Here ya go."

"That's hydraulic hose, you pussy!"

"That's my cock, you asshole."

Lieutenant Wallace summoned every last molecule of command presence he'd ever dreamed of, lowered his voice half an octave and said, "Quiet, men!"

The hoots grew wilder, the catcalls more personal, the whistles more leering. Finally, a new voice blew the noise out like a candle in a sudden gust.

"*Shut up!* Show some respect! We got the junior comms officer here!"

Engler swung his legs out of his rack. He wore no shirt. The reading light from his rack slanted across his upper body and shoulders, making his muscles seem immense. "Sorry, Lieutenant. What can we do for you today?" He put on his pale glasses.

"I need you to cover the radio room while I have a meeting with the XO. I'll relieve you as soon as I'm done."

"Who's gonna relieve me?" someone snickered.

"Your right hand, dickweed."

"I said *quiet!*" Engler commanded. "How come I got to lose sleep over it?"

"Look," Wallace pleaded, "there's no comms traffic to worry about. I'll take the hour off your regular watch."

A chant began. *"Two! Two! Two!"*

Engler shrugged, his expression one of helplessness.

Wallace held up his hand in defeat. "All right. Two."

The Alley Rats cheered.

Wallace was about to leave when he caught sight of something moving down at his feet: a small tube, a black hose yanked back into the dark with such speed he might have imagined it except for what it had left behind. He was standing in a small puddle of some liquid. The deck was wet.

"Baby Jesus just took a leak on the deck!"

Wallace tried to step out of it but just succeeded in spreading the puddle.

"Aw, jeez, Lieutenant." Engler moved gingerly around Wallace. "You're not supposed to let on how bad we scare you."

The Alley Rats bayed as Engler left Wallace standing in a spreading pool of urine.

"We're set," said COB as he shut the door to Steadman's stateroom. "All we need now is Engler."

Steadman turned the volume on the small radio up to full and sat on his bunk, his back against the curving wall of the hull, the radio in his lap. Browne placed the second radio and the recorder on Steadman's desk and switched them both on.

The sound of Scavullo's breathing filled the stateroom. *How long will it take us to get back there and stop him?* Steadman wondered. They'd have to negotiate a short passage, dash through Control—thank God Whalley had the conn and not Vann—and back through the aft doorway to the radio shack. *Ten seconds? Fifteen?*

There was a noisy click, then, *"Hey. Hiya doin', Lieutenant?"*

The clack of a shutting door came through the tinny speaker.

"All right," said Browne.

Steadman watched the tape cartridge spin.

Then, Scavullo's voice. *"What are you doing here? You're not supposed to be on duty."*

"Neither are you. Baby Jesus asked me to cover for him."

"You can call him Lieutenant Wallace."

"Yeah. Whatever. You busy? We need to straighten some things out. I don't want there to be any misunderstandings."

Scavullo said, *"There's no misunderstanding, Engler."*

"I know that little stunt didn't go over real well, but you know, guys do it all the time to each other."

"You call going after me with a pipe a stunt?"

"Keep talking," Browne whispered.

"No, I mean the tea bag thing. Everybody gets tea-bagged their first time out. You need a sense of humor."

"Tell me again how unzipping your pants and putting your penis on my shoulder was funny. I missed something."

"It was just for laughs."

"What about the fan room? Was that just a joke, too?"

"Fuck you. You almost fried my ass in there."

"We got him," said Steadman.

"Almost," said Browne.

"What do I have to do for you to call it even?"

"Four years in a cell at Quantico."

"Shit. You asked to be here. If you can't play with the boys, then go run home and cry on your girlfriend's shoulder."

"That's one thing about you that really mystifies me. You wear a wedding ring. You're married. I can't figure out what would make a woman want to stay with a psycho like you."

Browne looked up. "You tell her?"

"No." Steadman's heart jumped. Scavullo had just crossed a line.

"Leave her out of this, bitch."

"How do you keep her from running off? Do you have to lock her in the basement and beat her with a pipe?"

"I keep her happy with this."

Scavullo laughed. *"If that's all it takes to keep her happy, you'd better hang on to her. Believe me. She's one of a kind."*

"You fucking bitch."

One second she'd been in her chair telling him his wife was one of a kind. The next, a rock-hard ball struck between her breasts with enough force, enough fury, to send her sprawling. She hit her head on something going down and the fluorescent lights were slowly rotating.

Engler straddled her waist, then reached under her neck and raised her head up until her mouth gaped open.

She was still holding the pencil she'd been using at the console, and swung it overhand with all her strength and buried the tip in Engler's thigh.

His leg shot out straight. Engler fell back against a radio rack.

"Jesus Christ, Engler! On your feet! *Now!"*

It was Vann.

He plucked the pencil out of his thigh and threw it to the deck. The tip was red with his blood. "Captain!"

"What in the name of God is going on in here?"

He scrambled to his feet. "She fell off her chair and—"

"I'll deal with you later. Get out of my sight."

Vann waited until Engler had shut the door behind him. He walked over and threw the dead bolt with a *snap.* There was no way anyone could get in now without breaking down the door.

Her eyes were beginning to focus again. She pushed herself upright against a radio rack.

Vann stood over her and looked down with something like pity. "I will not have you throwing dirt over my reputation. I won't have you running to your Washington friends with lurid stories. Whatever you *think* happened to you here on *Portland,* it didn't. None of it. You will be silent. You will spend your remaining time quietly. When we put in, wherever that may be, you will leave us and forget you ever came aboard. I say this all for your own good."

She looked up at him in disbelief. "No chance."

"Wait. I'm not finished. You will prepare a statement admitting to inappropriate relations with members of my crew. Leave out the names for now. If necessary, I'll add them later. You will sign this document and I will keep it out of the public eye. That is, unless I need to present it to an investigative body."

"You can't make me lie for you."

"I don't have to. It will be your own, freely given sworn statement." Vann smiled.

"Never."

"You'll change your mind, Lieutenant. You see, you'll be with us for a while. If you cooperate, the weeks will pass uneventfully. If not, well, I can't be everywhere." The smile vanished. "I want your statement on my desk in an hour. Lieutenant Bledsoe will be there, too. You will sign it in our presence."

Scavullo watched him unbolt the door, then turn.

"You don't belong here. When we return, it will be plain to the rest of the world, too. And it won't be my word that pulls the plug. It will be yours. You're going to solve a lot of our problems." He left without looking back.

She got to her feet and staggered over to where the radio was nestled in the stacks of manuals. *No,* she thought. *You just solved mine.*

CHAPTER TWENTY-TWO

TO HERALD CANYON

9 AUGUST

Baikal

The Lomonosov Ridge soars twelve thousand feet above the bottom of the Polar Abyss, yet when *Baikal* topped it only an uptick on the paper drum of Markov's recording Fathometer marked the passage. They crossed the Mendeleev Ridge a day later.

Markov knew the approach to Bering Strait was a maze of deep ice and shallow water. More, their under-ice sonar had been wiped away in the collision and their powerful active system would betray them to anyone listening. And yet he was expected to sail the largest, heaviest submarine in the world through it. How?

The truth was he didn't know. He couldn't go back to Seal Bay. He couldn't hide in the polar sea forever. Ultimately, Markov would have to make a run for the Pacific, a big, deep ocean with room for possibilities, even hope. But to reach it, *Baikal* would have to evade the Americans and run Bering Strait. He wasn't sure which task was more formidable.

The strait was a funnel that tapered to a slender pass less than fifty miles wide. Its northern mouth was Herald Canyon. In a hundred nautical miles, twelve hours' sail at *Baikal*'s stealthy eight knots, the bottom would rise from two thousand meters to barely a hundred and then, in the strait itself, just over fifty.

Sheets of ice driven south piled up into underwater ridges forty meters deep. For a submarine thirty-six meters from keel to sail, it might as well be a wall stretching from Russia to Alaska.

"Passing the five-hundred-meter line now, Captain," said Navigator Borodin. "We're entering Herald Canyon."

Markov watched the men on duty in Central Command go about their tasks. They seemed to be only half-awake, under some spell. Markov recognized the syndrome, the spell, woven from too much time spent locked up in a steel cylinder, breathing stale air, terrified that the monotonous routine would be broken only by sudden catastrophe, by death.

Only Belikov still seemed himself. He was hunched over his screen, headphones on, listening over the passive sonar set.

Curious, Markov walked over to stand behind him. The screen was lit with random flickers generated by the snapping jaws of a billion Arctic shrimp. He watched a brighter, steadier line appear, then fade, then reappear. "Whale?"

"Male bowhead," Belikov said finally. "Look at his signal strength. I'm calling this one Pavarotti."

Maybe he'd been a little hasty in his appraisal of Belikov's state of mind. "You're naming whales now?"

"Look at his numbers."

Underwater sound is measured in decibels, and Belikov was right. This whale was singing his lungs out. *One hundred and nine decibels,* thought Markov. It was about the same as the noise made by a departing jumbo jet. "Let's hear it."

Belikov put it over the speakers. An unearthly song blasted out at maximum volume. Pavarotti's wails rose, wavered high beyond human hearing, then down low to a kettledrum bass. The sequence ended with a staccato bubbling sound that sounded a lot like a watery laugh.

Two uneventful days or not, everyone turned, shocked at the sudden noise.

Belikov dialed the volume back to something more tolerable. "I've been thinking about Bering Strait. It's going to be hard to find a way through without using sonar."

Or impossible. "So?"

"This whale song is carrying a long way. The Americans are out there somewhere listening to Pavarotti sing, just like we are."

Who cared what they were hearing, as long as it wasn't *Baikal*? "What are you getting at?"

"Pavarotti could help us find a way through the strait."

"A whale needs a single meter of water under his belly."

"I'm not saying we should follow him, Captain. But why not use his song as our sonar? It powerful enough. We can broadcast it through the UQC as loud as we want, and who cares if someone hears a whale looking for a wife?"

The UQC was an underwater telephone device, a holdover from the days when one submarine had reason to talk to another; reasons that disappeared when making noise became tantamount to committing suicide. *Baikal* was big enough to require three such systems, one forward, one atop the sail and the other aft. As far as Markov knew they'd only been used to talk with divers doing work on the hull. Even then the sound quality was like someone trying to shout and gargle at the same time. "How?"

"By playing Pavarotti through the forward UQC, then listening on passive sonar. We can time the return echoes off the ice. I think I can even rig something to show a line on the recording Fathometer."

"A kind of horizontal depth display?"

Belikov nodded. "We won't be able to see very far, but it might keep us from hitting something if we take it slow."

"Pavarotti won't sound much like a whale played through the UQC."

"He'll sound even less like *Baikal*."

Markov wondered how he got so lucky in finding men like Grachev, like Demyan, like Belikov. "What do you need and how soon can we try it?"

"I have to make up some cables. I should have something ready by the end of the watch."

Northwind SOSUS

The end of the Cold War brought a lot of changes to the network of undersea monitors known as SOSUS. Of the arrays that had once guarded the approaches to Alaska, only the Northwind Line was still active. It was this array that picked up the sounds of a heavy, twin-screw submarine approaching from the northwest.

Fifteen minutes later, a red silhouette flashed onto wall-sized displays at five U.S. Navy ocean surveillance centers. With a count of Russia's submarine force going on at full speed, the sudden appearance of a Typhoon where no Typhoon had ever appeared generated instant attention.

What were the Russians up to? The White House had gone to the Joint Chiefs for an answer. The Joint Chiefs sought assurances from the Chief of Naval Operations, who phoned Vice Admiral Graybar, the Submarine Force Atlantic commander, with a simple question: *You told me that damned Typhoon wasn't headed for China. SOSUS says she is. Who's right?*

Graybar had Vann's "clean sweep" message on his desk, but you don't get three stars for walking on bear traps. And so he said, "According to my most recent information she turned back two days ago."

"SOSUS says she's almost to the *goddamned Pacific Ocean*. The president wants an answer."

"You'll have it." Graybar looked at Vann's message, crumpled it up and threw it into the trash. It took a lot to disturb a three-star's equilibrium, but getting your tail chewed by the Chief of Naval Operations will do it every time.

John Graybar's salty sailor's curse, suitably transformed into printable orders, was heard all the way from his outer office to the other side of the globe.

USS *Portland*

If the control room is a submarine's brain, then its mess is surely its heart. Other spaces aboard *Portland* were dedicated to the submarine and its mission, and whatever was left was given over grudgingly to her crew. That was the rule, but the mess deck was its exception.

Here you could find photographs of babies born while their fathers had been away on patrol, clippings from hometown papers, notices of motorcycles for sale and the chart COB kept measuring each nonqualified man's progress toward the goal of winning his dolphins. There was the "Hero" case, covered with glass, containing *Portland*'s many awards as well as her official commissioning plaque. It was flanked by two damage control lockers and topped by a mounted red lobster big enough to wake a Down East lobsterman in a cold sweat.

Red-shirted messmates were busy serving up dozens of its smaller cousins in celebration of Commander Vann's forty-fifth birthday, his last as *Portland*'s captain.

The chief of the boat had even managed to run off another HOME OF THE INVISIBLES banner to replace the one that had mysteriously vanished. Browne had it hung over a folding table set up for the captain and the officers: Whalley, Dan Keefe and Tony Watson. The heads of the navigation, weapons and engineering departments, along with Bledsoe.

Everyone not on duty or too tired to rise from their racks was here and the space was jammed to bursting. Even the small jump seats bolted to the ends of the tables were occupied. Engler was there, along with all the denizens of Rat Alley he could muster. They busied themselves dipping lobster tails into big pots of melted butter and then, when there was no more lobster, mopping up the rest with big, doughy biscuits.

Finally, when the lobster was gone, when the final ear of corn had been stripped to the cob, it was time for the special cake Browne had arranged for the event. It was hidden under a domed stainless steel cover behind the juice dispenser.

"Captain?" said Browne. "Folks are waiting on dessert. I figure you got about a minute before the riot starts."

Vann pushed back from the table and stood. "Thanks, COB. I know when you say one minute you don't mean two." He looked around the mess. "I was starting to think I was going to end my career in the Navy as the oldest serving submarine commander. Not that it would be such a bad deal, but as you all know, when we get back I'll be leaving *Portland*." He nodded at the Hero case. "My name will go on a little piece of polished brass, and a new man will take my place. But it's been an honor and a privilege being *Portland*'s captain for this run."

The room was dead silent.

"We got handed a difficult job. We encountered challenges from within and without, and we met them. We did the things we trained for. We did our country's work and we did it well."

The officers applauded. The denizens of Rat Alley cheered.

"I want to thank you for following me where we had to go, and for still being willing to come and celebrate my birthday." Vann smiled. "I know I'd be in trouble if being your skipper was an elected office." He glanced at Browne. "How many votes could I count on, COB?"

"Depends on how much more you got to say, Captain."

Applause gave rise to a messwide chant:

Cake! Cake! Cake!

"Bring it on!" Vann told the messmates.

They picked up the big covered tray. They struggled it up as though the thing was made of solid plate steel and not flour, sugar, water and reconstituted eggs.

"Make a hole!" Browne shouted at the officers seated at the captain's table. Much to the amusement of the men, they did as COB demanded, and cleared room for the straining cooks to drop the heavy platter down. They swiped the sweat off their brows, picked up the domed lid and stood back.

The platter was empty except for a ribbon that read, *Happy Birthday to the Invisible Vann*.

The blue-suited young men hooted and hollered and laughed in the slightly crazed manner of people who hadn't found much to laugh at for too long.

"Well, Captain?" said Browne. "You gonna make a wish and blow out those candles?"

Vann was just as pleased as though a cake had actually been there. More. He looked up at the officers, then the men, and then closed his eyes, took a deep breath and was about to blow out the invisible candles, when the intercom tone sounded, followed by the XO's voice.

"Captain to control, captain to control."

"Start dishing the ice cream," said Vann crossly. "I'll be back."

"Sonar, Conn," said Steadman. "Any close contacts?"

"Nothing inside thirty thousand yards." It was Niebel, the duty sonarman who'd thrown his socks at Bam Bam Schramm.

"Very well," said Steadman. "All stations make ready for periscope depth."

Vann stepped through the aft door. "What's going on?"

"Comm alert over the trailing wire," said Steadman.

Vann eyed Lieutenant Choper. Slice and Dice was sitting dive. "Amazing. He hasn't cut it again?"

"He's doing just fine. We're getting ready to go to PD to raise an antenna to download it. I thought you'd want to be informed in case the message was important."

"All right. Make it quick. I've got a party waiting."

"Dive Officer," said Steadman, "make your depth sixty feet."

"Sixty feet, aye," said Choper, angry at Vann for the snide remark and pleased that the XO had stood up for him. Though from what he'd heard, the XO's support wasn't exactly the gold standard these days.

"I can let you know when the message is ready," said Steadman. He hoped Vann would leave. Indeed, he'd done his best to avoid the man for the last day and a half.

"I'm here, Mister Steadman. Don't waste any more of my time than you have to."

"Aye aye." Coming up for a message should have been a welcome change from the monotonous routine of cutting ovals in the Chukchi Sea listening for submarines. But Vann cast a dark shadow over nearly everything.

Vann was a deeply flawed man, and Steadman believed those flaws were deep enough to preclude him from ever taking another ship and crew to sea.

The tape he had in his safe could destroy him, and despite everything, he couldn't help feeling something like pity. For in one way they were alike: They both saw command at sea as a kind of ultimate achievement. Vann had it, but not for long. And Steadman? He was looking at the end of that dream. The difference was, he knew it. Vann did not.

"Depth now sixty feet, XO," said Slice and Dice.

There were comforts in routines, and Steadman now put everything away to concentrate on bringing *Portland* to periscope depth safely, copying the waiting message correctly and resuming their prowl around the approaches to Bering Strait. "Let's have an ESM sweep."

The Type 18 scope eased upward until a slender whip pierced the waves. It cut the barest feather of a wake. The ESM antenna atop the periscope's head sniffed the cold salty air for the telltale emissions of radar.

"ESM is quiet, XO," said the chief at the electronics countermeasure console. "Just those fishing trawler sets a long way off to the south."

"Radio, Conn. Stand by to copy message traffic."

The satellite receiver emerged from the waves. It was designed to listen for just one kind of signal, and the instant it cleared the surface it found those signals in abundance.

"Conn, Radio. We're downloading a high-priority flash message from COMSUBLANT in Norfolk," said Wallace. "It's running through crypto now." Then, "It's for CO's eyes only."

Steadman watched Vann step through the door leading back to the radio room, glad to be free of his presence. "Captain's on his way."

Waves have deep roots. When COB's calibrated feet detected a slight rolling motion he knew they'd come up to periscope depth. He felt the deck tilt as they dived again to patrol depth. Vann would be back any minute. He turned to the messmates collecting ice cream bowls. "Captain's on his way."

They brought another tray out from behind the serving line. It was as large as the first and covered with an identical metal dome. They set it down on the officers' table and removed the lid with a flourish.

Long and gray, the cake was made in the exact shape of a submarine. Not just any submarine, but a Russian ballistic missile boat, a Typhoon.

COB held out a hand and someone put a lighter in it. He snapped the blue flame to life and started lighting the forty-four candles on the Typhoon's foredeck. He was halfway to the bow when an alert tone sounded over the shipwide 1MC, followed by a voice:

"Corpsman to the radio room! Corpsman to the radio room!"

Portland's independent duty corpsman, her "doctor," was being summoned.

"What's going on?" asked Keefe.

COB had his radio out. He spoke softly into the microphone, then looked up. "The captain's taken ill," Browne announced to the whole room.

Baikal

Belikov made the final connections to the recording Fathometer, then stood back to examine his work. A bundle of cables connected the instrument with an output jack on his sonar console. The sound of a singing whale would pass through those cables and should make the needle on the Fathometer twitch in a meaningful way. He hoped.

Markov pulled down a *kashtan*. "Igor. Can you maintain depth and still hold a five-degree-up angle?"

"Why?" came an immediate, and suspicious, reply.

"I want to point the bow up at the ice. We need to calibrate a new sonar set."

"There are no new sonar sets."

Markov winked at the young sonar officer. "For once you may be mistaken. Belikov? How far away is the ice pack?"

"Two and a half kilometers, Captain."

"Let's hope Pavarotti agrees."

The bow rose, the deck sagged as tons of water weight astern began to have an effect.

Sound traveled through the sea at about a kilometer and a half per second. If the Fathometer twitched three and a third seconds after the whale began his song, then it had caromed off the ice and echoed back to *Baikal* correctly.

"Five degrees and holding, Captain."

Markov looked at Belikov and nodded.

Belikov switched on the recorded whale song. The eerie moans blasted from the bow and reverberated in ghostly echoes.

Markov clicked a stopwatch on. The sweep hand jumped.

One second . . . two seconds. Markov watched the Fathometer needle. It was motionless. *Three and . . .*

The needle jumped. The Fathometer pen made a sharp little mountain peak on the paper scroll.

"It worked?" asked Belikov.

Three point three seconds. Markov grinned. "Let Pavarotti sing. Bring the ship level. All ahead one-third."

CHAPTER TWENTY-THREE

THE CONVERGENCE ZONE

9 AUGUST

USS *Portland*
Herald Canyon

Portland's independence duty corpsman, Chief Cooper, stood outside Vann's stateroom with a bag full of his gear. An IDC wasn't the same as having a staffed clinic on board, but Cooper was trained to handle everything from heart attacks to food poisoning, even depression and minor surgery. He was a short, serious-looking man in bright, steel-framed glasses, with blond hair so closely cut it resembled a kind of white bristle.

Vann had fled the radio shack with Cooper in tow at the end of a stethoscope.

Steadman leaned in through the door to Control and motioned for Cooper to enter. They gathered over the plotting charts aft of the periscope stand. Browne joined them there.

"What happened?" asked Steadman.

"Lieutenant Wallace called and I came running. I found the captain sitting at the teletype. His skin looked gray and he was sweating. I asked him if he was all right and he didn't seem to hear me. By now I'm sure he's having a heart attack, right? I started taking vitals. His heart was running flat out. I asked him if he's having any pains, and he just looks at me like whoa, who are you?"

"His eyes seem normal?" asked Browne.

"No. I shined a light in one to watch for a response. He let me hold that beam for what, one, two seconds? Then he swatted it away. It was like it took him a while to notice. I told him I should attach a heart monitor in his stateroom and he said no. I started hooking him up anyway and he took off for Control with me hangin' on. He shut his cabin door in my face."

"They just copied some kind of flash traffic from Norfolk," said Browne. "Wallace ran it through the crypto gear and handed it to Vann. Skipper read it, then he sat down. Wallace asked him if he needed something, no answer. He asked him again and same deal. No answer. He went over to make sure Vann was all right, and when he saw his face, that's when he called for help."

Steadman asked, "Chief, would you say he's incapacitated?"

"Maybe for a few minutes there he suffered from some kind of attack, but I sure don't know what kind."

"You think he'll be okay in his cabin?"

"You mean could he have another episode? I don't know. I can't tell you what triggered this one."

"All right, Chief. Thanks."

The corpsman left them at the plotting tables.

"What do you make of it, COB?"

"You play much poker, Mister Steadman? A good player can look at a man's face and read his cards. You play with someone new to the game and there always comes that moment when he realizes he's in *way* over his head. He's staked more than he can afford to lose, and now he ain't got the cards. You can see it in the eyes. His mouth may be smiling, but his eyes, they go dead *flat*."

"You've seen Vann like this before."

Browne nodded. "If I had to guess, I'd say the skipper just got dealt some cards he don't like the looks of."

The message from Norfolk. Steadman picked up the intercom and dialed the radio shack. "Radio, Conn. This is the exec. I need a copy of that flash traffic right away."

"It was for the CO's eyes only." Then, "Is Commander Vann okay? I mean, if he's not, then you're CO, right?"

Steadman had spent hours poring over his copy of *United States Navy Rules and Regulations.* He'd memorized Chapter 10, Section 1088, paragraph 2:

In order that a subordinate officer may be vindicated for relieving his commanding officer from duty, the situation must be obvious and clear, and must admit of the single conclusion that the retention of command by such commanding officer will seriously and irretrievably prejudice the public interest.

"No. Commander Vann is still CO."

Belikov turned his crude whale sonar into something Markov could actually use to navigate the ship. Now instead of a single pen on the strip chart to mark the presence of ice, there were two: The lower pen displayed the ocean bottom, the upper, the ice. They'd have to keep *Baikal* in between the lines.

Markov swiveled his chair to face the helm. "Sounding?"

"One hundred meters and rising, Captain."

They were already beyond the head of Herald Canyon, where the steep upslope merged with the shallow continental shelf. They were sailing over a rising plain cut with gullies and troughs all meandering in the general direction of Bering Strait; the deepest one was known as Wrangel Trough. A grand-sounding name for what had been an ancient riverbed cut when the Chukchi Sea was a steppe connecting Asia and America.

Markov would have to find Wrangel Trough and follow it like a salmon struggling up a stream. Every meter beneath his keel was important, for the next deep water they'd find would be in the Pacific three sailing days away. "Make your depth eighty meters. Ahead slow."

He left his chair and walked over to where the recording Fathometer was mounted. The needles showed the sea bottom was rising; fifteen meters in the few moments since the helm had called it out. The upper pen that marked the ice was still dead flat.

Then the upper pen began to move. It hesitated, quivered, then began angling down. "Ice," said Markov. He was worried about finding it and relieved that the sonar still functioned.

As *Baikal* approached the first ice ridge, the pen moved down, down, then came level at the eight-meter mark. That was more than *Baikal* could surface through in her present condition, but thin enough to pass safely beneath. "Helm, left five degrees rudder. New course one seven nine."

Baikal swung her bow east. The pen hesitated, then began moving down. Eight meters of ice thickened to ten, then twelve.

South was not working. "Right ten degrees rudder."

The submarine pointed her bow at the thinner ice, but the gap between the ice above and the mud below was narrowing.

The ice pen started down again. Ten meters. Fifteen.

"Helm, *hard* right rudder to one four eight."

It was nearly a direct heading for Wrangel Island; it was Russian territory and all but uninhabited except for walruses and the polar bears that ate them. "Make your depth seventy meters." It would put his belly just meters off the bottom.

As the missile submarine planed down, the line marking the overhead ice stopped its descent and began to rise.

They were through. *Baikal* had passed its first test.

"Sounding now eighty meters, Captain."

"Hold your depth." A scant ten meters separated his keel from the mud. It was the absolute minimum he would accept. Markov looked back down at the strip chart. The upper pen was moving down again. As it passed the twenty-meter mark, Markov said, "Engines all stop!"

It was a wall.

Markov could see on the strip chart that it wasn't a single massive ridge ahead, but two. They left an open slot fifty-five meters tall, and *Baikal* needed nearly forty of it. "Rudder amidships. Ahead dead slow."

As they crept under the first ridge the pen neared the reference line that marked the top of *Baikal's* sail. Markov looked up and expected to hear the shudder and jar of steel striking ice.

A second ridge was dead ahead.

"Sounding."

"Seventy-six meters, Captain."

It was possible this ridge was as bad as any they might encounter. It was possible that beyond it there could be relatively easy sailing. It was also possible that the slot would neck down into a solid wall. He thought once more of his sailing orders: *Arrive Anadyr Gulf, Grid Square 22 NW, for rendezvous with Pacific Fleet escorts not later than 13 August.* Three days from now.

Go on, or turn back?

"Make your depth sixty-six meters. Ahead dead slow."

USS *Portland*

Steadman knocked on Vann's door. There was no answer. He knocked again, and was just about to rattle the handle to see if it was locked when Vann pulled it open.

"What?"

"Sir, I wanted to check in and see how you were doing. You gave Lieutenant Wallace a scare." Steadman saw the folded flash message in his breast pocket.

"Chief Cooper say I'm okay?"

"He thought you might have had some sort of an attack."

"Did he say I was incapacitated?"

"No, sir, he didn't."

"Then you have your answer. Don't disturb me unless it's necessary." He started to shut the door.

"Captain, was there anything in that flash from Norfolk I need to know about? Any operational matters we need to discuss?"

"We're still headed west? Sonar's keeping a close watch for submarine traffic?"

"Yes. Bam Bam's about to take over from Sonarman Niebel."

"Then what more could I possibly do?" said Vann, and then he shut the door in Steadman's face.

Bam Bam Schramm slid into his seat behind the sonar console and made a face. "I hate a warm seat."

Sonarman Niebel glanced at Schramm's ankles. "At least you remembered your socks. What's going on?"

"Slice and Dice is sitting dive again," said Bam Bam.

"That moron couldn't find the surface if you tied a balloon to his ass and let him go."

"COB is watching him. They got CNN playing down in the mess." Bam Bam slipped on the headset. "The Chinese are telling us to stay away or else."

"Yeah, it'll be a real hardship not to be able to buy a two-dollar pack of T-shirts at Kmart anymore."

"Fuck 'em."

"Fuck 'em," Niebel agreed.

The preliminaries finished, it was time to get serious. "Any contacts?" asked Schramm.

"Ice, trawler traffic along the coast and a ton of biologicals."

"Popcorn shrimp?"

"And a whale who can't sing for shit."

Bam Bam listened, made an adjustment to the acoustic filters. "Bowhead male." He listened some more. "Kinda garbled, too. We could be listening through a couple of CZs." Convergence zones, where underwater sound bent and bounced and often became distorted. "You work up a range on him?"

"He's a whale, asshole," said Niebel.

Bam Bam cocked his head and closed his eyes. "Something's screwy about him."

"I told you he couldn't sing."

Schramm manipulated the display controls to put the whale's sound spectrum up on the screen. He whistled. "Take a look at that." It was a kind of bell curve, though with the outlying frequencies to the far left and far right cut off so completely it looked like the work of a cleaver. In between the two cutoffs was the normal scatter of peaks and valleys.

"I'm looking," said Niebel. "So what?"

"You know the difference between a tree and a two-by-four?"

"Trees are round and . . ."

"This whale is square. Look at his frequency cutoffs. A real bowhead can sing across seven octaves. This whale ain't no whale at all. It's a recording."

Baikal

Markov stared in disbelief as the recording pen marking the ice swept steadily downward. *Twenty . . . twenty-five . . . twenty-eight . . .* "All stop!" he called out, frustrated.

They'd been nosing through a maze of ice corridors, gaining a little room here, losing it there, ending up nearer Wrangel Island than Bering Strait. It was like sailing an old windjammer against a gale. Every kilometer forward was won at the cost of five, or ten, spent tacking to either side.

Markov had followed the drowned riverbed southwest from the lip of Herald Canyon. The ancient stream had meandered south, then swung due west. They'd been blocked, nosed left, found an opening, proceeded. They'd even had to back down once to escape what turned out to be a one-way tunnel in solid ice.

Now they were a lot closer to Wrangel Island than Markov would have liked. If they could surface, they would likely be able to spot the island as a dark, rocky band on the southern horizon.

Following the old riverbed had demanded every reflex, every skill Markov could command. But in the end, it tricked him.

He'd sensed the waters opening up. The trough had widened into a kind of broad basin. There was room in it to turn, to maneuver, to hope that the worst was behind them. But it wasn't, for when he crept up to the southern shore of the ancient lake bed, the trough he'd been following dived into a slot and vanished.

There was no way through.

His first officer joined him at the recording Fathometer. Gasparyan glanced at the pinched space between the deep-drafted ice and the bottom. "Thirty meters of ice?"

"Who knows the polar sea better than Russia?" Markov said, mocking Fedorenko's stirring speech.

"What will you tell him?"

"The truth," said Markov. "Go find Fedorenko."

USS *Portland*

As Portland headed southwest, the bearing to the source of the strange whale song gradually shifted enough to permit Bam Bam to compute a range of forty-three miles.

Hearing a whale from so far away wasn't unusual. Real whales could sing across entire oceans, and their voices were rich with frequencies that carried immensely far. But when he transferred the bearing and range to a chart, Schramm found a surprise: if his numbers were right, *this* whale tape was being played in a deep-water channel off Wrangel Island.

It wasn't science that suggested to Schramm that whoever was broadcasting whale music was right where a submarine would be if she were trying to run Bering Strait submerged. It was the whispers of a muse, and like any artist, Bam Bam took them seriously. He reached for the intercom. "Conn, Sonar."

"Go ahead," said Steadman.

"Sir, I got something here you need to see."

Baikal

Markov drew the curtain that separated Borodin's cubicle from Central Command and ordered the navigator out.

Borodin left and after Fedorenko went in, Markov pulled the curtain shut. "It's not a matter for negotiation," he said. "It's a matter of reason and fact."

"What facts? What reasons? All I've heard are excuses."

"You saw the chart. You know how much room this submarine needs to pass. Show me a way."

"The chart says the ice is thirty meters deep and the bottom is seventy-eight. That's forty-eight meters of open water. *Baikal* requires forty. There's your way."

"You want me to sail my ship through a slot with *eight* meters of clearance? No one signed on to deliver this ship or die trying. No one agreed to a suicide mission, Fedorenko."

"All that is required is for each man to do his best. Including you. Is there room to pass? Yes. Is there a reason not to try? Only a perverse wish to see this undertaking fail."

"You have no idea what's beyond that ice wall."

"And neither do you. It could be the last obstacle. There could be open water all the way through Bering Strait."

"I'm a sailor, not a politician. I deal with what is, not what might be. Eight meters of water is insufficient. That's my judgment."

"Even if it means being brought up on a charge of dereliction of duty? Even if it means every one of your officers will face the same charge?"

"I'm captain. It's my responsibility."

"That's an argument you can try to make when the time comes."

It had the sound of an indictment. *Was there enough water? Well, yes, but . . .*

"And don't forget," said Fedorenko. "We're of equal rank. I can countermand you."

Markov wondered what would happen if he walked away from the helm and let Fedorenko take over. He'd be putting every man on the ship, his chosen crew, at risk, and that, in the end, he could not countenance. He looked down at Borodin's sea chart for some kind of an answer.

"Well?" said Fedorenko. "North or south?"

Markov walked away and swept open the curtain. "*Starpom*. Right full rudder. Ahead on number one, all back on number two."

Gasparyan acknowledged the commands. Markov's rudder and engine orders would spin *Baikal* away from the ice in little more than her own length. But where were they heading? Back over the pole for home? "What course, Captain?" he asked. "North?"

Markov saw Fedorenko take hold of the *kashtan* to countermand his order to retreat. He turned away and faced Gasparyan. "Zero nine zero," said Markov. "East."

Steadman put the headphones down. "How long have you been tracking it?"

"Niebel picked it up last watch. It's probably some kind of whale research."

"Maybe." He recalled the last set of orders Vann had been willing to show him: Establish a barrier patrol and identify and report the whereabouts of all submarine traffic headed to or from Bering Strait. An odd sound coming from the only deep channel leading to the strait didn't leave Steadman much room for pondering tactics. "That was first-class, Bam Bam. We'll go in and see what we're dealing with. If it's a ship we should be able to tell."

He picked up the intercom and dialed the CO's stateroom. It buzzed once, twice, a third time. Steadman tapped the cradle and dialed again. On the fifth buzz, Vann answered.

"Captain? We've got a contact."

"What kind of contact?"

"Somebody's playing a recording of a whale over and over. It's coming from a natural transit route for a submarine trying to make Bering Strait submerged. I think we should go check it out."

"You propose to take us into the ice?"

"Unless the last message from Norfolk changes our standing orders, yes. I do."

"'Kay. I'll meet you in Control." With that, Vann hung up.

Bam Bam looked up at Steadman. "Ah, sir? Is Lieutenant Choper going to sit dive?"

Steadman knew what Schramm was getting at. "It would be best if you can ID the source of that recording before we get too far into the ice."

"Don't you worry," said the sonarman. "I'll be *all* ears."

"Bottom is still rising, Captain," said Belikov as he watched the pen scribe the strip chart. "It's through sixty meters."

They'd been tracing the irregular shore of the ancient lake bed for some time now, seeking a way through. Each hint of a door leading south had quickly slammed shut. He turned to Fedorenko. "There's a permanent settlement on Wrangel Island called Ushakovsky. Fishermen live there."

"Why do I need know this?" said Fedorenko.

"Because we're about to go aground in their backyards."

Fedorenko slammed his palm down on the top of the sonar console. "We've found one way through. Why do you refuse it?"

"I refuse to sacrifice this ship or her crew so that your friends can collect their commissions. Helm," said Markov. "Right full rudder."

The Typhoon swung her bow away from the shallows, back in the direction of the ice maze they'd just threaded, and directly onto a course that would cross *Portland*'s path eighteen miles ahead.

CHAPTER TWENTY-FOUR

THE DISASTER

9 AUGUST

USS *Portland*
Wrangel Trough

Vann walked into Control and said, "I have the conn."

"Commander Vann has the conn!" shouted Browne.

Vann shot Browne a quizzical look. It had always been *Captain's got the conn*. Was calling him *commander* and not *captain* a subtle dig? *If Bledsoe leaked that message I'll kill the son of a bitch.*

He went to the ship's control station, scanned the old Hamilton clock to be sure the winding indicator showed correctly, and then tapped Choper on the shoulder. "Mr. Steadman will sit dive while we're in the ice, Lieutenant."

Slice and Dice was relieved to give up his seat, but when he turned to leave, Steadman held out his hand.

"I'll take over dive, but you should stick around," said Steadman. "It will be a good opportunity for you. I'm sure the skipper won't mind."

The skipper minded a lot, but he said, "Have it your way, XO." Why was everyone second-guessing him? Vann went to his small, sidesaddle seat at the front of the periscope stand and leaned back and raised his paper cup to be filled.

The messenger of the watch poured Vann's cup full.

Vann began crunching ice at a pace that made it plain to everyone within earshot that he was not happy.

"Conn, Sonar," said Bam Bam. "Bottom's two hundred sixty feet and rising."

Vann put down his cup and picked up the intercom. "Light off the high-frequency set, Bam Bam."

"Comin' at ya'," said Schramm.

The big flat screen mounted over the helm blinked, then came back up a solid dark blue as the sonar mounted under *Portland's* chin went to work.

"I don't see a bottom," said Vann. "Steer the sounder head down and put that whale contact over the speaker, too. I want to hear it."

A distant, low groan sounded through Control. It rose, higher, higher, then ended in a derisive burst of bubbles, a mocking, underwater strawberry that Vann found particularly annoying. "Damned nonsense."

COB heard the comment and turned. "Sir?"

"If it's some tourist ship trying to lure a whale in for a Polaroid moment I'm going to put Bam Bam out on the ice and let them take pictures of *him*."

"Here it comes, skipper," said Bam Bam.

A brilliant red band swam up from the bottom of the screen. Hot pink boulders streamed back and vanished as the boat moved ahead at a steady eight knots. The mud and rocks looked close enough to touch. The planesman unconsciously pulled back on his yoke. *Portland* gained a foot in depth, then another.

"Watch your depth," said Steadman. He sat behind the two men at the helm, leaning forward, keeping an eye on heading, angle and depth, but the view through the sonar screen had a powerful pull on him, too. He glanced up at the scrolling red plain, then back to the ship's control gauges.

He thought about Lieutenant Choper, and how Vann had evicted him, and decided it was probably the right thing to do. Slice and Dice had maintained a ten-foot-depth band reasonably well, but here it would be plus or minus one foot, plus or minus one degree, and on speed to within a . . .

"What the hell is that?" said Vann.

Everyone looked up. The picture on the screen had changed. A large, irregular object broke the red line of the undersea horizon. It was sitting on the bottom directly ahead and growing larger.

"Sonar, Conn," said Vann. "How tall is that rock formation?"

"I reckon about thirty feet high."

Closer, larger, the apparition swiftly grew, then swept by under *Portland*'s sonar eye. In the instant of its passage, the rock formation became a sunken fishing trawler seen from mast height. The wreck sat upright in the mud, wrapped in a tangled furze of torn drift nets. The HF picture had been detailed enough to show the dark blind ports of her wheelhouse.

"Sheeit," said the sonar tech with his ice cube bucket.

"Anyone believe in ghosts?" said Keefe.

"Save it for a sea story, Keefe," said Vann. The bottom became a featureless red plain again. "Zero the sounder head."

The red bottom fell away to pure, deep blue again.

"What do we have for a bottom, Bam Bam?"

"One hundred ninety feet and we're about to cross under the edge of the marginal ice."

The first ice ridge was easy to pass under. The second, less so. Forty minutes later Vann had used every rudder order in the book nosing *Portland* through a complex landscape of spires, sucker holes and blind alleys.

"Sonar, Conn. I need an ID on that whale ship."

"I'm not picking up any ship noises, skipper."

"How much ice do we have overhead?"

"Six feet and steady," said Bam Bam. "It's been looking kinda even. There's a basin out ahead that's covered over with fast ice. Stand by! I'm picking up some bearing change on that whale now. Designate him Sierra Nine. He's not a moored buoy. He's definitely moving."

"He's *got* to be an ice breaker," said Vann. "How about a range?"

"The bearing shift makes me think he ain't that far away."

"I want a number."

"Inside ten thousand yards. He'll pass down our port side if we continue. Recommend a five-degree turn to port."

Vann looked at the big screen. They'd come through an obstacle course. A single deep ridge was all that blocked them from the basin ahead. "Helm, left rudder. Steady on a course of one seven zero. Ahead slow. Turns for six knots."

Portland turned her bow back into the path of the mysterious object.

The whale song grew noticeably louder.

"Conn, Sonar," said Bam Bam. "I'm showing a deep ice keel dead ahead, range eight thousand yards. That whale noise is coming from the far side of it."

Vann peered at the HF display. The dim maroon band of a thick ice ridge was beginning to emerge at the top of the screen.

"You want to take her deeper, Captain?" asked Steadman. It was more a suggestion than a question.

"I'll let you know when I need something, Mister Steadman."

"Aye aye." But Steadman wasn't so sure. The ice ridge was coming at them at eight knots and even if there was open water on the other side it didn't look like they'd clear it by all that much.

"Turn that whale off, Bam Bam," said Vann.

In the silence that followed, the loudest sound came from the crunching of ice cubes. But then Vann cocked his head and looked up. It was faint, but he could still hear the whale song. "Check your switches, Sonar. I can still hear it."

"So can I, Conn. It's comin' right through the hull. Sierra Nine must be a lot closer than I figured."

"Ahead dead slow," said Vann. "Turns for four knots."

"Captain," said Bam Bam, "Sierra Nine will pass close abeam the port side. I'll have his range in a minute."

Baikal

"Try it now, Captain," said Belikov. "I ganged up two of the UCQ transmitters and doubled the signal strength. I think it will let us see another kilometer or so."

Markov examined the strip chart. The ice overhead was still nearly five meters thick but at last he'd found the pass he'd sailed through coming in. "As soon as we clear that deep ridge we'll give Pavarotti a rest and go back to normal sonar operations."

"Understood, Captain," said Belikov. "You should pick that ridge up soon."

"So you're giving up," said Fedorenko. "The master who can do anything with a submarine runs from a little ice."

"It's not a little ice."

"Little or a lot, I can't allow it."

"It's not for you to decide."

"Captain?" said Belikov. "I'm picking up echoes off the ice ridge. Are you seeing it on the strip chart yet?"

Markov welcomed the chance to turn away from Fedorenko. "Yes." He clicked on a stopwatch.

Fedorenko leaned close, pretending to examine the strip chart. Instead, he said, softly, "If you turn this ship north while there's still a chance to make Bering Strait, I will have no choice but to assume command."

"Be my guest. I can tell you now that no one will obey. You've never even been a member of a submarine crew. Our cook would have more authority than you."

"I've sailed on submarines."

"As what? A political officer? Excuse me, but those days are gone. You're not a submariner, Gennadi. We both know it and so does every man on this ship. Driving *Baikal* into that ice trap would be suicide."

"Suicide," said Fedorenko, "is what you're best at, I think."

Markov glanced at the stopwatch, then at the Fathometer trace. The bottom was growing deeper. It was nearly down to ninety meters. They had forty meters of water under the keel instead of a miserly ten, and the extra room made Markov feel like a rich man. "Helm," he said, "come left to zero two zero."

The habits of both hunter and prey are written in blood. And so it was only natural that Markov would use the oncoming ice keel to help mask his ship. *Twenty seconds.*

Markov would wait until the last moment to dive beneath the ice. It was a matter of instinct.

Ten seconds. "Belikov? Switch off Pavarotti and begin passive surveillance." *Five.* The stopwatch hand swept to zero. *Now.* "Helm, steady on course. Make your depth eighty meters."

The *michman* controlling the diving planes pushed forward on a small joystick that sprouted from his console, and gradually, smoothly, the deck tilted down and the ridge of deep ice swept by overhead.

USS *Portland*

Schramm wanted to give Vann what he wanted, but he couldn't. It wasn't a matter of inexperience, but trigonometry. The shift in Sierra Nine's bearing had just stopped. Either it wasn't moving or it had turned right at them, and there was no way to know which. Not with a wall of ice between them. He put up the regular waterfall sonar display on his screen, hoping to spot something, anything, that could help him solve the puzzle.

There was a cluster of bright lines dead center, bearing zero zero zero. That was Robo-whale singing his . . .

The lines faded, then vanished as though a switch had been thrown. The steady lines that filled the rest of the screen said the system was still on-line. The silence was real. "Conn, Sonar, we just lost contact with Sierra Nine."

"Try to pick him up on passive broadband."

"Searching." A bellowing whale made an easy target and even Schramm knew that he'd been locked onto its distinctive signal for too long. The sonar world is one of constant, subtle change. You couldn't keep staring at one place without losing the mental picture of what was happening everywhere else.

He swept the sea for different, fainter sounds. There was nothing manmade out there.

And then there was.

Whoa. A bright line appeared at the center of his screen, precisely where the whale signal had last shown up. It became one, two, then a dozen lines, all growing brighter even as Schramm watched. "Conn, Sonar, contact reacquired and it's *real* strong. I'm running it through the analyzer to ID it."

The analyzer put up the new contact's sound spectrum on Bam Bam's screen. It wasn't a recorded whale song at all. The curve didn't come close to matching. There were no tonals, no grunts, no bubbles.

Instead, there was a bright 50-hertz sizzle from a powerful electrical system, the torrential rush of water tumbling back over a great hull, and the distant *swish . . . swish . . . swish* of a pair of large screws turning very, very slowly. It had been masked by the ice ridge. It was now in plain view.

Sierra Nine was a submarine.

Oh shit. Schramm grabbed the intercom microphone so hard it nearly shot out of his sweaty hands like a bar of soap. "Conn!"

Vann heard the shout. But even as Schramm yelled out a warning, a flicker of movement caught his eye. He turned to the HF sonar screen over the helm.

The maroon band of the ice across the top of the screen was still there. But a new object, bright and dangerous red, had appeared just beneath it. A strange, flattened oval nearly filled the gap between the ice above and the bottom below. It swelled larger, became slightly elongate, even as Vann stared in disbelief, even as Schramm screamed over the intercom for someone's attention.

One second. The roar of storm surf filled Vann's ears as he watched the red oval grow larger, shifting off dead center to the left. Two seconds. Steadman was only now beginning to turn away from the screen in his direction. Schramm's shouts were jumbled into an unintelligible mass, yet Vann could hear each tick of the old Hamilton ship's clock perfectly.

Three seconds.

To his credit, when he finally spoke, Vann said the right words: *"All back emergency!"*

Time rushed from dead slow into fast forward.

Browne pulled a switch above the ballast board and the collision alarm began to screech. The red shape filled the HF sonar screen, blotting out the view to the ice, the bottom, the sea. It became the screen itself.

Four seconds after *Baikal* appeared beneath the ridge of ice *Portland's* screw began to thunder in reverse.

"What's happening?" Scavullo asked. But in an instant, the two officers in the wardroom with her were on their feet and halfway to the door. There was a distinct shuddering she could feel right through the deck. The door slammed open as the two men fled, but not before one of them yelled,

"Collision!"

Collision? She went to the open door. The passage was full of hurrying men. She'd get run over if she put a foot out the wardroom door.

The shuddering grew. The coffee urn walked off its stand and crashed to the deck. Storage bin doors popped open and books tumbled out to the deck. She turned, her instincts to stop things from spilling, when there was a heavy *crunch* from somewhere forward, followed by the *pop-pop-twang!* of HY-80 steel being ripped apart, and a sidelong motion that felt exactly like a car spinning out on black ice.

She found herself on the linoleum deck without knowing how she'd gotten there. The lights went out as the deck began to tilt down, down. She grabbed onto the frame to keep from sliding.

The roar of the screw thundered behind her, but now she heard a new sound, a terrifying sound: the unmistakable hiss of water where it had no business to be. She pulled herself out into the dark passage just as the emergency lighting came on.

Water foamed across the deck. There was no one in sight and that made her the senior officer present. She had to report. She pulled herself back into the wardroom and grabbed the intercom and clicked on the emergency 4MC circuit.

"Flooding outside the wardroom!" she yelled, not knowing whether anyone had heard her, whether anyone else was even still alive, for her own ears were filled with the thunder of collapsing steel and the rush of the invading sea.

CHAPTER TWENTY-FIVE

THE DILEMMA

Baikal

"Igor! Reverse on both engines! Maximum turns!" Markov could hear *Baikal*'s hull grinding against the ice. *I misjudged it,* he thought. *If we sink, it won't be Fedorenko's fault. It will be mine.*

A glancing blow would do no harm, but let *Baikal*'s damaged sail hit and he could lose the ship. He couldn't dive. The bottom was right below him. He couldn't turn. He had to get stopped.

The screws thundered in reverse, but the terrible sounds of tearing metal were growing nearer, louder.

"Damage reports!"

Gasparyan pulled a *kashtan* down and was about to speak when the noise from outside the hull rose to a screeching crescendo. Whatever was making it seemed to be right beyond the walls of Central Command. Then, from within the groans and cracks came the hiss and fizz of air escaping into the sea.

Markov snatched his own *kashtan*. "Grachev! We're losing air!"

"No pressure drops aft of Compartment One," came Grachev's calm answer. "There's water in the torpedo room so there could be some escaping through that bad breech gasket."

"I heard it, Igor. Something is venting."

"Not us."

If *Baikal* wasn't losing air, then what *was?* Ice doesn't hiss. He looked up at the curved gray steel. *Mother of God!* "All stop!"

The Typhoon rumbled on, seemingly unscathed. And so it would have been but for a jagged strip of *Portland*'s sonar dome.

The HY-80 steel panel was peeled back by the impact. It briefly caught on *Baikal*'s port bow plane, held its shape for an instant, then folded around it like a parachute snagged on an airplane's wing. It would have caused little harm if it had stayed, but it came free and tumbled aft to *Baikal*'s afterdeck. There, like a sheet of paper in a whirlwind, it flew up over the deck and wrapped around the tall, slab-sided rudder.

USS *Portland*

The collision alarm was still screeching, not that anyone needed it. The boat had gotten slammed and nearly rolled. *Portland*'s orderly spaces were strewn with pots and pans, clothing, bedding and yelling men with broken bones. Anything not solidly bolted down had been thrown into an inchoate jumble.

The reactor was unhurt but the shock disabled the subsystems used to monitor it. It automatically shut down, triggering another alarm.

"Emergency reactor scram!"

"Flooding in the VLS support area!" someone yelled over the emergency 4MC circuit.

An instant later, a woman's voice: *"Flooding outside the wardroom!"*

The turbines died. The lights in Control dimmed. Control consoles went dark. *Portland*'s nuclear heart was going cold, and with it her eyes, her ears, her lungs. She was dying.

"Captain!" Browne shouted. "We got to get the water stopped before the batteries flood out!"

"I can see that." But instead of firing off the sequence of commands needed to restart the reactor, pump out the flooding forward spaces and save the boat, Vann kept staring at the blank sonar screen. There were flashing red warning lights, alarms going off, the fluorescent tubes from the overhead fixtures were in shards on the linoleum. He calmly raised his paper ice cup, tilted the last cube into his mouth.

"Blow the fucking ballast!" yelled Lieutenant Keefe.

"Captain!" Browne shouted again.

Lieutenant Keefe lurched in the direction of the ballast control panel. The deck tilted downhill and the weapons officer nearly slid through the door to the sonar room before clawing his way back up to the ballast board.

"Water now in the battery compartment!"

Keefe reached up to trigger the two red Chicken Switches, but Browne was faster. Keefe managed to pry up the covers and had his fingers on the latches when Browne grabbed him and pinned his arms, to his side.

"Son, you do that and we'll bounce off the ice hard enough to bust what ain't already broke." He shoved him away. Keefe bounced off the seats at the helm and caromed into the forward passage.

Steadman unfastened his belt and got up. Slice and Dice was still hanging on to the back of his seat. "Take over, Dive!"

"I can't! We'll die!"

Steadman threw him bodily into the seat. "Then die sitting down." He lurched to the center of Control next to Vann.

The 4MC squawked. *"Gas in the battery compartment!"*

The giant batteries were starting to fume poisonous chlorine.

"Commander!" Steadman shouted. "We've got to get people on EABs *now!*" Emergency air breathing masks.

Vann looked right through him.

Steadman knew they had to be close to the bottom. How long before they hit, before the damaged hull gave way? "Commander!"

There was no time for prudent diagnosis. No time to wonder about right moments. He opened his mouth, but Browne was faster.

"XO's got the conn!"

Steadman pushed Vann down into his small, sidesaddle seat. "COB, line up all forward drain pumps to the battery compartment and gang-start them *now!*"

"I'm on it." COB flooded an aft trim tank to try to take some of the down angle out of the boat, lining up the valves while talking calmly over his headset with damage control parties fore and aft.

"Damage control parties forward! Don EABs!" said Steadman. He turned to Browne. "Blow forward trim! *Level the boat!*"

Browne sent a *whoosh* of high-pressure air into a depth-control tank and hoped to hell he wasn't sending it overboard through a ruptured line. Use up all their air for nothing and you had no way to get rid of the water and no way to head back up.

Portland headed for the bottom more slowly. Another *whoosh* and she slowly came level.

Steadman didn't know where the words were coming from, but he knew they were the right ones. "Secure the collision alarm! Shut the main and auxiliary water intakes! Engineering Officer! Get that reactor back on-line *now!*"

The alarms fell silent for only a moment.

"Water's still rising in the battery compartment!"

Steadman had to work to calm his voice, to dial it way, way down. "COB, put some pressure in the hull to slow that leak."

"Aye aye."

"What are you doing, Steadman? Get back in your seat."

It was Vann.

"I have the conn, Captain. Go to your stateroom."

"Like hell. This is my bridge."

"No, sir. Not anymore. You stand relieved."

"That's mutiny." He looked around and fixed his gaze on Lieutenant Choper. "You and Steadman steered us into an ice keel."

"No!" said Slice and Dice. He looked to Steadman.

Ice keel? "Captain, if you don't clear out of Control *now*, I will have you removed."

"You'll hang, Steadman. You and anyone dumb enough to stand with you. I'll live to see it happen."

"Not if we don't get control of this boat." Steadman grabbed the intercom. "Corpsman to Control!"

Vann slowly stood up and nearly fell forward down the sloping deck, but COB was quicker. He steadied him by the shoulders. "Let's go. We'll get this all sorted out in your stateroom, skipper."

"Goddamned right, COB," said Vann. "You know the score."

"Yes, sir, I do." Browne looked at Steadman. "I'll go forward and see where the water's coming from. Permission to leave Control?"

"Go." Before COB led Vann away, Steadman reached out and snatched a folded slip of paper from his breast pocket.

Scavullo fought her way forward. A cold mist filled the dim passage, pricking her skin like wind-driven sleet. Somewhere ahead of her the ocean was rushing in and the sea temperature was well below the freezing point of fresh water.

Where was it coming from? The passage was lit only by fat white sparks cascading down from a damaged overhead cable. She came to the Goat Locker, the Ship's Office. In between was a bulkhead with a heavy circular hatch set low. She didn't know where that hatch went, but the ocean was right beyond it.

Needle-hard jets sprayed from around its perimeter. A pool a foot and a half deep sloshed across the deck. She was about to see if there was a way to clamp the hatch more tightly, when someone grabbed her shoulders and threw her back.

"Goin' wading with a bunch of sparking cables ain't smart. I don't need no Kentucky-fried lieutenants." Command Senior Chief Jerome Browne had arrived with pipe clamps in one hand and an EAB mask in the other.

"I was just . . ."

"Here." He handed her the EAB. "You get this on *now*. You don't touch anything, you don't do anything unless I say so. Got it?" He didn't wait for an answer before keying his radio. "Conn? This is Browne. I'm at the scene and I am in charge. The water's coming in through the sonar tunnel hatch. The cables goin' through the bulkhead are damaged. The whole bow must've shifted."

"You're loud and clear, COB. Reactor's back on-line and the engine answers bells. What do you need to get the flooding stopped?"

Good question. "Give me back some down angle. If the Tunnel's only part-way filled it might slosh to the bottom." Browne reached up to the cables and traced them with a knowing hand. He got a 450-volt tingle. "Conn? The main power feed to the sonar beam formers is grounding out. Kill everything to the sphere."

With a *clank*, the shower of sparks stopped.

"I'll crack the hatch," he told Scavullo. "You be . . ." Browne was about to say she would be his talker when he heard a shout.

Three men hurried in his direction. Even in EAB masks he knew them: two men from the auxiliary gang and Radioman Larry Engler.

COB Browne made a snap decision. Scavullo wasn't qualified in submarines. Engler wore the dolphins of a qualified submariner. "You two head for the battery compartment!" he told the A-Gangers. "Let the water reach the terminals and you won't have time to drown." He looked at Engler. "You're my talker." He handed the radio to him.

Scavullo had her mask on but some of her hair was caught between the rubber and her skin and she couldn't get a good seal. "What do you want me to do, COB?"

"Just make a hole," said Browne as he splashed over to the leaking hatch with Engler in tow.

The hatch was barely wide enough for a man's shoulders. Beyond it lay a thirty-six-foot tunnel that extended all the way into the sonar sphere in the bow. Or what was left of it.

Browne checked a pressure gauge mounted beside the hatch. "There's air on the other side."

Engler relayed the report.

"Sonar tunnel's only partly flooded. The hatch is shifted off its seat," said Browne. "Request permission to break rig for dive and open it!"

Engler said, "XO says go!"

COB pulled a locking pin, then clamped a wrench onto the center bolt. With a grunt, he spun it off. Only then could the strongback mechanism be swiveled open. Browne pushed the heavy door in against the pressure of the sea. An explosion of air and foam knocked him off his feet. But the flood subsided, ebbing, its force drained. "I'll be damned!" he said. There was a leak, but it might not be a fatal one. A drain line. A pressure fitting. It might be something small. Something a person who knew what he was doing could fix. He called back to Engler. "I'm goin' in!"

Browne didn't wait for the acknowledgment to be relayed. He climbed through the hatch headfirst and belly down. The Tunnel was frosty cold. Using grips set into the walls, he pulled himself forward, hand over hand, deeper into the darkness, closer to where water was rushing in. He had his emergency lantern. His clamps. His EAB was still tucked inside his suit. His hands knew every square inch of *Portland,* as though his veins were laid out in builder's blueprints.

If any man could fix what ailed this boat, COB was the one.

Baikal

"Captain?" said Grachev. "We've got rudder problems."

Markov hadn't had a chance to let go of the *kashtan* for so long now his hand was beginning to cramp. "What is it?"

"I cycled the rudder to be sure it worked," said the chief engineer. "It jammed at five degrees starboard. I've tried everything to free it. Maybe it's a control arm, maybe its something simple. I can't tell from in here. We'll need to surface and go take a look."

"There's no place to surface, Igor."

"You'll be steaming in circles until you find one."

"Can you rig something to work until we reach open water?"

"I already tried. You'll have to use the engines to turn, Captain. Forget the rudders."

Using differential power to the screws could make her turn but she'd have the handling qualities of a log. The open waters of the Arctic Basin were just four hours back, but they might as well be four thousand, for without a rudder *Baikal* would never reach them.

But in the other direction, thirty hours would bring them through the strait and out into the open waters of the Pacific, and to the escorts waiting to assist them. If Markov was willing to bet on a guess, a hope, that he could somehow maneuver through the obstacle on the southern shore of the basin. The wall that had already turned them back once.

North to the Arctic? South to the Pacific?

USS *Portland*

Browne could hear the hiss of water in the darkness of the sonar tunnel. He was two-thirds of the way to the sphere, directly under the launch tubes for *Portland*'s Tomahawk missile battery and above a ballast tank. The cold was in him and he trembled uncontrollably. He pointed his lamp ahead and inched forward. Then he saw it.

A cat's cradle of water jets, *sprayers* in submarine parlance, and Browne knew at once the battle to save the sonar sphere was lost. This was no broken drain line, no cracked fitting. The whole damned *Tunnel* had been shoved hard enough to break the welds that connected it to the sphere. They'd have to abandon the Tunnel to the sea, and jury-rig a repair at the hatch.

"Engler!" he yelled back over his shoulder. "It's no good! The sphere's loose! Tell the XO to bring up some welding gear to the hatch! You hear me?"

"Tell him to get out of there," said Steadman. Browne's report of the busted sphere only confirmed what he'd expected. But as more reports filtered in, Steadman found room for hope. There were burns in the galley, broken bones down in the auxiliary machine room, water in the battery bilge, concussions, a machinist who got a noseful of chlorine gas. Their problems were serious but *Portland* was no longer out of control.

"Conn, Torpedo Room. Water level is falling in the battery room."

"Stay on EABs until we scrub the chlorine!"

The next report came from the engineer of the watch. "Conn, Engineering. All reactor indications are normal. We're ready to answer bells."

"Stand by." Steadman wasn't about to move the boat anywhere until Browne was out of the sonar tunnel. One shake might be all that it took to break it open and flood it. He was about to find out whether Browne was out yet, but he remembered the slip of paper he'd pulled from Vann's pocket. He unfolded it and read.

Z00043Z9AUG2002
NLOB*NLOB*NLOB
FM: COMSUBLANT
TO: CO USS PORTLAND
INFO: COMSUBPAC, CINCPACFLT
SUBJ: SPECIAL OPERATIONS
SECRET

1: TYPHOON CLASS SSBN DETECTED CHUKCHI SEA VICINITY
   WRANGEL ISLAND BOUND BERING STRAIT
2: INTERCEPT AND ID SSBN AND REPORT IMMEDIATELY
3: DELAY OF SSBN TRANSIT BERING STRAIT CRITICAL
4: ALL MEANS REQD SUCCESSFUL CONCLUSION THIS
   ASSIGNMENT ARE AUTHORIZED AND BY GOD DEMANDED
5: THE SAFETY OF YOUR COMMAND IS SECONDARY. IF YOU
   HAVE TO RAM HIS SCREWS TO STOP HIM, DO IT
6: YOUR CLEAN SWEEP PREMATURE. STOP BLOWING SMOKE
   AND START PERFORMING . . . GRAYBAR SENDS

He folded it back and put it into his own pocket, then picked up the
portable radio. "Where's COB?"

"I see him, XO," said Engler. "He's almost out."

Browne pushed himself back up the slight incline. He was already aft of the
VLS tubes when he heard the *pop! pop! pop!* of bolt heads shearing, followed
by a powerful rumble. He stopped and aimed his light at the sound and saw
that the sprayers at the sonar sphere welds had become a solid curtain. *Well,
shit. You couldn't have waited another minute?* He shouted, "It's breaking up!"
He had to get out of this trap before a wall of water blew him out into the
hatch like a pea from a straw.

He shoved himself back. The water was coming in fast, rising as he
backed away from it. "Tell Conn to put on more down angle!"

There was no answer from Engler.

Browne was almost out. His boot struck the lip of the circular hatch. He
shifted his legs to where the opening should be, but it wasn't there. He
doubled himself over and put his lamp on it.

The hatch was shut.

He started kicking on it as a groan echoed through the Tunnel. He pointed his light back down.

A boiling mass of foam was coming for him.

Steadman heard the *wham!* of water blasting into a sealed space. It made the entire boat shudder. "Engler!"

"COB! Shit shit *shit!* It just let go!"

"Engler, calm down and put COB on."

"Oh *Jesus!* I can't! He's still in the Tunnel!"

CHAPTER TWENTY-SIX

JONAH

9 AUGUST

Baikal

Markov left Gasparyan in charge and went forward to Main Engineering. "Have you tried isolating the rudders?" There were two, upper and lower. "It could be that just one of them is jammed."

Grachev was in his customary blue chair, watching a gauge register pressure to the stern hydraulics. "I've tried everything except going out and giving them a kick. It's no good."

Markov lowered his voice. "We can't maneuver through ice without a rudder, Igor. And there's no place to surface."

"What about the spinners?" *Baikal* had two auxiliary electric thrusters, one in the bow, the other in the stern.

"They're for docking, not maneuvering," said Markov. It was what the book would say.

"You know," said Grachev, "he could be right about that fucking slot."

Markov was brought up short. "Who?"

"Fedorenko. Finding our way back will be a trick. But what's ahead? We don't really know. There might be open water on the other side."

"Or a blind alley."

"I'm only suggesting that when everything known looks black, something that's gray seems brighter."

"Without a rudder we could be trapped in there forever."

"Aren't we trapped now?"

Markov thought about the terrible sounds he'd heard from the American *Los Angeles*. Here, the lights burned, he was warm, the air was fresh. The engines answered his command. And still, Grachev was right. They were trapped.

"Look. You're the captain," said Grachev. "But we're a lot closer to

Petropavlovsk than Seal Bay. I say let's limp in, walk off the ship and let Fedorenko figure out how to get her to China."

And the way to Petropavlovsk lay through the slot. "All right. Get the spinners ready."

USS *Portland*

Steadman gave Whalley the conn and told him to keep *Portland* exactly as she was—heading, depth and deck angle—until he heard otherwise. He paused by the ship's control station and said to Slice and Dice, "Plus or minus one foot, one degree. COB's life is in your hands, Lieutenant."

"Sir, maybe someone else should be—"

"No excuses. Do it."

Steadman made his way down to the flooded decks. The passage was lit by emergency lighting. Water sloshed against the forward bulkhead. Engler stood beyond the edge of the pool. The hatch was sealed and the center bolt snugged tight.

"I couldn't do nothing," he pleaded. "COB was backing out and it just let go. Jesus. I could see his legs and then he yelled for me to close the hatch. I didn't want to, but . . ."

"You fought your impulse to save him and shut it?"

"What could I do?"

Before Steadman could ask anything more, Lieutenant Bill Hennig, *Portland*'s damage control assistant, came forward.

"Whatever you do, keep some down angle on the boat," said Hennig. "There's an air bubble in the sonar tunnel."

Hennig was the officer in charge of the Auxiliary Division, the A-Gang. He wore large glasses and affected a slicked-back hairstyle. His sideburns skated close to, and sometimes beyond, the regulations.

"Enough for COB to be alive?" asked Steadman.

"He's *gone,* dude," said Engler. "The ocean got him."

Steadman looked at Hennig. "You agree?"

"Not necessarily. But COB's got three problems. Air, cold and pressure. There's no way to get air to him without opening the hatch."

"And no way to open the hatch with water pressure keeping it shut."

Hennig nodded. "We'll have to surface and even then it'll have to be forced. And if you rise too fast . . ."

"COB dies of the bends. Even if we find a place to surface we'll lose the down angle and the Tunnel will flood."

Hennig nodded. "We'll have to crack the hatch in a hurry."

"How long does he have?"

"No more than an hour if he managed to stay dry. If not . . ."

"He's already dead," said Engler.

Steadman thought Engler was sounding altogether too hopeful. "How is it you were his talker, Engler?"

"Scavullo was here but COB ran her off and handed the radio to me."

Steadman found it hard to believe but he got a nod of confirmation from Hennig. "I want a written statement from you."

"I thought all that shit was over. The skipper dropped it."

"Your information is a little out of date," said Steadman. "I'm in command of *Portland* now."

"No shit?"

"No shit." He turned back to Hennig. "Get some of your men in here with heat guns. Have them warm that hatch up until it glows. Some of it might get through and do some good. We need to buy enough time to work out the other problems. What about the sonar sphere?"

"I sure wouldn't shoot any juice into a flooded sphere before I knew about COB."

Steadman was in a box. Without sonar he couldn't find his way out through the ice. But if COB was still alive in there, he *had* to find his way out before the cold killed him.

Steadman couldn't do it. The navigator couldn't, either. There was just one man aboard *Portland* who might have an answer, a way out. "Lieutenant," he said, "find out if there's any way we can pipe air into the Tunnel and let me know."

"You'll be in Control, sir?"

"No. The sonar shack."

Samuel Johnson once observed that serving aboard a warship offered a man all the amenities of prison, with the added possibility of drowning. A submarine expanded on this short list considerably.

Browne's thoughts were less profound and more focused on the sealed hatch. There had to be fifty pounds per square inch holding it shut. How many square inches in a hatch? Too many to fight.

He was in an air pocket barely larger than his body. When he reached down into the absolute blackness below, he could feel roiling, frigid water, not rising, not receding.

The pressure pulse that slammed up the Tunnel was powerful enough to tear his flashlight from his hands. When he opened his eyes there was nothing at all to see, no way to even know they were open at all. He knew he was alive by the throb of his heart, by the clammy fog that blew against his cheek with each breath, and the burning cold water lapping at his legs.

The cold, the carbon dioxide in the air bubble he'd retreated to, the pressure of the surrounding sea. They were all in a kind of a race to see which one would kill him first. He'd heard them knocking on the hatch, and he'd tried to answer by pounding his fist on the tunnel walls, but he might as well have been banging against a vault.

There was enough air in the bubble for a few hours of calm breathing. The water pressure at this depth was considerable, but it would kill him only if the boat rose too fast, which, given the ice overhead, was unlikely as long as Steadman kept folks away from the Chicken Switches.

But the water inside the tunnel was barely twenty-nine degrees. It stung like live steam at first, but now his skin was numb. Soon, the rest of him would be, too. His thinking would slow, then stop; he'd close his eyes and never wake up.

"No fucking way," he said out loud.

He doubled up, trying to find another inch here, a quarter inch there, to turn around inside the Tunnel. He felt a jabbing pain in his hip, and realized what it was: a pipe clamp. He calmed himself, slowed his breathing, got an arm free and contorted it around until he got his fingertips on it. They brushed, threatened to push the clamp away, and then he had it.

He ripped it from his belt, put his hand through the steel clamp, made a fist and slammed it against the hatch.

"Where is that Typhoon now?" Steadman asked Schramm.

With the electrical system still shut down, only the emergency lights burned in the sonar room. Still, they were much brighter than the usual dim blue lamps. Schramm's screen was blank.

"Last look I got before the power went out he was just sittin' out there about five hundred yards to the east."

"What do we have that's still working?"

"The bow sphere is toast. Figure on the flank arrays, the under-ice gear up in the sail and probably the tail."

None of them is good enough to steer by. "Bam Bam, we need to find a place to surface. There's a chance COB is alive inside the sonar tunnel but we can't crack the hatch with water pressure fighting us. Can you find me a hole with what you have?"

"We could try cruising around. We might get lucky and find a thin spot to bust through."

"We don't have time for luck."

"You sure he's still alive?"

The speaker buzzed, then, "Sonar, this is Damage Control."

Steadman picked up the sound-powered intercom microphone. "Steadman here."

"Sir, I've talked this over with my leading chief," said Hennig. "We may have something. There are two fittings into the sphere I didn't know about. A drain line and a pressure line. The drain won't do much for us if the sphere is open to the ocean, but we can bubble in some air through the pressure line. It might find its way up into the tunnel if the angle is right."

"All right. Start blowing air in. Make COB's bubble as big as you can." Steadman dreaded having to ask the next question. "Still nothing from the other side?"

"We've been making a lot of noise here with the cutting saw."

"How about the heat guns?"

"They're warming the hatch up now."

Air and heat. "Let me know if you hear anything." He clicked off, then said, "Engineering. Reconnect the forward vital circuit."

"Aye aye, Mister Steadman."

The emergency lights blinked, went off and with a buzz were replaced by the soft blues. Schramm's sonar display flickered, went blank, then started going through a self-test menu. Finally, the sounds of the surrounding sea began to show up on the screen.

"There he is," he said, pointing to a cluster of lines off the port side. "That's his fifty-hertz line. He's got his lights burning, but there's no flow, no plant signature. He's just sitting dead in the water." Schramm looked up. "Maybe he's got problems, too."

For the first time and for a reason he would never have been able to anticipate, Steadman thought, *I hope not.* That Typhoon was *Portland*'s, and Browne's, only way out.

Baikal

"Both spinners are ready," said Grachev.

Markov glanced at his sonar operator. "Belikov?"

"The American submarine is still out there. His engine is stopped but I'm still picking up the sound of escaping air."

Was everyone on her dead? Dying? Sealed up in a few pockets of air as the water rose inexorably? "We might as well use our active sonar."

Belikov flipped a plastic cover away from the broad, red button that would trigger an active ping, and pushed.

A high, crystalline *PING!* blasted out from *Baikal*'s bow.

USS *Portland*

"Whoa!" said Schramm. His octagonal display had just lit up. "Active ping and lots of horsepower behind it!"

"Is he ranging us?" asked Steadman. He wouldn't put it by the Russian skipper to be dialing them in for a torpedo shot.

"I don't hear any flooding tubes. Just that one big old ping." Schramm watched the echoes reverberate off the nearby ice. "I'm gettin' a good picture of that ridge, though. And the basin on the far side, too." He looked back. "You think we could ask him to keep that up for a while?"

"I wish."

"Look," said Schramm. The sonar display was changing. New lines blossomed. A thicket of them. "He's moving."

"North?"

"Stand by." Schramm watched the play of light on his waterfall, the shift of lines degree by degree, then said, "No, sir. He's heading south!"

"Don't lose him!" he yelled, and he lunged for the door leading back to the control room.

Baikal

Baikal's engines surged, her great screws thrashed the water, and the ship began to move ahead.

"Bow spinner is running at fifty percent," said Grachev.

The effect of the jammed rudder was instantly apparent; it was like trying to steer a car straight with the wheels turned.

"Four knots," said Gasparyan. "Course is one six five and holding." He stared at the directional gyro mounted at the helm for the first sign of drift. It wasn't long coming.

"Five knots and one six eight."

"Igor," Markov said into his *kashtan,* "increase thrust on the bow spinner."

Grachev spun a knob to increase the turns on the electric docking motor in the hull. "Eighty percent." There were limits to what such a small device could do, and he sensed they were very close to them. "These motors aren't designed for this."

"I need more from the spinner, Igor."

"One hundred percent. You've got everything, Captain."

"Heading is coming back to one six eight."

It was an equation of forces, and Markov had just discovered that by running his bow spinner for all it was worth he could make seven knots straight ahead. But for how long? "Another ping."

The high, ringing tone sounded again.

"We're approaching the ice ridge," said Belikov.

"Make your depth eighty meters."

Baikal planed down beneath the deep ridge and into the clearer waters of the ice-locked basin.

"Borodin," Markov said to the navigator, "can you find that slot again?"

USS *Portland*

Browne had made all the noise he could. Nothing had happened, and he'd just heard a sonar ping coming through the hull. There was no question about what that meant: there was another boat out there, and likely not a friendly one. *Portland* had to move, and when she did, his bubble was going to move, too. When it did, he would die. The only question was whether the XO would worry about poor old COB and not do what he had to do. If that was a ranging ping, a torpedo would soon be headed their way.

He took hold of the steel clamp. Saving the boat was what mattered now. He and Steadman were friends, but now Steadman had to forget all that. He had to be *cold.* Even if it meant filling Browne's tunnel full of ocean. There were a hundred and twenty other men who might be saved. And one woman. Now why in *hell* didn't he leave her as his talker? *Too late.*

He reached out and started pounding on the hatch.

Clang!

He smashed the clamp against the hatch again.

Clang!

A frantic pounding came from the other side of the hatch.

Browne started tapping out a simple message in Morse code.

MOVE . . . THE . . . BOAT

There was a pause. He was about to begin rapping out the message again, when he heard a far-off rumble: the sound of ballast being shifted.

They'd heard him!

A second rumble, and the uphill slant of the tunnel began to sag. Almost at once, the water rose up to his knees.

His bubble was dying.

Browne heard the sound of the distant screw beginning to turn, felt the vibration through the hull.

He wasn't going to make it, but *Portland* had a shot at surviving. Browne had sold everything he had left to buy that final shot, and knowing it put a smile on his face.

The water was at his waist now. He felt something moving around his legs and lower body. He reached down.

Bubbles?

They're pumping in air!

Then he felt something even stranger on the back of his neck. He couldn't be sure. He wouldn't allow himself the folly of misplaced hope. But it sure did feel a lot like *heat*.

CHAPTER TWENTY-SEVEN

THE SLOT

10 AUGUST

Baikal

"There it is," said Belikov.

A solid wall marched from left to right across the sonar display. It was the same deep-keeled ridge of ice they'd found earlier in the day.

"Another ping, Belikov," said Markov.

Belikov pressed the broad red button and sent another sharp ping at the wall. It bounced back and the bright spokes glowed even brighter.

"Igor, train the spinners fore and aft. Twenty percent power."

"Understood, Captain." Grachev turned the azimuth wheels for both thrusters, tilting them against the locked rudder so that *Baikal* could move more or less straight ahead. He doubted they'd work much longer. Then what?

Gasparyan stood behind the two men at the helm watching the heading indicator. "Making two knots on thruster power."

All forty thousand tons of *Baikal* was being pushed through the water by the meager power of a 750-kilowatt motor.

"Captain, I have the slot."

Markov leaned over Belikov's shoulder.

There, off the port bow, the bottom of the wall was starting to look less solid.

"Maximum power to both thrusters."

USS *Portland*

"Conn, Sonar. Sierra Five is moving again."

"Where?" asked Steadman.

"Right at that ice keel."

"He'll have to squeeze under it," said Whalley from the chart plot.

"If there's room for him there's room for us," said Steadman. "Ahead one-third."

Tripod was sitting in his customary chair near Scavullo's rack when he heard the sound of running feet and looked up.

Larry Engler and four of his fellow Alley Rats were running down the passage, heading for the forward ladder.

"What's goin' on?" he asked. Then Bedford saw the Beretta M-9 automatic in Engler's hand. "Where did you get *that* thing?"

"The small arms locker, asshole." Engler stuck the Beretta into his waist and climbed up and out of sight.

Scavullo pulled her curtain open and swung out of her bunk.

"He's got a fucking gun!" said Tripod.

"Follow me," she said.

Baikal

"Gasparyan?"

"Heading is steady on one six one degrees. Speed two knots."

"Belikov go to continuous pinging."

Ping! . . . Ping! . . . Ping! . . . Ping! . . . Ping!

"Range one kilometer," said Belikov. The fuzzy zone at the base of the solid wall of ice was now an irregular crevice.

"Captain," said Grachev, "the bow thruster is running hot. The RPMs are starting to drop."

"We're almost there."

"Range to the ice now five hundred meters."

"Captain, we're losing the bow thruster."

"Secure it, Igor. Helm," said Markov, "all ahead flank."

Gasparyan swung and stared. "What?"

"All ahead flank!"

USS *Portland*

"Conn, Sonar. Sierra Five just stepped on the gas!"

"Range and bearing?"

"Three thousand yards off the port bow. Watch that ice keel, it's a deep mother. You want me to turn the BQS-15 loose on it and see just how big it is?"

"No. I don't want him to hear us in his baffles. Helm, five degrees left rudder. Stay with him, people."

"Commander Steadman!"

He turned aft and saw Scavullo and Bedford in the portside. "Not now, Lieutenant."

"Sir . . ." she persisted, but Steadman snapped, *"Not now!"* He had to stay with that Typhoon. It was the only way through the ice. It was COB's last chance.

The lines on Schramm's display abruptly vanished. *Oh shit.* The helpful Russian pings were no longer bouncing off the ice, leaving *Portland* running straight at a wall he couldn't see. "Conn, Sonar! Contact lost!"

"Okay, Bam Bam. He's through the ridge. Diving Officer! Don't you gain or lose *one foot.* Maintain your heading *exactly.*"

Slice and Dice only nodded. He was staring hard at the gauge as *Portland* swam straight at an invisible wall of ice.

Baikal

"We're through!" Belikov shouted.

"Still turning to port," said Gasparyan. "Speed is twelve knots."

A silence fell over the officers in Central Command as the ship slipped between the ice above and the mud below.

Ping! . . . Ping! . . . Ping!

"Thirteen knots."

There was a shudder that seemed to rise up from the very decks. The shudder grew into a series of sideways jabs and lurches. They were on the edge of the dead zone—the range of speeds where a Typhoon's rudder became ineffective.

Markov remembered the captain who'd discovered the dead zone by steaming into Kola Bay at just the wrong speed and drove straight onto the beach with his rudder hard over, useless.

"Fourteen knots."

The vibration came from swift-flowing water streaming across the hull and alternately striking the rudder and flowing around it.

"Heading is . . . stabilized!" Gasparyan sounded shocked.

"Watch your speed!" Markov shouted.

Too fast and the flow would reattach itself and the rudder would become a problem again.

"Belikov! What does it look like out ahead?"

The sonar operator looked at the circular display, manipulated the controls to see if his first impressions were trustworthy. "Stand by." He hadn't seen a screen like this since they'd ducked beneath the marginal ice back by Franz Josef Land. Finally, he turned to Markov. "Only fast ice."

"No ridges? No deep bergs?"

Belikov shook his head. "None."

"There's deep water off Cape Schmidt," said Borodin. "Sixty meters and better."

After the slot, sixty meters of water sounded like the open ocean.

USS *Portland*

"Conn, Sonar, Sierra Five is pulling away from us at fourteen knots."

"Can you tell me what we've got overhead?" asked Steadman.

"About twenty feet of ice."

"Commander," Scavullo broke in, "I need a word with you."

Steadman said, "In a minute, Lieutenant."

"God*damn*it, Commander. Engler broke into the small-arms cabinet and he's in talking to Vann right now."

Steadman turned. "What?"

"I saw him with a handgun. He was headed to the captain's cabin and—"

"Conn, Sonar! Ice is down to twelve feet."

Steadman snatched the intercom and dialed the Goat Locker. "Hennig?"

"Aye aye, Commander."

"Get ready to crack that hatch. Try not to damage it but use whatever force you have to. We're going to surface."

"You got it, XO."

"Ice is now six feet."

Steadman hung up the microphone. "Retract the bow planes."

"Conn, Sonar, ice is now two and a half feet!"

"Blow ballast!" Steadman switched to the 1MC and said, "Surface, surface, surface."

"Belay that order!"

Steadman swung around and saw Lieutenant Bledsoe lead Vann through the forward portside passage. Vann was supported between two enlisted men from Rat Alley. Vann looked woozy from sedative. Engler stood behind them all.

"Clear out, Steadman," said Lieutenant Bledsoe.

"No way," said Steadman. "We're surfacing."

"I'm warning you, XO. I have the conn!" Bledsoe said firmly. He turned to Vann. "Right, sir?"

"I designate . . . I designate . . . Bledsoe," Vann slurred.

"No, *sir.*" said Steadman. "You are on the sick list and no longer the commanding officer of this boat. All of you," he said, "off this bridge *now.*" Steadman said to the chief at the dive board, "Blow ballast. Surface this goddamned boat."

Engler eased from behind Vann. "I told you he'd need convincing." He handed the Beretta to Bledsoe.

Bledsoe pointed the M-9 at Steadman's chest. "You're under arrest for mutiny, XO."

No one was watching Scavullo.

She leaped to the ballast control board. Bledsoe's mouth was just opening as she reached up, grabbed both Chicken Switches and pulled the red handles down.

With a deafening *whoosh, Portland*'s ballast tanks were blown dry by a hurricane of compressed air. Seven thousand tons of submarine began to rise.

Browne heard the bow planes retract, heard the blow begin. It kept going on and on like an endless roll of thunder, and he knew that too much of a very good thing was not a good thing at all. The bow was rising fast, and he had the presence of mind to take two huge breaths before the air bubble that had kept him alive sloshed up the tilting tunnel and a wave of solid water came crashing down on him.

He grabbed onto something and held on like a limpet gripping a rock. He felt the grip of the sea begin to diminish as *Portland* rocketed toward the surface. His lungs were inflating like balloons, pressing hard against his ribs, trying to bust out through his chest and up his throat. Despite every impulse that screamed for him to hang onto every particle, every bubble of air inside him, he started letting it trickle out between his tightly clenched lips.

He felt a sharp pain in his chest and let out an explosion of trapped air. They were rising fast, maybe too fast for him to keep up with. And if he let out all his air now, when they did surface they would still have to . . .

There was a sudden *crash!* from somewhere forward as *Portland* struck the ice and burst through. Browne was caught in a black, invisible maelstrom. Water and foam surged one way, then another, slamming him against the tunnel walls, tearing at him, trying to dislodge his grip. He held on, letting air out of his lungs, hoping that whoever was on the other side of that steel was ready for him, because he figured they had a minute, maybe two, to get that hatch open.

It was a demolition–derby version of musical chairs. Anyone in Control without something to hang on to was not going to find one as the boat seemed to tumble end for end. The two enlisted men holding Vann had let go of him as the deck reared up. Now they were hanging on to the bulkhead beside the helm. Vann had collapsed and rolled right to Steadman's feet, and he would have kept going but Steadman knelt down and grabbed his wrist with one hand while holding onto his own seat with the other.

Bledsoe skated down the deck, bounced off the periscopes and caromed onto the chart tables right under the terrified gaze of the navigator. Whalley was looking for that Beretta, but the M-9 was skittering across the linoleum first aft, then forward, then port, then starboard, bouncing off people and machinery. Engler watched that gun, gauging its movements, waiting, waiting.

Scavullo saw the M-9 head her way and dived for it, but Engler was quicker.

He jumped, reached under her and tried to pry the weapon away, clawing at her hands. They both ended up beneath Lieutenant Choper's legs. Engler had the Beretta's barrel and Scavullo its handle. They were joined by the M-9, and neither one would let go.

She tried to slip her finger through the trigger guard and gave Engler the opening he was waiting for.

He gave the barrel a savage twist that broke Scavullo's finger with a *snap!* He yanked the weapon away as she rolled to the deck.

When she looked up, the automatic was pointed at her head. She scrambled to her knees, oblivious to the strange angle of her finger, to the pain. To everything but Engler.

Choper pulled an emergency lantern from the bulkhead and tried to swing it but Engler batted it away.

She didn't think. She didn't evaluate. The scream of pure rage that erupted from her lungs was no martial-arts stratagem. She was on her feet as the gun wavered back in her direction. Before Engler could react, she reared back and drove the toe of her shoe so far up into Engler's groin she could feel his spine.

Engler flew back against the chief at the ballast control panel, unable to do anything but register the nauseating waves boiling up from his testicles.

The chief at the BCP was a close friend of COB Browne. He plucked the lightweight pistol from Engler's faltering grip, picked up his much heavier coffee mug and smashed it against the radioman's temple.

Engler went down like a gaffed fish.

The chief held the Beretta out to Steadman. "Here ya go, skipper," he said. "I believe this belongs to you."

The boat was surfaced, but there was still thirty feet of water inside pushing against the sonar tunnel hatch. Two of Hennig's team of A-gangers knelt beside it, waiting for the order.

"Now," said Hennig.

They didn't waste a second trying to open it by hand. They spun the lock nut out, released the strongback, then slammed the end of a collapsible jack against the hatch and started cranking so fast their arms were blurs. The jack handle clicked madly as they ratcheted it out.

"Get ready," said Hennig. He got on the intercom to Control and warned them to get the bilge pumps switched on. He didn't get an answer.

The jack grew longer, pressing against the big flat bolt head at the center of the hatch.

Click! Click! Click! Click!

Fifteen cranks. Twenty. Thirty.

The hatch hadn't budged. But Hennig heard the bilge pumps come on under his feet. *Someone was listening.*

Click! . . . Click! . . . Click! . . . Click!

"More," said Hennig.

The aft end of the jack was resting on a steel frame. The frame was bending. The hatch hadn't budged.

Click! . . . Click!

Now it took both men on the jack handle to move it at all.

Click! . . . Click!

Another.

Click.

The steel frame was going to break.

Hennig joined them and put his weight behind the handle. All three of them managed to force it slowly to the deck.

Click.

"It's not . . ."

The hatch let go with the sound of a shotgun shell going off at very close quarters. A cylinder of foam and sea erupted out of the hatch and sent all three men tumbling. With the pressure off, the hatch door slammed open and the jack flew up into the Tunnel. They could hear it rattling as it headed for the sonar sphere.

The torrent of icy water subsided to a river, a stream, a trickle.

Hennig was first to his feet. He ran to the hatch and pointed a lantern down its black bore. It was empty.

"You see him?" asked one of the A-gangers.

"No!" said Hennig. "He must have gotten swept down into the sphere!" He stuck his head into the tunnel and yelled, "COB!"

"Oh, shit," said one of the aux men. "He's *gone.*"

"No, he ain't."

Hennig turned.

Browne had ridden the gusher right out of the Tunnel. He'd landed soaked, shivering but happy, on the deck.

Engler's Rat Alley friends had vanished. They would have to be found and dealt with but Steadman had more pressing concerns. He grabbed the 1MC and said, "IDC to Control! IDC to Control!" He hesitated, dreading having to ask the next question. He dreaded the answer even more. He clicked the intercom to the Goat Locker and said, "Hennig? Did you get COB?"

There was no reply from the damage-control party.

Vann roused himself from the deck, tried to stand at his accustomed place. He was spattered with sharp fragments of coffee mug. "What have you done?"

Steadman tried to read Vann's expression. He looked like an old man who'd taken a step off a curb and found himself on the street. "Captain, I know about the arrangement you had with Bledsoe and Engler."

"What on earth are you talking about?"

"You forced Lieutenant Scavullo to sign a statement you knew to be false, and threatened her with Engler if she refused."

"That's an outrageous lie."

"No, it isn't. It's all on tape, sir. Every word you spoke when you thought you were alone in the radio shack."

"You *bugged* me?"

"Yes, sir, I did. It's over now. For you, for Bledsoe. For Engler, too. The honorable thing for you to do is help establish the truth."

"He's bluffing!" Bledsoe burst out. "It's his word against yours!"

"No, it ain't."

The chief of the boat strode in through the forward door leading to the sonar room. Schramm was with him, as well as Hennig and his two A-Gangers. Browne had two pairs of handcuffs. "It's my word, too. Captain," he said to Vann, "I dived that sonar tunnel. Engler thought he locked me in and let the ocean swallow me up like Jonah. Well, Brother Jonah came back, and so did I."

"COB, you don't believe I had a hand in any of this!"

"Captain, you failed us back on *Baton Rouge,* and God help me, I let you get away with it. I ain't gonna make that mistake again."

Vann's mouth was working but no words escaped.

The corpsman hustled into Control.

"Lieutenant Scavullo injured her hand," said Steadman. "See to it, Chief. When you're done, help Commander Vann back to his stateroom."

"Aye aye, sir."

Steadman turned to the chart plot where Bledsoe was standing. "Mister Bledsoe, you're under arrest. Lieutenant Hennig? Secure him to something solid."

"Yes, sir." He advanced on Bledsoe with a pair of cuffs and with the help of both A-Gangers, clapped them on. The lieutenant stayed behind as they led him out into the aft passage.

Engler stirred.

Browne walked over to him and rolled him onto his back. He leaned over and stared into those pale eyes until they started seeing. Browne pinned him to the linoleum. "A shit screen like you can have too many options for his own good." He put his face so close to Engler's that an icy droplet fell on the radioman's forehead. He slipped the other pair of cuffs over Engler's wrists, snapped them shut. "I'm gonna limit them."

Chief Cooper had Scavullo's finger wrapped in a splint. He snipped off the end of the wrapping and bound it tightly.

"What now, skipper?" asked Whalley.

Steadman thought of the orders in his pocket. He and Engler were in the same predicament. They'd both run out of options.

TWENTY-EIGHT

BUSTAFISH

IO AUGUST

OM-142
Chukchi Sea

The fish spotter up in the tower tossed the empty bottle overboard, then yelled, "Throw up another!"

"Find us a whale. Then you can ask."

The captain of the whaler *OM-142* unscrewed a fresh bottle of something dangerously close to pure alcohol. He'd been a fisherman all his life, though this was only *OM-142*'s third trip up north, and whales, scientifically speaking, weren't fish. He took a long swig and felt the familiar, delicious burning down his throat.

It was a perfectly calm morning on the Chukchi Sea off Cape Schmidt, with hardly a ripple of wind or wave. The ocean was thick with brash ice. The dark line of the Siberian coast skimmed the southern horizon. The sea looked more like a vast lake in spring, just after ice break.

The spotter leaned down from his perch atop the high, spindly tower. "I don't see any whales."

"Look harder. We're done for if we don't bring at least one back."

Once, *OM-142* had been a scientific survey ship. He'd transformed her into something less academic but more useful. Gone were the beds, the washbasins, the bookshelves. He stripped out all the fancy interior fittings and swapped them for fishing gear, extra fuel tanks, an overhauled diesel. A welder walked away with the carved wooden bar from the galley and in exchange constructed a tower atop her wheelhouse from which spotters kept watch for the telltale plume of broaching whales.

They'd motor up to the creature and dispatch it with a rocket-propelled grenade to the head. It was a messy way to catch a whale, but very efficient. Death was instantaneous and the explosion filled the carcass with air. The buoyant whale, a bit worse for wear, would get lashed to the side and off they'd go to find another. When *OM-142* was flanked by a pair of bloody corpses, she'd turn around for Provideniya and sell the meat to the cannery, which, in turn, would ship it overseas to Japan.

"Come on. My eyeballs are falling out."

The captain took another drink. One whale paid the costs of food, fuel and a bit of folding money for the two men who sailed with him. The second whale was profit. No whales meant selling the boat to someone as foolish as he'd once been.

He let his eyes relax, become unfocused, as he gazed across the dark blue water, the white ice, the distant undulating line of land. It really did resemble Lake Baikal in springtime. He'd been born on its shores. Why had he been so anxious to leave? What was so much better *here*?

He was about to take another swig when he recalled the quaint ceremony the native Buryat fishermen of Baikal used to bring the fish up. They had a god of waters named Burkhan, and they'd make a sacrifice to him. Before they took so much as a single sip, they'd pour some onto their fingers and sprinkle it over the side, saying, *For Burkhan.*

It was likely a waste of good vodka. But nothing else seemed to be working. Should he wish for a fat bowhead, or a train ticket home to Baikal?

I wish for Baikal. He splashed some alcohol on his fingers, leaned over *OM-142*'s low gunwales and let the icy crystal drops fall to the surface of the sea. *"For Burkhan."*

Nothing changed. There was hardly a sound. Just the slap of water against the steel hull, the creak of the spotter tower, the . . .

"Hey!" said the spotter, pointing. *"Whale!"*

He stood up and looked in the direction of the spotter's outstretched arm.

The water was roiling just fifty meters away. Like a school of little fish racing around trying to escape bigger ones. The surface seemed to be heaped up, convex. Then, a white steamy jet of vapor erupted from the disturbed spot, and behind it, a dark fluke cut the surface of the sea. *Those Buryats were on to something!*

He ran to the little bridge and jabbed the start button, and the cutter's engine grumbled to life. He swung the wheel hard over.

The convex sea was now twice the size it had been just a few seconds before, and the dark fluke towered. He urged the boat in its direction, not wanting to let the whale sound.

"Look out!"

The captain looked through the grimy, salt-streaked glass of the wheel-house and said, "Mother of God."

A second towering spout blasted skyward. A third. A fourth. How many whales were out there, anyway? A pod?

The dark fluke loomed over *OM-142*. Black as midnight, taller, taller. Water pounded down on the wheelhouse roof from those titanic spouts. He spun the wheel to avoid it but something unseen, something powerful, grabbed the boat and heeled it over.

A sudden, freak wave boiled over his gunwales. The air was full of mist. The spotter was hanging on to the rails and screaming for him to do something but the boat was in the grip of a force beyond anything he might do to reverse.

He was thrown to the deck and when he scrambled back to his feet he saw a great black beast rising from the sea like an island, hissing jets of mist, white water rumbling off its flanks.

A steep, curling wave caught *OM-142* and she rode it like a bathtub toy, higher, higher. To his right, the fin. To his left, a bulbous black bow. And in between, a great black rectangle with a single word emblazoned on its battered front: *Baikal.*

The captain had asked Burkhan to help him find a way back home to Baikal, and Burkhan had delivered in spades.

He'd brought *Baikal* to him.

Baikal

"There was nothing on sonar," said Belikov. "He must have been drifting with his engines off."

The growl of the fishing boat's diesel could be heard through the hull. Markov pulled down a *kashtan.* "Igor, we need a repair party to go up and look at that rudder."

"I'll go."

Markov was about to say, *No, I'm keeping you below this time,* but instead he said, "We'll both go. And Demyan, too. And you'll wear a float vest."

"Pah."

"You wouldn't object if I joined you?" said Fedorenko.

"Let no one say we denied you a thing," said Markov, which earned him a dirty look from the chief engineer. Then Grachev made a little pushing motion, followed by a cocked head, a raised eyebrow.

Markov shook his head no.

Grachev and Demyan followed Markov up the ladder from Central Command to the elevated "Balcony." Fedorenko followed behind. There, Grachev cracked open the pressure-tight hatch to one of the emergency escape chambers and retrieved an armful of orange flotation vests.

There were two escape capsules built into the base of *Baikal*'s tall sail. Theoretically, in a disaster all one hundred and fifty members of her crew could fit inside them and blast to the surface safe and sound. But history taught that any accident bad enough to put a ship on the bottom would kill its crew long before they had a chance to use them.

Grachev distributed the vests. He even put one on. All four men climbed a second ladder to the inner hatch, and through it to the final hatch set in the O1 deck at the base of the sail.

Despite the brilliant day outside, the interior was dark, gloomy, filled with the echoing splashes and seeps of a deep, wet cave. Markov hadn't had much of a chance to look around the last time he was up here. The bent frames, the dented plates, the way the entire upper lip of the sail had been shoved back, all gave stunning, visual weight to the bet he'd placed back under the ice: that *Baikal* would not survive a brace of torpedoes, but she could hit the ice head on and come out alive.

Grachev went forward.

"The rudder is the other way," Fedorenko said acidly.

"Go back and see if you can find it," said the chief engineer. With that he cracked open the hatch in the sail and carefully stepped out onto the broad, flat expanse of the missile deck. Markov was right behind.

The sky was almost blindingly bright for eyes accustomed to a submarine's steady, even light. Markov spotted the fishing boat hurrying south at maximum speed. She cut a bright white wake, her bow planing across a flat sea the color of slate. To the north, the sea turned gray, the sky misty. *Ice,* he thought. They were out of the worst of it.

Grachev went forward along the centerline, walking between ten rows of interlocking muzzle hatches, looking for signs of the collision. Surprisingly, there was none until he'd made a football-field-long stroll, nearly a hundred meters. There, on the port side just aft of the slot into which the bow planes retracted, bright streaks of gouged steel gleamed like veins of silver from a hillside of black coal. The black rubber skin was peeled back in great sheets, and the hull below was dished in.

Grachev leaned over the side. "We ran the bastard over."

"Careful," said Markov. "Could he have survived?"

"He hit us hard enough to shove our outer hull against the inner. That took force." Grachev looked up. "American submarines have just one hull. Crack it and there's nothing to keep the ocean out. No. We don't have to worry about him again."

Markov stared down the curve of the hull to where the water rose, fell, rose and fell. "He could have been useful."

"The American? How?"

Markov didn't elaborate. He started back aft with a puzzled Grachev falling in behind him.

They retraced their steps to the sail, then worked carefully around it, keeping close to its vertical wall.

"There should be handholds along here," Grachev grumbled.

"They can weld them on in Petropavlovsk."

"You've decided to put in?"

"Why shouldn't we head for the nearest friendly naval base?"

"Those Chinese ships are between us and that naval base, Captain. They think we're going to Shanghai."

"Fedorenko can explain it to them."

Grachev paused, then, "So do you want that rudder or not?"

"Why?"

"You're cooking something up. I can see it."

"Let's go take a look at that rudder," Markov answered, or more accurately, did not.

USS *Portland*

Portland's hull steamed at the epicenter of a chaotic field of black water and shattered pack ice. Her violent surfacing had thrown plates of it fifty feet from the open water. They lay jumbled in heaps like wrack left by a tidal wave. White on top, gray in the middle, their bottoms an almost Caribbean blue.

"Well, I've seen worse, but only in pictures," said Browne. He and Steadman were standing atop the rounded hull, just aft of the vertical launch system tubes. "And those pictures were all taken in dry dock."

Portland's bow had absorbed most of the force. Looking forward, they could see that the twelve hinged lids to the Tomahawk tubes were intact, but everything beyond them was crumpled and bent. A large, jagged piece of the hull was simply missing.

Browne eased his way forward. He motioned for Steadman to join him.

They were on top of the steel sonar dome now, or what was left of it, and there, through a jagged rip in its skin, the hydrophones studding the sonar sphere could be seen. The baffling installed to keep it from being swamped with *Portland*'s own sounds floated in shards inside the dome. The sphere had been pushed down until it nearly touched the hull.

"This tub's gonna be on blocks so long they'll have to rechristen her the USS *Bustafish*," said Browne.

They stared down into the shadowed dome.

Steadman thought of Vann, down in his stateroom, sedated to the eyeballs. Engler and Bledsoe cuffed to matching torpedo racks. A broken crew, a broken submarine. "Can we sail?"

"Only to Pearl or Japan. They're both about three thousand miles away. Me, I'd break out the leis."

"You think the boat will hold together long enough to make Pearl Harbor?"

"If we take it slow and don't hit anything else. Six knots on the surface if it's calm, ten at shallow depth. But any way you cut the cake that's still the better part of a two-week run."

Steadman looked up. "If we can make ten knots submerged, then we can't head for Pearl. The flash message Vann was reading when he froze up? It was from COMSUBLANT. Some Chinese ships are waiting for that Typhoon down in the Anadyr Gulf. We're to stop him before he gets that far."

"Stop him how, exactly?"

It was the same question Steadman had asked Vann. It seemed a lifetime ago. "However we can. Admiral Graybar said the safety of the boat is not an issue."

"Hold on. You asked if we could *sail* this boat. Not *fight* her."

"If Bam Bam can find him and track him, if you say the boat will hang together, then I don't have a choice. We fight her."

Baikal

When Grachev had tried breaking the rudder jam by swinging it hard over, there'd been a fifty-fifty chance of success. He would either force it out, or draw it deeper. There was no way to know from inside, and in the end, he'd made the wrong bet.

The long strip of steel plate torn from *Portland*'s hide was caught between the movable rudder and the tall, vertical fin. Grachev, Markov and Fedorenko stood near the crater left by the Beast Buoy. Both screws were mostly underwater, but the tops of their protective shrouds were not.

"It looks like a piece of hull," said Grachev. "It's going to take more than tweezers to pull it out." Grachev eased down the short slope to the waterline, then stepped nimbly up onto the shroud without even getting the soles of his boots damp.

"Next you and your engineer will tell me there's no way to fix it," said Fedorenko. "That you're both disappointed, but we're stuck here until angels come down and carry us to Shanghai on their wings."

"On the contrary. We can get underway for the Anadyr Gulf at once," said Markov.

Fedorenko eyed him suspiciously. "How?"

"*Baikal* has two rudders. The upper one you can see and a second below the waterline you cannot. They're meant to move together but they have independent hydraulics. Unlink the two and the bottom rudder will answer the helm with the top one still jammed. It wouldn't work submerged, but we could sail around the world on the surface."

Fedorenko might be unsure where Markov was leading him, but he was certain it was not a place he wished to go. "We can't sail through Bering Strait like some cruise ship."

"Well, we can always wait here for help."

"You know as well as I there's no help that can reach us here in time. Our escorts are waiting for us a day's sail away."

"Then call them. Tell them we need a tow."

"There is no way to call them."

Markov didn't answer.

Grachev walked along the vertical fin until he could actually touch the piece of bright, twisted metal. He gave it a push.

The steel didn't move.

Grachev returned. "So. The metal is thin but it's no ordinary steel. It's like a spring."

"Can you pull it out?" Fedorenko asked.

"It will take time."

"How much?" asked Fedorenko.

"A day. If it stays calm. If we're lucky."

"We don't have a day."

"Then you'd better start pulling."

Markov turned to Fedorenko. "You have your choice. Stay here and repair the rudder or run the strait on the surface. You don't trust my judgment. The decision is yours."

Fedorenko saw the outlines of the trap. If the order to steam on the surface came from him and it ended badly, Markov would be off the hook. *Fedorenko issued the order.* Markov had dithered his way across the top of the globe, wasting time at every opportunity, but if they missed their rendezvous, who would be blamed? "You've presented me with two impossible choices."

"Sometimes that's what command of a ship at sea is about."

Fedorenko looked off to the southeast. Bering Strait was out there, and not far beyond were ships that would guarantee this mission, no matter what Markov had in mind. "Get that rudder clear," he said to Grachev. "And if you do it before the next watch comes on at noon, there will be something in it for you."

Grachev glanced at Markov, then said to Demyan, "Go bring the drill, some cutting oil, ten meters of braided cable, a pad eye and the lifting lug for the stern planes."

After the assistant engineer left, Grachev said to Fedorenko, "What kind of something?"

"Get us to that rendezvous and you'll collect your bonus."

Grachev held up two fingers. "Double bonus."

"Double?"

"Double," said Grachev.

"There was a time when that would be called profiteering."

"Sure," Grachev agreed. "Back when we were selling the Chinese AK-47s. Not atomic submarines."

"Very well." Fedorenko scowled. "But only if you fix the rudder in time." He turned on his heel and stalked back to the sail.

Markov said, "Double?"

"It's not for me."

"Demyan?"

Grachev looked surprised. "How did you know?"

"He came to talk to me in my cabin. When did you find out?"

"Last year," said the engineer. "Why do you think I brought him along on this run? It was his only chance. But you still haven't told me what you're planning."

"You're right."

Even with some of the junior officers standing watch, even with Bledsoe down in the torpedo room cuffed to a rack, the wardroom was packed to capacity. All the chairs were filled. The heads of Engineering, Operations and Weapons sat at the table with Steadman. Their assistants formed an inner ring while Hennig, the damage control assistant, Scavullo, Browne and the corpsman, Chief Cooper, and a select group of senior chiefs occupied the perimeter.

Steadman put COMSUBLANT's orders on the table. "You heard them. Anyone want to read them, too?"

"Is the admiral serious?" said Keefe.

"Admirals usually are," said Steadman. "The question is whether we're in a position to do anything about it."

"What about Commander Vann?" asked Tony Watson, *Portland*'s engineer. He was in charge of the boat's reactor, and was a lieutenant commander like Steadman and Whalley. Like Vann, he was a "supernuke" who'd spent all his career around machines. "What's his status precisely?"

When Tony Watson said *precisely*, he meant it. "I'll let the man who examined him tell you." Steadman looked to the corpsman. "Chief?"

"Commander Vann suffered some kind of attack while he was reading those orders you just heard. Apparently he had another one after we hit that Typhoon. He's in his stateroom sedated now."

"You said he 'apparently'?" said Watson.

"I wasn't in Control to see it, sir," said Cooper.

"I was," said Browne. "The boat was headed for the bottom and Vann was staring into the HF screen. It happened on *Baton Rouge* just the same way."

"That's not what the Board of Inquiry said."

"But I was there," said Browne.

The engineer still wasn't satisfied. "Chief Cooper, are you saying Vann is unfit to command this boat?"

"He is now."

"Don't be cute with me. You know what I'm asking."

"Sir, I can't give you an honest answer. Burns, sprains, broken bones. If I can see the problem I can fix it. It's my opinion that something broke inside Commander Vann, but it's nothing you can see."

"You mean he suffered from some kind of psychological episode?"

Cooper nodded. "I think so."

"Are you a trained psychologist?"

"No, sir, I'm not."

"Then you can't offer an expert opinion, can you?"

"Tony," said Steadman, "your questions aren't wrong, but we don't have time to hold a hearing out here. I guarantee there will be one when we get back. I'll have to answer for what I did and I'm prepared to do it. But for now, I need two things from you all. First, I need to know if *Portland* is capable of carrying out the mission COMSUBLANT gave us. Tony? We might as well start with you."

The engineer was clearly unhappy with getting sidetracked. "There's nothing wrong with the engine or the plant."

"I take that as a go. Lieutenant Keefe?"

"The VLS is inop," meaning the Vertical Launch System. "All my electrical connections to the missile tubes are gone."

"Torpedoes?" asked Steadman.

"We shot four fish out of twenty-six. We're not going to run out anytime soon."

"What about sonar?" Steadman asked.

"I'd prefer to let Petty Officer Schramm answer that, sir."

Steadman turned to the sonar man. "Can you find that Typhoon again, Bam Bam?"

"Active sonar is gone, sir. That leaves the tail and the port and starboard wide apertures but they'll only work if they get a cue from the sphere or the tail. Can I find a Typhoon with what I got? Maybe. But finding him and *doing* something about it are different. I might get you in the neighborhood but you can forget about underhulling him, or messin' with his screws or putting a fish through his mail slot. It won't happen."

Lieutenant Keefe spoke up. "We can use the torpedo's sonar as an off-board sensor to track him. You get us in the neighborhood, Chief. I'll make sure the mail gets delivered."

Two green lights. Steadman made a mental check mark. "Whalley?"

"Nothing broke. We can navigate and communicate."

"Lieutenant Hennig?"

"Sir, we've fixed all the immediate problems that could put us on the bottom. The sonar tunnel hatch is secure and the water that accumulated down in Battery One is pumped. The chlorine level is down and we're ventilating the boat to get rid of it all. But if you start moving, I mean *maneuvering*, there's no saying what might happen. The bow could fall off and take the sphere with it, and if it did I doubt the hatch would hold."

Red light. Steadman looked to Browne. "COB?"

"Captain," he said deliberately, knowing that the word would carry weight, "we hit the biggest son of a bitch of a submarine that's ever put to sea and we're still afloat. Can we make Pearl? Yes. Can we stop that Typhoon and make Pearl? You want my honest answer, I'd say we're here by one miracle and I wouldn't go askin' for another."

"You vote no?"

Browne shook his head. "Ain't a matter of voting. You want my take, there it is. The rest is above my pay grade."

Two greens, two reds. "That brings me to the last matter. I put Commander Vann on the sick list. I've taken command of this boat in accordance with naval regulations. I believe I can justify my actions. But I have to justify them to all of you first." He picked up the orders. "You've heard what COB said and it makes a lot of sense. But these are not ambiguous orders. We're supposed to get the job done and then figure out how to make it home. COMSUBLANT means for *Portland* to go into harm's way and without our bow sonar, we're going to have to go in blind. I have to know that all of you will follow me. No qualms. No questions."

The wardroom went dead silent. At last, someone spoke.

"I will," said Scavullo.

There was a general wave of consent, with one exception.

Steadman looked to the chief engineer. "Tony?"

Watson grimaced, swallowed, then said, "You point the front of the boat. I'll make sure the back gets you there."

"Anyone else have doubts?"

"Not about you, XO," said a chief from the periphery. "But could you kindly order up a new boat?"

"I'll see what's available on the lot down in Pearl." Steadman stood up. "Lieutenant Scavullo? I'll have a message drafted to Norfolk for you to transmit in five minutes." He paused, looking out over the faces of the men, and the woman, who'd placed their lives in his hands. "Dismissed," he said. "Let's get ready to move the boat."

On the way out, Browne pulled him aside. "There's one more problem I didn't mention in the open. I checked the small-arms locker to change the lock and make a count."

"You lock up the Beretta Engler swiped?"

"Yes, I sure did," said COB. "And that's the problem. We left port with four twelve-gauges, four M-14 rifles and a dozen M-9s."

"And now?"

"There's eleven."

CHAPTER TWENTY-NINE

THE STRAIT

Baikal

Grachev screwed the lifting lug onto the stern plane, then hooked a stainless steel cable to it. He still had to attach the *other* end to the chunk of steel jamming his rudder, and it was tougher than it looked.

He tried drilling it and broke three bits without making an appreciable dent. Spraying oil on it while the drill screamed only made it smoke. The material seemed to possess a split personality: hard as armor plate and flexible as spring steel.

Frustrated and mad and nearing Fedorenko's deadline of high noon, he sent Demyan below to fetch a spike made from a superalloy and Thor, a massive sledgehammer.

The sun was directly overhead when he started pounding the spike into the metal. The ocean might be lethally cold, but Grachev stood sweating and shirtless astride the great shroud over the starboard screw. He looked like a blacksmith, not a nuclear engineer. Sparks flew as he hammered. His arms quivered with exhaustion before it went through.

Grachev leaned against the vertical fin, panting.

"Are you all right?" yelled Demyan.

Grachev waved an arm to show that he'd heard. But he was thinking, *If this is what they make their hulls from, it's no wonder they only need one skin instead of two.* You could break diamonds with a wedge of this steel.

He worked the small hole larger until he could jam the cable through. He turned to Demyan. "Raise the stern planes!"

At first nothing happened. Then there was a low hum from deep beneath Grachev's feet, and the great slab of the stern plane began moving, rising, slowly, until Grachev yelled, "Enough!"

He fed the cable through the hole until it was taut, then fastened it with a clamp. He jumped down off the shroud and onto the stern. "Give me that."

Grachev grabbed the walkie-talkie. "Lower the stern planes! All the way to the stops!"

The horizontal plane started back down toward the sea, taking up the slack as it dropped. Just before it splashed into the water, the cable drew tight. The plane submerged and the cable began to hum like a piano wire.

The walkie-talkie squawked. "Hydraulic pressure is in the yellow zone," came a voice from below.

"Keep going."

The jammed steel was moving, elongating like taffy.

Suddenly, with a crescendo of *snaps* and *twangs*, both cable and steel whipped away from the rudder, flew across the sea, skimmed, bounced, caught and tumbled to a stop in a fan of spray.

The stern plane slammed down to its bottom limit with a *thunk* that shook the forty-thousand-ton ship.

"Raise the stern plane and shift the rudder," said Grachev.

There was the familiar hydraulic hum, and the stern plane rose back from beneath the surface. Then the rudder began to move. It didn't stop until it came to rest against the starboard blocks.

Grachev said, "Captain?"

"Listening, Igor. Is everything all right up there?"

"You have your ship back."

Fifteen minutes later the screws began to churn the sea to froth, the great black hull jetted tall streams of vapor and she slipped beneath the waves.

COMSUBLANT
Norfolk, Virginia

Vice Admiral Graybar threw the message from *Portland* to his desk and said, "Jesus *Christ*. Who does Steadman think he is?"

"He's a young XO, admiral," said his chief of staff, Captain Joseph Welch. *At least, he was,* he thought, for if *half* of the message on Graybar's desk was true, Steadman would be lucky to keep his head on his shoulders. "He was supposed to go to PCO school last year, but Vann didn't recommend him."

"So now Steadman's kicked the guy who bilged him off his own bridge. Jesus. If this doesn't stink I don't know what does."

In some ways Joe Welch was Vann's double. Like Vann, he'd specialized in nuclear engineering. Like Vann, he'd been given a hard-luck boat, the USS

Hyman Rickover, and turned her into one of the best submarines in the Atlantic fleet. There the similarities ended. His years at sea were accident-free. He'd risen while Vann was sidelined.

"An XO is supposed to take over if his commanding officer can't hack it," said Welch. "Steadman could be doing his job."

"Vann is sneaky and persistent and I need someone like him up there, on his feet and not drugged to his eyeballs. If that renegade Russian makes it through the strait, you know what's going to happen?"

"Sure. We'll have to put two Chinese tin cans and all those little *Kilos* on the bottom right next to her."

"And that means a real war," said Graybar. "Not a little operation we can keep quiet. It will be right out where the whole goddamned world will see it."

"Any boats we can spare to help them out?"

"*Corpus Christi* is heading up there from Guam."

"That's three days' sail. Why can't the bird farms do some honest work for a change?" It was the derisive term submariners used for aircraft carriers.

"All the carriers are committed off Taiwan. No," said Graybar, "this is going to be a knife fight and Steadman just broke my only goddamned blade." He looked up at Welch. "I won't have a mutiny breaking out on one of my boats. Vann isn't some two-bit Captain Queeg, for Christ's sake. He's had his troubles but he turned *Portland* around. What's Steadman done?" The admiral paused, letting steam build back up. "I swear I'll fry him in butter."

"You'd be right to," said Welch. "If he doesn't deliver."

Graybar waited for him to elaborate, and when he didn't, he said, "Well?"

"I'm only a captain, and you can tell me to shut up if you want, but if that message is accurate, then that lieutenant commander you're so anxious to fry has got his hands pretty full right now. He's got a busted-up boat with no sonar. He's blind and he's got a shallow-water run ahead of him that's dangerous in a sub with all the bells and whistles working. He's got a crew problem, and he's in a tail chase with a boomer who can outrun him, outsee him, and is about to join up with some nasty friends. You gave *Portland*'s CO the authority to risk his boat, his life, to stop that Typhoon. For better or worse, right or wrong, Steadman's the CO you've got."

"A kid who hasn't even been through PCO school!"

"A kid who was there to take over if Vann was incapacitated," Welch repeated.

Graybar pointed his finger. "You don't know that he is."

"And *you* don't know that he *isn't*. In the end it doesn't matter. Steadman's the man on the scene and he took you at your word. He's doing exactly what you or I would do if we were younger, and you know what, Admiral? His chances aren't so good. Give him a break. You may be surprised."

Graybar raised a bushy salt-and-pepper eyebrow. "You know something I don't?"

"All I know is that Vann let that Typhoon get by him at Kola. Then he sent you a sitrep that was smug as hell and dead wrong. Maybe Steadman will do a better job. You'd better hope so. If that Typhoon gets handed over intact, it won't just be green XOs who'll end up sautéed. They have plenty of pans in Washington for the big fish, too."

"Comforting thought. Just how do you propose I tell the CNO that our best chance at avoiding a war with China is in the hands of a kid his own CO wouldn't recommend for command?"

"I wouldn't presume to suggest the wording of an admiral's message to the Chief of Naval Operations."

"You'll hand me the rope but you won't wear it."

"Yes, sir. First thing they teach you at command school."

Baikal

Markov ran parallel to the Siberian coast, sometimes in Russian waters, sometimes not. They approached Cape Dezhnev, the bony finger of land marking the inner gates to Bering Strait. His options were growing as tight as the waters. His escorts were a day away. Just as he would have to thread *Baikal* through the narrows, he would have to find a way between the ships out there and Fedorenko right here.

"Captain," said Navigator Borodin, "turn coming up in eight minutes. Our new heading will be one nine eight degrees."

"Where will that put Ratmanov Island?"

"We'll pass to starboard," said the navigator. "It's a longer track to our rendezvous point but the American side of the strait is ten meters deeper."

When did ten meters matter so much? For all the power and majesty of *Baikal*, it was designed for the open deeps, not this undersea jungle of rocks and shoals.

"Where is Fedorenko?" he asked, as though speaking to himself.

"In the officers' dining room," said Gasparyan. "Pavel made *pelmenyi* again." Siberian ravioli. "Do you want him?"

"No. Let's all enjoy his meal in peace."

"Captain," said Belikov, "I'm picking up a lot of surface contacts out ahead in the strait. They sound like fishing trawlers. Several small ones and a bigger contact. Perhaps a factory ship."

"It's fishing season." Markov wished he had a periscope that still worked. Those trawlers might be dragging kilometer-long drift nets.

"Turn coming up in four minutes."

Markov longed for a look at the rocky coast of his homeland. Cape Dezhnev was barren and probably uninhabited, but the far Siberian shore was still Russia. It was a view he hadn't had since leaving Kola Fjord, and he had every reason to think that another chance would not come his way soon.

"One-minute warning," said Borodin.

"Depth now fifty-eight meters, Captain," said Belikov.

He looked around at the officers on duty in Central Command. They'd met two of the greatest challenges any Russian submariner could face: the polar sea and American torpedoes. The ship wasn't exactly as good as new, but she was still sailing under her own power. They were still standing on their feet. It was a victory the American submarine he'd left behind could not claim.

"Helm," said Markov, "make your depth forty-five meters."

They crossed the fifty-five-meter curve with her keel a scant ten meters off the flat ocean floor. *Baikal*'s sail was so close to the surface the trough of a wave would expose it. The sea would rise in a sudden, turbulent boil as though breaking over a reef, though this was a reef moving southeast at twelve knots.

"Five, four, three, two, one and *mark!*" said Borodin.

"Helm, five degrees right rudder. New heading will be one nine eight degrees. But gently," said Markov. A quick turn would tend to heel the ship over, and in waters this shallow that could ground them in an instant.

Baikal swung her bow south and entered the narrows of the strait. As she did, her bow sonar became flooded with diesel grumbles and the rattle and clank of trawler gear.

"Multiple contacts now dead ahead. They're out beyond Ratmanov Island and the small ones are definitely trawlers, Captain. Single-screw diesels. The big one is something different."

The factory ship. "Are they moving?"

"The trawlers are working southeast. The larger contact is remaining behind."

Then we'll have to slow down to keep from getting tangled up. "Helm," he said, "turns now for six knots." It made Markov smile to think a great warship containing enough destructive power to end the world, driven by two atomic plants of near infinite power, could be stopped by a barrier woven of fragile fishnet.

"Captain? We're entering the strait," said Borodin. "Passing abeam Cape Dezhnev."

"How far to land, Borodin?"

There was something in Markov's tone that told the navigator his captain was asking a slightly different question. "Nine kilometers. You could see it if the weather is good up there."

Markov felt a magnetic pull, an almost physical ache to see Russia. No doubt the cape would have an old military installation on it from Cold War days. Perhaps a sizable one. Perhaps it was still manned by soldiers who'd given their superiors reason to banish them to Russia's most distant corner.

There would be wooden buildings. A radar site. An old airstrip with sunflowers sprouting from the untended concrete. Maybe even a rail spur still in use. A spur that would connect with a branch that would link up with the Trans-Siberian main line. And from there it would be just six days' travel to Moscow, another day north to Murmansk, to his street, his building, his apartment. To his Liza, to Peter. To his life.

"Captain?" said his first officer, Gasparyan. "Perhaps you'd like to surface to take a visual bearing off the cape."

Sometimes it was comforting to be known so well, to be understood by the men he commanded. But not this time.

"Maintain heading depth and speed," he said.

USS *Portland*

Scavullo and Wallace were in the radio shack when the trailing wire antenna picked up the signal for incoming radio traffic. A tone sounded, a light glowed. Wallace picked up the intercom and said, "Conn, Radio. We've got a message alert tone."

"All stations make ready for periscope depth," said Steadman. He looked at the contact evaluation plot. There was nothing on it, which didn't mean much with *Portland*'s primary sonar dead. "Sonar, Conn. Are you holding any contacts?"

"Conn, Sonar. Negative. But all I've got to go on is the tail," said Bam Bam. "It doesn't see too well ahead."

All the books said you *never* surfaced without knowing what was up there. But Steadman couldn't afford the book answer, the safe answer. Not if there was a whisper of hope of finding that Typhoon and delaying it. "Diving Officer," he said, "make your depth sixty feet. Helm, slow to four knots."

"Sixty feet and four knots," said Slice and Dice.

It wasn't much of a rise, for *Portland* was cruising at just one hundred feet. The mud lay just twenty-six beneath her keel. Nor did it take much to slow to periscope speed. *Portland* could barely make ten knots without stirring up an unholy racket from her damaged bow.

The boat clattered up from the darkness, heading for the filtered green light above.

Steadman watched as the Fathometer crept up to the proper value and froze as though seven thousand tons of submarine had been mounted on a pedestal. *Rock solid.*

"Sixty feet."

"Raise the mast," Steadman ordered.

"Message from COMSUBLANT coming in," said Lieutenant Wallace. "We're running it through crypto now."

Was it a recall message ordering *Portland* to head for Pearl Harbor? A directive to place himself under arrest and to hand the bridge back to Vann? Steadman wouldn't have bet either way.

A few moment later, Scavullo appeared at the aft portside door. "Permission to enter Control?"

"Come."

She had the paper in her unbandaged hand. It would have been impossible for her not to have read it, and so Steadman tried to gauge her expression for some hint about its contents. "Are we still in the game, Lieutenant?"

"Aye aye." She handed it to him and said, "And it's in overtime."

Z090043Z10AUG2001
NLOB*NLOB*NLOB
FM: COMSUBLANT
TO: CO USS PORTLAND
INFO: CINCLANT, CINCPACFLT COMSUBPAC
SUBJ: SPECIAL OPERATIONS

1: ALL PREVIOUS MISSION DIRECTIVES REMAIN IN EFFECT
2: PLAAN TF NOW NORTH ST LAWRENCE ISLAND

3: NEXT 8 HRS CRITICAL

4: HOPES AND PRAYERS ARE WITH YOU

5: GET THE BOOMER . . . GRAYBAR SENDS

North of Saint Lawrence Island? If the message was accurate, the Chinese warships were right on the other side of Bering Strait!

"Conn, Sonar."

Steadman folded up the message, slipped it into his pocket and grabbed the intercom. "Go ahead, Bam Bam."

"Sir, if you could make an easterly run across the strait, I might be able to pick up something with the tail, then cue it to the flank arrays. It's kind of an ass-backward move but it might get us some contacts."

Steadman looked to his navigator. "Whalley? How far to the strait?"

"Twenty miles to the beaches of sunny Cape Wales."

Twenty miles. Maximum torpedo range.

"Captain?" said Browne. "Bam Bam's a good sonarman, but he's *thinkin'* like a sonarman."

"What's on your mind, COB?"

Browne stood up from the ballast board and took Steadman aside. "A Mark 48 torpedo has a pretty good onboard sonar."

"It should at three million bucks apiece. You want me to fire one at nothing as a scout?"

"Just a thought."

"Conn, Radio," said Wallace. "Acknowledgment sent and confirmed."

"Retract all masts." Steadman walked back forward to the small seat at the head of the periscope stand. "All right," he said. "Helm, make your depth eighty feet. Turns for ten knots. Steady on one eight five degrees."

"Eighty feet, ten knots and one eight five, aye."

"Mister Keefe?" he said to the weapons officer. "Make Tubes One, Two, Three and Four ready in all respects."

"Sir?" Keefe said. "We don't have any contacts."

"Not yet," said Steadman.

Down in the torpedo room, the order to make all four tubes ready for firing brought a sudden flurry of activity. Two weapons were already loaded and ready to go. The other two were rolled from their storage racks onto the loading trays, and the torpedomen had to work around two unfamiliar obstacles:

Lieutenant Bledsoe and Radioman Engler. They were handcuffed to the outer port and starboard storage racks.

"If your order didn't come from Commander Vann," Bledsoe said, "it's your duty to disobey."

"Is that right, Lieutenant?" said Chief Babcock. Like most leading chiefs, he was happy to chew holes in anyone, no matter the rank or rate.

"You drop that fish on my fingers and I'll make you eat it," said Engler, as 3,400 pounds of Mark 48 torpedo was manhandled off the rack and onto a loading tray. He strained at the cuff like a fox caught in a leghold, putting himself in the way of the torpedomen, which was never a good idea. They were big men in a hurry, and Engler was knocked flat to the rack.

He tried to stand but Chief Babcock shoved him down. "Son," he said, "if you don't shut your mouth, the next torpedo we slide is going to be greased by none other than you."

"And you're a fucking dead man."

The inner breech doors were unlocked and open, and loading rams slid the twenty-foot torpedoes into their tubes. A torpedoman attached the weapon's data link wire, shut the breech, locked it and put a sign on the locking handle: *WARSHOT LOADED*.

In Control, two green lights on Lieutenant Keefe's panel became four.

"Tubes One, Two, Three and Four are ready to flood," he told Steadman. "Sir, how do you want me to set them up?"

"Straight run, depth fifty feet, swim them out at forty knots and start them pinging at ten thousand yards. Ripple fire at thirty-second intervals. If the first fish finds him, I want the second one ready to take out his screws."

"Presets accepted."

"Flood Tubes One and Two and open the outer doors."

There was a faint rumble as water rushed into the two ready tubes.

"Tubes One and Two flooded."

"Shoot one."

Keefe jammed his palm down on the big red mushroom button. There was a louder rumble as the first Mark 48 was shot from its tube on a column of water. Its two counterrotating screws spun up into a furious whine.

"One's away."

"Reload the tube with another Mark 48." Steadman watched the second hand tick ever so slowly around the face of his watch. *Fifteen . . . twenty-five . . .* "Shoot Two!"

Keefe jammed the firing button down again.

"Two's away. Both fish running hot, straight and normal."

Baikal

"Passing Ratmanov Island to starboard," said Borodin.

"The Pacific Ocean," said Fedorenko. "At last."

"We're barely through the strait," said Markov. "It's a little early for celebrations."

"Captain," said Borodin. "There's something strange about that factory ship ahead. She's no diesel. I'm hearing steam turbines and twin screws. And she's got a medium-frequency hull sonar dialed way down low."

Steam turbines? Sonar? "She's a warship."

Belikov pressed the heavy black headphones more tightly to his ears. "She sounds like a *Sovremenny* destroyer."

"She is," said Fedorenko. "Or at least, she was."

Markov turned. "Who's out there, Fedorenko?"

Hangzhou or her sister ship, *Fuzhou*. One or the other."

"Chinese? So far north?"

"Standing orders were to move the rendezvous north if *Baikal* ran into any difficulties. Releasing the emergency buoy seems to have triggered the correct response."

"No one thought to mention it in *my* standing orders."

"Captain!" said Belikov. "High-speed screws astern!"

Fedorenko was immediately forgotten. "What kind, Belikov?"

Belikov watched the white sound spike flicker faintly at the bottom of his circular screen. The white line grew brighter with familiar, and frightening, speed. He looked back over his shoulder. "It's a torpedo, captain. A Mark 48 at maximum range."

"You're sure?"

"I've got bearing change. It's not coming at us." Belikov concentrated hard, then said, "A second torpedo! Both are beyond twenty kilometers."

"Who fired them?" said Fedorenko.

"A submarine." The first sound spike suddenly brightened to almost incandescent intensity.

"The weapon is pinging!"

"From twenty kilometers? At what?" said Fedorenko, baffled.

"Second torpedo has gone active! Range now eighteen kilometers to the first."

Both of them fired in the blind, Markov thought. *Why?* Sometimes it was done to force an undetected adversary to reveal himself. No one could afford to sit still while one homing torpedo hunted you. Was there another *Los Angeles* up there?

"Left ten degrees rudder, Gasparyan. Hold depth and speed." Markov watched as both weapons cut an absolutely straight path down his starboard side.

"Captain!" said Belikov. "New contact bearing zero four five! A single-screw submarine running on batteries! He just came out of nowhere!" A new sound spike brightened and began to move away from the original bearing. "He's really digging holes in the sea to get away!" Another bright spike. "Warning! *A third* torpedo is in the water! A Type 53!"

A diesel boat firing a Type 53 torpedo? "That makes him a *Kilo.*" Markov looked to Fedorenko. "More Chinese?"

Fedorenko seemed transfixed by the play of light and motion going on across Belikov's screen. "Chinese officers and crew with a dozen Russian advisors."

Markov watched the little diesel submarine scrambling away from the Mark 48s streaking in from behind. It was a race between a seventeen-knot submarine and a forty-knot torpedo. A race that could end only one way.

CHAPTER THIRTY

TIGER AND SEAL

USS *Portland*

The torpedoes saw their world in shades of sound. Noisy was bright, quiet dim and silence was the black of a moonless midnight. Their views were transmitted back to *Portland* along furiously unwinding spools of fine cable. There it popped up onto Lieutenant Keefe's fire control console screen first, and then on Bam Bam's up forward in the sonar shack.

At first both screens flickered only with the reflected noise of the Mark 48s' own buzzing screws. Then the seeker head in the first weapon went active. The effect was like a halogen headlamp switched on bright.

"Contact bearing zero zero three," Keefe called out. "Range seven thousand one hundred yards."

"What kind of a contact?" Steadman demanded.

"Conn, Sonar," said Bam Bam. "That's a submarine. Designate her Sierra Ten. She's cavitating something fierce."

"A Typhoon?"

"Not unless she's only got one screw running."

A single-screw boat seven thousand yards out, thought Steadman. Whoever she was, Sierra Ten was inside the Mark 48s' lethal range.

The sonic view brightened again.

"Second fish has started pinging, Captain," said Keefe.

Bam Bam watched the blade count rise, then stop. "Conn, Sonar. No plant noise at *all*. For sure she's runnin' on batteries."

"Diesel boat," said Browne. "Might be Russian, might be Chinese. She could even be Canadian."

Steadman was about to tell Keefe to steer the weapons away when Keefe shouted, "Torpedo in the water! Sierra Ten just fired a snapshot down our bearing! It sounds like a Type 53!"

"Forget the Canadians," said Browne. "She's a *Russian* boat."

"Or Chinese. Rig ship for depth charge," Steadman ordered. "Whalley," he said to the navigator. "Which way to open water?"

"Turn to port. You've got good water for the next six miles."

"Left ten degrees rudder," said Steadman. "Ahead one-third."

"Left ten degrees, aye," the helm acknowledged.

"Conn, Sonar. Confirm that torpedo is a Type 53," said Bam Bam as he watched the characteristic soundprint on his screen.

"A 53 doesn't have the legs to reach us up here," said Browne.

Steadman allowed himself to relax as much as anyone could with a smart weapon headed his way. They were lucky the captain of that *Kilo* was so easily spooked. It would have been all too easy to stumble onto him at close range. But what to do about him?

Steadman's orders said he could shoot at a Chinese ship but only if shot at. That *Kilo* had fired a torpedo, but if *Portland* took him down, everyone in the North Pacific would hear it. *He's not the one I want.* "No other contacts, Bam Bam?" he asked.

"Stand by," said Bam Bam. "It's gettin' kinda noisy . . . Whoa!" he said. "Surface contact bearing two zero eight. He's out beyond Sierra Ten." He worked the acoustic filters to bring the new contact into clearer focus. "I've got a twin-screw ship and she just started pinging. Designate him Sierra Eleven. It's a Bull Horn set, skipper."

"Destroyer," said Steadman. "Looks like we just fired two fish at the whole Chinese Navy." He turned to Keefe. "Weapons. Set up Tubes Three and Four for Sierra Eleven. Flood them both and open the outer doors."

Steadman thought, *A destroyer and a* Kilo *boat.* They'd found the Chinese task force, or part of it. Where was the Typhoon?

Two lights on Keefe's console went from red to green. "One hundred fifteen seconds to impact." He turned and looked at Steadman. "Sir? Do we take him?"

"This one gets away. Steer number one to starboard and keep it pinging. That Typhoon is out there somewhere. He could be out there hugging the Russian coast."

"Aye aye." Keefe typed in the commands. "Terminal run aborted. It's lost lock on Sierra Ten."

"Steer number two to starboard."

Steadman had put two multimillion-dollar chips on the table in a bet to find that Typhoon before she could join up with her escorts. So far he'd found the escorts. Where was that Typhoon?

"Something's happening," said Belikov. "The first torpedo is going to miss our friend." Then, "It's heading west."

A cheer went up in Central Command. The submarine community was small. If there were Russian advisors on that *Kilo,* they would almost surely know their names, their wives, their favorite place to drink. They could be neighbors.

"Firing a torpedo back at the Americans frightened them off," Fedorenko said. "You see? They're not invincible."

"No one said they were," said Markov. Though he doubted the Americans had been frightened away by a torpedo that couldn't possibly reach them. *No,* he thought. *He saw that* Kilo *and chose not to sink her.* It was a measured move, not reckless, not bloodthirsty. It didn't fit. *Who are you?*

"Captain? The *Kilo's* torpedo just went dead," said Belikov.

His opponent's approach, his tactics, had subtly changed and now Markov's thinking would have to change to match them. He knew what he would do in the American's shoes. *He spared the* Kilo *because he's hunting bigger game. But why use a torpedo sonar?*

Then he stopped.

The collision. It had bashed in a section of *Baikal's* hull. What did it do to the American's delicate bow sonar? *Can he still be alive?* He watched Belikov's screen for only a few seconds more, then said, "I think the second torpedo is going to turn our way."

Belikov looked back. "It's still tracking the *Kilo.*"

"Wait."

Belikov watched as the radial spoke on his screen froze at the two-o'clock position. If it was following its mate the spoke of light would begin to dim. Instead, it was growing brighter.

"Confirmed. The second torpedo turned our way."

"How the devil did you know that?" asked Fedorenko.

Markov ignored him. "How far away is it, Belikov?"

"Inside ten kilometers."

"I want an *exact* number." The American submarine might be blind but his torpedo was not. *How far could a Mark 48 swim?*

"Range is eight point five kilometers," said the sonar officer.

"What's your plan?" asked Fedorenko. The brightening spoke of light on Belikov's screen was making him plainly nervous.

It wasn't such a bad question. Make rendezvous with the Chinese and *Baikal* would go to Shanghai. The Chinese would own *Baikal,* along with her missiles. No.

Remain at sea, lose himself in the vast Pacific? That was appealing, but he'd have to put in somewhere. . . .

"*Markov!*"

"Relax, Gennadi. I don't think it can reach us."

USS *Portland*

"We just lost the wire from number one," said Keefe.

"Any sign of a boomer?"

"Not yet," said Keefe.

Steadman was about to order Tube Three shot to serve as scout, when Bam Bam said, "Conn, Sonar. Contact at six thousand two hundred yards, bearing one eight six. And she looks big."

Another destroyer? A fishing trawler? Or a Typhoon? "Keefe, how much run do we have left on Two?"

"Three minutes even, Captain."

That was good for 4,500 yards. The fish would come up short. "Can we slow it down and squeeze out some more range?"

"Yes, sir, but if that target out there accelerates . . . ?"

"We'll worry about that later. Drop the speed back to thirty knots. Bam Bam? What's that contact look like?"

"Stand by." Schramm watched as his screen began to fill with a pattern he'd grown only too familiar with. The sound of water rushing over a vast hull. The sheer size of the return, so big it could fool a less capable ST into thinking he was seeing a *normal* submarine from up close. But no. Look at the range! *Five thousand yards and it shows up as a real ship, not a dot!* "Conn! It's our old friend Sierra Five. Seeker range five thousand yards!"

Baikal

"Four kilometers, still coming straight in," said Belikov.

Markov grabbed a *kashtan*. "Igor," Markov said to the chief engineer, "we're cutting this too close. Ahead two-thirds and *do not cavitate.*"

"Understood," said Grachev. It was only smart to be cautious with a torpedo around. He sent more steam into the turbines, keeping a close watch on the cavitation light mounted above the throttles. *Still dark.* He inched the steam controls forward and was rewarded with a brief flicker, then pulled the throttles back.

Grachev had to make sure neither one of the seven-bladed screws sent a shower of bubbles upward. The sea pressure would collapse them like imploding popcorn and make a noise impossible for a homing torpedo to miss.

"Torpedo is three kilometers astern," said Belikov. "It's slowing down."

Markov glanced at the digital speed display above the helm. *Sixteen knots.* The Americans had seen him. Why slow down? Could it be that they had cut things too finely, too?

USS *Portland*

Bam Bam watched the play of light and shadow on his octagonal screen. Something was definitely changing. *More plant noise, more flow, higher blade count.* "Conn, Sonar, I think Sierra Five is on to us."

"Is he turning?" asked Steadman.

"No. He's still heading southeast. The blade count says he's making sixteen knots and picking up speed real slow."

"Two thousand yards to go," said Keefe. "Two minutes twenty to hit. The seeker should lock him up any second now."

Steadman said, "Put the fish into his screws."

"Aye aye." Keefe brought up an option menu on his console and commanded the Mark 48 to head for the *swish swish swish* of the Typhoon's great propellers. "Ninety seconds' run to target."

Baikal

The steady *ping . . . ping . . . ping* from the weapon's seeker shifted into a more urgent, higher tone as it swept in from astern.

"Range two kilometers," said Belikov. He said it calmly, without emotion, as though it were the distance to some tropical island, and not a high-tech kamikaze filled with three hundred kilos of high explosives.

Markov glanced again at the digital speed display, willing it higher than the meager eighteen knots it displayed.

"One kilometer astern," said Belikov.

"Do something," said Fedorenko. His pale forehead glistened.

"Gasparyan, stand by to throw the rudder hard over to starboard. Igor? On my command, all-ahead emergency."

"Understood, Captain."

Ping! . . . Ping! . . . Ping! . . . Ping!

"Here it comes," said Belikov. He could hear the whine of the torpedo's screws.

"Left full rudder! Grachev! *Now.*"

Baikal's screws slashed the sea into froth as the ship began to turn, leaving enormous whorls of disturbed water in its wake. Curtains of bubbles rose, then collapsed with the sharp reports of a furious small-arms battle.

The torpedo saw through the ruse and instantly discounted it. Its guidance computer had been programmed to know that when there was a rich source of sound dead ahead, it didn't just disappear when a sonic fog rolled in. Those thundering screws were still out there. The Mark 48 swam through the turbulence, the chaos of bubbles, and beheld once more the goal it had been commanded to reach, and destroy.

But it had to get close to trigger the proximity fuse in its warhead. Exhausted by its marathon swim, the Mark 48 began to falter. The motor sputtered on the last drops of fuel, then stopped. With its seeker head still pinging plaintively, it nosed down, heading for the soft mud on the bottom.

USS *Portland*

"Ten seconds," said Keefe. "Nine, eight, seven, six, five, four, three, two and *mark.*"

Steadman listened, knowing that it would take a bit more time for the sound of an explosion to reach *Portland* from so far off. "Bam Bam?"

"Nothing from the flank arrays, nothing from the tail. Not a damned thing on any . . . Whoa!"

A low rumble shook *Portland* like distant thunder.

"Explosion in the water bearing one eight three!"

"Did we hit him, Bam Bam?"

"The timing was almost right. We'll have to run up there and look around to know."

Steadman now found himself in a position not unlike the one Vann had encountered at the edge of the ice. He'd done his best to kill that Typhoon, and he might have. He'd surely alerted the enemy to his presence. Only now there were more enemies to deal with. A *Kilo* and a Chinese destroyer. In a better world, he'd turn his tail to them and speed away on a flank bell.

"He sure ain't makin' it easy, is he?" said Browne.

Baikal

The powerful explosion shook *Baikal* from stern to bow. The ocean sprayed in through the multiple seals of her propeller shafts, and an icy shower cascaded down her main trunk in the sail. As the ship shuddered, as the lights flickered off, then back on, Markov wasn't even sure the torpedo had missed. "Gasparyan?"

"Damage reports are coming in, Captain."

"Igor?"

"Both reactors are normal, engines are normal. Ballast and air systems normal. But that was too fucking close."

"I agree." Markov glanced at their speed. *Twenty-one knots.* Much too fast for such restricted waters. "Helm, all stop. Belikov. Any contacts astern? Whoever fired that torpedo might be foolish enough to follow it." *Not that we could do anything about it.*

"Passive sonar is still degraded. Give it a moment to clear."

"Captain?" said Borodin, the navigator. "Saint Lawrence Island is fifty kilometers ahead."

Fedorenko said, "All that's left is to join our escorts and follow them home. Let them deal with the Americans."

"My home is in Murmansk," said Markov. "Gasparyan? You have the command."

Markov walked over to the curtain that gave the navigator a bit of privacy and went in. "Pull the charts for the sea near Petropavlovsk."

Borodin went to a steel cabinet, pulled open a flat drawer and took out half a dozen detailed navigation charts. "Which one, Captain? We can start with the far north and—"

The intercom buzzed and Belikov said, "Captain. Possible contact."

Markov had to return to Central Command. But before he left he said, "I want you to find deep water. Some very deep water. Not too close to land, and not too far. Understood?"

"Understood," said Borodin, though as he watched Markov go he thought, *No. I don't.*

Markov hurried back to the sonar console. "Where?"

"Dead ahead. It's on the surface, so it might be that trawler traffic we picked up before."

Markov glanced at the speed display. *Fourteen knots.*

Belikov sat up suddenly in his seat and began manipulating the sonar controls.

"What is it, Belikov?"

"Submarine bearing zero zero five. It just came out of nowhere. It's close! Range is under three kilometers!"

If it was a *Los Angeles,* they were dead. "The American?"

Belikov shook his head. "A diesel boat on batteries. One second it wasn't there, and now it is. He's making strange sounds."

"Strange?"

"I think you should listen."

Markov walked back to the sonar console and pressed the headphones to his ears.

The sound was distorted, watery. Markov had expected the *swish* of screws, the *clank* of diesels. This was something very different. It wasn't a sound made by a machine at all, but rather, a voice, saying the same two syllables over and over.

". . . *ooo . . . lao . . . ooo . . . lao . . . ooo . . .*"

"He's using an underwater telephone frequency," said Belikov. He was just as puzzled.

Markov said to Belikov, "Put it over the speaker."

". . . *lao . . . ooo . . . lao . . . ooo . . .*

Fedorenko broke out into a broad smile. "Do we have the ability to respond?"

"On our underwater system. What does it mean?"

"Captain! Second underwater contact bearing one three five," Belikov sang out. "It's another *Kilo.* Now a surface contact, bearing zero one two. Twin screws and a steam turbine. Just started up. I think it's a destroyer."

"*Laohu* is Mandarin for 'tiger,' " said Fedorenko. "Our countersign is *Nerpa.* And it means we don't have to find our friends. They just found us."

USS *Portland*

The noise of water flowing over the damaged bow seemed to grow louder as *Portland* crept south. *Maybe something up there is coming apart,* thought

Steadman. They were surely advertising their existence to anyone nearby. "Helm, turns now for six knots."

Whalley looked up from his charts. "Saint Lawrence Island off the bow, XO. We can run five miles before we have to turn."

That Kilo is out to the west. We'll have to turn east. But where did that Typhoon run off to? "Sonar, Conn. Any contacts?"

"I was trackin' that *Kilo* with the tail for a while but he ran west and disappeared."

Steadman wanted to say, *Gentlemen, anyone have a brilliant idea, now would be a good time to share it.* "I think this is where the cavalry shows up over the hill."

"Or the Indians," said Browne.

Baikal

Belikov lined up the switches correctly to transmit over the underwater telephone, then handed Fedorenko the microphone.

Fedorenko waited for the garbled, watery voice coming through the speaker to pause, then clicked the microphone and said, *"Nerpa."* Seal.

Fedorenko switched to Mandarin.

From the speaker came, *"Huanying dao Taiping yang."*

"You qianshuiting zat zhui women," Fedorenko answered.

"Women huz zujie tamen. Nimen zaodao sunhai le ma?"

Fedorenko smiled and turned to Markov. "We're speaking to Captain Bai Yao, commander of the attack submarine *Lin San Liu.* He says welcome to the Pacific. I told him we have a tail and he's offered to cut it off for us. He wants to know about damage."

"Tell him we're able to proceed."

"Women keyi jixu hangxing."

"Fuzhou zai women de nanmian sige gongli chu. Nimen genzhe ta dao Shanghai. Mingbai ma?"

"What is he saying?" Markov asked. He'd heard something that sounded a lot like *Shanghai.*

"There's a destroyer. The *Fuzhou.* She's four kilometers south. We're supposed to follow her to Shanghai. Captain Bai Yao wants to know if that's understood."

"Tell him I understand."

Fedorenko put the microphone to the underwater telephone to his lips and said, *"Mingbai."*

As Fedorenko spoke over the UQC, Markov caught Gasparyan's eye and with a nod gave him command. He stepped through the forward hatch to Main Engineering to find Grachev.

Grachev looked up from his consoles. "Whatever you were thinking, it's too late."

"Not yet. Who do we have on board who speaks English?"

"Why?"

"You know that Fedorenko is having a conversation back there with the Chinese?"

"You want to have conversations with the English?"

"It gave me an idea. Can you operate the stern underwater telephone from there?"

"Naturally."

"Who would you trust to get a simple message across?"

"It's not a matter of trust," said Grachev. "The underwater telephone can be heard, what? Four, five kilometers? The Americans can shoot us from fifty. How do we get close enough to be heard without getting a torpedo in our face? You don't need someone who speaks English," he said. "You'll need a psychic."

"Then find me a psychic who speaks English."

Fedorenko was still talking over the UQC when Markov returned to Central Command. When he glanced at Gasparyan, his first officer nodded in the direction of the sonar officer.

Belikov had a sheet of paper out on his console. Markov walked over. At first it looked like a curious geometric doodle. An arrowhead shape whose points were made of smaller and larger circles. A large circle at the apex, two small ones to each side, and the largest of all at the bottom.

He didn't need labels to know the biggest circle was *Baikal*, and the others represented two *Kilo* submarines and their destroyer mother ship. *Baikal* had sailed right among the silent diesel–electric boats without detecting them. "So?" he asked.

Belikov picked up his pencil and placed it on the paper and drew a long, wavy line from *Baikal* to the bottom of the page. There he drew another circle, larger than the one he'd made for the *Kilo*s, smaller than for *Baikal*. He drew the ubiquitous nuclear symbol of whirling atoms beside it, then a number: *12*.

Now Markov understood. It was a nuclear boat twelve kilometers to the north. *I was right.* The American *Los Angeles,* and likely coming in blind. The instant Fedorenko stopped talking those *Kilo*s would detect it.

The Americans were sailing into a trap.

Fedorenko spoke what sounded like a final phrase, then turned to Markov. "Everything is established. Everything is understood," he said. Then he noticed something in Markov's expression. "What's wrong?"

Markov had searched for some currency that might buy the Americans' trust. Here it was. He reached over Belikov's shoulder, flipped up the guard that protected *Baikal*'s active sonar transmitter and jammed his fist down onto the broad red button.

BAH-WAH!

A sphere of pure sonic energy blasted out from *Baikal*'s bow, decibel for decibel as loud as an ocean liner's foghorn. It shattered the dark, silent world like a bolt of lightning flashing across the night sky. Even the stunned silence that followed seemed to echo with its thunder.

CHAPTER THIRTY-ONE

CONTACT

One minute Bam Bam was groping through a pitch-black sea. Then came the Russian sonar pulse and *Portland's* steel hull rang like a struck bell. "Conn, Sonar! That was a *big* active pulse from a Skat sonar dialed up to the max. I've got *multiple* contacts out ahead, surface and submerged. It looks like the whole fleet."

"Thank you, Mister Typhoon," said Browne, relieved, and also curious. *Why would he go active? He had to know it could draw another torpedo like a magnet.*

"All stop," said Steadman. He was thinking much the same thing. "Right ten degrees rudder."

Slowing down, going silent and turning away from a sudden cloud of threats were the right commands. But the orders in his pocket said it without a trace of ambiguity: GET THE BOOMER. He was to do everything in his power to keep that rendezvous from happening. Even at the cost of his boat, his life. Now it had happened, and Steadman was on his own.

Now what? Head for Pearl with his tail between his legs? Trail them and hope to get in a shot at that Typhoon without being detected and sunk by his friends first? Try to sneak in and pick the Typhoon out of the herd?

And why the active ping? It had helped *Portland*. What had it done for that Typhoon?

He glanced at the Fathometer above the helm. The waters here were so shallow that *Portland* could have her keel on the bottom and still be at periscope depth. "Radio, Conn. Send someone forward to pick up a message for immediate transmission."

"Conn, Radio, aye," said Lieutenant Wallace.

Scavullo appeared just as he finished scribbling a quick message for COMSUBLANT. "How's the finger?"

"Hurts." The finger Engler had snapped was cased in a bandage, but the flesh was swollen and angry.

"Have Chief Cooper give you something for the pain. We'll have your mast up for only a few seconds. Be ready to send."

She took the paper. "What about the confirmation?"

"Don't wait for one." Steadman walked aft to the periscope stand. "All right. Let's have a *real* fast ESM sweep."

The electronics mast barely broke the surface before the technician sitting at the radar console sang out, "Top Plate radar bearing one nine zero. Level three return."

That's got to be the destroyer, thought Steadman. "Down the ESM mast. Radio, Conn. Is that message formatted and ready?"

"Aye aye," said Wallace.

"All right, people," said Steadman. "This is not going to be a Hollywood observation. Up the search scope."

Steadman crouched down and let the scope rise into his hands. It was a backbreaking pose, but he didn't want an extra inch of the instrument exposed. At first all he saw was black water. Then the black turned green, green turned to white froth, and the scope head broke through to the air.

The quartermaster's stopwatch was already running.

"Two seconds."

A wave drowned the lens, pulled back, then blotted out the view again. But in the instant between, Steadman saw a dark mast, a gray square radar, a white superstructure.

"Chinese destroyer and he's close."

The water sloshed back over the scope head, and when it pulled away again, Steadman got a quick, almost subliminal view of a long, white hull with the number *136* painted on its side. A quick turn revealed the masts of another warship farther south.

"Conn, Radio. Message sent."

"Six seconds."

"Good work. Down scope."

As the scope slid back into its well, Steadman made a fast 360-degree sweep. *Clear.* "Keefe. Do we have any firing solutions?"

"I've got two destroyers and two *Kilos* stacked and racked, XO," said the Weapons officer. 'We're close enough to throw rocks and be guaranteed of hitting something."

"Same goes both ways, Mister Steadman," said Browne. "They hear us fire it'll be a shooting gallery with four guns and one duck."

"Set it up, Mister Keefe. Tubes One, Two, Three and Four. Run One and Two five thousand yards west, then back in. Send Three and Four five thousand yards east, then back in."

Browne saw what Steadman intended and didn't think much of the ruse. "Those *Kilos* and that skimmer are close enough to hear our fish clear the tubes. Might as well run 'em hot, straight and normal and get the job done before they know what hit 'em."

COB's right. They could get four shots off, but there was no way they could evade the inevitable return fire. There was no point in being subtle now. "Mister Keefe? Make One, Two, Three and Four ready in all respects. Set them up the way COB said."

"We've got four contacts, XO. You want one fish per?"

"No," said Steadman. "Put all four into the Typhoon."

Baikal

Fedorenko looked physically stunned. "What did you do?"

Markov folded the sheet of paper with Belikov's diagram. "While you were having a long conversation with your Chinese friends, whoever fired those torpedoes was moving closer. It seemed a good way to end the conversation and get us moving again."

"But I was copying down our instructions. They've set up an elaborate plan. The submarines here, the destroyers there, the helicopters searching in an arc ahead of . . ."

"I can save them a lot of time and effort," said Markov. "Rule number one: A submarine can protect a destroyer. A destroyer cannot protect a submarine. Tell them to proceed on course. They can use the helicopters to search ahead. We will guard their backs."

"That's not what was agreed."

"It's what will happen." He turned to the navigator's cubicle. "Borodin?" The curtain to the navigator's cubicle pulled open.

"Lay a course to the west of Saint Lawrence Island. Keep to the deepest channel."

"Two seven nine looks best. We'll have sixty-meter water. And Captain? I have the chart you asked for."

"Inform the Chinese of our intentions, Gennadi," said Markov, and then he joined Borodin.

Markov closed the curtain. A paper chart of the ocean off the Kamchatka Peninsula was spread open on the table.

"Avacha Canyon," said Borodin. "It's marked off as a restricted area. The Pacific Fleet dumps old reactor cores into it." He peered closely at Markov, trying to guess and gauge him. "Was there something else you needed?"

Markov looked up. "Not now. Thank you, Borodin." He pulled the curtains open and left for Main Engineering.

Grachev had made a quick search for an English-speaking crewman and came up with Senior Midshipman Maxim Glubov, a diesel-engine technician who spoke some English.

Markov took Grachev aside. "Glubov? The one who brews beer in his cabin that I'm not supposed to know about?"

"He's all I could find on short notice."

Markov faced the midshipman. "Say something."

"Nice to meet you." Glubov said it with a bright smile that made him look simple and stupid. "Sir, about the beer . . ."

"Forget it. Give him the microphone, Igor."

Grachev handed it to Glubov.

"What will you have me say, Captain?"

Markov thought about it, then said, "This is the Russian Federation missile submarine *Baikal,* calling the *Los Angeles.*"

"Palm trees. Blondes. Boards for water sports. Now, Captain?"

"Now, Glubov."

USS *Portland*

"All tubes are ready to flood," said Keefe. "Range to the Typhoon is approximately ten thousand yards. Run time will be five minutes thirty-three seconds."

Steadman picked up the intercom and clicked it, sending a hum throughout the boat.

In every space, in every compartment, from the torpedo room on the bottom deck to the sonar shack on the top, everyone heard the hum, stopped what they were doing and looked to the nearest speaker.

"This is Lieutenant Commander Steadman," he said. "I want all of you to know where we are, what we're about to do and why."

Steadman took out the piece of paper he'd taken from Vann, and read. "We've made it through Bering Strait. We're just north of Saint Lawrence Island. We could throw a stone and hit Alaska, or Russia. As for why we're here, let me read you our orders."

After Steadman finished, Bam Bam broke in and said, "Conn, Sonar. The fleet's starting to move south."

"The Typhoon?"

"He's tail end Charlie, but he's moving, too."

"Very well," said Steadman. He clicked the 1MC back on. "We've got that boomer in our sights now. The only problem is, he's surrounded by a bunch of Chinese ships. They won't be too happy when they realize what's happening, so we'll have to do a couple of other things pretty fast.

"First, we're going to put four Mark 48s into that Typhoon. Then we're going to outrun some Chinese torpedoes and fool the ones we can't outrun. Finally, we're going to set a record for the shortest transit time between Bering Strait and Pearl Harbor. If anyone thinks we're not up to all that, now is the time to say so."

Steadman waited. He turned to each of the men in Control. Keefe at the attack console to starboard. Browne at the ballast board to port. Whalley at his charts aft. Lieutenant Choper and the sailors at ship's control.

"Piece of cake, skipper," said Browne.

He raised the microphone to his lips, but stopped when he saw a stooped figure in the forward portside passage.

"Carry on," said Vann. His eyes were hollow. His khakis hung from him like sails on a dead calm day. "I can't stay in bed with all those records about to be broken."

Steadman turned to Keefe and was about to say, *Shoot One,* when Bam Bam Schramm's nasal twang intruded.

"Conn, Sonar. I got something comin' over the WQC-6." It was the underwater telephone. "I *think* it's some Russian dude."

"Shoot him," said Vann.

Who is he talking to in English? "Put it over the speaker."

"*. . . Russ . . . mees . . . Bai . . . Los Angeles . . .*"

"You've got him dialed in. Do it, for Christ's sake," said Vann.

Steadman listened to the wavering, watery voice repeat the same phrase over. It still made no sense. Nor would it even if the words had been perfectly clear.

Keefe looked up from the weapons console.

"Goddamn it," said Vann. *"Shoot!"*

"Hold on," said Steadman. He grabbed the intercom. "Radio, Conn. Send Scavullo up here *now.*"

Scavullo hurried forward from the radio shack. "Sir?" She looked up at the speaker.

". . . Russian . . . mar . . . Baikal . . . Los Angeles . . ."

"Jesus," Vann spluttered.

"What is he saying, Lieutenant?" asked Steadman.

"I need it over a headset."

Steadman snapped his fingers, and one was produced. She put it on and closed her eyes,

"You're letting him get away again," said Vann.

"Sir!" Scavullo's eyes popped open. "Sir, that's a native Russian speaker saying he's on the Russian missile submarine *Baikal,* and he's calling the *Los Angeles.* I think he means us."

Steadman pulled down the special microphone connected to *Portland's* underwater telephone. He handed it to Scavullo. "Tell him this is the *Los Angeles.* Ask him what he wants. Then tell him he's got one minute to state his intentions before we fire."

Baikal

Glubov's face froze, smile and all, his mouth dropped open.

"What is it?" said Markov.

"He says . . . I mean, she says what do we want or they will shoot us in one minute!"

"Who are you talking to?"

"Who is this?" said Glubov.

The answer filtered back through layers of shifting water. It came in Russian, but it was perfectly, ominously clear.

"What did she say?" Markov demanded.

"That we have forty seconds. I think she's Russian!"

"Give that to me!" Markov grabbed the microphone. "This is Captain First Rank Markov. I am the commander of the heavy submarine missile cruiser *Baikal*. There are four Chinese ships with us. Shoot at me and you'll be dead a minute later. Answer."

There was a pause, then:

"Twenty seconds."

"Put down your fucking clock and listen to me," said Markov, angry. "Think for a moment what would happen if we destroyed one of your missile submarines. Moscow knows you are here. They will know what happened if we vanish. So go ahead and shoot. Let the world be on your conscience." He eyed the sweep hand on the large clock over Grachev's consoles. *Ten seconds left.*

USS *Portland*

"I don't believe it," said Vann. *"By God,* I may be a son of a bitch of a captain, but I'll take that over a pussy-whipped lieutenant commander any day. You heard the admiral's orders. *Get the boomer."* He looked directly at Keefe. "Shoot them, Mister Keefe."

The weapons officer turned to Steadman.

"Hold your fire!" Steadman turned to Browne. "COB! Get someone up here to escort Commander Vann back to his cabin!"

"Got it covered, sir," said Browne, who was already whispering into his mouth microphone.

Steadman turned back to Scavullo. "Tell him he's bought himself some time. Tell him to explain himself, and if it doesn't make sense, then let the world be on *both* our consciences."

"Abyasnee sibya!" said Scavullo.

Baikal

Markov watched the second hand sweep by, the Americans' deadline, then heard the woman say, very rudely, *Explain yourself.* Whoever she was, she spoke in simple, direct sentences.

He put the microphone to his lips, and with the same free fall of feelings a suicide experiences stepping off a bridge, he said, *"Podlodka ni pai idyot f'Kitai. Podlodka pai idyot toda, gdye nikto ne naidyot yeyo."*

He immediately saw the effect his words had on Grachev. He had to wait a few moments longer for the Americans to react.

"What's he saying, Scavullo?"

"His submarine is not going to China. It's going where no one will find it."

Markov's words came over the speaker in Control again.

"He knows our sonar is damaged. He says not to worry about the Chinese. That if we can follow him, he'll take care of everything else."

"Follow him where?" asked Steadman. *And how?*

"Someplace called . . ." She listened, nodded, then said, "Avacha Canyon."

"Whalley! Find Avacha Canyon!" To Scavullo he said, "Ask why should we trust him."

Scavullo repeated the question, and when Markov answered, the scorn in his tone needed no translation.

"He says you were headed into a trap but I . . . but he revealed it. That we don't deserve saving but he saved us . . . anyway."

"Ask him if *Baikal* is going to Petropavlovsk."

Scavullo relayed the question.

The answer was immediate. *"Nyet, nyet."*

"Then what are his intentions?"

Markov spoke quickly, animatedly.

"He says . . . okay. Not Petropavlovsk. He . . . he wants . . ." Scavullo stopped and spoke over the underwater telephone for clarification. She listened, shaking her head, "That can't be right."

"What did he say, Lieutenant?"

"I *think* he said he wants us to *buy* his ship."

CHAPTER THIRTY-TWO

THE VOTE

COMSUBLANT
Norfolk, Virginia

Admiral Graybar had the unenviable job of telling the Chief of Naval Operations that a Russian submarine had just been handed to the Chinese Navy off Alaska, and there was nothing he could do to stop it. For a couple of two-bit naval powers to pull this off within spitting distance of the United States was like saying a Little League team had not only made it to the World Series, they were two runs ahead.

He was about to place the unpleasant call when his chief of staff, Captain Welch, buzzed from the outer office. "Come!"

"I've got fresh news from *Portland*."

"Tell me he sank that boomer."

"Sorry. But he did make contact with her."

"Contact?"

"With her CO. Over his underwater telephone. He—"

"I'm about to get my head handed to me by the CNO, the Chinese are about to kick us out of the Taiwan Straits, and he's *chatting up some Russian*?"

"Negotiating is more like it. You'd better read it."

Graybar took the message. "Is this serious?"

"Steadman seems to think so."

"You expect me to tell Washington that a green XO is suggesting we buy a renegade boomer from her captain?"

"Steadman isn't suggesting anything. He's giving you options. You read the message. He can take *Baikal* down, but he thinks *Portland* will end up on the bottom next to it. You ask me, Admiral, whatever the Russian wants is a bargain compared to that."

"Avacha Canyon is right off Petropavlovsk," said Graybar. "That's where *Houston* got a bloody nose last week. The Russians are sanitizing the whole damned coast. How is *Portland* supposed to sneak in there with a busted bow and no sonar?"

"All I know is Steadman thinks he can."

"Jesus. If he pulls it off, I swear it's coming out of his pay for the next six hundred years." He picked up his telephone. "How are we going to stuff a boomer crew into *Portland,* anyway?"

An hour later, a message was sent to *Portland*:

1. DETERMINE CO BAIKAL'S REQUIREMENTS

USS *Portland*

Scavullo brought the message forward from the radio room and handed it to Steadman.

"Let's see what the Russians have in mind," he said. "Get on the UQC and hail him. What's his name?"

"Markov." Scavullo slipped on the headset and picked up the microphone. *"Baikal, Baikal, Baikal. Vui slushitye?"*

The reply came quickly. "Chief Engineer Grachev listening."

"We have a message for your captain."

"Go ahead. I'll pass it on."

"It's for Markov."

"I am an officer of the Russian Navy. Who are you?"

"If you're smarter than you sound you may find out someday," said Scavullo. "Now put Markov on."

Baikal

"She's rude," huffed Grachev. "She refuses to speak to me."

Markov slipped into the blue chair beside Grachev. "I believe she is annoying you, Igor."

"Pah. Let's see how well *you* do with her."

The captain pressed the transmit key. "Markov listening."

USS *Portland*

"We've got him," she said to Steadman.

"Tell him we've been authorized to listen to his requests."

Scavullo listened to the reply, jotting down notes as she went. "He says they're not requests. If we want his ship, we'll pay the Russian Federation the same as the Chinese."

"How much is that?"

She listened, and her eyes widened. "One and a half billion dollars. And he wants us to pay the ship's company what they've been promised, too." She looked up.

"Tell him no deal. We already bought his ship once."

Steadman waited, then Scavullo said, "He says so have the Chinese. He asks, who wants *Baikal* more?"

"This is not an auction." Steadman looked at the weapons console and saw the four green lights marking four ready torpedoes. "His crew will be taken care of. The only question he must answer is whether they'll live to spend their money or not."

A distorted, watery voice answered, "The same can be said of yours."

COMSUBLANT
Norfolk, Virginia

1. 1.5 BILLION, PAYABLE RUSSIAN FEDERATION
2. 3K EACH 45 RATES, PAYABLE OFFSHORE ACCT
3. 4.5K EACH 25 CPO, PAYABLE OFFSHORE ACCT
4. 6K EACH 30 RANKS, PAYABLE OFFSHORE ACCT

A billion and a half, thought Graybar. That would be a straight-across trade if it did nothing but save *Portland*. The Russian CO was offering to throw in the Typhoon for free, and the rest was petty cash. On a new sheet of paper, Graybar wrote the reply Washington had dictated:

1: TERMS ACCEPTABLE PROVIDED RUSSIAN FUNDS
   RESTRICTED TO SCRAPPING REMAINING TYPHOON HULLS
   UNDER INTERNATIONAL SUPERVISION

Then, he added his own message:

2: IF CO BAIKAL BALKS, EXECUTE STANDING ORDERS
3: UNODIR, ADV AND PROCEED AVACHA CANYON . . . COM-
   SUBLANT SENDS

"International supervision means spies," said Grachev.

"Who cares if they spy on a rusting Typhoon? The only ones who will suffer are Fedorenko's colleagues. They won't be able to steal as much. Everyone else comes out even."

"Where is that slug, anyway?"

"In his cabin taking a well-deserved nap," said Markov. He picked up the microphone, thought about the implications of his next few words. For himself. For the crew, their families. For Russia and the world. He decided on simplicity. "I'll give you my answer in one hour. *Baikal* out." He let go of the microphone. It dangled from its cord, swaying like a metronome.

"An hour?" said Grachev.

Markov looked up. "I'm calling a quick meeting in the wardroom. I want you there, too."

"What kind of a meeting?"

"There's going to be a vote."

"Who am I supposed to vote for?"

"Not that kind of a vote, Igor."

Pavel the cook was busy overseeing preparations for the noontime meal of fried lamb cutlets, *tvorog* cheese and kasha when the order came down from Gasparyan.

The big cook dried his brow with the back of a sleeve, then turned to another messmate. "You! Prepare a *zakuski* tray for the officers! Smoked fish, bread, cheese and jam!"

"When do they need it?"

"Next Christmas." When the messmate seemed confused, Pavel said, *"Right away.* Use the supplies I set aside for the arrival ceremony." He turned. "You! A thermos of coffee and tea! And don't forget the cream! Understood?"

"Understood!"

"Everyone! Get moving!" *Fucking officers,* he thought as he watched his lunch plans derail. He checked the kasha pot to make sure it was perfect and fluffy, then turned the electric coils beneath the lamb cutlets down. *I ought to send them fucking shingles instead of meat,* he thought. What good was a meal plan when they screwed up everything with an unannounced party?

Pavel surveyed his ranks and rows of gleaming pots and pans. They were all first-quality, commercial-grade. Far better than anything the Navy had tried to dump on him. He'd looked at the battered, burned cookware they'd delivered to *Baikal* and ordered it thrown into a box and sent back, then went down to Murmansk to see his older brother.

His brother owned a small but very profitable restaurant called *Na Skoruyu Ryku,* At the Quick Hand. It was a deeply Russian version of a fast food restaurant, a small, stand-up café where the city's best borscht could be bought for a price nearly anyone, even a sailor, could afford. *Unlike fucking Pizza Hut.* You could spend a month's rent on a meal there.

Pavel had borrowed a full set of German cookware, including a set of cutting knives that belonged in a museum. They came in individual leather pouches. He'd promised to bring all of it back safe and sound. He needed his brother's goodwill, after all: Pavel's sailing bonus would go to opening a chain of similar cafés. There would be one in every Navy town at first, and then he would slowly expand to the bigger cities, though not Petersburg and surely not Moscow. Between the thieves in government and those on the streets, the cost of doing business there was too high.

A large silver platter heaped with delicacies appeared. Insulated carafes filled with hot tea and coffee were next. Pavel made some adjustments to a great slab of smoked fish, then nodded. "They don't deserve it. Now take it."

The officers' dining room could have been a private restaurant in any large Russian city, which is to say the materials were lavish and the workmanship poor. The bulkheads were paneled in light birch with the edges left splintery and raw. Mirrored pillars containing pipes and electrical conduits divided the space. Repairs had to be strung around them in tangles of wires and pipe runs that assumed the complexity of sculpture. The deck was carpeted in a vast acrylic oriental that screamed *fire hazard.* A series of round paintings meant to suggest portholes looked out onto mountains and a sapphire lake.

Markov walked in and found his senior officers already present. Borodin, Belikov, Gasparyan and Grachev sat at the captain's table: a long, polished wooden slab cut from an enormous tree and lacquered to a high gloss. At the "table of second rank" sat Nosikovskiy, the lieutenant in charge of communications; Vasiliev, lord of *Baikal*'s engine rooms and a master when it came to her diesels; and Kuznetsov, who commanded the controls section back in the maneuvering spaces.

A beautiful tray of food lay untouched at the captain's table.

"Our passenger is asleep in his cabin," Markov began even before he took his place. Everyone knew who he meant. "He won't stay asleep forever, so I'll come straight to the point. There's no way to keep a secret on a submarine, and so all of you know about the rockets. Now I'll tell you what you may not know. The Americans are also aware of what's in our silos. I called you all here to come to a decision about what to do about it."

"What's to decide?" said Vasiliev. "The Navy ordered us here."

"The Navy ordered us to deliver an unarmed submarine. If any of you can tell me some way to do this, I'm prepared to steam into Shanghai harbor immediately."

There was no response.

"I couldn't think of one, either." Markov looked at each of his men. "Every one of you volunteered. You were promised money to deliver *Baikal* and more to stay on as a trainer. Strictly speaking, we're mercenaries. By whatever name, you placed your lives in my hands. I take this responsibility seriously. I also take my responsibility to Russia seriously. Does anyone doubt it?"

"We're listening, Captain," said Gasparyan.

"We think of *Baikal* as a ship. Our ship. But the truth is *Baikal* is a weapon meant to intimidate and destroy. It is my belief that giving the Chinese such a weapon is insane. I am not insane."

"Too late," said Kuznetsov. "We're already surrounded by them."

"It may not be too late," said Markov. "The Americans don't want *Baikal* in Shanghai. It's why they've been trying to sink us. I've established communications with one of their submarines. They've been trailing us for some time now."

"Americans?" said Vasilyev. "Why aren't we dead?"

"Because if they kill us the Chinese will kill them. Because I told them that if they pay Russia, and each of us, what we were promised, the Chinese will never get their hands on this ship."

There was a moment of stunned silence.

"You're *selling Baikal* to the *Americans*?" said Vasiliev.

"Only an interest in her. Not the ship."

"How can you promise this?" asked Belikov. "If we move out of formation the Chinese will know. If they don't, Fedorenko will."

"I can lose the Chinese. And I have a plan for Fedorenko."

"Plan or no," said navigator Borodin. "We can't spend our bonus money in a prison camp."

"Or after they shoot us," said Vasiliev, the engine room commander. "Making deals with the Americans is treason."

"This ship was already sold to the Americans once. Was that treason? Look, I can't promise there won't be trouble when we return. In fact, given the terms the Americans are imposing, trouble is likely. But I give you my word, no American will ever walk these decks."

"How can you be so sure?" asked Gasparyan.

"It would be better that none of you know the details," said Markov. "I ask for your trust and your faith. You can decide for yourselves how the risks add up. Either way, Shanghai or no, I'll abide by your decision." He stood and looked down at the heaped platter. "You can enjoy a meal and vote in private."

Markov didn't make it to the door.

"Captain? No one is hungry and it's not necessary to vote," said Gasparyan. The *starpom* looked at his fellow officers and said, "If you say something is right, it's enough. But what about Fedorenko? We can't just open the hatch and throw him out."

"No. Fedorenko is essential."

"Him?" said Borodin.

"Yes," said Markov. "He's going to be the one to save us all."

USS *Portland*
off Cape Chukotka

"They agreed," said Scavullo.

Steadman turned to Lieutenant Choper. "Dive Officer. Come to periscope depth."

"PD, aye," said Slice and Dice. His old panic over screwing up was gone. Choper had lost his stutter. A few more weeks and who knew? He might even sound like a submariner.

"Scavullo? Be ready to transmit the instant the mast is exposed." The whip was hard to spot even if you knew where to look, but not impossible. All it would take would be one lucky Chinese lookout with a pair of good binoculars.

"It won't take long."

The burst transmitter made short work of Steadman's message to Norfolk:

1: PROCEEDING AVACHA CANYON . . . STEADMAN SENDS

Bam Bam worked up a solid bearing and range to *Baikal* using the Typhoon's underwater telephone broadcasts. But he had only a vague idea about the Chinese ships. Out beyond *Baikal* in a wide arc were two destroyers and four *Kilo* submarines, all heading south. Or so he hoped, for the plot he'd developed from *Baikal*'s booming sonar pulse was growing older and less reliable with every minute. The *Kilo*s were doing some kind of leapfrogging advance, with two on the surface snorkeling while the other two lurked silently beneath the waves listening.

"Conn, Sonar," he said. "Bearing to the Typhoon is one seven five, range six thousand yards."

"What about the *Kilo*s?"

"Two to port and the other two to starboard," said Bam Bam. "They're alternating surfaced and submerged. At least, they were the last time I got good bearings and ranges. You don't suppose we could get the Typhoon to fire off another active pulse for us, do you?"

"Not likely." Steadman looked at the contact plot. Bam Bam was right. To remain in range of *Baikal*'s underwater telephone, they had to remain dangerously near the screen of Chinese ships. Fall behind and they might lose *Baikal* for good.

Browne could see what Steadman was thinking. "How far you gonna trust this Russian CO?"

"Until he gives me a reason not to," said Steadman.

Baikal

Markov pulled the curtain to the navigation cubicle and stepped inside. Borodin looked up from his chart table. "Captain?"

Markov closed the curtain and peered into the pale, flickering computer screen. It displayed a digital version of Borodin's chart. Their course was drawn in brilliant magenta. "How much does Fedorenko know about our navigation system?"

"More than he knows about navigating. He came in to ask when we'd updated the computer with a satellite fix, but then he hardly looked at the charts. What kind of a captain trusts a computer over a hand-drawn log?"

The useful kind. "The computer's accurate?"

"Accurate enough but I still don't trust it. Why?"

"Would it matter if it malfunctioned?"

"Not to me."

"I thought not." Markov walked over to the keyboard that controlled the display and tapped in a command. A new course that was parallel to but off-set from the real one showed up on the screen as a faint gray line. He touched another key, and the gray line flashed magenta. The white cross jumped to it and the old, true course faded to gray.

The intercom squawked. "Captain to Central Command!"

He looked up. "Carry on, Borodin," said Markov, and he left with the altered display on the screen.

"Captain? A Chinese submarine is hailing us over the underwater tele-phone," said Belikov.

Markov nodded for Fedorenko to take the microphone.

Fedorenko listened, then turned to Markov. "They'd like to increase speed. We're to move south at twelve knots."

"Very well," said Markov. He grabbed a *kashtan*. "Igor? Ahead one-third on both engines. Turns for twelve knots. Make sure everyone is informed."

Fedorenko gave him a questioning look. Informed?

"We're moving south," said Grachev brusquely. "We'll be making twelve knots. Acknowledge."

There was no answer from the Russian-speaking woman on the Ameri-can submarine.

He repeated the message in the simple, direct words of an officer speaking to a dull *matros*. Instead of saying, "*Acknowledge*," he said, "*Panyatna*?" Get it?

USS *Portland*

"They're moving south," said Scavullo. Her right forefinger was hurting again, but the pain gave her something to concentrate on, something to help keep her mind clear. "He wants us to make twelve knots."

"Tell him I can only give him eight. At twelve knots we'll make too much noise."

Scavullo spoke, then listened, and then said, "He says we will do as his captain has ordered."

"Tell him we're unable."

Scavullo had a mental image of the man on the other end of their tenuous connection. A Russian captain would like being told what he could and could not do by an American woman about as much as an American captain. And so she answered Grachev in a way she knew he'd understand.

"We will proceed at eight knots," she said curtly. "Use your fingers to count if you need to. *Tolka vosyem! Kak znaitye?*"

"What was that all about?" asked Steadman.

"Cultural literacy."

Baikal

"They will give us only eight knots," said Grachev.

Markov saw that Fedorenko was watching him closely, suspiciously.

"Another problem?" asked Fedorenko.

"A matter of power distribution," said Markov. "Tell our escorts we can make only eight knots until Grachev figures it out."

CHAPTER THIRTY-THREE

THE MONSTER

14 AUGUST

USS *Portland*

The shallows gave way reluctantly as the small fleet sailed south across the Anadyr Sea. One hundred feet shelved down almost imperceptibly to three hundred, five hundred, six. Then, off Cape Navarin, the bottom plunged to nearly three thousand. The continental shelf was behind them. Ahead lay the Bering Abyss.

In theory, sailing close behind a submarine as big as *Baikal* should have been easy. No book, no war games could have prepared Steadman for keeping *Portland* within hailing range of a Russian ballistic missile boat without using sonar for two solid days.

"He says . . ." Scavullo wiped away a lank bang of sweaty hair from her forehead. It had come loose from her ponytail and she didn't have the energy to pin it back. "Come further right."

"Helm. Right five degrees rudder." *She's going to collapse,* thought Steadman. Scavullo had been on duty for eighteen hours.

"Conn, Sonar," said Bam Bam. "I just picked up one of the *Kilo*s again."

"Good work! Where is he?"

"Eight thousand yards ahead of *Baikal* and snorkeling. I can hear his diesel real clear, sir."

Even though there were three other *Kilo*s out there, Steadman was relieved to know the exact location of one of them.

"Stop turn," said Scavullo.

"Helm, rudder amidships." *I'm not conning the boat. She is,* thought Steadman. "How are you feeling, Lieutenant?"

"Like someone's been vacuuming my head for two days."

"Can you hang in there for one more?"

"If that's what it takes."

"Conn, Sonar. Transient from that snorkeling *Kilo*. They just killed their engines. It sounds like they're beating on something with a hammer."

Scavullo let her eyelids drop. Lower, lower, they were nearly shut when Belikov's voice returned with a message that sent a jab of cold adrenaline straight to the heart. "They're stopping!"

"Helm! All stop!"

Simple physics ordained that stopping forty thousand tons takes more sea room than stopping seven thousand. Even with her screws windmilling, *Baikal*'s mass drove her onward. When she finally drifted to a stop, *Portland* had fallen out of position. She was no longer five thousand yards behind her, but nine.

Baikal

"They're busy beating an induction valve to pieces up there," said Grachev.

"It may be the chance we've been waiting for," said Markov. "The whole task group is paying attention to that *Kilo*. Can you think of a better time?"

Grachev shrugged. "You're the captain."

"All right." Markov lowered his voice. "In ten minutes, Belikov will detect the American submarine."

"Good. Fedorenko will shit in his pants."

"He'll also want to alert the Chinese. I assume the forward underwater phone can be controlled from here?"

"They won't hear a fucking thing."

"We'll dive below the layer, sprint and then drift. By the time the Chinese realize what's happened, we'll be gone."

"What about the Americans?"

"We have to warn them." Markov took the microphone hooked up to the aft underwater telephone and clicked it. "*Baikal* calling *Los Angeles*. Can you hear me?"

There was no answer.

USS *Portland*

"So did the XO restrict me to quarters, Bedford?" asked Vann.

"No, sir."

"I'm glad to hear it. Then there's no reason why I can't go to the head? Take a shower? Eat a sandwich? Walk my own decks?"

"I guess not." But Bedford wanted to ask COB first. He started to say so, but he didn't get the chance.

Vann went forward to the ladder heading down to the middeck. "They still call you Tripod?" he asked as he started down.

"Hang on! Yes, sir."

"Miss your wife pretty bad, son?"

"We were married two weeks when we left Norfolk."

Vann stepped down onto the middle deck and headed aft in the direction of the wardroom. "I'm sorry for you, Bedford. You're going to have it pretty rough."

"I sure am looking forward to Norfolk."

"That's not where Steadman is headed."

"Hawaii's a better spot for a honeymoon anyway."

"I wouldn't put money on Hawaii, either."

"Sir?"

Vann walked by the door to the wardroom. "The officers who took my boat are going to go up before a court martial if we ever get back. The charge will be mutiny. You think they're anxious to see U.S. territory?" Vann stopped at a ladder leading down to the bottom deck. "You really don't know where Steadman is going, do you?"

"No, sir."

"Petropavlovsk. The biggest Russian navy base on the Pacific Ocean. Now, why do you suppose he'd do that?" said Vann as he started down. "You better hope the Russians let your wife visit you in Siberia, because that's where this boat is pointed." With that, Vann descended out of sight.

Siberia? Bedford stood there for a moment, letting Vann's words percolate. "Captain!" he said, realizing that Vann wasn't waiting for him. He jumped to the ladder. "Wait up!" he called, then slid down so fast the rungs burned the palms of his hands.

There was no sign of Vann at the bottom. Aft was Rat Alley and the auxiliary machine room. Forward was the torpedo room, and that was where Bedford found him.

Vann stood next to a torpedo-loading tray, jabbing a finger into Engler's chest.

"Engler," Vann said, "you were a problem I inherited. I can't say that I expected much from you, and you surely have not given me a reason to change my opinion. But you," he said to Bledsoe, "you're an officer. It was *your* job to ride herd on the people in your division. Lieutenant Bledsoe, you failed us."

Bledsoe looked down. "I'm sorry, sir."

"Hey, skipper," said Chief Babcock, "are you supposed to be wandering around down here?"

"He's not restricted to quarters," Bedford volunteered.

Vann nodded. "Thank you, son."

"Well, Captain, this is *my* space and it ain't visiting hours," said Babcock. "I got four warshots loaded and I don't have time for tours. These two shit-birds," he said, meaning Engler and Bledsoe, "are definitely restricted. You need to stand away from them."

"I understand completely. Carry on, Chief," he said.

Baikal

"Captain," said Belikov, "contact bearing zero one four, range nine kilo-meters." He adjusted his receiver so that even Fedorenko would see it. "Steam noise and no blade count. It smells like a nuclear boat."

Fedorenko saw the spoke of radial light on the screen. He could see other radial lines that represented the Chinese ships. "Will our escorts detect him?"

"Probably not. Our sonar is better than theirs," said Markov. "It's why we're guarding the rear."

"They must be warned."

"Absolutely," said Markov. "Do it quickly, Gennadi. We're in range of their torpedoes. This is a dangerous spot for lingering. Use the forward telephone."

Fedorenko took the *kashtan* and tried to reach Captain Bai Yao. He got no answer. He looked to Markov. "Now what?"

"We'll have to lose this wolf and then rejoin our escorts." Markov looked to the two warrant officers at the helm. "Left full rudder. Ahead full! Do not cavitate!"

"What depth, Captain?" asked Gasparyan.

"Four hundred meters. Take her deep."

PLAAN Submarine Lin San Liu

Baikal's ballast tanks were large enough to swallow a *Kilo* submarine whole. For the sixty men sealed up inside her, a tank would have been just about as comfortable. The little *Kilo* was meant for short voyages. After two weeks underway, her tight passages, her tiny equipment spaces, her nooks, her crannies took on the smell and feel of a Third World prison.

At least the twenty Russian trainers had their own bunks and the excuse of being paid for their discomfort. One stood duty at the *Rubicon* passive sonar console. The *Rubicon* set was far less effective than the American sonar and it was nearly blanketed with racket from the *Kilo* making repairs. Still, it retained enough capability to detect *Baikal*.

"What the fuck is he doing?" the Russian sonarman cursed.

His Chinese counterpart leaned over his shoulder, breathing on his neck. The Russian petty officer's nerves were worn bare by the closeness of the *Kilo,* the smell of Chinese cooking, and the fact that they'd sailed around in circles for three days waiting for *Baikal* to show up. *"Uchadi!"* the Russian said, and grabbed the nearest *kashtan.*

By the time Captain Bai Yao hurried to see for himself what the commotion among the Russian advisors was all about, *Baikal* had plunged beneath an acoustically opaque layer of the sea.

The *Kilo* with its induction flapper valve jammed open was left to solve her own problems. *Hangzhou, Fuzhou* and the three remaining *Kilo* boats turned their bows in the direction *Baikal* had fled.

Antisubmarine helicopters clattered off the aft decks of the destroyers, but their dipping sonar was able to penetrate the thermocline no better than Captain Bai Yao's. When *Baikal* was not found, a message was sent to the Russian base at Petropavlovsk.

The ships and submarines of the once-mighty Russian Pacific Fleet were now mostly derelict. But that was not the same as saying that nothing could be done.

Once, American submarines had been able to creep right into Avacha Bay, tapping undersea phone lines and listening in on radio communications. In response, an ultra-low-frequency sonar net called the Avacha Sea Monster had been developed to sanitize the sea of the invading Americans.

Huge sonar transmitters the size of rail cars were seeded across the ocean bottom off Petropavlovsk, extending south to Cape Lopatka, north to Cape Kamchatka. When the Sea Monster roared, it emitted a deep, rich bellow powerful enough to boil seawater.

It was a sound able to cross whole oceans, loud enough to deafen whales. A sound able to penetrate and dissect the ocean's many layers and reveal every object, natural and unnatural, Russian or American, hidden within them.

USS *Portland*

"Conn, Sonar. Something's happening out ahead."

"Go," said Steadman.

"That destroyer just put on major turns. She's burning rubber headed southeast."

"Out to sea. What about the *Kilos*?"

"The tin can left them in the dust. Then . . . Stand by." Schramm watched his screen pulse with the regular flicker of active sonar. "Conn, Lamb Tail sonar bearing one six eight and he's close."

"A helicopter set," said Steadman. "What's he doing?"

"Second Lamb Tail set just went off somewhere ahead. I can't give you a bearing but they're sure hunting for *someone.*"

Us? wondered Steadman. Had the Russians alerted their escorts to his presence? Scavullo was on a break. He walked over to the microphone connected to the UQC-6, and keyed it. "*Baikal Baikal Baikal,* do you read?"

There was no answer.

"Bam Bam, do you have any contact with the boomer?"

"No UQC. No screw noise, no plant and no flow. He could be gone."

Steadman looked at Browne and said, "I think we've been had."

An invisible tidal wave of sound came roaring out of Avacha Bay, boiling the sea, killing fish, sending whales seeking shelter from the sonic storm. By the time it traveled the two hundred miles to where *Portland* lay still and silent, it had lost scarcely any of its punch.

Rose Scavullo's head was down on the table in the wardroom when it struck. She was fast asleep. An untouched chicken breast sandwich and a glass of orange bug juice lay nearby.

All through the boat, people stopped what they were doing and looked around. As the magnitude of the wave kept building, each one was sure that something bad was happening close by.

The damage control party finishing up work at the sonar tunnel hatch was sure the bow was coming loose and the tunnel was ripping away. The torpedomen on the deck below them heard the buzz of a Mark 48 running hot inside a tube. Bam Bam was sure *Baikal* had turned about and her bow was right beyond the hull, pointed at his eyes, an instant away from ramming. In Control, it was an electronics console about to explode. In the reactor spaces, a meltdown in the core.

Though none of these catastrophes had taken place, a dozen hands reached for a dozen alarms, certain that they had.

Scavullo's ears were not as well attuned as a submariner's. And she was exhausted. She slept through the first waves. At first, the surface of the bug juice shimmered in concentric rings. As energy poured into the submarine's hull, making it buzz and hum like a struck tuning fork, the liquid surface began to jump, to fizz.

There was a shout loud enough to wake her up, and when she opened her eyes, her orange juice was erupting like a carbonated volcano.

She could hear panicked voices and pounding feet from out in the passage. A fluorescent tube shattered with a *pop!* The room went dim, then dark. She lunged for the door and got her hands on the handle. The vibrations eased, then stopped, as the Sea Monster's endless roar swept right through the boat, and out to sea.

Any one of the alarms ringing in Control would have sent Steadman into adrenaline-powered fast forward. But all of them? It was a puzzle that Bam Bam Schramm quickly answered for him.

"Conn! Sonar! That was a hundred-hertz pulse from the mother of all sonars!"

Steadman ordered the alarms disabled. "Who pinged us? The boomer?"

"No way, sir. I'm still listenin' to aftershocks bouncing off stuff." The boat trembled. "That was another one."

"A pulse?"

"An *echo*. The source is somewhere to the south. For *damned* sure we just showed up on *someone's* screen."

Now what? The Chinese were hunting for something to the south. The low-frequency sonar was south, too. West was the Russian coast. East was looking a whole lot better.

"Conn, Sonar. That blast stopped the helos for a while but one of them is at it again. I've got one pinging away at three five zero. He's too far to pick us up but he's moving. . . . Conn! The second helo is pinging and he's going to be close."

Steadman reacted instantly. "Helm, *left* full rudder! All ahead flank! Take her down to three hundred fifty feet *smartly.* Be ready to fire a noisemaker!"

Portland left a swirl of turbulent water in her wake as she twisted away and dived.

"Two hundred feet," said Slice and Dice.

The high pings of helicopter sonar sounded through the hull.

Ping! Ping! Ping! Ping! Ping!

"He's got us," said Bam Bam.

"Like hell he does," said Steadman. *Will he drop on us?* It would be an act of war, though using one of *Portland*'s torpedoes as a sonar scout would have seemed like an act of war to the *Kilo* it had chased.

Ping! Ping! Ping! Ping! Ping!

Steadman waited as long as he could stand to wait before acting. "Helm! Shift your rudder!"

Portland left another great swirl in the water astern.

"Three hundred feet," said Slice and Dice.

Then Steadman got his answer.

"Conn! Sonar! Torpedo in the water aft! I say again, we have a torpedo in the water bearing zero eight five!"

"Fire the noisemaker."

"Noisemaker away!"

A chemical canister spat out of the three-inch launcher. It reacted with the salt water by bubbling furiously.

Steadman watched the Fathometer click off the feet as *Portland* raced to get below the temperature layer.

There was no sound, no physical sensation at all to mark the submarine's plunge beneath the thermocline. But the water temperature dropped eighteen degrees in forty feet.

"Three hundred fifty feet," said Slice and Dice.

"Conn, Sonar. Both helos are pinging on our noisemaker," said Schramm. "Bearing change on the torpedo. It's a miss!"

"Ahead one-third," said Steadman. "Left ten degrees rudder. Steady on course one seven six."

Steadman thought, *We got away from a pair of helicopters but that low-frequency sonar pulse could find us again.*

When it did, he intended to be far from the Chinese ships. He could only hope that when he got there, *Baikal* would be there, too. One way or another, Steadman would have to find him. Even if it meant chasing him right to the pier at Petropavlovsk. For the alternative, that he'd been taken in by a fast-talking Russian CO, that Vann had been right, would be a failure that made Vann's seem like shoplifting.

CHAPTER THIRTY-FOUR

THE FLOOD

Baikal
Emperor Seamounts

"Belikov?"

"No contacts."

"Have we lost the American?" asked Fedorenko.

"It would seem so." Like *Portland, Baikal* had boomed and groaned in demonic harmonies for a full minute. Markov felt the low reverberations right in his gut. But then his instincts took over and he pointed the ship in the direction of a chain of extinct undersea volcanoes called the Emperor Seamounts.

Where are the Americans?

If their captain knew his business, he should be far away. But with a damaged ship? With no sonar to guide him? That woman hadn't answered Markov's call. What if they were still back there waiting for *Baikal*'s guidance?

They'll catch him and sink him. If not after one pulse, then surely after the next.

"How do you propose to rejoin our escorts?" asked Fedorenko.

Markov looked pensive, as though he were actually weighing possibilities, evaluating moves. "They'll move south along the expected route. Borodin?" Markov said to the navigator. "Plot a southerly intercept course. Assume a ten-knot speed of advance."

"Stand by, Captain."

"Why not sail at full speed back north where we left them?" asked Fedorenko

"Think," Markov said patiently. "The sonar operators who sent that pulse might know where the American went but they haven't told us. I'd prefer not to meet him."

"He'd be a fool to stay around for another dose."

"No doubt."

"And here it comes," said Belikov.

Markov felt the second wave of sonar energy in his feet, transmitted right through the deck plates. It made the glass faces of his instruments buzz. It was louder than a sonar hundreds of kilometers away had any right to be. But sheltered in the lee of an extinct volcano, *Baikal* would not show up on anyone's screen. To the men who operated the Sea Monster, and to the Americans, *Baikal* would have simply vanished.

Central Command went silent as the rumble of distant thunder became a single, low note that finally subsided to silence.

"Captain?" said Borodin. "Our best course is two zero five. We should find them again along that line."

"What kind of water will we have under us up there?"

"Four hundred meters, but it gets *very* deep just offshore. Six thousand five hundred meters," said the navigator. "The new rendezvous point is west of a formation called Avacha Canyon."

"Helm," said Markov. "Left fifteen degrees rudder. Ahead two-thirds. Steer two zero five. Let's go find our little friends."

USS *Portland*

It was like listening to a whale song from inside the whale. Once more the steel hull rang with low tones. Once more the deck shook with its power and men looked up in honest fear.

"Avacha Canyon is fifty miles dead ahead," said Whalley. "We still going there?"

"Still," said Steadman, though he'd raised an antenna and sent word back to Norfolk that they were no longer trailing *Baikal,* that they had no idea where she was. Only hopes about where she might be. "Bam Bam? Did you get a recording on that one?"

"Conn, Sonar, aye. Two hundred forty-three decibels. That pulse must screw up the water something fierce. I reckon they can't fire it off without waiting for the bubbles to clear. I tell you what. I'd hate to pay the electric bill for that sucker."

"Keep a close watch for those helicopters, Bam Bam. Whoever's manning that sonar probably knows where we are and could be telling his buddies." *And that means there's no reason to creep.* "Helm, make turns now for ten knots." It was as fast as Steadman dared to go.

"Ten knots, aye."

Portland was running south eighty miles off the Kamchatka coast, caught between the hammer of the Chinese behind and the anvil of the low-frequency sonar ahead. It was Steadman's plan to find *Baikal,* pick up her crew and clear the area before the two could meet.

If only *Baikal* would be there.

The torpedo room had the tense, electric air of a cocked rifle waiting for a target to appear in its sights. But a hair trigger cannot remain poised forever. After a while, even the unusual sight of four tubes bearing placards that read *WARSHOTS LOADED* became just another part of the scenery.

Engler knew the signs. Like those placards, having men handcuffed to the port and starboard torpedo loading trays had become part of the scenery, too. And so, at the change of the watch, as Chief Babcock briefed the incoming leading chief, Engler said to a young torpedoman, "Hey, Red. I got to hit the head."

The torpedoman had short curly hair that paled to almost a carrot orange under the sun. Inside the hull, under the blue fluorescent lights, it remained a more subtle, autumnal shade of russet. "Why tell me? I'm outta here for some chow."

"Go tell your fucking chief I need to take a crap."

Red broke into the chief's private conversation. Three faces turned Engler's way, and with a disgusted look, Babcock nodded.

The red-haired TM returned with a key to Engler's cuffs. "You better figure out how to wipe your ass with no hands."

"Aw, man. Come on. Have a fucking heart."

"It's up to you. Be nice and I might let you have one of your hands. Be an asshole and you stink."

"Say the word. You want my hands in front or back?"

Red thought about it, about Engler's reputation, and said, "Back."

The cuffs came unlocked from the torpedo tray, and Engler held his hands together behind his back. Red refastened them with a sharp *click.*

It was dead quiet as they made their way through the narrow passage between the stacked bunks of Rat Alley. Eyes watched as Engler was led through in cuffs. If Engler went down, who would be next?

A young sailor in the deck division named Bronson had a special interest. Bronson was a big, slow kid from Topeka. It usually took a while to earn a nickname in the boats, but he'd come with his ready-made: Bronto. He'd been trying to get a recommendation to radio school, and Engler had been a help. If his ass was in a sling, then Bronto would be chipping paint a long, long time.

The lower-level head was a small space lined with linoleum and stainless steel. Red opened the door for Engler.

Engler stepped into the open stall and turned, his arms still behind him. "You want to pull my pants down, Red?"

"Turn around. And remember, if you give me any trouble, I'll lock you to the head, open the valve and when the shit storm is over they'll call you Freckles."

Engler obliged and Red unlocked the cuffs, then relocked the empty one to a vertical support, leaving one of Engler's hands free. "You're a pal, shipmate," said Engler. "I'll remember you."

"Do me a favor. Don't."

Engler dropped his poopy suit and squatted. After making enthusiastic noises and with a look of enormous relief, he reached for the toilet paper, unrolled a wad, then leaned forward to apply it.

When his hand emerged, the paper was gone, and he had a small key in his fingers.

Red was looking at his bleary eyes in the mirror. He didn't notice anything amiss until he heard the *click*. He half-turned in time for his face to meet a bright, glittering cuff swung with all of Engler's considerable strength. It caught him across the forehead. He staggered back against the sink, hit his head on it as he fell and dropped to the deck without another sound.

"Sorry, shipmate," said Engler as he snapped one cuff on Red and the other to a pipe.

"Conn, Sonar. Lamb Tail sonar astern bearing zero one four. I'd estimate twenty miles plus."

Right where we were two hours ago, thought Steadman. So far he was staying ahead of them. Just.

"Thirty miles to Avacha Canyon," said Whalley.

Time, thought Steadman. "Radio, Conn."

"Radio, aye," said Lieutenant Wallace.

"Scavullo still on watch?"

"Sort of," said Wallace. "Actually, she's asleep."

"Wake her up and send her forward."

"You still don't get it, do you?" said Engler. "He fucking *drugged* the skipper and took over. You approve of that shit?"

"No," said Bronto. The voice coming out of the darkened rack seemed childlike.

"Then tell me where you stashed it."

"I just want to get back home."

"Your fat ass is gonna get tossed over the fucking side if you don't tell me where you put it."

"Tell him!" someone yelled. "I heard an officer say the XO is taking the boat to Russia."

"Russia?" said Bronto.

"Isn't *that* something?" said Engler. "You want your family to read about how you handed over your submarine to the *enemy*?"

Five men yelled together, *"Tell him!"*

"Bow planes grease pump access," Bronson blurted.

Engler reached over and slapped Bronson's face. "Dumb shit deck ape," he said, and then ran forward, then up to the middle deck.

The bow planes grease pump lived behind a door set right into the bulkhead between two crew racks, just aft of the Goat Locker and the yeoman's office. Engler found one of the beds occupied and yanked a sleepy sailor out and onto the floor. He spluttered in outrage but Engler ignored him, reached over the warm bedding and opened the access panel.

The missing Beretta M-9 was right where Bronto had said.

"What are you doing up here?"

Engler grabbed the weapon and spun.

It was Chief Babcock. The chief was standing at the door to the soggy Goat Locker. The flood had made him homeless, and he was carrying away some books and photographs for drier keeping.

"Who let you out?" Babcock demanded.

"This." The M-9 came out.

Babcock froze.

"Remember what I told you?"

"Don't do it, son."

"I ain't your son." He pulled the trigger hard, letting the firing mechanism advance. A second pull, and there was a loud *crack* and Babcock flew back into the Goat Locker, his windmilling arms grabbing at the door frame for a hold and failing. The chief skidded across the deck, leaving a trail of bright red.

"What . . . what . . . " the now wide-awake sailor said. "You *shot the chief*!"

"He was working for the enemy, asshole." Engler leaned down over Babcock's face. His eyes were open, his mouth working but no sound escaped other than the wheeze of air leaking out through his ruined chest. "I keep my promises."

"Engler!"

The radioman spun on the sailor. "Some officer assholes arrested the captain and now they're taking the boat to Russia. I'm not gonna let them. How about you?"

"Russia?"

"Siberia. You in or are you a fucking traitor, too?"

The sailor eyed the gun. "I'm in," he said.

Bam Bam didn't hear the shot though *Portland*'s noise-monitoring system, the AN/WSQ-7, surely did. But with the boat running at ten knots, with her damaged bow creaking and shuddering, the sharp report was just one of a thousand new and unfamiliar sounds the system had to cope with.

And now, the helicopters were back.

"Conn, Sonar, Lamb Tail sonar bearing zero one five degrees true, range twenty thousand yards. He's pinging above the layer."

"Helm, make turns for six knots," said Steadman. The helos were getting too close and there was no reason to give them any more noise to listen to than was absolutely necessary.

"Conn, Sonar, there's the second helo. Bearing three five oh true, range twenty-two thousand yards. He's below the layer."

They were working together, cued by the big land-based sonar. Eventually they'd find him. A helicopter could run him down a lot faster than he could run away.

"Avacha Canyon dead ahead," said Whalley.

Steadman unhooked the microphone linked to the underwater telephone and handed it to Scavullo. "Lieutenant?"

Scavullo's eyes were red-rimmed with sleep. Her cheek looked bruised from resting it against the hard surface of a radio console. It seemed to take a lot of effort for her to raise her arm and grasp the black microphone, but she did with the grim look of a marathon runner gazing up at one last hill. She shook her hair back away from her eyes, blinked, then said,

"*Baikal, Baikal, Baikal, vui sluyshetye?*"

Baikal

"Go refill the teakettle, Demyan," said Grachev.

Demyan left Grachev alone on Main Engineering. The chief engineer walked over to the missile hatch hydraulics panel on the forward bulkhead. From there, the mechanisms for raising and lowering the heavy, bank vault hatches could be commanded by way of a tangle of piping and valves. There was a row of twenty small indicator lamps, all of them showing green for shut.

He couldn't launch one of those damned rockets. It would be a lot easier on everyone if he could. What Grachev *could* do was unlock a muzzle hatch and raise it. With finger-loose bolts on the access panels down at the base of the silo, a little crack would go a long way. Under pressure, a small leak would look like a torrent.

He pushed the green lamp marked *16*. The light began to flash as if to say, *Do you really mean it?* He pushed it again and the green went out, replaced by amber. When he was certain the system was functioning properly, he pried up the plastic switch cover and smashed the bulb dark with his thumb, then snapped the lens back in place.

The process of opening a hatch was fully automatic, but not quick. Depending on depth, it could take as much as five minutes to fully open. But when it did, Rocket Alley would become a river.

"Approaching the rendezvous point, Captain," said Borodin.

"Belikov?"

"Stand by." The sonar operator made a careful search, allowing *Baikal*'s passive sonar to sift the waters a full 360 degrees around. It would have revealed the presence of any ship within twenty kilometers, except that he'd adjusted the range to its minimum setting. Even at that, a radial spoke brightened.

"Active sonar contact, Captain. It's well to the north and close to shore. It sounds like a helicopter set."

"I was wrong," said Markov with a look of surprise. "They're hugging the coast."

"It was a mistake to run so far south," said Fedorenko.

"Why don't you go work out an intercept course with Borodin?" Before Fedorenko could express his surprise, Markov said, "It will be good practice."

Fedorenko went into the navigator's cubicle. He ignored the paper chart open on the table and consulted the video screen. The white cross marking *Baikal*'s position showed her over the continental shelf off Petropavlovsk. To the east, the bottom plunged eighteen thousand feet to the bottom of the Avacha Canyon.

"Sonar places the escort groups here," said the navigator, jabbing the computer display some distance to the north. "Right off Cape Kozlov."

"I told him we should return immediately to our escorts."

"The captain has his own ideas."

Fedorenko peered at the cool glass display. "Have you decided about Shanghai, Borodin? The offer is still on the table. You could spend a year there and then come home rich enough to retire from the Navy."

"Yes. I've made up my mind."

"So?"

"If *Baikal* goes there, so will I."

Fedorenko clapped him on the shoulder. "Good boy." He picked up Borodin's *kashtan* and said, "Markov? Turn this boat around. Your course will be zero four five degrees."

"Zero four five," said Markov.

Fedorenko felt the deck heel under him, but he kept his eyes on the little white cross on the screen. It pivoted and began to inch its way back in the direction of the Chinese ships.

Satisfied, he was about to go back and rub Markov's nose in the fact that he'd been so wrong when a blood-curdling *whoop! whoop! whoop!* sounded over the ship's intercom.

"Flooding alarm!" yelled Borodin.

Fedorenko pulled the curtain back. Markov was talking to someone on one *kashtan*. Gasparyan was talking over another. "What is it?"

Markov ignored him, pointed a finger at Gasparyan and snapped it. The first officer nodded and turned forward to the hatch leading into Main Engineering, then saw Fedorenko. "Shut that damned horn off!"

The alarm went silent.

"Water intrusion in Silo Sixteen," came Grachev's raspy voice. "Something must have broken loose."

Fedorenko rushed over. "What's happening?"

"There's water in Rocket Alley," said Markov.

"Grachev is going forward to check and he needs some help. What about the radiation in there?"

"The emitters are quite small."

"Good. You know where they are. You can go help."

"Me?"

"Is there some problem?"

Fedorenko knew the men in Central Command were looking at him for a sign of weakness, of cowardice. He needed to set an example if he hoped to convince them to remain in Shanghai as trainers under his command. "Of course not."

"Excellent," said Markov. "Grachev is waiting for you."

Grachev had a big canvas satchel full of tools slung over his shoulder. He was already wearing his lead foil radiation suit and was about to slip on the hood when Fedorenko undogged the aft watertight door and stepped over the coaming.

"Are you lost?" he asked Fedorenko.

"Markov said you needed some help."

"The last time I looked there were no Chinese in Rocket Alley." Grachev tossed the hood to the deck and grabbed a *kashtan*. "Captain? I need a submariner up here. Not a *zampolit*."

"Fedorenko has special knowledge, Igor. Trust me. He can help you."

Grachev looked deeply dubious.

"There are twenty silos with rockets in them," said Fedorenko. "And five radiation emitters. I know where they are."

"Radiation emitters? What are you talking about?"

"Markov didn't tell you?"

"I'm just an engineer. Nobody tells me shit." He put the *kashtan* to his mouth. "He wants to go for a swim? Fine. We're on our way." He slapped the *kashtan* into its cradle and said to Demyan, "Give him the tools, Demyan. You have the duty here."

"Understood." Demyan handed the heavy satchel to Fedorenko.

Grachev spun the locking wheel to the watertight door leading into Rocket Alley and pushed it open. In came a mist carrying the cold, wet smell of the sea. Grachev stepped through and motioned for Fedorenko to follow.

USS *Portland*

Vann switched off the cabin lights and stretched out on his bunk. He felt sorry for Steadman. He'd been in a position to walk away a winner as long as that Typhoon ended up on the bottom. Steadman had only to say, *Shoot!* to go home a hero.

Vann had a few things to explain. He'd been wrong to place his trust in a weak officer like Bledsoe, or to allow him a free hand in steering that maniac radioman. But was there the *slightest* doubt in *anyone's* mind that if he had been in command, the Typhoon would now be dead?

Instead, Steadman had tagged after that boomer like a puppy too small to mount a bitch. He'd brought them to the enemy's backyard. Just what in the name of God did he *think* would be waiting for him off Petropavlovsk? A fireboat spraying streams of water? A brass band?

There was a quick, urgent knock at his stateroom door. He quickly switched off the display and stretched out on his bunk.

The door opened. "Captain?"

He pushed the book away. It was Engler. "It's about time."

Baikal

The dim lights in Rocket Alley made the tall, narrow compartment seem like a tunnel. Grachev switched on his light and let it lance through the swirling mist. The forward end of the compartment was lost in the gloom. He turned to Fedorenko. "Dog that hatch tight and let's go."

Fedorenko slammed the heavy watertight door closed and spun the locking wheel. When he turned, Grachev was far ahead. "Hey!" He hurried to catch up, the heavy tool bag clanking as he ran by the first rows of silos.

The sound of splashing water grew louder as they moved forward to their source. The air was thick with fog. It condensed on the cold silos and ran down them in rivulets that Fedorenko mistook for more leaks.

"You'll know the real thing when you see it," Grachev said. "Where are those radiation sources?"

"Under Silos One, Eight, Twelve and . . ."

"Sixteen?"

"Yes."

"Wonderful. That's where the fucking alarm came from. What are they doing there anyway?"

"They're very small."

"If they're so small you can dive the bilge and find out why the pumps aren't keeping up with the leak."

The hatch back to Main Engineering vanished behind. The sound of the leak grew, as though they were nearing a small but vigorous waterfall. Grachev's light fought to penetrate the fog that enclosed them. Silos Ten. Twelve. Fourteen. Finally, both the beam and Grachev came to a stop.

"So."

Water was pouring out from around the perimeter of an access hatch in the side of Silo Sixteen. No, not *pouring*. It was jetting across the aisle, exploding into mist when it struck the wall of the opposite silo.

"We're lucky." Grachev put the lantern down and snapped his fingers at Fedorenko. "Tools."

Fedorenko was staring at all that water and wondering how a torrent filling up the submarine he happened to be riding might be considered *lucky*.

"Hey! Pay attention!" He stalked over, grabbed the tool bag and pulled out two large socket wrenches and a collapsible steel handle. "It's not serious yet."

"But look at it."

"I didn't say it shouldn't be fixed. Your friends back at Seal Bay forgot to tighten the bolts on the access panel. We've got to seal it ourselves. Here." He handed Fedorenko a wrench and the long extension bar. "You start tightening the bolts on your side of the hatch, I'll do the same on mine."

"How tight?"

"You'll know when the water stops."

Fedorenko pulled the handle out full, attached it to the wrench and set it onto the first bolt head.

Grachev was right. They were loose. Dangerously loose. It was either sabotage or criminal negligence, and either way, someone would pay. *Those yard workers will see the inside of a cell for this,* he thought as he pulled the bolt tighter. When it would turn no more he attacked the next one.

It wasn't as loose as the first. He grunted as he leaned against the handle and put his weight into it. Tighter, another quarter turn, an eighth. A sixteenth of a turn.

There was a sudden *snap,* then an entire series of snaps. The handle flew away and Fedorenko tumbled forward, off balance, into what seemed like the ocean itself. The blast threw him across the aisle and against a silo. This was no *spray*. This was no *leak*. The *Pacific Ocean* was roaring in.

"What have you done?" Fedorenko yelled above the roar of a sudden violent torrent flooding from the base of Silo Sixteen. "You've sunk the fucking ship!" Grachev ran to the *kashtan* and yelled, "Breach in Silo Sixteen!"

You've sunk the ship. Not the timid Markov. Not his insolent engineer. But *Fedorenko*. He looked at Grachev. The engineer was smirking in silent victory. No doubt this had all been planned. No.

Fedorenko got to his feet and swung the wrench at Grachev's head as hard as he could. It must have made a sound when it hit, for he could feel bones yield. But he heard nothing as Grachev flew back and hit the wall of a silo, yanking the *kashtan* out by its cord, and sagged down to the rising water.

FRIENDLY FIRE

Scavullo keyed the microphone again. *"Baikal, Baikal, Baikal."*

"Helm, make turns for four knots," said Steadman. "Right ten degrees rudder. Let's take her around again."

COB showed up in Control and slid into his accustomed seat at the ballast control board. He'd grabbed something to eat and a quick rest, but his eyes were bloodshot. He was weary to the bone. He saw Lieutenant Choper. It looked like he hadn't moved a muscle. "You doin' okay, Lieutenant?"

"It's automatic, COB," said Choper.

Browne took out his portable radio and put it on the console. He saw Scavullo with the underwater telephone mike in her hands. "Anything?"

"Not yet."

"Be real embarrassing if they don't show up. Where are we?"

More than embarrassing. "Avacha Canyon," said Steadman. "Steaming in circles. The Chinese are still beating the bushes."

"Baikal, Baikal, Baikal, vui sluyshetye?"

The radio call light on Browne's handheld was blinking. He grabbed it and wearily inserted the earpiece jack.

"Sonar, Conn. How long before I have to worry about those helicopters?"

"You can start anytime now," said Bam Bam. He watched a bright line pulse on his display. "I'm watching helo two, bearing zero two three, range eighteen thousand yards. His pal's been off the air for the last fifteen minutes. Probably had to head back to the barn for fuel."

Or another torpedo. Eighteen thousand yards, thought Steadman. If *Portland* surfaced they would spot him for sure. That would complicate getting any of those Russians over onto . . .

"God*damn.*" It was Browne. He slapped the radio down onto the console. "Engler's gone!"

Steadman was about to say, *Gone?* when Bam Bam shouted, "Conn, Sonar! We've got a helo dropping a line of buoys across our course. If he keeps to his pattern the next one will be close."

Fedorenko ran aft through the dark, narrow compartment chased by a swift rising tide. He splashed across the high-water mark at the big yellow silo marked TEN. Half of Rocket Alley's deck was now flooded. He could hear the rush of water behind him. The sound was no longer a waterfall's spray. It had the lower, deeper note of breaking surf. He reached the aft watertight door, spun the locking wheel hard and pulled. The door swung in and with it came the noise of a dozen new alarms going off in Main Engineering.

"What happened in there?" Demyan demanded. "I'm showing water as far aft as Silo Eight." He looked through the open hatch. "Where's Engineer Grachev?"

Fedorenko pulled the hatch shut. "He's finished."

"With what?"

"He's dead. We were securing a loose silo hatch when it just let go. The steel hit him across the face. It nearly took his head off."

Demyan looked at the sealed hatch. He'd dived into the polar sea and pulled Grachev back up. Getting knocked off your feet by a little water and bumping your head wouldn't, couldn't, kill the chief engineer. He yanked a *kashtan* down and said, "Captain, this is Demyan. There's been an accident in Compartment Two."

Markov saw the alarm annunciators flashing on Gasparyan's damage control board and thought, *It's too late to turn back. Everything is in motion.* "What's going on with all those flooding alarms, Demyan? It started with just one and now I see a dozen. Is Grachev working on the problem?"

"He's still in Rocket Alley. Fedorenko left him. Send someone forward to man the consoles. I'll go forward to bring him out."

He's still in there? That wasn't the plan. "Where's Fedorenko?"

"Here. He claims an access hatch blew open and knocked Grachev down. He says he's dead."

Markov felt a silence close around him, a blanket that muffled the ringing alarms, dimmed the flashing lights. "Put him on."

Demyan handed the *kashtan* to Fedorenko. "It's true. I was standing behind him holding a lantern when it happened. The hatch exploded in our faces."

"And you left him *behind*?"

"He ordered me out with his last breath!"

Markov was about to call him a liar when Belikov said, "Captain. Sonar contact bearing two six three, range five kilometers. I think it's the Americans."

Kamov 25

A Russian helicopter pilot flying from the Chinese destroyer *Hangzhou* turned his Kamov 25 farther out to sea. The sky was overcast, the horizon an indistinct haze blending sky and sea into an indeterminate gray. Behind his tail, the Avachinsky Volcano that loomed over Petropavlovsk pierced the western horizon. The Sea Monster had detected a submarine in this area, and he could only hope it was *Baikal*. It still astonished him that something so big could have been made to vanish. After all, the Monster was supposed to be able to spot a sardine. His job was to reestablish contact with *Baikal* if he could, and make sure the American submarine lurking in the area didn't find her first.

"Stand by to drop," the Russian sonarman said.

Even by helicopter standards, the Kamov 25 was an ungainly flying machine. It had four wheels, two rudders and two counterrotating rotors spinning madly over a fuselage with all the elegant lines of a baked potato.

If anything, her crew was even more awkward. A Russian pilot, a Chinese copilot, a bilingual radio operator and two men, one from each country, huddled at her small sonar station. The copilot was also in charge of their weapons, which for the moment consisted of a single Type 40 torpedo.

"Mark!"

A sonobuoy dropped from the clattering machine. A small parachute popped open to slow its brief fall before it splashed into the slate dark sea. The buoy with its radio and antenna remained on the surface as a hydrophone reeled out from its bottom, plunging deep beneath the waves.

The sonarman called out, "Passive sonar contact! Possible submarine!"

The pilot wheeled the Kamov around until it hovered in midair.

"*Baikal?*" his copilot asked.

He nodded. "We'll drop an active one this time. That should wake him up enough to surface and explain what he's up to. Sonar! Stand by for an active drop."

"Steer one seven five."

The pilot lowered the nose and the Kamov clattered south.

"Something's wrong," said the sonarman. "It's a single-screw ship. A Typhoon has two, doesn't it?"

USS *Portland*

Scavullo tried to block out all thoughts of Engler free and prowling *Portland*'s decks. She put her headset on, turned the volume up high and keyed the underwater telephone. *"Baikal, Baikal, Baikal, vui sluyshetye?"*

There was nothing but the steady hiss of flowing water.

It wasn't as though Engler could stay lost on a submarine. Where would he go?

She keyed the mike. *"Baikal, Baikal, Baikal, vui sluyshetye?"*

And then it struck her, and hard: *Vann*. The one place Engler could go was the captain's stateroom. She was about to tell Steadman this when a subtle change crept into the watery slosh in her headset. There was a lower note, a wavering *thrum* that hadn't been there a moment ago. So faint that when she concentrated on it, when she tried to summon it from the random sounds, it was gone.

"Baikal, Baikal, Baikal, vui sluyshetye?"

"Scavullo?" asked Steadman

She pushed her headset back and said, "You know, if Engler was going to find help anywhere, he'd go right to—" but then she stopped.

"Los Angeles, Los Angeles . . . mui vas slushayem."

"What is it?" asked Steadman.

"It's *Baikal!*"

Suddenly, three icy-clear tones sounded right through *Portland*'s hull. *Ping! Ping! Ping!*

"Conn! Sonar! That helo just dropped an active buoy right on top of us!"

Steadman said, "Helm! Right full rudder! All ahead full!"

Baikal

The tons of water accumulating in Rocket Alley would have sent *Portland* straight to the bottom, but the added weight put *Baikal* down by the bow by just a single degree. Not enough to worry Markov. It would take a lot more to sink this ship. There were scuttling valves down on the bottom deck. He was prepared to open them, but not with Grachev still in Compartment Two.

"Gasparyan," he said, "go forward and take over Main Engineering. Line up all the scavenge pumps and start them."

"Even the ones under the dry silos?"

"By the time you do it they won't be dry. And we may have to pressurize the compartment to slow the leak."

Gasparyan knew that Grachev had come up with something, though he wasn't privy to the details and didn't wish to be. When they got back, there would be a lot of questions and he didn't want any more answers in his head than was absolutely necessary. "If the hull is open, all you'll do is pump high-pressure air over the side."

"I said slow the leak. Not stop it."

The *kashtan* buzzed and Markov plucked it down. "Markov."

"Captain? There's water coming into Compartment One." It was Lysenko, the torpedoman who'd gone up on deck with Grachev and Demyan up in the ice.

"The torpedo tube?"

"No. From Compartment Two."

"Seal the watertight door."

"We did. The water's still coming through."

"How much water, Lysenko?"

"We're not swimming yet."

"Don't wait. Get your men out of there. Come back aft by way of the berthing decks. Report when everyone's out and we'll try to stop it with air pressure. Understood?"

"Understood."

Markov faced Gasparyan. "There's water in One. The watertight door isn't stopping it. I want Demyan *and* Grachev out of Compartment Two before the whole bow floods."

Gasparyan was an expert in damage control and knew better than almost anyone the implications of both Compartment One *and* Two completely flooded. A Typhoon had a lot of reserve buoyancy built into it. But not an infinite amount. "Captain, if both spaces fill, we may not be able to maintain depth control."

"Then we'll blow ballast and fight our problems on the surface. Now *go*!"

When Gasparyan went forward to Main Engineering, Belikov said, "Captain! Active sonar bearing three five zero! A helicopter set!"

Demyan was about to head forward whether Gasparyan relieved him or not, when the first officer stepped through the aft watertight door.

"What's our situation?" Fedorenko asked anxiously.

"We're one degree down by the bow and there's flooding in the torpedo room," said Gasparyan.

"Did they close the hatch?"

"They did. More bad seals. We might lose a hundred-billion-ruble ship because of a few kopecks' worth of rubber." Gasparyan went to the watertight door leading into Rocket Alley. There was a pressure gauge mounted beside a pair of valves on the bulkhead beside it. "It's too high. The door won't open."

"You'll have to raise the atmospheric pressure in this space," Demyan said to the first officer.

Fedorenko said, "You should be working to save the ship, not recovering dead bodies!"

Gasparyan slid behind the engineering controls. "Close the aft door. I'll raise pressure."

Demyan swung the watertight door leading aft shut, sealed it and hurried forward to the door leading into Rocket Alley.

Fedorenko's ears popped. "What are you doing?"

Demyan watched the pressure gauge, waiting until the needle indicated the same pressure as that in Compartment Two. "Stop! It should open now."

Demyan undogged the forward door. He leaned a shoulder into it, pushing with his legs. It didn't want to move, but then, with a *hiss,* it swung in. Demyan stepped through and slammed it shut behind him.

Fedorenko went aft, spun the wheel on the watertight door to Central Command and then tried to pull it open.

It wouldn't budge.

"Don't touch that door," Gasparyan ordered. "The compartment is pressurized. We need to hold on to the air we've got until Demyan comes back with Grachev."

"Hell never find the body in all that water!"

"Then you might as well sit down, Captain. We'll be here for a while."

Kamov 25

"Contact! *Los Angeles*-class submarine confirmed! He's running to the east and making a lot of noise doing it!"

The pilot banked the Kamov out to sea. "Radio!" said the pilot. "Let the ship know. Do we still have authority to attack?"

He waited while his command was heard, understood and translated into Chinese for transmission back to the ship.

There was a flurry of Mandarin over the radio that his copilot acknowledged.

"What was that all about?" asked the pilot.

"Fly south!" he said.

The pilot banked right, miffed at having been demoted from aircraft commander to chauffeur. What exactly were they going to do?

He got his answer when the copilot flipped open the guard on the ARM switch on his panel. A second switch opened the Kamov's small bomb bay. The trigger was on his cyclic stick, and a single pull on it would drop their one and only SET 40 electric torpedo on an American submarine.

"I want a confirmation," the pilot growled. "In Russian. Before you start a . . ."

But the copilot had already pulled the stick trigger.

Baikal

Demyan was up to his ankles in icy water the moment he stepped through into Rocket Alley. "Engineer Grachev!" His voice should have echoed down the long, tall space, but it was lost beneath a steady, cataract rumble that filled the darkness ahead. He switched on his lamp and pushed the bright white circle forward. "Engineer Grachev!"

Silo Four, and no sign of him.

A flood in Compartment Two. Water leaking through faulty seals into Compartment One. How many other leaky seals would the water find?

Silo Eight and Demyan was knee-deep.

"Engineer Grachev!"

Silo Ten. Demyan hesitated. The water was now around his thighs in two burning cold rings. He could see a glassy rise, a kind of standing wave, where it was coming in at the base of Silo Sixteen. There was no sign of

Grachev. He pointed his lantern aft. The door to Main Engineering was no longer visible.

The surging water nearly knocked him off his feet. It rose into an eerily smooth, almost oily, convex shape, a powerful wave spreading out in all directions, folding over and breaking against the adjacent silos, pushing him hard enough to make his footing doubtful. He was about to turn back when he saw something loom from the dim forward reaches of the space. He turned his lamp on it and found not Grachev, but a nightmare.

A white face painted in dark, liquid streaks loomed like a mask from beyond Silo Sixteen. Only the pointed goatee was familiar.

Demyan forgot about the force of the water and charged forward. He was slammed aside by the surge, thrown back against a silo wall, but he charged again and this time got hold of Grachev's hand and pulled him aft. His feet were swept out from under him and they rode the breaking, endless wave aft.

"We've got to get out," said Demyan, pulling Grachev away from the standing wave. "There's water in the torpedo room."

Grachev somehow got his feet back under him. His forehead oozed streams of blood. "What are you doing?"

"I've come to get you out."

"Of where?" said the chief engineer, then collapsed into Demyan's arms.

USS *Portland*

"Diving Officer," said Steadman. "Make your depth six hundred feet. We've got to lose that helo."

"Six hundred feet, aye," said Slice and Dice.

"We'll pass under the Typhoon and come back alongside from the west."

"No, Mister Steadman. You will not."

Steadman turned and saw Commander Vann in the forward port door. Engler was beside him, armed with the stolen M-9. The weapon was level with Steadman's chest.

Choper watched the gun with interest. Steadman had taken a clumsy, frightened supply lieutenant and turned him into a qualified watchstander. He had shown faith in him, more than was smart, and faith could not be repaid on the cheap. He watched the black barrel in Engler's fist, gauging, measuring. He'd been just another screwup from the surface fleet before. He had become something else, something more. Submariners expect a lot from one another. Choper would not be found wanting.

"You're too young to remember the *Pueblo*," Vann said to Steadman. "She was an intel ship the North Koreans decided to grab, and damned if her skipper didn't allow it to happen. By God, I won't go down that road without putting up a fight."

"Sir, nobody's grabbing anything," said Steadman calmly.

"You're sailing in formation with a Russian ballistic missile boat within spitting distance of one of their biggest bases? Whatever for, Mister Steadman? No. Don't answer. It's too late."

"Captain," said Browne. He stood up. "You are makin' a *hell* of a big mistake."

The barrel moved in Browne's direction. "Sit the fuck back down," said Engler.

"You're right, COB," said Vann. "I've made mistakes. But they're going to end right here." And with that, Vann walked right across Control, straight to the weapons consoles. "Mr. Keefe? We're going to stop the nonsense and conduct some business." He saw the four green lights, four ready weapons, and reached for the flat red button that would send them at *Baikal*.

"Conn, Sonar! High-speed screws astern! Torpedo in the water! I say again, torpedo in the water astern!"

Browne saw Engler look to Vann for direction. He coiled to spring at Engler's knees.

But Lieutenant Choper was closer. Slice and Dice seemed to fly from his seat behind the helm, rising like a missile, heading straight for Engler with his arm out to grab the barrel of the gun.

The M-9 shifted. "Fuck!" said Engler, and he pulled the trigger.

Baikal

"Gasparyan?" Markov said into his own *kashtan*.

"Demyan's not back yet."

"Captain, the American submarine is diving," said Belikov. "They're going to pass underneath us." Belikov stopped. A brilliant white radial line appeared on his scope. *Mother of God.*

"Belikov?"

"Torpedo!" Belikov turned. *"They fired at the Americans!"*

"Who?"

"The helicopter!"

There was no time to wonder whether it would find the ship Markov was depending on to save his men. He calmly keyed the *kashtan* again and said, "Gasparyan? Blow ballast now."

"The bow groups, Captain?" said the first officer, thinking Markov was trying to put the ship back on an even keel.

"*All* of them. Emergency surface *now*!"

"Understood!" Gasparyan reached up and punched a series of buttons illuminated by blue lamps. There were sixteen of them, and with every press, the blue extinguished, to be replaced by white.

As the first rumble of high-pressure air began to force the sea from *Baikal*'s ballast tanks, Markov reached up to the red lanyard over his chair and pulled it down hard. The loud, desperate *whoop! whoop! whoop!* of the collision alarm sounded throughout the massive ship, echoing in her passages, her compartments, from the hot machinery spaces aft to the empty, flooding spaces forward.

The small SET-40 barely had time to arm itself before locking onto *Portland*'s bubbling trail. But then, *Portland* dove beneath the thermal layer and stopped its screws.

The computer in its guidance system was not as sophisticated as the one inside a Mark 48. But it did not give up easily. It switched on its active seeker and immediately was rewarded with a target that seemed to encompass the whole ocean, a vast, silent wall of steel.

The tail fins deflected. The SET-40 shallowed its dive, and centered its full attentions on a fat, stationary target growing larger at the rate of fifty knots.

Ping! Ping! Ping! Ping!

A blast of high-pressure air and the rumble of displaced water confused it for an instant. But there was no hiding a Typhoon. The guidance computer measured its swift approach, and as it streaked in from the starboard beam, commanded a sharp downward deflection of the torpedo's stern planes.

The SET-40 dove beneath *Baikal*'s keel just forward of the sail. There, skimming beneath a solid overcast of steel and titanium, the pistol initiator fired and 150 kilograms of high explosive detonated in a white sphere of force and fire.

CHAPTER THIRTY-SIX

PATIENT ENEMIES

Baikal

Demyan had just put Grachev down so that he could undog the door out of Rocket Alley when he heard a hurricane of high-pressure air rushing into the ballast tanks. Markov was surfacing the ship, and from the sound it would be a very quick rise. He was about to tell Grachev that they'd soon be standing out in the open, drying out under the warm Pacific sun, when the deck suddenly jumped under his feet, followed by a distant, muffled *thud*.

What was that?

He let his lantern play across the yellow silos, up to the mid-level catwalk, then down again. Had a tank blown? He decided there was nothing he could do about it in here, and besides, it wasn't his problem.

In this, Demyan would soon be proven wrong.

Main Engineering resembled a gaudy Moscow nightclub flashing in a dozen urgent colors. Something had tripped both main power buses offline and killed nearly all the consoles. *Baikal*'s designers, like the empire that had built her, took centralization seriously. While there were local control stations scattered through the ship, they were afterthoughts. Everything—her reactors, the engines, her steering, her power distribution and fire protection, hydraulics and air—was meant to be managed from here. Now Gasparyan had authority over none of them.

He was still in the blue terrycloth seat. His hands went by instinct to the emergency backup power bus; it would reconnect *Baikal*'s essential circuits to a special battery room armored against all conceivable misfortune. He would never try to argue the point with Grachev but he knew these controls nearly as well as the chief engineer. He expertly switched it from ARM to ON.

The battle lamps came on just as there was a loud *hiss!* A painful shift in pressure made his ears pop.

Gasparyan suddenly remembered Fedorenko.

"Don't!" he yelled.

Fedorenko had opened the air bleed at the aft hatch to Central Command. Now the door clanged against the bulkhead as the great ship trembled and rocked in the roiled water left by the torpedo's blast.

Both the air pressure that would allow Demyan to open the missile room hatch, and Fedorenko, were gone.

With her ballast tanks blown dry, *Baikal* was already rising, and once forty thousand tons began to move they were nearly impossible to stop. A hundred kilos of high explosive going off under her keel only added to the upward impetus.

Water is incompressible, and so the full force of the explosion penetrated her steel outer hull, dishing in the outer plates, breaking an air line, severing a hydraulic circuit, cutting electrical conduits. The shock to *Baikal's* electrical systems tripped her old, mechanical circuit breakers. Though restoring them would take time, though the blast would have sent *Portland* to the bottom, *Baikal's* five inner hulls were flexible, strong and intact.

Compartment Eight at *Baikal's* stern was as far away from the explosion as any space could be. But the sea is a patient enemy. It hunts for any weakness, and it was there, where the great propeller shafts pierced the inner hull, that it found one.

Lieutenant Kuznetsov was in trouble. Water was coming into Compartment Eight through the shaft seals. The small explosion had rippled through the hull, flexed a propeller shaft and broken a bearing already damaged by *Baikal's* collision with the ice. The broken bearing allowed the propeller shaft to whip like a slender twig, breaking other bearings as well as the remaining seals.

Five steel and rubber rings the size of truck tires were supposed to allow the shaft to turn while keeping the ocean out, and four of them had failed. Only the fifth and final ring remained and it was never meant to resist full pressure alone. Now water was spraying through the gap between the shaft and the seal, and there was nothing Kuznetsov and the four warrant officers who manned the space could do to stop it.

Kuznetsov was about to say the hell with it, let's go and find out why the bilge pumps aren't running, when a high-pressure air line broke free from the overhead, fell and snapped.

The air line went to one of the stern trim tanks outside the hull, and it was as big as a man's wrist. The sudden blast of air blew a wrench off an electric motor casing. The wrench struck a hydraulic fitting already leaking oil and broke it off.

Oil under pressure sprayed across the hot motor and burst into white flame. Fed by the air, it became a blast furnace.

Where an instant before the trouble had been one of flood, now it was fire. Fire and smoke. Kuznetsov yelled for his men to run while he went to a damage control cabinet and pulled out an extinguisher. He hauled it over, aimed the nozzle and emptied it into the flames.

The instant the flow stopped, they sprang back to life, brighter, hotter than before.

He threw the fire bottle down and joined the others at the forward watertight door. The fire was being fed with fuel and air, and there was nothing anyone could do to stop it from inside the compartment. Their only hope was that once out, with the hatch sealed, they could stop the flow of air and flood the space with Freon and smother it.

Fire sensors in the space flashed an overheat warning to the watch engineer's panel in Main Engineering, where it blinked on a vast, flat plain of dark consoles.

"Depth now one hundred meters and rising."

Markov had felt the torpedo's blast with his feet. He'd attracted that torpedo for a reason, knowing there was little it could do to harm him or his ship. *Less than a pinprick.* But it had been enough to douse the lights in Central Command. Only a dim nebula showed at the helm where the needles and faces of the gauges had been painted with radium.

The calm voice of one of the *michman* at the helm had his face right next to the Fathometer. "Depth eighty meters."

Now even Fedorenko had a way out. If Grachev could point a finger at him, then he could point a finger at the Chinese. *They put a torpedo into us!* Part of him was sorry that he would get away so easily.

"Sixty meters."

The battle lamps suddenly winked on, revealing a surprisingly normal scene. The consoles were being brought back system by system. That was Gasparyan's doing, no doubt.

"Fifty meters."

She kept rising.

"Sail is clear!"

Her sail broke the surface of the Pacific and emerged and still she kept rising. The sail's rounded base, her weather deck with its missing Beast Buoy, her missile deck with the muzzle hatch to Silo Sixteen still raised, the stern planes. The bronze screws in their great rounded shrouds. She kept rising as though *Baikal* had been transformed from a ship of the sea to one of the air.

"Ship is surfaced," said the *michman* from the helm.

"What indicators do you have?" Markov asked.

"I have no indications at all except the manual Fathometer."

"Controls?"

The *michman* manipulated the small joysticks and tapped the pedals that should have moved the rudder and planes. "No response."

Markov pulled the *kashtan* down. "Compartment Six! This is the captain. Can you hear me, Vasiliev?"

"Vasiliev listening."

"What happened to your reactors?"

"They're in safety-shutdown mode. I'm trying to bring them back now."

"Don't. That might take too long. Get the diesels running. We need power to the pumps immediately. I'm depending on you."

"Understood."

"Gasparyan? Can you hear me?"

"I can hear you," Gasparyan replied. "What blew up?"

"A small torpedo."

"The Americans?"

"No. It was our friends the Chinese. Put Grachev on."

"I can't. They're still not out of Two. The hatch is jammed. That bastard ran off and bled away the pressure. I can't restore it."

Fedorenko bled off the pressure? Where had that shit run to? "Can you raise them on the intercom?"

"No. But *someone* is banging on the hatch, I can't force it open. There's too much pressure on the other side. And too little here."

No way back, no way forward. Demyan and Grachev are trapped. "I'll come forward with some help. We'll get a jack on that hatch and break it down if we have to."

"What do you want me to do, Captain?"

"Come back to Central Command and take over. The diesel generators should be running soon."

A frantic voice broke in over the intercom.

"Fire! Fire in Compartment Eight!"

"Slow down! Who is this?" Markov demanded.

"Kuznetsov! I'm in Seven! There's a big fire in Eight! The lines heading aft are all burned through. We're getting smoke in Seven now!"

Fire in Eight. Smoke in Seven. Water in One and Two. The one thing Markov knew above all else was that when smoke appeared anywhere in a submarine, sooner or later it would be everywhere. "Make sure everyone is out of Eight, then flood it with Freon."

"We can't stop the air! It is feeding the fire!"

And neither Markov nor Gasparyan had control over the air. The fire would not be contained for long. "Move everyone forward now."

"Understood!"

Markov switched his *kashtan* to sound throughout the ship. "This is the captain. All compartments are to evacuate to Central Command *now.* Don't stop to pick up anything. When the last man is out, dog down the watertight doors and go. This is not a drill. Move out *now.*"

In Compartment Six, the reactor room commander Vasiliev punched a start button and the second diesel generator shook itself awake. The lights instantly brightened, but there was a problem with the flow of air to the giant engines.

A pair of valves as large as manhole covers were supposed to open when *Baikal* was on the surface, letting in air for the diesels to breathe, and letting out the toxic exhaust.

Only one of the valves, the exhaust line, had opened correctly. The intake was cycling open and shut as though it had grown a mind of its own. Every time it thumped shut, the engines drew air from the interior of the submarine, causing a pressure pulse powerful enough to suck air from Vasiliev's lungs.

Only if he kept his finger on the intake control, ready at an instant's notice to cycle it open, would the diesels the captain needed to save the ship be willing to run.

He felt the pulse coming before the instruments displayed it. He jabbed his thumb down on the OPEN button even as the diesel sucked away the air in his compartment. *Too bad we can't suck out the air from Eight,* he thought. At least it would kill the fire.

He eyed a thin streak of brown smoke coming in from a cableway that penetrated the aft bulkhead to Seven. It was supposed to be absolutely watertight. Perhaps it was, but it wasn't stopping *smoke.*

Then Kuznetsov and his men came in from Seven. He saw the soot on their faces. He'd also heard Markov's order. You didn't run off when your captain told you to keep the diesel engine going.

Vasiliev got all his men moving forward, and when the last of them stepped through into Compartment Five, he slammed the hatch shut and returned to his duty station at the diesel panel.

A potent, stinging smell in the air made him stop and look up at the air vents.

Smoke was beginning to flow from them now, too.

In Compartment Five, Pavel the cook was screaming in pain. He'd been bringing a fresh pot of soup to the serving line when the blast had caused him to trip and drop the scalding liquid over his legs. At Markov's command, the mess emptied of diners as though a plug had been pulled, and Pavel followed them out into a crowded passageway filled with pushing, shoving, yelling men, all making their way forward, and up.

He'd made it up the middle deck of Compartment Four, directly under Central Command, when he remembered the gleaming pots and German knives.

"Where are you going?" one of his mess assistants asked.

"I forgot something!" he yelled, angry at himself. "Go!"

The men off duty in their four-man cabins grabbed photographs, books, foul-weather gear and bottles from secret stashes. They ran out into the dim passageways lit by battle lamps, heading forward and up. Those resting in the lounge threw down their magazines and ran. Warrant Officer Zubov had been serenading the others with his guitar. He carefully placed it back in its case and brought it along, heading forward, and up.

Torpedoman Lysenko showed up in the forward port doorway of Central Command. He'd been heading there from the flooding torpedo room with the three warrant officers from his crew when the torpedo had struck. They were the first to appear.

"Get a collapsible jack," Markov ordered. "And follow me."

The lights burned steady. *Bravo, Vasiliev,* thought Markov. He and Lysenko left Central Command through the forward passage and joined Gasparyan in Main Engineering.

The lights were on and so were a dozen alarms. The fire sensors on Compartment Seven were flashing red. Ominously, those in Eight, the source of the blaze, were dark.

"The wires to Eight are gone," said Gasparyan. "I can't shut the valves. I can't stop the air. We should dump Freon in Six and Seven but . . ."

"Wait until Vasiliev is out or he'll smother. What about pumps?"

"Running as you ordered."

Markov took out a muster roll and gave it to Gasparyan. "Get everyone out on deck. Make sure there's a mark beside every name."

"You have my word, Captain." The first officer took the sheet.

"I want you to take command and get everyone ready to jump into the rafts if something lets go. If she starts to sink she'll go fast. If it happens before I'm out, shut the clamshell and paddle like the devil. She'll pull you under if you don't."

"What about you?"

"I'll use one of the escape capsules. I brought Grachev on board. I'm going to bring him out. Go."

Kamov 25

The sonar operator picked up the roar of the explosion, and the helicopter pilot spotted the white boil of an angry, disturbed sea at once. It was barely three kilometers away. Then the black shape of a submarine emerged from its center. He lowered the nose of his ungainly machine and called to his radio operator that he had a submarine in sight and on the surface.

"The American?" came *Hangzhou's* urgent reply.

"Stand by."

As he approached her, the sheer size, the massive sail, the long missile deck forward told him all he needed to know. This was a ship unlike any in the world. He turned to his Chinese copilot.

"You put a fucking torpedo into *Baikal*!"

"Conn, Sonar," said Bam Bam. "That Typhoon took a hit. I say again, that was a hit. She blew ballast and is sitting on top."

Lieutenant Choper's body lay wedged between the empty seats at the helm and the outboard control yoke, shoving it full forward, forcing the submarine into a steep dive. A dark stain spread across his back and dripped bright red to the clean, waxed linoleum deck. The two sailors who were supposed to be at the helm had scrambled away at the shot and were sheltering behind the periscopes, trying to put something, anything between them and the smoking barrel of Engler's gun.

"Who's next?" Engler taunted. He looked to Scavullo. "You?"

The chief of the boat stood straight and exposed. "Son," he said, "it's time to give it up."

"You and the XO's bitch were going to hand the boat to the fucking Russians. And I ain't your fucking son."

"Nobody is getting *Portland,*" said Steadman. "We're taking on a boatload of Russians. Not the other way around." *Six hundred feet.* Steadman could see the Fathometer click. *Six-fifty.*

Vann turned left to Steadman. "What did you just say?"

Steadman slowly reached into his breast pocket and pulled out a folded sheet of paper and handed it to Vann. "From COMSUBLANT."

Vann scanned the short message.

1: PROCEED AVACHA CANYON . . . COMSUBLANT SENDS

"Conn, Sonar. What's going on? What's with this angle?"

Proceed Avacha Canyon? Vann folded the paper and looked to Steadman. Graybar *ordered* Steadman here? "There's some mistake."

"And you made it," said COB.

"What the fuck?" said Engler. *"Mistake?"*

"You killed Chief Babcock," Browne said. "That was another mistake."

Engler turned. "He tried to stop me, skipper. I'da never made it to your cabin otherwise. You said we were all goin' to Siberia! Tell them!"

"We all headed for the bottom and that's the truth," said Browne. "Give the skipper that gun and then we can correct *all* your *profound* misunderstandings."

The world, the universe had shifted out from under Engler's feet. All the reasons were gone. Hate was all that was left. "We don't have anything to talk about."

"Then listen to me," said Vann.

Twenty degrees down angle, Steadman thought. *Eight hundred feet.* He looked to see if Vann had noticed the fact that the boat was diving out of control, that the great fist of the sea was closing around them. New, she was good to over a thousand feet. But *Portland's* bow was torn up and there was just one hatch in the sonar tunnel keeping the water out. Sooner or later, something would let go.

"We both did what we believed was necessary. We were wrong. Honestly wrong," Vann said. "I promise you'll get a fair hearing."

Nine hundred feet. Twenty-five degrees. Steadman had to hang on to the overhead to keep from sliding right down the deck into Engler's gun.

"I did this for you," said Engler. "Right from the beginning. You owe me more than a fucking fair hearing."

"Engler . . ."

"You told me to fuck her up so she'd run away and never want to look at another boat again. Was that another little mistake?"

The silence was punctuated by the creaks, rifle-shot cracks and groans from a hull getting squeezed, squeezed.

Scavullo thought, *I was right.*

"I don't give a shit," said Engler. "Do it for you. For the service. For the fucking Navy. You all got yours. Now I want mine."

Nine hundred fifty feet. Steadman could hear the hull complain in a thousand subtle and not so subtle ways. Even the air took on a strange heaviness. Each breath took extra effort.

"No one ordered you to assault an officer," said Vann. "And no one gave you authority to shoot one, either."

"Figures you wouldn't give a shit about Babcock. But then he wasn't a fucking officer."

One thousand feet.

Vann said, "You won't take all the blame, Engler. But right now we have to get this boat back under control." He held out his hand. "Give me the weapon."

"Fair hearing. That means *you* get early retirement and *I* go to fucking Leavenworth. No deal. I want it made right." His luxuriant mustache was plastered to his lip with sweat.

"You have my word. I'll speak on your behalf," said Vann. His hand was still out, palm up. Fingers almost touching the M-9.

"Your word? You couldn't even keep your fucking bridge."

"Give me that gun!"

Eleven hundred feet. The deck at Steadman's feet bulged up as the hull contracted. There was no time left for talking.

"Engler," said Steadman, "Vann. Me. Browne. How many of us do you think you can shoot before we get you?"

"And me," said Scavullo.

"Easy," said Steadman as he started moving in.

Engler's weapon went from one to the next and came to rest on Scavullo. "You win."

"Conn!" Bam Bam's shout made Engler jump.

Vann reached out and grabbed for the barrel.

Somewhere in its arc, Engler pulled the trigger.

The sound of the shot echoed through Control. Vann staggered back against Keefe's weapons console, reaching behind him as though to find something pinned to his back, then sat down.

Twelve hundred feet!

The radioman was staring at Scavullo. "You think you have me beat, bitch? You think you have me beat?" He raised the gun again.

Steadman bellowed, *"Engler! No!"*

He laughed and put the pistol to his head. "Come and get me," he said. Engler was looking right at her when he pulled the trigger again.

CHAPTER THIRTY-SEVEN

PERILS IN THE DEEP

Baikal

"The fire's in Seven now and there's a lot of smoke coming into Compartment Six," said Vasiliev. "The pressure is pushing it right through the cableways in the bulkhead. It's getting smoky."

"Put your OBA on and get out," said Gasparyan.

"I have my mask on," said Vasiliev. "The diesel isn't stabilized. There's a problem with the intakes. I'm controlling it manually but if I let it go we could lose power."

"You have five more minutes. After that, leave the controls and get up to Central Command."

"The battle lanterns might not—"

"Just get up here!" Gasparyan sensed the gathering catastrophe. Water forward, fire and smoke aft, no controls. Markov fighting to break open the hatch into Compartment Two and now smoke invading the ship's air supply. They'd be lucky to get everyone out alive.

He hurried up to the balcony above Central Command and cracked open the hatch to one of *Baikal*'s two emergency escape pods. He pushed the heavy hatch in, then climbed through.

The pod was the size of a small windowless bus, a bare steel cylinder with spherical ends furnished with wooden benches. A metal box was mounted beside the hatch. Inside was a bright red button. Should something terrible happen to *Baikal,* the crew could climb into the pod, seal the hatch, punch that button and in theory everyone would bob safely to the surface.

Gasparyan started tossing life jackets through the open hatch and out onto the deck of the Balcony. Five, ten, twenty orange foam vests. A growing crowd of men anxiously passed them out and slipped them on. Even up here, a burned, chemical smell was making itself apparent.

Gasparyan kept tossing float vests until there were no more, then stepped out to the Balcony.

Had the smoke been this strong a moment ago? The space was wall-to-wall vests and eyes. Some faces were sooty. All of them scared. "You!" he said to a senior warrant officer. "Crack the lower hatch and open the clamshell."

A senior warrant officer spun the locking wheel and the heavy bottom hatch swung down and forward, revealing a smooth-bore tunnel leading up to the O1 deck.

"Quickly!" said Gasparyan.

The *michman* swarmed up the ladder. His boots vanished.

Gasparyan went to the ladder and looked up. His thoughts were shared by everyone there: if that bastard of a hatch up top doesn't open, everyone would be trapped.

There was a clang, and a splash of cold water poured down on Gasparyan's grinning face. But now the hatch became a chimney, sucking contaminated air from the entire ship, and the smoke became dense. First one, then another man began to cough.

Gasparyan's eyes watered. "I need the rafts broken out of the deck lockers. Who volunteers?"

Every hand went up. Who wanted to wait down here?

Gasparyan pointed. "You four go to the forward locker and get the rafts inflated." He picked out four more. "You go aft and haul the other two up to the missile deck and *then* inflate them. Everyone else assemble on the missile deck."

"Are we going to have to swim for it?" asked someone.

"The water temperature is five degrees. Make your own determination. All right? Get moving."

The men needed no encouragement. They rushed Gasparyan in a solid wave. "Wait!" He pulled out Markov's muster sheet and a pencil. "Say your name on your way up!"

"Borzhov! Torpedoman!"

"*Go!*"

"Shevchuk! Controls!"

"*Go!*"

"Sablin! Engineering!"

"*Go!*"

The men streamed by Gasparyan, hacking from the yellow, acrid smoke, and laughing at their great fortune to be at the head of the line.

"Corpsman to Control!" Steadman called out over the 1MC. "Engine room! Restore diving plane control to the helm!"

Chief Cooper was already near Control, summoned by a call over Browne's radio. He showed up at the after door. "Jesus."

Lieutenant Choper lay sprawled on the deck. He'd taken a 9-millimeter round through the chest. One look at the color and Cooper knew his heart had stopped.

Vann was another story. He was sitting against the fire control console with a thin stream of blood running out between his fingers. "My back," he said in a quick gasp between breaths.

COB hustled the two helmsmen back to their seats and took over both the ballast board the diving officer's position. "Recommend we blow the forward tanks *now* and take this angle off!"

"Do it, COB."

Blood was smeared across the diving plane yoke. The planesman seemed reluctant to touch it.

"I need you to pull that yoke, son," said Browne.

"Aye aye, COB." He grasped it and hauled it full back.

"One thousand three hundred feet."

Steadman looked to the helm. "Stand by to blow all ballast."

Down on the middle deck and all the way forward, Lieutenant Hennig stared at the small hatch leading into the flooded sonar tunnel. That one piece of metal was keeping the ocean out. Water sprayed from its full circumference.

"One thousand three-fifty."

He felt the steep angle gradually diminish, but *any* down was a bad direction to be going. Just beyond that hatch, the ocean pushed at more than five hundred pounds a square inch. He figured if the hatch let go, his eyes might register the sudden explosion, but the signal would never have time to reach his brain.

The needle sprays coalesced. The hull groaned. Every time Hennig heard a click, he winced. Would he have any warning?

"One thousand four hundred feet."

The water hissed. The air filled with fog. Something clicked, then began to crackle like distant fireworks. *Here it comes.* He closed his eyes, then he thought, *Why not see it happen?*

He opened them and couldn't believe what he saw. The whole of the elliptical bulkhead bulged inward as though the steel were the skin of a balloon about to blow.

"One thousand three hundred feet."

Hennig looked up at the speaker.

What did he just say?

Then, as though the XO had heard him, "This is Steadman. We're heading back up. All stations make ready for periscope depth."

Portland's corpsman gently probed and felt what he'd hoped not to. *Oh shit.* "How ya' doin', skipper?" said Cooper as he tried to maneuver Vann's torso without severing what might be left of his spinal cord. "Can you hear me, sir?"

Vann spoke between hard breaths. "My . . . back . . ."

"Yes, sir. Now how about moving a foot. Just one foot. Can you do that for me, sir?"

There was no movement.

Cooper looked to Steadman. "Sir, I need some help getting the captain to his stateroom."

"You'll have some in about ten seconds," said Browne. He'd already summoned two auxiliary men. "Through five hundred feet."

Two men showed in the after door right on schedule. Cooper waved them forward.

Steadman gave himself one moment to feel sympathy for Vann, but it was all he could afford. "Sonar, Conn. I need a fix on that Typhoon and that damned helicopter. We can't surface up through him."

"Conn, Sonar, aye. I *think* he's out on a two five zero bearing a half mile astern. I don't have anything on the helo."

"Two hundred feet."

"Not one foot more than seventy," said Steadman. He wasn't about to broach *Portland* into an unknown situation up on top.

"Seventy feet, aye," said Browne.

As the sea relaxed its grip, *Portland*'s hull relaxed. The arch in the deck plates became subtle, then disappeared.

"PD," said Browne.

"ESM sweep." He turned aft and remembered Scavullo. She was still there, holding the WQC-6 microphone. "Lieutenant, I need you on the radio. Are you able?"

Scavullo nodded.

"All right. Then go back and power up your gear." The ESM antenna broke the surface.

"Helo search set and close!" said the petty officer at the ESM board.

Does he know he just put a fish into Baikal?

Steadman went aft to the periscope stand and wrapped his arms around the handles. The quartermaster had already turned it to the Typhoon's last bearing. "Up the number-two scope."

"That helo will see it," said COB.

"I think he's got more to worry about right now than us." Steadman bent double and gradually straightened as the scope rose. The view through the eyepiece went from black to green, to white foam, then dark slate. He stopped the scope's rise and shifted it slightly to starboard. "God."

"You see her?" asked COB.

"Yes." The view was from the starboard bow looking aft. The Typhoon was a black silhouette against a gray sky and so close he had to elevate the head to zoom in on the top of her sail. So close that she would have run *Portland* down if she were underway, but there was no hint of a wake, no foam at the black bulge of her bow. The figures moving on her decks looked too small, but it was a trick of scale. There were men out on her missile deck and more near her sail. Then he saw the muzzle hatch. "She's got a silo open. They've got people all around it looking down." He saw something black billow up from their midst. *A raft.*

Kamov 25

The helicopter pilot banished the Chinese radioman from his post and gave the duty to the sonarman. Someone he trusted, someone who spoke honest Russian. He buzzed over the black decks of the surfaced Typhoon.

Men were streaming out onto her decks. A thin brown haze rose from inside her sail. A missile hatch yawned wide open. The wash of his rotors nearly blew a raft over the side.

"Tell them it looks like the whole crew is coming out," he said to his radio operator.

He banked around again to the east, and spotted a tiny white scratch on the rolling swells of a faultless dark sea. "What the devil is that?"

USS *Portland*

Scavullo said nothing as she slid into her seat in the radio room. Her skin felt ice cold, her head hot. She snapped on her receivers and the familiarity of it helped to banish, or at least shift, the terrible pictures filling her mind.

The intercept antenna atop the search scope picked up a flurry of signals. A loud Russian voice boomed in her headset.

"One raft. It's already inflated."

"Are they sinking?"

"No. There's a silo hatch open and it looks like a problem. There's water in it. Just . . . stand by."

There was a pause, then,

"Periscope sighted!"

She snatched the intercom. "Conn, Radio. They spotted us!"

Steadman watched the Typhoon's crew wrestle with a raft that had caught the wind when suddenly the view of black sea and pearl sky changed to bright, billowing red. "Marker smoke! Down scope! Emergency dive! Ahead *flank* and hard right rudder!"

They'd been spotted, and all Steadman could do about it was to run so close to that Typhoon that whoever had seen him wouldn't dare to drop another torpedo.

Baikal

If Senior Midshipman Dmitri Mirtov had a rifle, he would have shot down that damned helicopter making low passes overhead. He and three other men were struggling to pull open the stern raft locker. The cover had been painted shut and the perimeter had to be cut before the door could be pried up with the blades of their knives. But just as they started to pull it free the helicopter sent a hurricane of wind across *Baikal*'s after deck, threatening to send them all tumbling over the sides.

Maybe it was good luck that they didn't have the raft out. It would have surely blown away.

He watched it clatter off to the east. "Okay! Let's get these bastards out while there's a chance."

All four pulled and the door came open.

Mirtov gagged at the stink rising from the locker. It was a foul, burned smell, and when he tried to pull the first raft out, he saw why.

The top raft was melted to the one beneath. The bottom raft was nothing more than black taffy. Mirtov spat on his finger and reached down to touch the bare steel of the hull.

It sizzled.

Gasparyan stared down into the open missile silo. The hatch was tilted up with its inner locking rings and pressure dome exposed. Below, the gray bullet nose of a rocket emerged from a silo full of sea.

"It's not draining," said Gasparyan. "The pressure is keeping it in the silo."

"And the water is keeping the pressure in," said Borodin. "He's going to have to come out of there, you know."

"Grachev?"

"Markov."

"Sir!" said Mirtov.

Gasparyan turned. "Where are the rafts?"

"Melted. Both of them. There's fire below under the stern locker. A lot of it. The deck is too hot to touch."

Gasparyan looked to Borodin as though this had some bearing on a discussion they'd just had.

Borodin thought, *Markov.* "How many left below?"

Gasparyan checked the muster sheet. "Seven. Lysenko, Demyan and Grachev. Vasiliev and the captain. And Pavel the cook."

"That's six."

"Fedorenko, too. Fuck him. He can swim home."

"Captain Fedorenko isn't below," said Mirtov. "I saw him inside the sail."

"Hiding?" asked Gasparyan.

"He had a radio out and was talking to someone."

Gasparyan and Borodin exchanged looks, then Gasparyan said, "You're in charge up here now. Get everyone forward. If something blows in the stern, be ready to jump."

"How will a hundred men fit in two twenty-five-man rafts?" Borodin asked.

"They'll find a way." Gasparyan walked aft, stepped through the open door and saw Fedorenko. Just as Mirtov had said, he had a radio in his hand and two seabags at his feet.

Fedorenko had let out the pressure in Main Engineering, trapping Grachev and Demyan in Compartment Two. Would it be such a great loss if he forgot to tell him about the fire raging aft, that he might not have very long to go fight for a spot in the remaining rafts?

No. He walked over to him. "Stop talking and listen."

"I'll be ready," Fedorenko said into the radio, then turned. "Wait," he said to Gasparyan rudely and with no appreciation at all for the importance of his message.

Gasparyan fumed. Did he think he had all the time in the world? He saw bright red smoke billowing on the surface of the sea. *Marker smoke?*

"Yes. Unbelievable. I know. They can blame no one but themselves. Out." Fedorenko clicked off the radio. "The *Chinese* fired that torpedo. If they lose this ship the fault will be theirs alone."

But if Grachev and Demyan go down with it, the fault will be yours, thought Gasparyan. "I'm going below to bring the last men up. Your duty is to remain by the clamshell. No one is to go back down. *No one.* The fire's spreading fast. If something blows, shut the hatch. Do you understand? Before you run away and jump into a raft, *shut the hatch.*"

"Do young first officers issue orders to captains of the first rank now?"

"We'll see what they make of your rank when I tell them what you've done," said Gasparyan. Before Fedorenko could answer, he put on his OBA mask, threaded a fresh oxygen cylinder on the end of its hose and went to the clamshell.

The lights in Main Engineering burned yellow through smoke and haze. Gasparyan couldn't see Markov, couldn't see Lysenko, couldn't even see the nearby bulkheads. He took a deep breath from his cylinder, then pushed his mask away from his mouth. "Captain!"

"Here!"

Gasparyan put the mask back on and made his way forward.

The jack bore down on the hatch into Rocket Alley. The bottom was wedged against a heavy structural hull ring. Markov and Lysenko were both leaning against the handle, putting their weight into it. Neither one wore an OBA.

There was a *hiss!* A *crack!* And then they were on the floor, sprawled across the jack.

The hatch was open, and there was Demyan. He saw all the smoke, then turned away from the hatch.

"*Starpom!* Is everyone out?" asked Markov. His face was covered in sweat-streaked soot. His breathing came hard.

"Almost. Vasiliev and our cook haven't checked in up on top yet. I've spoken with Vasiliev. He should be out by now."

"What about Pavel?"

"I don't know. We could organize a search but you should know the rafts in the aft locker are all melted."

"It's going to burn through the hull," said Markov. He turned away from his *starpom* and yelled into the hatch. "Grachev! Demyan! Wake up and get out *now*!"

When Demyan pulled Grachev through the hatch Markov saw his worst fears realized: Fedorenko had been right. Grachev was lost. His face was expressionless and empty. One side of his forehead was solid purple. The rest, waxy and dead white.

But then the chief engineer opened one eye and sniffed the air. "What's burning?"

Demyan bent down to support Grachev's shoulder when he stopped and looked aft. He heard a faint, high whistling. Like a teakettle left on a stove, but far away.

"What's that noise?" asked Gasparyan.

Demyan didn't wait. He dropped Grachev, ran to the aft hatch leading to Central Command and slammed it shut.

Kamov 25

The helicopter pilot set the Kamov down on the afterdeck of the big submarine. He would have preferred the forward deck, it was wider and flatter, but there were too many people milling around and the last thing he wanted was a mob trying to climb on board. The Russian sonarman slid the side door open. Fedorenko sprinted to the idling helicopter, threw in his bags and dived in after them.

"Go!" he said. "It's getting hot!"

Hot like radioactive? The pilot brought in power to the rotors, but then some movement caught his eye. *What the devil?*

The rubber skin of the ship was sloughing off into the sea in great black sheets, exposing rusted steel and waves of heat. Like a great whale being carved up by a flensing tool, *Baikal* was being laid bare before his eyes. He could feel the heat on his face.

The ship was going to blow. He twisted full power and brought in maximum pitch on the collective. It was a risky maneuver because it left the machine vulnerable to engine failure, but *Baikal* was melting underneath him.

The Kamov jumped straight up off the deck as a broad section of her deck steel collapsed down into a chaos of fiery reds and yellows. An instant later, a tremendous concussion rocked the climbing Kamov, and enveloped it in a cloud of acrid steam.

USS *Portland*

"Conn, Sonar! Something just blew up topside! A mean *major.*"

"Torpedo?"

"If it was it was way bigger than the last one."

"Radio, Conn. Tell the Chinese to remain clear," Steadman snapped. "Tell them we're in international waters and engaged in a rescue at sea."

"Aye aye," said Scavullo.

"Helm! All stop. COB," said Steadman. "Take her up. Take her all the way up."

There was a rumble of air, and then Steadman announced on the 1MC, "Surface! Surface! Surface! Line handlers expedite to the main trunk for duty topside! And bring the line shooter!"

Portland broke the surface a quarter mile away from *Baikal*.

"Sail is clear!"

"Up the number-two scope!"

Steadman looked into the eyepiece and at first thought that a fog had rolled in. There was no sign of the boomer anywhere. Only solid white. Had she gone down that fast? But then he swung the scope and saw her bow emerge from that cloud, the raised muzzle hatch, and then the men huddled on her decks. "There's a ton of smoke. It's blowing in our direction. She's still afloat."

"Can you tell what's burning?" asked COB.

"The whole submarine. Down scope." He went forward to the main trunk. "I'll conn the boat from the topside bridge!"

COB watched him go and thought, *You forgot your damned float vest again.*

Kamov 25

The helicopter buzzed noisily over the surfaced American submarine, keeping a safe distance from the thunderhead of smoke and steam billowing up from *Baikal*'s stern.

"Who is this woman giving us orders?" Fedorenko demanded.

The pilot shrugged. "She speaks Russian. She says to stay clear, they are going to rescue people off *Baikal*."

"Tell them our ships are already on the way."

"What ships?"

"Just tell them."

"*Hangzhou? Fuzhou* won't show up for hours."

"I have given you a direct order."

The pilot didn't know why his pushy passenger was so anxious to see the crew of that burning submarine go for a swim, but there was no denying that a captain first rank could ruin the life of a mere lieutenant. More, it had been his helicopter that had launched that damned torpedo. Sure, the Chinese back on *Hangzhou* had ordered it and his Chinese copilot had pulled the trigger, but someone would fry. Why should it be him?

"Understood," he said.

USS *Portland*

"He ordered us to stay clear," said Scavullo. "He says that they have ships on the way."

"Thank him for his information and tell him we're a United States Navy ship and we do not take orders from helicopter pilots." Steadman turned. "Shoot."

The quartermaster had a laser rangefinder out. He pressed the trigger and read off the numbers projected onto the Typhoon. "Four hundred yards."

The Kamov came clattering down in a steep dive like a bird trying to frighten away a fox. It roared right over Steadman's head, then banked away. He kept moving *Portland* in on *Baikal* at a shallow angle. "Rudder amidships," he said into the small radio. "Ahead dead slow."

"Rudder amidships and ahead dead slow," COB acknowledged. "I'm sending up a vest for you, too."

A machinist's mate came up from below carrying an M–14 rifle fitted with a line thrower. He had an orange float vest on and another for Steadman.

"Three hundred yards."

Steadman eyed the approaching cliff of black steel, its top a solid line of men. How were they going to transfer all those people onto *Portland*?

The pall of smoke rose high into the sky until it merged, gray on gray, with the overcast. He was bringing *Portland* in slightly behind it. He could catch glimpses of the Typhoon's tall rudder wreathed in smoke and steam.

"One hundred yards."

"Right full rudder," he said.

"Right full rudder, aye," said COB.

"Fifty yards."

"All stop!"

"All stop."

Portland's bow swung smartly away from the stricken submarine until the two hulls lay nearly parallel.

The sea state was not nearly as flat as it had seemed through the periscope. A lane of black water rose and fell between the two submarines. Every third or fourth wave would rise to a freakish height and grow a white crest of foam and tumble. It washed against *Baikal*'s sides like surf against a seawall, but the foam covered *Portland*'s deck.

"Stand by to shoot a line!"

The man with the M-14 climbed out of *Portland*'s sail through the small "ice door" set in her port side. He clipped his "monkey tail" into the recessed safety track on her rounded deck and flicked the line ahead as he went, followed by a second crewman with a big coil of yellow line. They managed to keep their footing though waves were rolling over *Portland*'s topsides, leaving them knee-deep in ice-cold water.

High overhead, the Russians were shouting and waving at the line handler to hurry.

"Line handler!" said Steadman. "Shoot!"

The first crewman elevated his rifle high above the Typhoon's deck and with a loud *crack!* sent a thin yellow line sailing into the hands of the waiting Russians.

The Russians hauled in the line until it was taut. They were in a real hurry. For even before Steadman could give the order to tie a second, heavier line to the first and send it up, they leaped from the Typhoon's missile deck and began streaming down, hand over hand, one after the next.

"Get Scavullo up here fast!" he yelled into the radio as the thin line skimmed the waves under the weight of the panicky Russians.

Then Steadman saw the reason for their hurry.

The stern of the great missile submarine was going under. As he watched, the tall rudder shortened to a stub, and with a billow of live steam, vanished.

Baikal

The yellow line was tied off around the open muzzle hatch and dropped in a long curve down to the deck of the waiting American submarine. Borodin had to hold men back to keep their weight from dragging it in the sea. The water was deadly cold, and no one wanted to dip so much as a finger in it if they could help it.

But then came the rumble of a subterranean explosion, and Borodin felt the deck jump. He didn't stop to wonder what energy could make a ship this big shake like a snake in a terrier's jaws. The orderly line of men waiting to descend the line to the American submarine became a rushing mob.

The first raft went over the side and landed right side up. The second did not. The men lost all their inhibitions about the water and slid down after them feet first, but as the curve grew steeper, steeper, then perpendicular, their runs became tumbles and their tumbles became dives. One after another they splashed into the sea and paddled over to the rafts and flopped aboard as best they could.

Borodin faced aft. It was like looking down a black steel ramp being fed into a blast furnace. There was no sign of Gasparyan. He faced the tremendous cloud of smoke and steam.

And a new sound, the low roar of surf rising, rising, then breaking across *Baikal*'s back.

Someone yelled, "Come on! She's going under!"

There were still men on deck. "Here!" Borodin thrust the muster sheet into his hands. "Take it and jump for it! Get into the rafts!" he yelled. "Paddle away as fast as you can! You'll get pulled under if you don't!" Then he took off at a dead run.

The roar grew terrifyingly loud as Borodin sprinted aft. He could see a rolling wall of solid green water rising up behind the sail as he ducked through the forward door. From under his feet came the ragged *pop!* . . . *pop! pop!* of bulkheads giving way.

Fedorenko hadn't shut the clamshell.

The main trunk hatch gaped wide open and a volcanic column of smoke and steam blasted from its mouth. Not every name on the muster sheet had a check beside it. Who even knew if the list was accurate? He could no more summon the missing from below than whistle at a whirlwind. He didn't know how anyone could be left alive, but he knew what duty meant, even if Fedorenko did not.

He grabbed the clamshell and flung it with all his strength. It toppled over the opening and clanged down onto its seat. He spun the locking wheel shut as walls of water burst through the open doors leading out onto the deck. A wave of white foam tried to knock him loose, but he spun that hatch lock until it wouldn't move.

He was clutching it even as the sail flooded, even as the light turned foamy white, then green, then dim and black.

Even as the great hull accelerated in its final dive, as the sea closed in around him, Borodin was uplifted. Fedorenko had forgotten his duty. He had forsaken the faith.

Navigator Pavel Borodin had not.

CHAPTER THIRTY-EIGHT

THE PLUNGE

USS *Portland*

"We're going to have to get them off faster," Steadman told her.

"God," said Scavullo. The Typhoon didn't look like a ship, like anything manmade, so much as a mountain, a volcano of black steel and steam incongruously set out upon the ocean. Vast and powerful, yet dying; the water had swallowed up her stern deck and was rising up the sides of her slablike sail.

Men still clung to her missile deck. She looked down and saw upturned faces bobbing in the dark lane of water separating the two submarines, each clutching onto opposite ends of what appeared to be a guitar case. Those Russians lucky enough to be in rafts could only watch as their less-fortunate mates hung on to anything they could in the freezing water.

The roar of cascading water and foam grew louder as the Typhoon slipped under. Steadman knew the waves, the cold, the suction of the great hull going down would claim the men in the water unless he got them out *right now.* "Come with me," he said, then dropped down from the bridge to the free-flood deck at the base of the sail.

The coil of heavy line meant to follow the original one up to the Typhoon's deck lay in a heap. He grabbed it and shoved it into Scavullo's hands. "Tie it off." Steadman pointed to the short ladder going up to the open ice door.

COB poked his head out of the main trunk hatch. "Hey!" he shouted to Steadman. He had an orange vest. "Put this on *now.*"

Scavullo disregarded her broken finger and tied off the heavy line while Steadman slipped the vest on. He grabbed the free end of the line, stepped through the ice door and dropped down to the exposed deck. Browne followed on his heels.

The line made a railing for the dozen Russians already on deck. They staggered aft as Steadman held it taut. They clambered up through the open ice door and met Scavullo.

"Buistra! Buistra! Idyete v'podlodku!"

They didn't stop to wonder at a woman ordering them below. They dropped into the open bridge hatch and vanished.

Forward, COB and Steadman hauled in one overloaded raft and pulled an endless succession of arms and legs up the side of the hull. As the Russians scrambled back to the ice door, they pulled in the second raft.

There were still men up on *Baikal*'s missile deck.

"Come on!" Steadman yelled to COB.

"What . . ." COB began, but Steadman was no longer standing beside him. He'd jumped into one of the rafts.

"Shit shit *shit.*" Browne leaped over the side and landed inside Steadman's raft. He had the thin yellow line and was pulling them toward the Typhoon hand over hand. COB caught hold of the men in the water and hauled them in as they passed. A half-sunk guitar case gushed water into the raft, and Browne was about to throw it back when one of the Russians grabbed it and hugged it to his chest.

The laden raft stopped beneath the steep black cliff of the Typhoon's hull.

Steadman saw the white, foaming wave boiling up. He cupped his hands and yelled, "Come on! Jump!"

The men up above slid, then fell. The raft tilted and threatened to spill them all into the sea as one, two, three Russians leaped into it from above. A fourth, a fifth.

Browne heard a roar and turned to look aft. The view was terrifying. "Oh man."

A steep wave reared up higher than *Portland*'s deck, curving over and falling into what seemed to be a bottomless hole. It surged up under the raft, propelling it skyward, then hollowed to a wall, a breaker, tipping over in an avalanche of green sea that swamped the raft to the gunwales and drew it over the falls.

The yellow line parted with a *twang!*

The raft spun crazily. The whole world was tilting down, down, as the raft surfed the walls of the powerful eddy, swirling closer to its dark heart. COB was sure they'd all follow that big mother down, but then a great boil of air and foam rose up and shoved the raft aside. It tilted, nearly flipped, but the sheer weight of the men inside made a kind of human keel, and it righted.

The whirlpool moved on. When it passed, Steadman was gone.

———

Steadman tried kicking and stroking away but he couldn't make the smallest progress. The vest was barely keeping his head above water, and then it couldn't. He took a quick breath as he went under. It was as though the water beneath him had vanished, and he was falling to the bottom of Avacha Canyon, falling into the very heart of the sea.

He looked up and saw the bright, mirrored surface recede as he was drawn down, down. He could feel the pressure building against his ears. Something brushed against his face, a frayed, parted line, and he snatched wildly at it without knowing what it might be, without caring whether it was tied off to the sinking Typhoon, or to *Portland*.

The line went limp, then with a sudden yank it pulled so hard he nearly lost it, but Steadman held on. He held on, not knowing whether the stretching line was taking him up, or down.

"Buistra! Buistra! Idyete v'podlodku!" She hurried the last Russians below, then looked up to where the Typhoon had been.

It was gone, but Scavullo saw a tiny orange speck riding a great boil of whitewater rumbling up from where the black hull had vanished. She didn't know who it was, and it wouldn't have mattered if she had. She picked up the radio Steadman had left behind and said, "Helm! Left full rudder! Ahead dead slow!"

"What the hell?" Below in Control the two sailors looked at one another. Could she give them rudder orders?

"Goddamnit, helm! Do it!"

They snapped to and swung the rudder hard over and rang up the throttle command.

Portland swung her bow over to where the lone figure floated on an oily sea, rising, then falling, as the rollers passed under him.

"Rudder amidships! All back!"

The screw rumbled in reverse, biting the sea and slowing the boat's forward motion to a creep.

"All stop!" said Scavullo, smiling. She was close enough to that orange vest to see the face at its center.

COB spotted the yellow line that had once connected the two submarines floating on the surface.

Then it twitched.

Browne sprang and dove for it. The icy water exploded against his face, but he didn't notice it. He grabbed the line and paddled back to the raft, then swung himself back aboard and began hauling in on it.

There was something on the other end.

Raft, *Portland* and swimmer arrived at the same spot more or less at the same moment. Browne reached over and grabbed a fistful of vest and pulled Steadman in.

He flopped to the bottom of the raft, his face pale, his lips blue with cold. "COB?" he said.

"Yeah," said Browne with a broad grin. "Maybe next time you'll remember your personal flotation device on your own."

Baikal

Markov opened the hatch to Central Command and a hot choking mist of steam and smoke poured into Main Engineering. It enveloped the five men in a toxic, scalding haze. "Everyone on OBAs!"

He could hear the cracks and groans of the hull as water flooded in and burst the bulkheads and smashed the doors and hatches. But the lights were still burning in Central Command; not the battle lanterns, but the normal, overhead lights.

Gasparyan saw it and thought, *My God. Vasiliev is still back there!* He spun. "Captain! Vasiliev might be trapped!"

Markov spotted the blinking numerals from the Fathometer at the helm. Like the lights, it was still running, and it read *52*.

They were no longer on the surface. The sail was already under. Vasiliev was doomed if he stayed at his post.

"I've got to go find him!" Gasparyan turned to run but Markov grabbed him by the collar and yanked him back.

"No! Bring Grachev! We're going to have to use the pods!" He ran to the ladder leading up to the Balcony and motioned for the others to hurry.

Lysenko went up first, then Demyan pushed Grachev up the ladder like a sack. When the engineer's boots thumped out onto the deck above, Gasparyan looked beyond them and saw the shut clamshell. *You did one right thing,* he thought of Fedorenko.

There was the sound of distant thunder. The deck shook. Gasparyan leaped for the ladder and found himself sprawled on the deck of the Balcony without knowing quite how he'd done it.

Markov yelled, "Into the pod!"

"You don't have forever!"

"Go!" Markov looked aft. He could sense the ship's gathering plunge, feel it accelerate. There was a shudder, and another *crack!* loud enough to make Markov look up to see whether the hull had split open.

He returned to the most familiar place in all the world, the blue swivel chair in the middle of Central Command. His chair.

For now, for surely the last time, he was alone here. The lights in Central Command projected his silhouette onto the smoke and mist. Shifting shadows, as though the ghosts of all the men who'd lived and worked here were gathering to ride *Baikal* ten kilometers down to the bottom of Avacha Canyon.

"Captain!" called Gasparyan again.

Markov took down the SUBMARINE LIFE IS NOT A SERVICE, BUT A RELIGION plaque and slipped it into his overalls.

Another loud *crack.*

Markov ran back to the ladder and climbed up. The pod hatch was open. He dived through barely in time to keep Demyan from slamming it on him.

Grachev sprawled against the bare steel hull. Lysenko spun the locking wheel. The small white-faced gauge on the bulkhead next to the firing button was a mechanical Fathometer. Its needle was moving swiftly through a hundred meters.

The rise would be violent. "Sit down! Hold on!" said Markov. The others barely had time to sit before Markov swung open the gray metal box and slammed his fist against the red button.

There was a *spit,* then nothing.

The bolts didn't fire.

Hangzhou

The Kamov landed on the fantail of the Chinese destroyer *Hangzhou,* and Fedorenko was met by an officer who escorted him to the bridge. Up there, through the thick glass, Fedorenko could easily see the great white cloud of steam on the southern horizon that marked *Baikal's* final dive.

"Good day, Captain Fedorenko."

He turned away from the glass. Two elderly men stood in the aft passageway. They wore spotless dark uniforms decorated with enough metal and braid to sink a small submarine, and were flanked by lesser officers.

In the old Russian Navy, a destroyer like *Hangzhou* would have been considered a second-rank ship, and her captain would be, accordingly, a second-ranked captain. The Chinese Navy did things its own way, apparently, for standing before Fedorenko were Rear Admiral Li Xiukang and his boss, Admiral Wang Yongquo, commander of the East Sea Fleet.

"Gen women zou," said Admiral Wang.

Fedorenko tried to parse the meaning of the demand to follow them. Not even a courteous *please*? He followed them to a sparsely furnished wardroom just off the destroyer's bridge. The other officers, captains, senior lieutenants all, remained outside and shut the door quietly behind Fedorenko.

"You have been through a difficult experience," said Admiral Wang. He spoke Mandarin. "Do you need medical attention?"

"There's no time to treat my injuries. Quick action is demanded."

"Action?"

"As you know, torpedoes were launched against *Baikal*."

Admiral Wang looked stung at the mention of the error. *"Shei zuode hui shou cheng fa!"*

"The punishment of those responsible is exactly what I wish to address," said Fedorenko. "I refer to the Americans."

Wang glanced at Li. Neither said a thing.

"They fired two torpedoes at *Baikal* at the entrance to the polar sea. Two more while under the ice and two just north of here in the Bering Strait."

"That was an act of piracy."

"Indeed," Fedorenko agreed. "Would it not be wise to let them reap the fruits of their crimes? A torpedo struck our ship on the way to join your country's navy. It would be embarrassing if it appeared that torpedo had been launched by Russian hands. Or Chinese." He saw the impact his words had on the senior officers. *They've had this discussion,* he thought. *And your necks are on the line just like mine.*

Wang caught on at once. "The American Navy will know it was not their doing. Their submarine will make a report."

"Not if they are on the bottom along with *Baikal*."

"Tingqilai, ni dui ni tongbao de shengming bu zhenxi," said Admiral Wang. *You speak lightly of the lives of your countrymen.*

Fedorenko shook his head. *"Wo shuo de shi zhuanbai weisheng."* Then, in case he had not been understood, repeated himself in Russian: "I speak of turning disaster into victory."

The Chinese officers exchanged another look, then Rear Admiral Li said, *"Ni keyi zou."*

The door behind Fedorenko opened. He'd been dismissed.

In the time it took to walk back to the bridge, the destroyer and her sister ship had stopped dead in the water. But the two *Kilo*s had not. Their rounded, bulbous bows stuffed with heavy, ship-killing torpedoes were pointed south.

Baikal

Gasparyan watched the needle on the small depth gauge continue its inexorable fall. "Six hundred meters."

Markov could feel the ship pick up speed in the dive. Now that her bow was pointed down, gravity and mass were turning *Baikal* into a forty-thousand-ton arrow aimed at the bottom of Avacha Canyon. "We could try the other pod," he said.

"Seven hundred meters," said Gasparyan. The gauge stopped at one thousand.

The sounds of the dying ship filled the small pod. A crash of water coming in under great pressure beat at the hatch as though it knew they were inside the pod, sheltered behind a flimsy piece of steel. As though giving them notice that it would soon be coming for them.

"The clamshell's gone," said Demyan.

"Eight hundred meters."

The beating ended in a *crack!* so close and loud it made Markov jump. *How will it come?* As a wall of water made hard as steel? Or will the walls simply collapse and crush them?

"One thousand meters."

"Oh, shut up, Gasparyan," said Grachev. "You'd count the posts in Saint Peter's fence."

Markov looked down at his chief engineer. Was it a blessing for him to have awakened in this steel bubble heading for the bottom? "I'm sorry, Igor. The bolts didn't fire."

A heavy vibration coursed through the steel skin of the pod, as though they were in the back of a truck running too fast over an uneven road. It became more intense, until it no longer seemed to be coming from anywhere, but instead, from everywhere.

"Flow turbulence," said Markov. "We must be really moving. Forty, fifty knots. Maybe faster."

The pod tipped over farther, until it was no longer possible to sit on the wooden bench. The deck had become the bulkhead, the bulkhead the deck.

To be crushed, to drown. Markov wasn't afraid. Indeed, he'd half expected to ride *Baikal* down. He was only sad that good men were riding it down, too.

A low, animal moan came from the juddering hull. It ended in a shriek, a snap, as some structure was pulled apart by the speed of their dive.

"You know," said Gasparyan, "we might make it to the bottom. The impact might blow us free."

"The pod won't take the pressure of eight thousand meters," said Markov. "It won't take two thousand."

Gasparyan looked at the gauge. The needle had come to rest against its stop.

USS *Portland*

Portland was a madhouse packed with a hundred extra bodies on board. They were shoulder to shoulder from the bottom deck to the top, from the torpedo room at the bow to the hatch leading into "nuke alley," the reactor spaces, aft.

Steadman told Scavullo to find the Russian captain, then gave the conn to Whalley with a terse, "Get the boat underway for Japan *now*. Take her down to two hundred feet. Right full rudder. Turns for six knots."

"Sure, but . . ."

"No buts, Whalley. Do it."

Portland shouldered beneath the sea and turned away from land, heading out into the open ocean that was her true home.

"Helm, take us all the way around to about two zero zero."

The chief sitting dive said, "About?"

"Just two zero zero."

Whalley had managed to shoo the wet, bedraggled Russians out of Control, but they were in the forward and aft passages and were talking in such loud, excited voices he could hardly make himself heard over the din. He was glad that they were all so happy to be alive, but he wished they'd do it someplace else.

It was going to be a long run to Japan.

"Conn, Sonar. That big bastard is breaking up."

"Why tell me?"

"Because . . . Stand by! We're being pinged by two sonars bearing zero four zero and zero three two. They sound like Shark Gills," said Bam Bam. "I think we've got a pair of *Kilo*s out there."

"How far away are they?"

"Inside ten thousand yards."

The boat was in range and in trouble. "Helm! Turns for twelve knots! Let's get out of Dodge."

"We can't go fast and quiet," someone reminded him.

"Then *ten* knots. Keefe! Make your tubes ready to shoot."

"At what?" said Keefe. "I don't have any targets stacked up."

"Send the weapons down the bearing of those two *Kilo*s!"

"Two hundred feet."

Bam Bam listened to the steady pinging in his headset. It was growing louder, closer. Then suddenly, it stopped.

"Shit," he said. "Conn, Sonar. I think they're on to us."

Baikal

"God," said Gasparyan. His voice shook with the tremendous vibration set up by the swift flow of water beyond *Baikal*'s plummeting hull. He was standing on the bulkhead, the wall, of the pod, looking at the depth gauge between his feet.

The pod was like *Baikal*. So tremendously overbuilt it could withstand pressures beyond the ability of a depth gauge to register. Yet the bolts. The damned bolts had doomed them. *When will the walls go?*

Grachev groaned and pushed himself upright. His head was swimming. He turned to face the swinging door to the firing button. *Contacts,* he thought.

"All . . . of . . . you . . ." said Markov. "I'm . . . sorry. . . ."

Grachev crawled uphill to the firing box. He took an old knife from his pocket and stabbed the red button.

"Igor . . . !"

Grachev levered the plastic cover away and exposed a plastic membrane meant to protect the brass contacts beneath. The contacts were green with corrosion.

There was a screech, a tearing, an almost-human shriek, and the pod lurched, then tumbled.

"She's . . . coming . . . apart!" Gasparyan yelled.

Grachev scraped the green terminals with his knife, then thrust the blade across the dirty contacts. "Ahhh!" he yelled as a sizable jolt sizzled through his arm, but he kept the knife where it was, bridging the contacts.

There was a fat blue spark that illuminated the pod's interior with a harsh flash. Lightning, followed an instant later by the loudest clap of thunder any of the five men had ever heard.

Submarine *Lin San Liu*

"Open the outer torpedo doors now," said Captain Bai Yao. He felt the glow of the coming victory suffuse him like powerful drink. How many years had gone by since a Chinese ship had destroyed an American? Had it *ever* happened?

Never mind his submarine had been built in Russia. Never mind that his crew took orders from him but looked to the Russian advisors. Many wrongs were about to be made right. China had suffered bad luck for too long. Now, it would be America's turn.

"Final range and bearing?" he asked the Russian sonarman.

"Six thousand meters, angle on the bow, port five."

Captain Bai Yao turned to the weapons officers. "Match final bearings, Tubes One, Two, Three and—"

"No!"

The captain turned to the sonarman.

"High-speed screws inbound! Two torpedoes!" His small screen blossomed with bright new lines. "*Four* torpedoes!"

USS *Portland*

Steadman heard Bam Bam's initial warning as he put on a dry uniform. Then the boat began to move, and an instant later, "Torpedoes in the water!"

He sprinted out of his stateroom, turned right and found himself swimming up a river of wet Russians, all of them trying to tell Scavullo something.

"Where's their captain?" he asked her as he shoved his way into the mob.

"He didn't make it," she answered.

Didn't make it? He pushed through and found Control only a little less chaotic. Whalley was in overload. He could hardly finish a sentence before starting another.

"Put our stern to them! Make your . . . No! I mean, the *Kilos*. Not them! . . . Bam Bam! Where are they anyway?"

"Conn, Sonar. Where are *who*?"

Steadman stepped in and said, "I have the conn."

With a look of pure relief, Whalley said, "XO has the conn!"

"All stop! Hold your depth!"

The Russians began talking again, loudly and all at once. Steadman could scarcely hear himself. He snatched the intercom. "Sonar, Conn! What have we got?"

"Two *Kilos* eight thousand yards northeast. They dialed us in on active and then four fish popped up in the south."

We're sandwiched. "Chinese torpedoes? Russian?"

"Not unless they're shooting Mark 48s."

Mark 48s? He looked at the contact board. It was a spaghetti of bearings, ranges and guesses.

"Conn, Sonar. Two torpedoes to port, two others to starboard, all of them astern. Range two thousand yards. They're running hot, straight and normal at fifty knots plus."

"Scavullo!" Steadman yelled. "Shut those Russians up!"

She said something. They paid no attention.

Then Scavullo took a deep breath, aimed herself at a Russian *michman* and fired straight into his face: *"Malchi! Torpedye vas mogut uslichat!"*

She'd told them to shut up or else the torpedoes would hear them, and it worked. The passage went dead silent.

"Conn, Sonar, here they come."

A high-speed whine sounded through Control, rising up the octaves as it swept in from the stern, falling away as it swam by.

"One," said Steadman.

Another, closer, for when it passed by he heard the bubbling of its furiously spinning screws.

"Two."

The sounds were now a blend of approaching and departing torpedoes. In the center of this Doppler symphony was *Portland*.

"Three . . . and *Four*."

As the last of the salvo hurried north, Bam Bam said, "Conn, Sonar, the fish are going after the *Kilos*!"

Submarine *Lin San Liu*

"Torpedoes have gone active," said the Russian sonarman. He picked up a cigarette and lit it.

"No smoking in the Control room!" Captain Bai Yao snapped.

"Fuck off," said the Russian, and took a deep drag as the first Mark 48 began pinging.

"Fire noisemakers! Ahead flank!"

The *Kilo* spat out a string of chemical bubbles as it slowly moved away from the torpedo streaking in from astern.

"Ten seconds," said the Russian. He would have to hurry to finish the cigarette. "Weapon is in terminal mode."

Ping! Ping! Ping! Ping!

The captain changed his mind about running. "Emergency surface! Blow ballast tanks now!"

A hand was reaching for the controls when a warhead sized to take down a Typhoon detonated six feet from the *Kilo*'s hull.

The little diesel split open, filling instantly, shedding a cloud of debris like a cracked-open piñata. The second torpedo mistook the fragments for the submarine and attacked them. Another warhead detonated, turning even the larger pieces into a blizzard of black, jagged snow.

The second *Kilo* was less fortunate. Its crew had to listen to *Lin San Liu*'s death, and then wait another twenty-nine seconds before it joined it on the long, silent journey down to the bottom of Avacha Canyon.

USS *Portland*

"Periscope depth," said Browne.

Steadman was ready. "Up the number-two scope. Scavullo?"

"Conn, Radio. Stand by." She let the scanner sweep through all the regular frequencies until it locked onto a transmission. She listened to a fast, frightened voice from the destroyer *Hangzhou* plead for help. It was going out in accented Russian, in the clear, unencoded. When a big, booming transmission replied that there was no help to send, the destroyer then asked for permission to enter Avacha Bay itself.

"Conn, Radio. The destroyer's running for Petropavlovsk. Or at least she wants to. The Russians haven't said okay yet."

They're rattled, thought Steadman. They were going to deliver the coup de grâce on a blind, helpless target, and ended up short two submarines and without a clue about where the fatal blow had come from. "Up scope."

The head rose from the scope well and Steadman swept it in a fast, full circle before stopping. "I've got a destroyer bearing zero zero three. She's making smoke and running off to the west at high speed." So high, in fact, that her graceful clipper bow was nearly fully exposed, planing like a ski boat's.

"Conn, Radio. The Russians just gave *Hangzhou* and *Fuzhou* the okay."

"Very well." Steadman swept the horizon again, and then stopped. "What the hell is that thing?" He increased the magnification. "Okay. I have some floating debris bearing two four eight. It looks like a ballast tank."

There was a low buzz from the Russians watching from the forward passageway. One of them, a tall, slender man with a sharply angular face, jutting jaw and buzz-cut black hair, stepped forward. His dark blue coveralls were marked *Kp-3T*, whatever that signified. "Scavullo. Come forward. I've got a situation here."

He's an officer, thought Steadman. But then, it seemed almost all the Russians were officers.

The Russian pointed to his chest and said, *"Belikov. Sonar."*

"Lieutenant Commander Steadman. I'm *Portland*'s executive officer."

"Starpom." Then Belikov pointed to the periscope. *"Da?"*

"Nyet," said Steadman.

Scavullo appeared in the rear door.

Belikov looked relieved to see her. He pointed to the periscope. *"Eta* ne *vadayom. Ne vadayom. Eta nash kapitan. Nash kapitan."*

"He says it's not a water tank, it's his captain."

"He doesn't know what he's talking about." Steadman motioned for Belikov to take a look.

Belikov grasped the handles expertly. He shouted to the dense knot of Russians gathered in the forward passage, *"Nash kapitan!"*

"His captain!" said Scavullo.

Steadman said, "Diving Officer. Surface the boat."

"Aye aye," said Browne as he sent a blast of high-pressure air into *Portland*'s ballast tanks.

Portland emerged from the slate gray sea five hundred yards to the east of the floating tank. Steadman slipped on a float vest, then gave one to Scavullo and Belikov and climbed out onto the bridge.

It looked no more like anyone's captain from up here than it had through the search scope. But when Belikov saw it he pointed and grinned like he'd just won the lottery and then, to Steadman's utter amazement, he began to weep.

"What's wrong with him?"

"I think he's happy," said Scavullo.

Steadman brought the boat alongside the black steel tank. It rolled heavy and low in the sea, tipping one way, then another, looking very much the worse for wear, as though a child had taken a hammer to a tin can. The sides were dished in, the spherical ends flattened. There were streaks of acid yellow in flower-burst patterns at regular intervals along its thirty-foot hull.

A larger wave rolled it almost completely over, and when it did, Steadman saw the hatch. "*Jesus!* Helm! Right full rudder! Ahead dead slow!"

Portland crept closer, then bumped the tank hard, rolling it completely over. "All back!" The stern churned white with froth, then, "All stop!"

The surface detail secured it to *Portland*'s flank, then used more lines to roll the hatch up and away from the water.

Belikov could stand it no longer. He jumped down from the bridge and was out through the ice door in the sail before anyone could stop him. He ran out along the deck as though it were a level track in a stadium and not a curved hull rolling in moderate seas.

He jumped for the pod, sailing across a narrow gap of water, landing next to the hatch. His weight shifted the tank and he nearly went for a swim, but the lines held fast and he started pounding it with his fists and shouting, *"Vui hadditye! Vui hadditye."*

"He says come out, come out," said Scavullo.

The hatch fell open with a *clang!*

"Bridge, Radio," squawked the intercom beside Steadman.

He picked it up as the first Russian pulled himself free of the hatch. He reached back down and a second face rose into view. A third, a small dark man peeked out suspiciously, as though he might be entertaining the notion of staying. A fourth, and then a fifth.

How many people are in that thing? And then Steadman wondered, *Where will I put them all?* "Go."

"The CO of *Corpus Christi* sends his regards. They're standing off a quarter mile south at PD. He says the eyes of Texas are upon us, and he wants to know if we could use any more help."

Steadman turned and caught sight of a slim white feather of a wake. "Thank them for the good shooting. Tell him I'll rendezvous with him fifty miles east."

Belikov led two of his crewmates aft with the injured one draped between them. They were followed by a bald officer with a mustache. When they got to the ice door, the others stayed back and let the bald one climb through first.

He looked up at Steadman from the bottom of the bridge ladder and shouted up a quick question.

"He asks for . . ." Scavullo started, but Steadman knew.

"Tell him permission granted."

Markov climbed five feet up to the open bridge. With Scavullo there was hardly room to turn.

"I'm Captain Markov. *Baikal* was my ship. I have an injured man who needs medical attention."

"I'm Lieutenant Commander Steadman. *Starpom* of the USS *Portland*. Welcome aboard. Have your man taken below. The corpsman will see him at once."

Scavullo translated, but she knew Markov understood.

As Grachev was passed below, Markov said, "Your ship is very small. Where are all my men?"

Scavullo translated and Steadman answered, "Your men are below. We tried to rescue them all."

Markov nodded when she finished the translation, then said, "You're an officer?"

"Lieutenant Rose Scavullo."

"I didn't know women served on American submarines."

"You're not the only one."

Markov turned to Steadman and said, *"G'dye kapitan etoy podlodkoy?"*

"He asks, Where is the captain of this submarine?"

Steadman had expected it. Commanding officers, no matter the color of their uniforms, no matter which flag their ships might fly, talked to commanding officers.

"You're looking at him," he finally said.

EPILOGUE

The only space large enough for the Russian crew to gather was the mess deck, and they quickly filled it to overflowing. They attacked the coffee urn and drained it, then the juice dispensers, even the condiment bins.

"Attention!" shouted Gasparyan. "Captain on deck!"

All eyes turned to Markov as he pushed his way through the crowd to stand beside a big television at the forward end of the jammed space. He was still in his soaked uniform.

Markov held a sheet of paper. He waited until the last voice went silent, then said, "It's good to see you all."

The response was automatic.

"Greetings, Comrade Captain!" they roared in unison.

Markov looked at the list, but then he folded it up and put it away. He knew all the names from memory.

"Belikov, Viktor."

"Present, Captain!"

"Borodin, Pavel."

Silence.

Markov scanned the faces. "Has anyone seen Borodin?"

"Still on patrol, Captain," said Mirtov, the seaman who'd seen him running aft as the ship was going under.

Markov put a hand out to the nearest table for a long second, another, and then said, "Gasparyan, Sergei."

"Present, Captain!"

"Grachev, Igor!"

"The American doctor is looking after him, Captain," said Gasparyan.

Markov went down his mental list of officers without calling Fedorenko's name.

"Vasiliev, Alexander!"

Gasparyan looked physically ill. He collapsed as though someone had struck him with a hammer. The room was too tightly packed for him to fall. The men to either side held him up as tears poured from his eyes. "I told him . . . I said five minutes . . . only five! It's . . ."

"Still on patrol," someone called.

Markov started in on the warrants and seamen. To each name he heard, "Present!" until he came to, "Ossipov, Pavel!"

Then someone said, "Still on patrol, Captain."

Between his gleaming pots, his museum-quality knives and this antiseptically clean American galley, Pavel the cook had fallen off the world.

When he was finished, when every name had been called and accounted for, Markov said, "I propose to honor *Baikal* and the men who served her in the traditional manner." He looked around as though waiting for something. "Who's hiding a bottle?"

Someone produced a flask spirited off the sinking ship and gave it to Markov. Ceramic mugs were passed out. The vodka was meted out drop by drop into a hundred and five mugs. Enough for a splash in every one. A smell more than a proper drink. But then, this wasn't a time for drinking.

Markov raised his mug. "To those we have left on the bottom of the sea," he said. "To our ship and to the world. I pray we served them both correctly and well." His eyes glistened, his body swayed as though a wind had gusted through the packed wardroom. He put the mug to his lips and smelled the sharp scent of raw alcohol.

When he tipped it back, perhaps a single drop found its way to Markov's lips, where it met, and mixed, with his tears.

City of Corpus Christi sprinted ahead, then drifted, listening with her good sonar for threats. There were none. The ocean that had seemed so full of peril had turned innocent.

At ten knots, it took the better part of a day to sail clear of Russian waters. There, a hundred miles off the Siberian coast, fifty men, half of *Baikal's* homeless crew, were passed over the side to *Corpus Christi*. A single raft shuttled the men across.

While on the surface, *Portland* received orders from Norfolk.

"Conn, Radio. New message traffic received."

"Bring it forward," said Steadman.

Lieutenant Wallace handed Steadman the decoded message.

COB sat at the ballast board and read Steadman's expression as quickly as Steadman read the message from Norfolk. "Bad?"

"Looks like you'll get to wear that lei after all, COB," said Steadman. "They're sending us to Pearl by way of Shemya."

"*Shemya?* That's Alaska."

"We're medevac-ing Vann off the boat and bringing Admiral Graybar's chief of staff on. He'll be CO for the run down to Pearl."

"Joe Welch. Good CO."

"I hope you're right." Steadman folded the sheet and put it away. "COB, I'm going to need to assemble some paperwork."

"Deck logs? Sonar contacts? Navigation tracks? Already done, sir. From the moment we crossed the Blue Line back at Kola to today. It'll be there for Welch to review." He lowered his voice. "In case anybody's been messin' with the books, Bam Bam's been keeping his own."

"I didn't hear that. But if I did, I'd advise Bam Bam to stuff it in the TDU and send it to the bottom before Captain Welch arrives."

"I believe Sonarman Schramm has already received that advice."

"Conn, Radio. We've copied a special CNN broadcast."

"Send it down to the screens in the mess decks and the wardroom," said Steadman. "Nav?" he said to Whalley.

"Captain?" Whalley's tone had changed. They were still the same rank, but the lightness, the irreverence, the bantering was gone. When those two Chinese boats started pinging he couldn't bear up under the weight of command. Now he was counting the hours until he could step across the brow and never look back.

"We've been ordered to stand off Shemya Island to meet a helicopter. Plot the course and get us headed there right way. *Corpus Christi* will keep us company. You have the conn," said Steadman. "I'll be in the wardroom. Call if you need me."

Steadman went down to the middeck and aft to the wardroom. When he opened the door, the television was already playing. Lieutenant Rose Scavullo sat at the big table while Chief Cooper rewrapped her broken finger.

"How's Vann?" asked Steadman.

"Bad. We could lose him. Same goes for the Russian. They need a real hospital."

"Keep them going for a couple of days and they'll get one."

"Aye aye," said Cooper, and left them alone in the wardroom.

"I can go if you need to work," she said.

"Stay put, Lieutenant," he said as he went to the coffee urn and poured himself a cup. "I'll fill you in on what's happening." He looked at the screen. A ship, an American aircraft carrier, was coming into port somewhere. Her decks were lined with white-clad sailors and there were fireboats shooting giant arcs of spray into a faultless blue sky. "Maybe you ought to tell me."

"CNN says we forced the Chinese to cancel a military exercise and open negotiations with Taiwan. Listen." She turned the volume up.

". . . while a long road lies ahead for these two countries, the crisis that began with the suicide bombing of a mainland diplomat does appear to be easing. The American aircraft carrier Kitty Hawk's *jubilant arrival in Keelung Harbor today has the unmistakable feel of a military victory, though if so it was a battle won by the threat of force rather than the use of it."*

"Will the real story ever come out?" she asked.

"Not if a submariner has any say about it. How's Markov doing?"

"He told me he'd rather have one friend than a thousand rubles. But he said he still has his faith. I'm not sure what he meant."

"Losing men in an accident would be bad enough. Losing them from something you set into motion must be unbearable." And of course, he thought about Vann. Was he feeling that, or was he so over the edge he couldn't see what was right in front of his face?

"We're going to meet up with a helicopter off Shemya Island," he said. "Vann and the Russian will be taken off. We'll head south for Hawaii. COMSUBLANT's chief of staff will come aboard as the new CO."

"They're not letting you bring *Portland* home?"

"I'll be lucky to stay out of Leavenworth."

"Sir," she said, "I'm sorry. I didn't mean to drag you . . ."

"I didn't volunteer to fight your battles. I did what I thought was right."

"You think they'll see it that way?"

He smiled. "Maybe that's what Markov meant about faith."

COMSUBLANT
Norfolk

"You've decided to fry Steadman," said Captain Welch.

"In deep fat," said Admiral Graybar. "There was a goddamned *shootout* on his bridge. He's bringing back three bodies in the freezer compartment, a crippled CO and a boat so busted up it'll take a year to make right. I've bilged COs for grounding their keels on a sandbank. Tell me why I shouldn't crucify Steadman."

"Because he got your job done," said Welch. "What else do you want from the guy? He's just a lieutenant commander, for Christ's sake."

"What about mutiny?"

"We don't know that it was. I'd take a real close look before I made up my mind."

"Well, we do agree about that, at least."

Welch raised a black eyebrow. "About what?"

"You're going out to *Portland* to take that close look. A little sea time will do you good."

Welch had the uncomfortable feeling that he wasn't steering Graybar anymore. "What about the girl?"

"You have an opinion?"

"If it were in my hands, if she comes out clean, I'd send her straight to Groton."

"She's already been to spook school."

"Not spook school. *Submarine* school."

"She's a rider who asked for a boat. No. She *whined* until she got one. I gave it to her."

"You gave her Vann. What's *that* going to sound like at a Board of Inquiry?"

"What if she makes it through sub school? What do I have on my hands *then*?"

"A submariner," said Welch, simply.

Provideniya, Russia

The mild Kuroshio current flows north from the Central Pacific, passes Japan and brushes the Siberian coastline before colliding head-on with the frigid Anadyr countercurrent. The waters mix and swirl, and a powerful eddy is born that sweeps the sea clean of floating debris and deposits it in a bay near the fishing town of Provideniya.

All through the first weeks of September the fishermen who used the rickety old pier for crabbing knew that *something* had happened beyond the fog-bound horizon. Drifts of yellow insulation, burned-smelling and foul, dusted the surface of the gray sea. Steel flasks, broken sheets of wooden paneling, waterlogged papers and small glass bottles came in with every tide.

The crabmen sifted through the flotsam for anything useful, sellable or drinkable. They argued and speculated about the ship that had gone down, the details of its misfortune, its crew and cargo as they pulled up their crab traps. One after another, the wire cages were hauled up from between the legs of the old pier bristling with fat Kamchatka crabs.

The last trap rose to the surface, but then it stopped, caught on something. A weak lantern was produced. The crabmen looked down to where the tide surged around the barnacled legs of the pier, and saw the swimmer.

He was on his front, his upper body, his shoulders and arms in constant motion. The dark water around him was white with his frantic splashing. He seemed to be trying to climb on top of the crab cage, which was understandable given the temperature of the water.

"Hold on!"

He could be a fisherman fallen off an anchored boat, or a drunk who'd walked into the sea, or a thief trying to steal crabs. Whatever had put him there, he was a man in very cold water and they were watermen who understood, who shared that nightmare.

They ran for the ladder. Someone found a gaff.

The trio climbed down below the rotting deck of the pier. Down to the water where the weak lantern revealed not a swimmer, but a body. It was covered in the shredded remnants of navy blue coveralls and armored with a clacking, quarreling mob of feeding crabs.

They gaffed the body closer and scraped the crabs into the sea. A wave sent the body against the pier, and it rolled, exposing an eyeless face, a hollowed-out belly trailing streamers of white flesh, and a white identity strip above his breast pocket: K1 FEDORENKO.

Tripler Army Hospital
Honolulu, Hawaii
4 December

Vann spent September at Tripler Army Hospital. He figured he was being kept on the island so that when the Board of Inquiry convened, he could be called to defend his actions, and himself.

He spent October with a cheerful physical therapist named Tui. The big Samoan assured him that he could lead a perfectly normal life without the use of his feet, his legs. Really? He'd once commanded a ship and now he wasn't in command of his own bladder.

He spent the first three weeks of November building his case. It filled a large box full of yellow legal pads. Vann might never walk again, but he itched for the chance to bring his guns to bear on the man who betrayed him.

Tripler was festooned with cutout turkeys and pumpkins the week before Thanksgiving, when a visitor arrived.

Once, a long time ago, Captain Brooks Loeffler had been Vann's CO. He'd been the one to recommend him for PCO school. Now he was one of two former fast-attack skippers who taught the prospective commander's course over at Naval Training Facility Pacific.

Loeffler was a small man with a broad, open face and snowy white hair. His eyes were piercing blue. His skin was the kind of pink that burned easily under the Hawaiian sun. As kindly as Loeffler seemed, he was an uncompromising demon at the helm of a boat. Any PCO student who assumed an easy nine weeks lay ahead was making a career-ending error.

"You look shitty," Loeffler said by way of a greeting.

"Me and my boat both," said Vann.

He gazed down at Vann. "You need something? The bed moved? Something to drink?" His eyes came to rest on the bag hanging on a stand, hooked up to a tube that vanished under Vann's covers, then Loeffler looked away.

"You can tell me what's on your mind, Brooks."

"Steadman. What's the good word?"

Vann's forehead went reptile cold. If Loeffler was asking, then Steadman's name must be on a list for PCO school. Which meant the Board of Inquiry had either finished its work without Vann, or else there had been no Board of Inquiry. "What do you want to know?"

"Nothing I'm not cleared for. It's like a wedding. The preacher says if anyone knows some reason these two should not be joined let them come forward now or forever hold their peace. So?"

"Someone getting married?"

"Someone with a lot of stars requested a background check."

"I had the chance to recommend him last year and I couldn't. It embittered him to the point of committing mutiny."

"You wouldn't recommend him for a boat?"

"Jesus, Brooks. I'd recommend him for a firing squad. We're talking about *mutiny*."

Loeffler hesitated, then said, "We're talking about the man who just made commander."

Commander? Vann felt the bile rise. "How . . . how can that be? Who would recommend him?"

"A golden boy from COMSUBLANT's office. Name of Welch."

"Joe Welch?"

"The same. Now, I don't trust golden boys so I went out with your old XO to see for myself. Steadman doesn't have alligator blood in his veins. He's not a killer like we were. But he's done things for real the rest of the fleet only practices. How many warshots have you ever fired? How many live fish have you evaded in earnest?"

"But . . ."

"It's no reflection on you. But our war? It's over. We won. Even heroes have to go home sometime."

"No. That's wrong, Brooks. You're mistaken. He fooled you."

"Maybe so." Loeffler checked his watch. "It's graduation day over at the school and they expect me to say something profound. By the way. You want to be a guest lecturer next term? Say the word and I'll set you up with your own room."

"Sure, Brooks. That would be fine."

"Take care of yourself, Jim. Okay? Don't take this too hard. It could eat up your life."

As Loeffler walked to the door, Vann said, "Brooks!"

Loeffler turned.

"What about *Portland*?"

"They're sending her back to EB," he said, meaning Electric Boat in Groton. "She's been sitting over at Number One Drydock."

"When does she leave?"

"They're flooding the drydock today. You want to go see her before she leaves? I'll make the arrangements with security. Least I can do." And with that, Captain Loeffler went out and closed the door.

**Drydock #1
U.S. Navy Ship Repair Facility,
Pearl Harbor, Hawaii**

"We could have been anybody," said Vann, fuming. "He didn't even check any ID."

"Be happy they didn't take your camera, Cap'n V," said Tui. He switched on the windshield wipers and looked up into the rearview mirror. "You got to cut people a little more slack."

"The hell I do." Vann's khakis were cleaned and pressed until the creases were sharp enough to draw blood. He'd polished his gold dolphins until they gleamed.

"Take you," said the young Samoan. "You had your rehab class tonight and here you are playin' *hooky.*"

"Tui, there is no good reason for a crippled man to go swimming."

"Talk like that, you gonna get me fired."

"Take the next left."

A warm rain turned the shipyard road slick and the streetlights into yellow globes as Tui drove Vann out to the water.

From the East Quay Vann caught a glimpse of the white *Arizona* memorial, indistinct enough behind a curtain of rain to be a ghostly ship riding at anchor.

"Where'd you say your ship was, Cap'n?"

"Drydock One. And it's a boat, Tui. Turn here."

Tui swung the van onto the road paralleling the main Ten Ten dock. Massive traveling cranes stood high above them, so tall they had red lights blinking from their summits to keep airplanes away.

A pair of immense gates rose from the water immediately beyond the southern end of the Ten Ten Dock. Beyond them, Vann spotted a scaffold of yellow steel, and inside it, bathed in sodium lights, was the pitch-black rectangle of *Portland*'s sail.

They drove down the road beside the flooded drydock.

Vann felt a chill and looked down at his lap. *Dear God.* He'd wet himself. His khakis were dark with a spreading stain. "Stop here!"

Tui pulled over. The wheels bumped across tracks meant for the big rolling cranes, and then he had to stop at a concrete barricade.

The headlights poured through a gap in the barricade, revealing two yellow chains guarding the edge of the drydock. *Portland* was afloat, secured to the sides by a cat's cradle of crisscrossing lines. Temporary railings made a narrow walkway along the spine of her rounded hull. Awnings covered the forward and aft escape hatches and a larger one protected the bridge. A long metal brow extended from the edge of the drydock to a point just aft of the sail.

"What's your pleasure?"

"I want to get out and see my boat."

"In the rain?"

"Why the hell not? I'm already wet."

The Samoan looked back over the seat. *Oh shit. They definitely gonna fire my ass now.* "You know, we should just head back to the hospital and get you a brand-new set of—"

"Tui, don't make me crawl out to her."

"Sure, sure. Keep cool, Cap'n."

Tui opened the van's back door and took out the wheelchair. "Rain's stopping," he said as he rolled it up to the back door of the van.

Vann eased out and allowed Tui to strap him in tightly. More tightly than usual, he noticed.

"I ain't pushing you out on that bridge thing so don't even ask."

"The brow. I don't want to board her. I just want to look at her."

Tui rolled Vann through the gap in the barricade and over to the railing chains.

With the rain stopped the water around *Portland* grew calm, grew clear. The still surface reflected the yellow work lights strung along the scaffolding until it seemed she was afloat in a black sky ablaze with stars.

He could see beyond the scaffolding, see through the black rubber skin of her hull. He took in her slim, tense gracefulness, her rounded shape, her trim, orderly insides as though the whole of her lay open beneath a brilliant sun. There was the Engine Room. There was Maneuvering, the reactor space, Control, Sonar and then his own stateroom. Right there.

He could see it all. Machinery and men welded together by unbreakable chains of duty, of responsibility. A world unlike any other, and now forever barred to him because of one man.

Commander Steadman.

He felt the fury build in him, but try as he might, Vann couldn't conjure his face. The harder he tried, the faster it seemed to slip through his fingers. One man. One man. *One man.*

When a face finally rose up from the deep, when the ripples of its surfacing were spent, when the waters turned mirror flat, it wasn't Steadman's face Vann was looking into, but his own.

"Well, Cap'n? You seen enough?"

Vann patted his lap, then looked up at Tui. "I left the camera back in the van. Would you get it for me please? For my scrapbook."

"Then we can go?"

"Then we can go."

Tui gave the railing chains a shake to be sure they were secure. The links were thick and heavy, threaded through rings set on steel poles. He locked the wheelchair and left Vann to find the camera.

He hunted for it everywhere. On the backseat. He saw the wet stain on the upholstery and knew he was going to catch it for not connecting Vann up to a new bag before they left the hospital, even though he had. The old man was just too full of piss for his own good.

He heard the pattering of drops on the roof of the van. It was raining again. It was time to bring the old guy back home.

He slid the door shut and made his way back through the concrete barrier to where he'd left the wheelchair.

The Samoan stopped.

The wheelchair was still there, but he could see right through the tubular back to the lights beyond.

Oh, man. He ran to the chair and found Vann's golden dolphins on the damp seat. He went to the edge of the drydock, leaned out over the chains and looked down into the black water.

Bright reflections shimmered crazily as an expanding circle of light lapped along *Portland*'s hull, fading, calming, then growing still.

Submarine Base New London,
Groton, Connecticut
11 July

With winter gales scouring the Arctic, *Portland* returned to her spawning grounds by a southerly route: through the Panama Canal, the Caribbean, up the Atlantic coast to Long Island Sound and finally to New London, Connecticut, and its river Thames. There, laid up inside a floating drydock, *Portland* required eight months of repairs before she was ready to feel the sea beneath her keel again.

With a new war in the Middle East on the horizon, Electric Boat worked round the clock to make her ready to sail. Steadman did much the same.

After graduating from PCO school, he rotated through a dizzying schedule of training at Naval Reactors, seminars on human resources and leadership. At the end came half a month working under the gaze of COMSUBLANT, Admiral Graybar. It was a race to the wire, for if *Portland* was ready before he was she'd go out with a different captain.

But when the invitations went out to the change-of-command ceremony, Steadman's name was on them.

The ceremony was as ritualized as Kabuki. Dress whites, gloves and swords, processionals, recessionals, patriotic music and prayers. Even the tide tables were consulted to make sure *Portland,* now free from drydock and tied up to a pier at Navy Submarine Base New London, would not sink ingloriously from view.

The band fell silent as Steadman walked across the brow and back onto the submarine he knew so well. A covered platform had been built on her after deck, offering shade to a sparkling array of admirals. He saluted the colors, then the topside watch, while a bosun's whistle piped him aboard with *"Commander United States Navy arriving."*

Captain Welch took the podium and said, "I will now read my orders."

When he was finished, Steadman took the podium, read his own orders, then turned to Welch. "I relieve you, sir."

Welch said, "I stand relieved, sir."

Welch's words were the same ones the United States Navy had used since the Revolutionary War.

And then, Joe Welch winked.

By 1100 the next morning, the platform built on *Portland*'s weather deck was gone, along with the striped tent set up on the pier for guests. The chairs where the band played "Ruffles and Flourishes" for Admiral Graybar were empty. The Thames was just another lazy river, the air rich with the smell of brown water and tar under a hazy sun.

Portland was scheduled to sail at 1230, and a scattering of men watched her make ready for departure at the turn of the tide.

Steadman looked on from inside Welch's car as the tugs *Sea Tractor* and *Paul* stood by to nudge *Portland* away from the pier.

"About time to take her out," said Welch.

Steadman nodded. "I appreciate all your help with the admiral."

"Admirals are like barges. Cranky and tough to steer. They need a good captain to make sure they end up where they're supposed to. You'll see what I mean someday."

Maybe. But right now his eyes were on *Portland*. The Navy said she was his. How would it feel to walk her decks? Familiar, or haunted?

"Jesus, I envy you, Steadman. I really do."

Steadman understood. There was no reason to ask why.

"Command at sea. Don't let anyone tell you it's just a rung. It's the top of the ladder." He nodded at *Portland*. "I spent, what? A couple of weeks on board? She was never really mine, but damned if I didn't resent giving her to you anyway." Welch held out his hand. "Good luck with her."

Steadman grasped Welch's hand, then looked back at the buildings of the submarine school.

"I mean *Portland,*" said Welch. "You'll have to handle Scavullo your own way."

"At least she won't have any excuses for being late." Scavullo was most of the way through the officer's course at Navy Submarine School, located a quarter mile away from where they were sitting. He wondered how she was going to take being yanked away for another Russia run.

"Things may get a little hairy while you're underway. It might be a while before you put back in at Norfolk."

"Someone once told me that a submarine was always at war. We'll be ready."

"All right then, Commander. Move your boat."

"See you in Norfolk, Captain." Steadman opened the door and the heavy, hot air spilled in. He closed it quickly and walked out to the pier. The deck crew was standing by, everyone in an orange float vest, the heavy lines in their hands, as Steadman crossed the brow, saluted the colors, then the topside watch. A bosun's whistle trilled and a voice boomed out over the 1MC loudspeaker:

"Attention! Portland *arriving."*

"Welcome aboard, skipper," said the chief with his clipboard.

"Everything set?"

"Aye aye. Crew's on board and the boat smells brand-new."

"What about our rider?"

"Lieutenant Scavullo hasn't checked in yet."

"Send her up to me when she does."

Steadman climbed up through the ice door to the open bridge and joined the two lookouts already there. He spotted a car racing out to the pier from the direction of the sub school gate.

"Tell the tugs we're ready," he said.

The signal was flashed and chuffs of dirty smoke rose from *Paul* and *Sea Tractor*. They gingerly approached *Portland*'s glistening black hull, ready to pivot her bow out into the slack current.

The car screeched to a stop and Scavullo exploded out the door at a dead run with a seabag over her shoulder.

"Lift the brow," he ordered.

"Sir?"

"Lift it. But just one foot."

The crane roared and the cables stiffened as Scavullo ran across the gangplank. She had to jump down to *Portland*'s deck.

She saluted the flag, then tossed the bag down the forward escape trunk. She glared up at him, squinting into the brassy sky. Her expression turned to surprise when the chief told her to start climbing.

Her face was sweat-streaked and dusty when she stepped onto the open bridge. "Lieutenant Scavullo, reporting aboard."

"You're late again, Lieutenant."

"I'm sorry, sir. I had to see all my instructors and beg them not to wash me out and start me all over in a brand-new class. Graduation was in two weeks, you know. Was this your idea?"

"I don't assign riders, Lieutenant."

"I meant raising the brow."

"Good thing you weren't any later." He looked across the still, sluggish waters. "Go below and check in with the yeoman. You know where he is?"

"I think I can find him this time."

She stepped into the main trunk hatch and started down, but she paused and said, "Commander? I don't know if you had anything to do with sending me to sub school, but . . ."

"Don't thank me, Lieutenant. It's a new Navy."

She smiled. "Not yet. But I'm working on it." With that, she vanished below.

I just bet you are. Steadman took a long breath, let it out slowly. He watched the young men in their orange vests looking up to the bridge, probably wondering who this new captain would turn out to be.

He also thought about *Baikal*'s crew, and Markov.

What had he said? Sailing submarines wasn't a profession, but a religion? If so, thought Steadman, it was an Old Testament kind of faith. One that rewarded believers and meted out harsh punishment to sinners.

Commander James Vann's heart hadn't quit at Avacha Canyon, but it might as well have. Vann hadn't violated rules and regulations so much as the simple, common faith that bound submariners together. You followed your orders, but above all, you kept the faith. In yourself, in your ship and in your crew.

Then, as a cool, salt sea breeze filled the colors behind him and made them stir, a thought filled Steadman and stirred within him, too: a captain who understood these things would never go too far wrong.

He keyed the intercom. "Maneuvering. This is the captain. Stand by to answer bells."